PENG

People

Catriona Stewart lives in San Francisco and works in communications. Her writing has appeared in *HuffPost*, *The San Francisco Chronicle*, *Jewish Currents*, *Lilith* magazine and more. *People Pleaser* is her debut novel.

# PEOPLE PLEASER

## CATRIONA STEWART

PENGUIN BOOKS

PENGUIN BOOKS

UK | USA | Canada | Ireland | Australia
India | New Zealand | South Africa

Penguin Books is part of the Penguin Random House group of companies
whose addresses can be found at global.penguinrandomhouse.com

penguin.co.uk

First published 2025

001

Copyright © Catriona Stewart, 2025

The moral right of the author has been asserted

Penguin Random House values and supports copyright. Copyright fuels creativity, encourages diverse voices, promotes freedom of expression and supports a vibrant culture. Thank you for purchasing an authorised edition of this book and for respecting intellectual property laws by not reproducing, scanning or distributing any part of it by any means without permission. You are supporting authors and enabling Penguin Random House to continue to publish books for everyone. No part of this book may be used or reproduced in any manner for the purpose of training artificial intelligence technologies or systems. In accordance with Article 4(3) of the DSM Directive 2019/790, Penguin Random House expressly reserves this work from the text and data mining exception.

Typeset in 10.4/15pt Palatino LT Pro by Jouve (UK), Milton Keynes
Printed and bound in Great Britain by Clays Ltd, Elcograf S.p.A.

The authorised representative in the EEA is Penguin Random House Ireland,
Morrison Chambers, 32 Nassau Street, Dublin D02 YH68

A CIP catalogue record for this book is available from the British Library

ISBN: 978–1–804–94945–0

Penguin Random House is committed to a sustainable future for our business, our readers and our planet. This book is made from Forest Stewardship Council® certified paper.

For my grandmothers

# Maggie

Maggie didn't know where she was, but she knew that she was dying. Splayed out on a dirty concrete floor with blood pooling around her, she felt warm and light. There was no pain anymore, even though there should've been. Now, there was just a soft ringing in her ears, which wasn't unpleasant. Her vision flickered, as if someone was turning on and off the light. She wondered what was to come, but didn't have the strength to think it through.

She was drifting. But she came back to herself as someone moved beside her, cradling her head, speaking softly to her. *It's OK, Mags. It's almost over,* the voice said. She relaxed, letting herself be comforted, cradled. She drifted farther. She waited for her life to flash before her eyes, as they say it does. But it never came; her unspooling consciousness didn't present a montage of her worst and best moments, of all the things that made up her life.

And then, suddenly, Maggie could no longer feel anything at all.

She closed her eyes. Too quickly, it was over.

# Jill

*Three and a half months later*

The restaurant Dave had chosen for their first date was called Taco. It was casual, but nice enough that it signaled he wasn't trying to be cheap. It was probably a first-date spot that he'd used before, given how quickly he'd suggested it. But Jill was mostly fine with that.

She got there five minutes late, but he wasn't there yet (he was so sorry, work was crazy and he'd got held up at the office) and a hostess seated her outside. There were at least three other first dates around her, which she tried not to let irritate her. Rather than continue to eavesdrop, she perused the menu and decided she would get a margarita and two fancy tacos: a quail egg taco and a mushroom and feta taco. When in Rome.

She looked at her phone, as if checking work email and doing something important. But her inbox was empty, and Amanda was on set so couldn't text her nonstop. Instead, she scrolled through Instagram Stories until she had none left to watch. And when that became boring, she opened her phone's camera and turned it to selfie mode to double-check her lipstick and make sure there was nothing in her teeth. She was in the middle of plucking some gray hairs that'd recently begun growing in her curly brown bangs when she felt a tap on her shoulder.

"Jill?" a man said. She dropped her phone, hoping her date hadn't noticed her discard a gray hair by flicking it to the ground. But she looked up to see it wasn't Dave. It took her a second to place who it was.

Theo Cooke.

She hadn't seen him since Maggie's funeral, and even then, she was so focused on supporting Emma that she hadn't interacted with him beyond the obligatory *I'm so sorry for your loss*. He wore a navy sweatshirt and sweatpants (were they cashmere?) and his chin-length brown hair was tied up in a messy knot at the nape of his neck. Even from a couple feet away, he smelled stale, as though he hadn't washed himself or changed his clothes in a few days. His face was pale, his eyes bloodshot and tired. Somehow, even in his diminished state, he was scarily handsome. She looked down and saw he wasn't wearing a wedding ring anymore—wasn't that a bit unusual? He'd only been widowed three and a half months ago. She took mental notes for Emma, who'd want every detail about her brother-in-law's current state.

She stood up to give him a hug, which he returned with surprising warmth. This restaurant was not a place she would've expected to find him; it was far too normal. He seemed happy to see her, which felt strange; they'd never had a close relationship.

"How are you holding up? Are you OK?" She drew back from their hug, but he kept his palm on the spot in between her shoulder blades. She regretted this word choice as his face fell; she could see he was about to cry. She looked around to check if anyone had noticed. The couple on a first date to her left definitely had, and averted their eyes as soon as she looked over.

"Ah, sorry." He caught a tear with the palm of his hand before it had the chance to drop down his cheek. "It's awful. I'm not doing great. But yeah, I'm living around here now. At least until they finish investigating our house." His face crumpled again. "So sorry. It's just a little weird seeing you."

"Oh my God, don't apologize. It's horrific. The fact that you're eating"—she gestured around her—"is encouraging. So, you're living in Silver Lake?"

"Just off Glendale, in a shitty condo," he told her. Jill knew from Theo's Instagram that "shitty condo" meant a gorgeous three-bedroom with a huge balcony, but she let it slide. "It's honestly good I can't be at our place. I needed to get out of there. There were too many memories of Maggie. But it's also bad not being there, because that's where our life together was. And I just fucking miss her." His voice cracked.

Theo had never shared more than pleasantries with her, but she guessed this was normal behavior after your wife got murdered. Still, it felt a bit odd seeing him this emotional, like watching a dog stand on its hind legs. She needed to change the subject. "Are you back to work?" she asked.

"It's harder to do the influencer stuff right now, given that my life is in shambles and no one wants to see that. Even though everyone says vulnerability is the new 'thing,' I just don't feel comfortable posting selfies crying, you know? 'My wife is dead, buy this shaving cream' doesn't quite work."

"That sounds really difficult," she said.

"I made my bed and now I have to lie in it." There was a note of resigned anger in his voice. She wasn't sure what he meant by that, but it felt rude to ask. "I have to make a living, so I'm doing one or two sponsored posts a week. It's really not so bad."

Out of the corner of her eye, she saw a man who matched Dave's photos on the dating app. His eyes widened as he saw her standing there and talking in close proximity to Theo. She felt, all of a sudden, self-conscious toward both of them.

"I have to get going," she said to Theo as he eyed up her date.

"I'll leave you to it." He nodded at Dave. "I'm just grabbing some takeout. Jill, don't be a stranger. And give Em a big hug for me," Theo said, squeezing her shoulder before he walked away.

"I will," she said, waving, and turning toward Dave.

He went in for a weak hug. "Good to meet you," he said as they sat down. "I have to ask, was that Theo Cooke?" She reluctantly explained to him that yes, it was Theo, and that she knew him because he was her best friend-slash-roommate's brother-in-law. Was he still Emma's brother-in-law if Maggie was dead? Jill wasn't sure, but she wasn't about to ask Dave what he thought.

Unsurprisingly, Theo's appearance derailed the date, because Dave had an endless supply of inappropriate questions. She accepted her fate, allowing him to verbally poke and prod at her as she ate her quail egg taco (quail eggs, as it turned out, tasted like regular eggs). She took big sips of her drink, which was so sweet that it bordered on being undrinkable. Dave droned on, discussing his theories about Maggie's murder until she couldn't take it anymore.

"I actually have to get going," she said, after half a margarita helped her work up the courage to end the date. She'd never before left a date early.

"So soon!" He sounded disappointed. "I had more questions."

"I'm sorry." She silently pleaded with whatever gods existed that he wouldn't fight her too hard on this.

"And I wanted to order cardamom churros for us!"

"Those sound amazing," she said, hoping to seem disappointed. "But I have a work emergency." She tried to look like she was responding to something urgent on her phone.

Finally, he relented, and she got up to leave. When she got to her car, she saw that he'd requested $43 on Venmo—her portion of the meal. She clicked on the request, deleted it, and drove home.

# Emma

It was in the middle of Emma's TikTok stupor that her phone pinged with the sound of an email. She saw in the preview that it was from the detective, and dragged her finger across her phone to open it. It was after work hours—an odd time for him to get in touch.

Emma's days, including this one, consisted of lying in bed for hours on end and scrolling through apps whose algorithms presented an endless stream of content that spoke uncannily to her specific circumstances and interests. TikToks detailing the best barbeque spots in Koreatown. Tweets making jokes about capitalism. Instagram Stories of butches skateboarding. She interspersed the more "mindless" scrolling with YouTube videos about Maggie's murder and the investigation, largely from conspiracy theorists and celebrity gossip accounts.

The LAPD detective who was working on her sister's case was a short and unfriendly man in his mid-fifties named Daniel LaClair. Emma had gathered, from watching the other cops talk to him, that he was one of those people who just went by his last name. Over the past three months, LaClair had barely been in touch. He'd interviewed Emma twice, for two hours each time. And until today, she'd heard from the LAPD just four times, mostly asking logistical questions and saying there were no updates. This email just said: *Emma, please come to Santa Monica station at earliest convenience. DL.* Not for the first time, she wished she'd been assigned a detective with a better bedside manner.

Nonetheless, Emma felt a burst of anxious energy she hadn't experienced in weeks. She looked down at her unmade bed, with the sheet peeled off one corner and a large yellow stain populating the spot where she slept. Hoping it was sweat but fearing somehow it was urine, she stripped the bed; she'd deal with it when she got back. She opened her curtain and let the early-evening light in, which felt blinding and wrong but also necessary, as if the room itself needed vitamin D.

She went to the bathroom to wash her face and brush her teeth, and examined herself in the mirror for the first time in months. She looked terrible. Her mousy blonde hair was at the awkward, grown-out phase that she hated. She could almost hear Maggie in her ear: *Time for a haircut, Em. Should I call my stylist and make you an appointment?* But Maggie was dead, and the effort it would take to find a hairdresser she could actually afford felt insurmountable.

Growing up and even into her adult life, she'd always been called lanky. But since Maggie's death, she'd become skin and bones; any semblance of slight curves was gone. Saliva was crusted around her mouth, and she couldn't remember the last time she'd brushed her teeth (her toothpaste was Maggie's SmileWhite brand). Her skin was dull and pale, and the lines in between her eyebrows and on her forehead had deepened. She swirled some mouthwash around (where was her toothbrush?) and splashed water on her face, digging the crusted saliva off with her fingernails. She'd come back and shower after her meeting; there wasn't time now. Instead, she sprayed her hair with some of Jill's expensive dry shampoo that was supposed to smell good but instead reminded her of the scent of the women's bathroom at a wedding. The skin around her wrist was red and raw from where she'd been scratching it—an anxious habit from childhood that had come back after Maggie died. She applied calamine lotion to it, which stung.

When she got to the station, she looked down at her hands, which were trembling. Was it because she was nervous? She wasn't sure. Maybe she hadn't seen the light of day in too long, though it was starting to get dark. She shoved her hands into her pockets as she waited on a vinyl chair to be called into Detective LaClair's office.

"Emma?" She turned to find Detective LaClair walking over in an ill-fitting blazer; he was about five foot seven and was swimming in it. It wasn't as if Emma—who was a lesbian, after all—couldn't appreciate a good oversized suit. But this was not that.

He was bald and had a goatee streaked with gray. As he got closer, she saw that he had a few crumbs stuck in the wiry beard. LaClair, in turn, eyed Emma with skepticism. She must've looked like a depressed dirtbag, because even a guy wearing a blazer he'd purchased twenty years ago felt comfortable judging her. LaClair motioned for her to come into his office and sit down, which she did. It was cluttered, and smelled of old coffee. There were no pictures or personal effects on his desk, or on the shelf behind him. Just a framed award that read "Hot Wings Challenge Winner 2009."

"I'm afraid the update I have is probably not what you want to hear," he said.

Emma shifted in her chair. "How so?" Her mouth was dry with anticipation.

"Well, there's no easy way to say this, but we're going to announce in a press release first thing tomorrow that we're declaring the investigation into your sister's murder inactive."

Adrenaline pulsed through Emma as she tried to keep her face neutral. "What do you mean, inactive?"

"It's now a cold case. There are no leads, and it's taking up staff time that we just don't have." LaClair's voice was flat.

"But it's only been a couple months," Emma protested.

"It's been almost four months. And we can't make special allowances for this case just because your sister was famous."

"That's not what I was saying, I just—"

"There's no use arguing about this. I called you here as a courtesy. I know it's hard to hear, but there's just nothing we can do. The crime scene was . . ." LaClair paused. "I'm sorry, there's no other word for it. It was meticulous. There was nothing to work with. We've done everything we can."

"How can that possibly be true?" Emma was trying not to cry, but tears clouded her eyes anyway.

"Look, I know this is tough." LaClair was trying his best to sound soothing. "We looked into the only leads we had, but they have strong alibis and we can't keep badgering them if there's no hard evidence."

"Javier? He's no longer a suspect?" Maggie's housekeeper and her husband were the focus of many internet conspiracy theories surrounding the murder, as CCTV footage had surfaced of Javier's car driving a few blocks from where Maggie's body had been found half an hour after the estimated time of death.

"You know I can't confirm or deny any specifics. But we can always reopen the investigation if new evidence emerges. Or someone comes forward." He handed Emma a tissue box, which she took reluctantly.

"It feels like you're giving up." She blew her nose.

"Don't think about it that way." The detective leaned back and took a deep breath, as if she was annoying him. LaClair eyed her wrist, and Emma realized she'd been scratching it again. "Have you looked into those support groups I sent you? I really think that could be helpful for you in your grief process."

Emma considered picking up his Hot Wings 2009 award and throwing it against the wall. "I should be going," she said instead.

"I'm sorry this is so emotional," LaClair said.

Emma couldn't sit there anymore. She threw her tissues in the trash and made her way to the door. But before she could stop herself, she turned back. "Do you have a family? A wife? Any kids?"

He looked at her, his eyebrows knit in annoyance. "I don't disclose personal information to victims."

"Well, let's say you do. Let's say you have a kid. Or a wife. And they're all you have. They're your only family. And something terrible happened to them, but the LAPD refused to help even a tiny—"

He cut her off. "This isn't relevant. We did everything we could, and it's time for you to go."

When Emma got home, she felt drained; the earlier adrenaline rush had left her system. She crawled back into bed even though it no longer had sheets on it; the laundry would have to wait until later. She was half watching an episode of *Seinfeld* when she saw her door open and the light stream in from the hallway. It was Jill, clearly dressed for a date in her usual ripped jeans and "sculpting" bodysuit. She was a good six inches shorter than Emma's five foot nine, with curly brown hair she wore most days in a clip on top of her head or in a ponytail. She described herself as "an LA six but a New Jersey nine." This irritated Emma, who was at best an LA five in that scenario.

Emma sat up and turned off her TV.

"You're not looking so great. Did you eat today?" Jill tucked one of her curls behind her ear and sat next to Emma on the bed. "Also, where are your sheets?"

"I ate dinner. And I'll deal with my sheets tomorrow," Emma said, impatient. "I had a shitty day."

"How so?"

Emma explained that the LAPD was closing the investigation into Maggie's murder, and Jill sat, wide-eyed, nodding at the right moments. "It's fucked." Emma started to cry. "Sorry. All I do is cry these days. It's just so frustrating."

"Don't apologize," Jill said. "I'm sorry. I wish I knew what to say."

"It's not your fault."

"I know. But it still sucks," Jill said. "I know how badly you want answers."

"I think I'm out of luck on that front." Emma lay back down in exasperation.

Jill stood up to leave, but hovered in the doorway. "I wanted to let you know I ran into Theo tonight. It was weird."

Emma sat up again. "Whoa. How did he seem?"

"He seemed emotional, and he rambled on. It felt out of character. I know you've never found him particularly forthcoming," Jill said. That was an understatement. "Anyway, I ran into him while waiting for my date. Which, by the way, was bad. He saw me with Theo and grilled me about him and Maggie the whole time."

"Oh God." Emma felt guilty. Maggie's murder had taken up so much space in Jill's life. Jill hadn't complained to her, but Emma knew that it took its toll.

Jill continued: "Apparently Theo is living in a 'shitty condo' in Silver Lake. He seemed lonely." Emma rolled her eyes at the idea of Theo's supposedly shitty condo. "Yep," said Jill, agreeing with the eye roll. "The whole thing was odd, even running into him at a taco place. I realized I've never seen him eat food that wasn't, like, a green smoothie.

But whatever, the man is grieving. Except, you know, he wasn't wearing his wedding ring anymore. But maybe that's normal?"

Emma snorted. "That was quick. He's probably seeing someone." Her brother-in-law had always made Emma uncomfortable—it was some combination of the reality TV thing, the quickie wedding, and the over-the-top obsession with his appearance. But when Maggie had been alive, she'd implored Emma to be nice, to give him a chance. And now, just a few months after they'd buried her, he was wandering around town sans wedding ring, probably hoping to meet women. What a dick.

"I should let you sleep," Jill said. Even though she was tired to the bone, Emma knew she wouldn't be able to sleep. It was the kind of bizarre day that she'd never had before Maggie had died. The kind of day that made her want to crawl into a hole or scream into the void or walk into oncoming traffic.

"I can't believe they're declaring it a cold case." Emma's voice was bleary.

"We can talk about it tomorrow. Sleep well, Em. I love you," Jill whispered.

Emma was kept awake by thoughts of her conversation with LaClair, and of Jill's run-in with Theo. It was possible he hadn't contacted her since the funeral because he was angry about the money. Maggie had left a detailed will, ensuring Emma would inherit half of the value of her and Theo's house—which they'd bought for around $15 million—whenever he decided to sell it.

She was on unpaid leave from her job in a writers' room for a children's TV show called *Mrs. Ladybug*, which aired zany but educational half-hour episodes on topics of interest to children, all featuring the eponymous Mrs. Ladybug as host. Emma had been deep in rewrites on an episode about trucks when she'd gone on leave. *Mrs. Ladybug* was her first actual screenwriting gig, and despite the fact that it wasn't exactly the kind of prestige dramedy she'd hoped to be working on by thirty, it was the best job she'd ever had.

After college, she and Jill had moved out to LA together to try and make it as screenwriters. Emma knew this was a pipe dream, but was happy to go along with it because Jill's parents paid their rent for the first year out of school. They sent packets to every writers' room, for every type of show, and no one so much as offered them an interview. Out of desperation, Jill got a part-time job nannying for a major producer. The producer eventually helped her get an assistant gig at a big talent agency, which she'd done for six years before going on to work for Amanda Lehman, an actress, writer and showrunner. Emma held out a bit longer, living off her savings from her college barista job. But she eventually took a job as a copywriter for an ad agency, working her way up the soul-crushing corporate ladder to become an account manager.

That was, until Maggie became famous. Then all it took was an introduction to a friend of a friend who was the executive producer on *Mrs. Ladybug*, and Emma was hired. Nepotism worked.

She'd been in the *Mrs. Ladybug* writers' room when she'd gotten the call about Maggie's death. Her phone rang and rang for twenty minutes straight, and finally she stepped out and into the hallway to yell at the caller to leave her alone. *Mrs. Ladybug* shared a building with a popular daytime talk show, and busy-looking production assistants and suited executives and camera techs milled about as she clicked answer.

"Emma Lathrop? This is Detective Daniel LaClair with the LAPD."

Her heart raced. "Yes? Is everything OK?"

"I'm very sorry to tell you this"—his voice was calm—"but two days ago, your sister was murdered. She was stabbed nine times in the chest and abdomen. Her body was found at a warehouse where she was scheduled to do a photoshoot."

Emma was silent for a long moment. For some reason, her instinct was to laugh, as if it was some weird joke. Because this was Maggie. The same Maggie who had just spent the afternoon at her house helping her reorganize her closet—what was it? Three days ago? Maggie was alive. She was extremely alive. "No. Sorry. I don't follow."

"It's a terrible thing, but we will do everything in our power to find out who did this and bring them to justice. Do you have someone you can call right now to take you home?"

"What?" Her mind was blank. What was he talking about? Where was she? What was happening?

"Ms. Lathrop, do you understand what I've said?" His voice was almost quiet. "Your sister was murdered."

It was then that she let out a piercing, strangled scream. She dropped to her knees. Her phone fell out of her hands.

Her vision went spotty. She remembered nothing about the next half-hour, and had no idea how she'd gotten out of that building. How she or her car made it home. All she remembered was LaClair's mystifyingly calm voice, the feeling of her knees hitting the floor, the sound of her own scream.

And even though she would forever associate her job with the worst day of her life, some part of her missed it. She missed working, and writing—even if it was an extended scene about how many tires are on a big rig. Now that she had millions of dollars coming to her at some point in the future, she hadn't panicked yet about her dwindling savings. But it was almost time to make a choice about whether she would go back for the upcoming season or take more time off. They'd been so understanding about her bereavement leave, and had made it clear they wanted her back. But it seemed impossible to face the people who'd heard her scream bloody murder in the hallway outside of their brainstorm on how to make trucks feel fresh in a saturated market.

Maybe the inheritance was why Theo hadn't returned any of Emma's texts or made any effort to see her since they'd worked together on funeral arrangements. Or maybe it was just that they didn't like each other, and they could give up the charade now that Maggie was dead. And because Emma had no parents, and no other family, there was nothing else tying them together.

Despite the fact that Theo was Maggie's husband and also a famous person and far more comfortable with crowds than she was, when they planned the funeral, he begged her to do the eulogy instead of him. ("I won't be able to get through it in one piece," he told her.) Emma, who couldn't so much as make herself toast without sobbing, agreed, fearing that if she didn't speak, no one else would.

But the day of the funeral, she realized it was a mistake to have agreed to eulogize. She should've just forced Theo. She knew it as soon as she got to the church, standing outside on that cold day to greet the guests who were there to mourn Maggie. She recognized almost no one, but it appeared that every attendee except her and Jill had had professional hair and makeup done. The idea felt foreign to Emma, who, despite Maggie's best efforts, was only able to competently apply a few swipes of mascara. The first person to arrive at the funeral was a woman Emma had never met before, who introduced herself as Lisa Clement and gave a handshake so firm it was almost painful.

"Your sister was so special to me," Lisa said, dabbing at a tear with her extra-long acrylic nail. Emma wondered, idly, how she buttoned her pants. Lisa smelled good, like cedar, and wore a drapey silk jumpsuit.

"How did you two know each other?" Emma eyed her own black shift dress and black puffy jacket self-consciously. She'd bought the dress from Target's business-casual section five years ago to wear to her ad agency's annual gala.

"We worked together," Lisa said. "She was a brand ambassador for us at VagFit. She was just so amazing. Her posts were incredible. So many of our ambassadors struggle to make posts because, like, how do you advertise for a

Kegel weight brand and make it cool? But she figured it out!" Lisa shook her head, as if remembering just how compelling Maggie's Kegel weight content was.

"I'm so glad." Emma tried to make eye contact with the next person in the receiving line that was forming. So far, she'd recognized a few of Maggie's friends, but there were so many strangers there. Strangers who made her feel so dowdy and ungroomed that she wondered if she was a different species entirely.

The next person in line was a blonde who had the largest fake boobs Emma had ever seen in real life.

"You must be Maggie's sister?" She reached out a manicured, glowy hand to shake Emma's, which, in comparison, looked like it belonged to a pale old witch. "I'm so sorry for your loss."

"Yes, thank you." Emma tried not to stare at the woman, who looked like a replica of a human being instead of a real person. It was something about her skin, or her proportions, or maybe both. She wasn't sure. "How did you know Maggie?"

"We were on *LoveShack* together?" she said, as if it were a question, not a statement. This woman expected Emma to recognize her, but Emma had never seen the show. When it originally aired three years ago, she'd offered to throw a viewing party for Maggie. But her sister refused. She hadn't wanted Emma to watch it, saying it was embarrassing. So Emma, in keeping with Maggie's wishes, didn't watch. It was never an issue before, because Maggie rarely socialized with her castmates. "My name's Sunny. Is it OK if Zeke from my team livestreams?" She motioned to the guy behind her, who wore a black suit, a black shirt, and, for some reason, a bolo tie.

"Livestreams what?" Emma asked.

"The funeral, plus some commentary about my relationship with Maggie on the show. I have eight hundred thousand followers on Instagram so it'll get really good traffic for you. Maybe we can get you for a quick interview, too?" Sunny said, as if that was a sweetener.

"Oh . . ." Emma paused. "I'd rather not—"

"Sunny, do you think that's really necessary?" a man behind them in line asked. Sunny rolled her eyes at this.

"Can you stay out of it, Finn?" Sunny was doing her best to look irritated, but her face was so frozen that she couldn't convey much. "I just want to honor Maggie."

"I think I need to get back to the rest of the guests," Emma said. "Thank you for that," she whispered to the man as Sunny walked away.

"No worries," Finn said. He was tall, maybe six foot two, and clearly in great shape. She could make out the shape of his biceps underneath his suit. His hair was dark and he sported what looked like an intentional five o'clock shadow along his absurdly square jawline. Even though she wasn't the slightest bit straight, she could see that this guy had a certain *je ne sais quoi*—the glow that people like Maggie and Theo also possessed. The thing that set them apart from normal people, like Emma. "I know we come off badly sometimes, but we're not all awful. And I'm so sorry for your loss."

"Thank you." She nodded. "Who is 'we'?"

"Oh, you know, 'content creators.'" He made air quotes.

When she looked at him blankly, he continued, "That's the fancy term for influencers. Sunny and I were on the show with Maggie. And now we all hawk stuff on social media. Anyway, I'll let you get back to it." At least he was self-deprecating about it. It was strange, now she thought about it, that she'd barely met anyone from the cast besides Theo.

Emma's ex-girlfriend Liz was the next person in the receiving line; Jill must've called her to tell her about Maggie and the funeral. Her presence was comforting, even though they'd had a messy breakup two years prior. Liz looked cool: her red hair was longer than Emma had ever seen it, and she wore a black leather blazer and Doc Martens. It was the outfit Emma should've worn. They hugged, and she kissed Emma's cheek. "Are you OK?" Liz asked as they pulled away.

"Absolutely not." Though no part of Emma missed dating Liz—they hadn't had sex for the last six months of their relationship and fought constantly (including about Liz's belief that Emma and Jill's relationship was "codependent")—she felt the desperate urge to be held by her. "My sister was murdered. And I'm at a funeral with the worst group of people I've ever met."

"I saw that woman with the huge fake boobs. Something looks really wrong with her," Liz said.

"She was a delivery from the uncanny valley," Emma said. They both laughed, which felt good.

"I should let you get on with it. If you need anything at all, I'm here." Liz gave Emma a tight hug.

"Can't you just stay here and talk to me instead?" Emma

said into Liz's ear, only half joking. What she actually wanted to do was fall into Liz's arms and ask: *Can we just ditch this so I can go cry about the fact that I am not only an orphan but now the only living member of my immediate family, that I had to bury my mother and now my sister, and that I'm all alone in the world with the exception of maybe Jill?* But she didn't, and Liz just gave her a sad smile and a squeeze on the arm before she walked away.

The next person in line was a normal-looking human in black slacks and a black blazer who introduced herself as Priya. "I'm a producer on *LoveShack*," she said.

Emma shook her hand. "Thanks for being here."

"Just checking, but you won't be mentioning *LoveShack* in the eulogy, I hope?"

"No, but why would that matter?"

A wrinkle appeared in between Priya's eyebrows. "It's been tough for us at *LoveShack* to lose your sister, and we miss her terribly. She wouldn't want the show that launched her career dragged through the mud, right?"

"I don't know if—"

But Priya interrupted: "Thanks so much for your understanding. And I'm so sorry for your loss."

The funeral was surreal, partly because she didn't know many of the attendees besides a handful of Maggie's and Theo's friends and staff who sat in the first couple of rows, plus Jill and Liz. As she recounted memories of her sister, she couldn't help but focus on the strange group of actors, models, reality stars and influencers who'd come together to mourn her.

"Maggie took care of everyone in her life," Emma said to the crowd. "She had this warmth to her that was magnetic. She wasn't just my big sister; she was America's big sister." Out of the corner of her eye, she noticed that woman Sunny, holding up her phone to film. And there were two or three people behind her as well, all filming. Someone had even set up a tripod. She clutched the lectern, steadying herself.

*Don't lose it.* She took a deep breath, but it was no use. The words escaped her mouth before she could stop herself. "You know what? I can't believe I need to say this, but if you are filming, you can leave. This is a funeral, for fuck's sake."

Oh God. Had she just said "fuck" in a church? There was murmuring in the crowd as people put their phones away. She looked at Jill, who gave her a slight smile and a supportive nod as Emma began to give the rest of the eulogy.

Theo had taken care of planning the reception, which was held in a nearby restaurant he claimed was Maggie's favorite. It was called Lover's Quarrel, and sold upscale vegan dim sum. They'd never gone there for Maggie's birthday—she'd always chosen a fancy burger place in Santa Monica. Given they'd spent their childhood in Kansas eating casseroles and corn, Maggie's palate had never been the most sophisticated. She tried to picture her sister eating a jackfruit xiao long bao, but found she couldn't.

She was regretting letting Theo choose this place as she sat down at a booth in the back of the restaurant with Jill, downing a cloying lychee cocktail.

"This feels like a dinner party or something. Not a funeral," Jill said.

"Yeah, well. It's not exactly what I would've chosen." Emma finished the last dregs of her drink. "I'm gonna go get another one of these."

At the bar, she tried her best to wave down the tattooed bartender nearest to her, but he was in deep, flirtatious conversation with a pretty blonde woman whom Emma recognized from Instagram. She was having a hard time recalling who exactly this woman was—a celebrity chef? One of the hot Mormon mommy bloggers?—but she'd seen her before.

"Hi," Emma tried, but the bartender didn't look away from his conversation. "I'd love to order something," she said as loudly as she could muster without embarrassing herself. But the bartender didn't hear her. Or maybe he was ignoring her. She called out to him one more time, but to no avail. She wasn't used to being in places like this, places where she was invisible. It was probably time to cut her losses and find the dim sum carts instead; she realized she was gripping the bar so intensely that her knuckles had turned white.

"Are you OK?" she heard someone ask, and turned around to see it was Theo. He was accompanied by a group of people she surmised were from the show, including his best friend Bryan, Sunny the would-be livestreamer, and Finn.

"This bartender is ignoring me. And I just want another drink. At my sister's funeral. Is that too much to ask?" She tried to sound like she was making a joke, but the words came out harshly.

"Doesn't seem like it," Bryan said. "Here, let me help." He stepped up to the bar, and immediately the bartender turned his attention toward their group. Emma couldn't help but roll her eyes in irritation, but took the opportunity to order two lychee martinis.

"We were just talking about some of our favorite memories of your sister from the show," another woman from their group said to her. Emma smiled politely.

"Maggie was a riot. She was always telling jokes, keeping us all entertained," Bryan said. Emma nodded as if this was bringing up fond memories. But that didn't sound like Maggie at all. Not that Maggie wasn't funny—she was. But she wasn't funny in an outgoing way. She wasn't a joke-teller; she was shy in groups. Emma was always the funny one.

"That's sweet," Emma said as the bartender prepared her martinis.

"She was so real. She wasn't superficial at all," Sunny said. That also sounded nothing like Maggie. Maggie would never leave the house without a full face of makeup and, at minimum, a blowout. She'd got thousands of dollars' worth of Botox and fillers and cosmetic surgery a year starting the second she could afford it. Maggie had been a lot of wonderful things, but "real" was not one of them.

"I really appreciate the memories." Emma needed to get out of there as soon as possible.

"She talked about you all the time," Finn said, and Emma turned to look at him.

"She did?"

"I knew about you way before I knew anything else

about her. She always brought up how excited she was to move to LA full-time after the show wrapped, so she would be closer to you. She told a great story, once, about you as kids," Finn continued. "She stepped on a bees' nest, and got stung a bunch of times, and you had to give her an EpiPen? Even though you were, like, eight?"

"Oh my God." Emma let out a surprised laugh. "Maggie's foot swelled so much we thought it was going to burst." This was the only time that day anyone had offered a memory that resembled the Maggie she knew: the older sister who, starting at ten, was put in charge of Emma after school while their mom worked. Who took Emma on adventures to the creek near their house and held her hand while they crossed it, stepping on rocks and giggling when their feet got wet.

Theo laughed, but it sounded shallow. "I've never heard that one," he said as the bartender returned with her two drinks. "Enjoy those."

"All I know is that you were her favorite person ever," Finn said.

"Thank you for saying that." She smiled and slipped away with her martinis.

And that was the last time she'd interacted with Theo in three and a half months until tonight's rendezvous between him and Jill. Besides, of course, the obsessive internet stalking she did of his social media profiles and anything or anyone related to Maggie. Instinctually, needing her fix, she reached for her phone. But as the screen lit up, she stopped herself. She'd lost too many nights to internet rabbit holes. Plus, she wanted to sleep; she was exhausted. She wanted to stop thinking about Theo, about money, about Maggie, about all those weird influencers at her sister's funeral. So she dug around in a drawer in her bedside table for a couple of extra-strength Tylenol PMs, which she took without any water. In about fifteen minutes, a dreamless sleep overtook her.

# Amanda

Amanda got out of her Uber, walked up to the sleek Beverly Hills office space, and pressed the call button. She was late for her appointment with Beth, a beautiful 55-year-old who wore her hair in a severe jet-black bob that featured a silver-gray streak. She was what Amanda referred to—in a way she hoped came off as self-deprecating—as a "therapist to the stars."

Beth's office was in a three-story building with valet. Its interior was furnished with uninviting but architecturally interesting chairs, and a couple of original Cindy Sherman prints. The prints, a set of large photos of older women in ill-fitting pink wigs and badly drawn lip liner, were an odd choice for an office housing five expensive therapists.

"Come on up," Beth said through the intercom. As Amanda climbed the stairs to the office, past the scary Sherman prints, she felt the usual thrill at the bottom of her gut, knowing she was on her way to talk about herself for the next fifty minutes.

Beth's door was open, and Amanda entered her office to find her sitting in her chair, legs crossed. She wore red mules and had her toenails painted a deep purple.

"How are you doing?" she asked.

"I'm good." Amanda set down her beaded Susan Alexandra purse, which she'd bought herself after her first Emmy win. "Well, I'm just OK." She slumped onto the couch and took her place in her usual position (right cushion). "Work kinda sucks right now."

"How so?"

"I still have this suspicion that everyone hates me. Which I know is paranoid. Except maybe it's not paranoid? Like on Tuesday, our assistant producer kept cutting me off during our production meeting. And when he does this to anyone else, everyone tells him to shut up and stop interrupting because he pulls this shit all the time. But because it was me, no one said anything. And I'm the EP?"

"Hm." Beth uncrossed her legs and crossed her arms instead. "That sounds difficult. And that's different from how they've treated you in the past?"

"I don't know. It's at least different from how I was treated when I was working on *Anxiety*. A male colleague would never have to deal with this."

"How do you think a male colleague would be treated?" Beth asked.

"People continue to judge me for things I did when I was still using. But men are only seen as tragic and wounded if they do dumb shit on drugs." Amanda felt the uncomfortable sensation of watching herself through Beth's eyes.

"Is there something in particular you're reflecting on, that you're worried they're judging you for?" Beth said.

"I don't know." She paused, thinking. "I mean, obviously the stuff with Trevor. Is everyone always thinking about that? When they look at me, do they think of that? Or is that just in my head?"

"Let's examine that for a second. Why would that matter to you if they continue to associate you with Trevor?"

"It matters for a hundred obvious reasons." Amanda sighed. "Sorry, not to be rude. But people think I'm a bad person because of it."

"Do you think you're a bad person?" Beth leaned back in her chair.

"On most days, no. But like I said, I don't want *other* people to think I'm a bad person. We've talked about it a million times and I've forgiven myself for most of the stuff I did when I was using. I'm past it. I just think other people aren't."

"Hmm." Beth looked at her skeptically.

"And you know, I'm worried about the *LoveShack* stuff, too. It's been on my mind because that cast member, Maggie Lathrop, was killed. You know that Maggie was Jill's roommate's sister? Isn't that wild? What if people found out about my involvement in the show? I'd get canceled again, somehow."

"I'm curious. Why would your involvement in the show get you canceled?" Beth paused. "Is it possible that you're simply having a trauma response to your past experiences of public scrutiny?"

"Of course it is. But that's beside the point. I would get canceled because of the rotten moral core at the center of the *LoveShack* franchise. Because people like Maggie are dead."

"But how does the show, or more importantly your involvement in it, have anything to do with that woman's murder? Even if she was Jill's roommate's sister, as you say?"

This whole endeavor was somehow $380 for fifty minutes a week, a price that made Amanda feel stupid, but also special. This session alone cost more than the limited-edition Anna Sui alligator belt she was wearing.

"It doesn't, obviously," Amanda said. "It's just the optics. Everyone already disapproves of me. It makes me want to hole up and never work on another show again. Maybe I should just do projects on my own, like another book. Something I can have full creative control over."

"That's a great idea," Beth said. "I think some of this anxiety might be coming up because you're a little bored. A new project makes sense."

They had about twenty minutes left in the session, during which Amanda listed the kinds of projects she could take on: mentoring younger screenwriters; throwing together an essay collection; starting a production company. It wasn't that helpful to talk it through, but it was a good enough way to pass the time.

The best part of seeing a "therapist to the stars" was running into other famous people in the waiting area. One would think they'd have a more discreet system, but she figured therapy was cool now, so maybe people wanted to be seen. Amanda talked about therapy all the time in interviews, and had also written a whole essay about Beth in her last book ("Are you mad that I wrote about you?" she'd asked Beth. "Do you think I should be mad that you wrote about me?" Beth had said).

Last year, she had seen Hailey Bieber in the waiting room

a few times, which alone made the price tag worth it. She always wore a fun outfit just in case someone interesting was there that day. And part of the game was, of course, pretending not to recognize the other famous people if you passed each other in the hallway or sat near them on the horrible chairs. Rather, you needed to appear engrossed in your phone, looking business-y and distracted, while you texted your friend: *omg Seth Rogen also sees my therapist????*

# Emma

As LaClair had promised, the press release from the LAPD came out first thing in the morning. It caused a new wave of sadness that felt, somehow, different from the waves she'd experienced in the months prior. Not only was she sad, but she was sick of being sad.

She could tell that Jill was worried, because before she left for work, she set out a full pot of coffee and Emma's favorite breakfast sandwich from the local bakery. Emma took it into her bedroom, got back under the covers (still no sheets), and took a bite. But she could hardly get it down. Jill's attention to her well-being was both welcome and uncomfortable; she felt ashamed to need her friend so much. Jill liked to care for people in her life, but Emma didn't want to take advantage of that generosity. It was days like these that she wished, more than anything, that she had some family, any family, with whom she could share the burden of this grief.

When Maggie and Emma's mom got sick with pancreatic cancer almost nine years ago, the sisters were a team. It all happened so fast once their mom had to quit her job after she started to deteriorate. When she lost her health insurance, Emma and Maggie served as her full-time hospice care to keep costs down.

One night, near the end, their mother was sleeping—breathing in that labored, shallow way that dying people do—and Maggie suggested they watch a movie together, just to have something to do that wasn't changing their mother's diapers or feeding her mashed potatoes or adjusting her morphine pump. So they lay together on Maggie's twin bed from their shared childhood bedroom while Maggie streamed *The Parent Trap* from her laptop.

"We're regressing," Emma said.

"Possibly," Maggie conceded. "But given the circumstances, I think it's allowed."

As they watched Lindsay Lohan do her secret handshake with her butler, Maggie played with Emma's hair. "Can you braid it?" Emma asked. Her hair was still long then, and she hadn't washed it in seven or eight days. It was covered in saliva and sweat and tears.

"Course," Maggie said. She handed Emma the laptop, who took it and put it on the ground next to the bed. They sat, wordlessly, while Maggie brushed out the matted parts of Emma's hair. She pulled it into two sections and braided each tightly. Emma kept those braids in until their mother died a few days later, when Maggie insisted it was time to wash her hair.

That was the first time she'd felt soul-crushingly depressed, and it had shocked her. It was impossible to get dressed, to eat, to shower. Maggie went into full older-sister mode, organizing the funeral and picking out

Emma's outfit for it. She was the best version of herself: caring and protective, but not patronizing. She wrote emails to Emma's professors asking for extensions on assignments. She decided where to bury their mom and what the gravestone would say. She organized her stuff and drove bags of it to the Salvation Army. It reminded Emma of being in eighth grade, when she had starred as a Pink Lady in *Grease* and had developed horrific stage fright two nights before their weekend of performances. Maggie, who was a sophomore in high school, had sat in the front row every night, mouthing the words along with her, giving Emma strength.

Maggie was in charge in all the ways that mattered, so Emma could fall apart. And if Emma was honest, there was something that felt good about it. Or, maybe not *good* exactly, but right. She'd completely succumbed to her sadness, and it allowed her to feel whole again. She emerged from the grief feeling empty and light. Now, with Maggie gone, Emma was alone in the world. No parents, no grandparents, no siblings. Nothing. It was just her. Her and Jill. And she was in charge of her own miserable life.

Maggie and Emma had grown up in Kansas, about an hour from Topeka, in a small split-level on the edge of "town"—a tiny community made up mostly of farms, a post office, a dollar store, and a small grocery store. Their mom, Melinda, worked as a paralegal and raised them by herself. Melinda was the first in her family to go to college; she went to Kansas State on a full scholarship. After graduating, she commuted an hour to the same law firm in Topeka until she got sick. They never knew their dad, and Melinda didn't share much. They knew only that he suffered from addiction, and that he'd been in their mom's life for enough time to get her pregnant twice. Emma had no memories of him, and Maggie didn't remember much either, but the topic was off-limits. Thus, without anything to satiate it, her thirst for information about her dad ran dry over time. The Tallahassee police called their house one day, when Emma was thirteen and Maggie fifteen, to let their mom know he'd died of an overdose. They didn't attend the funeral; it was in northern Florida, and there wasn't exactly any money lying around for flights.

While Maggie had a rags-to-riches orphan story, she never talked about it publicly. Maggie told Emma that on *LoveShack* her image was all apple pie, girl next door from Kansas—nothing about their dead parents. And though Maggie could've easily graced the cover of *People* with an exclusive about the sad story of her mom and dad, she never did. Even in the coverage of Maggie's death, it was just a footnote. It took up two lines on her Wikipedia's "Early life" section. Her Wikipedia didn't mention the years of debt, of striving, of trying to be anything but the boring, pretty girl from Kansas.

The truth was, Maggie and Emma had loved their childhood. They'd loved being on their own with their mom, receiving her full attention. They were working class, sure, but they never wanted for basic necessities. And the expectation was always that they would go to college and get an education so they could get good jobs. Emma was an excellent student and got a scholarship to school. Even though she wasn't making a lot of money right after college, she always sent some back home to her mom—not a lot, but enough to help with the bills. After Maggie hit it big, it felt as though the Lathrop girls had made something of themselves. Now, the idea that any of this had ever mattered to her was laughable.

Emma forced herself to eat a quarter of the breakfast sandwich, which made her feel nauseous. It was time to dig into what she thought of as Maggie Content Hour—time she'd allotted herself each morning to dig through social media conspiracies, trying to find anything useful about Maggie's murder. It gave her a sick sort of pleasure to open Google and search Maggie's name. The first hit was the best, of course. Anything felt possible with that first look. The day still held the possibility that maybe she'd solve Maggie's murder with aggressive googling. And then, as she carried on, switching from one platform to the next, refreshing and refreshing and refreshing, she started to feel empty and lethargic.

She could easily spend all day doing this, which was why Jill had suggested she set some boundaries to keep her internet sleuthing to a slightly healthier level. But it was hard to stick to.

Everything that morning was about Maggie and the announcement about the LAPD declaring her murder investigation a cold case. Maggie's murder had, unsurprisingly, generated a massive amount of media interest—after all, she was famous and gorgeous and had millions of fans. Reddit and TikTok were filled with conspiracy theories, mostly about Lucía and Javier, and the chatter online hit a fever pitch after any major announcements came out about the case. Paparazzi occasionally parked themselves outside of Theo's condo after something big happened, hoping for a statement.

Before she died, Maggie had mostly worked from home, leaving her house only for influencer events and a constant stream of planned appearances in full hair and makeup to places like Nobu and Erewhon. She hated getting swarmed by paparazzi, which happened a lot after her video content with Theo took off. But with these outings, she could court the paparazzi on her own terms. Her team would call them and tell them to show up, and in exchange, they'd leave her alone for things like dentist appointments and family dinners. But usually Maggie would send a car to get Emma and bring her to the house in Calabasas, a mansion-filled suburb just north of Malibu, which she and Theo had bought a year and a half after starring on *LoveShack*. They spent most of their time together in her backyard, chatting and eating whatever Maggie's personal chef had put together. Being at the Calabasas house was nice, but they were never alone there. Maggie had endless staff present at all times, and Theo was often around. Post-*LoveShack*, Maggie was on a unremitting schedule, dictated by the people around her and the demands of her life as an influencer: hours set aside to film content, personal training appointments, glam for events, conference calls with product collaborators. Even though they were living in the same place for the first time since high school in Kansas, after

*LoveShack* it felt as if they saw each other less than they'd used to when Maggie was in New York and Emma in LA. But every once in a while, Emma was able to convince her to come hang out at her and Jill's apartment. Those were the best moments they had together as adults—far better than when Emma spent time with Maggie in their Calabasas place. Emma would cook them something simple, like chicken parmesan (which Maggie would pick at and not really eat, because she never ate real food), and they'd watch something stupid on TV.

Now, she couldn't remember the last time she'd gone food shopping, or seen a friend besides Jill, or gone on a walk. She resolved that tomorrow would be the day she actually got out of bed and got her life together. She hoped. She placed the rest of her breakfast sandwich, which had now gone cold, on her bedside table.

She felt itchy, as if she needed to do something. She needed to see Maggie, to talk to her. She lay on her bed and closed her eyes, trying to breathe, to empty her mind. But it was impossible. She pulled out her phone and began scrolling through old photos of her and Maggie that she'd looked at a million times. It felt so good to see her sister like that: happy, alive.

She was struck by the idea that maybe she should just watch *LoveShack*. It was footage of her sister she'd never seen. Footage where she was probably happy, and definitely alive.

It was a brilliant idea.

Why hadn't she thought of this before? Maybe it'd help her get a clearer picture of the parts of Maggie's life she knew little about—the parts she was trying to uncover with fruitless social media scrolling. Sure, Maggie had specifically told her not to watch. It had always struck Emma as silly, but she'd complied. But now Maggie was gone, so it was up to her.

She sat upright and turned on her TV.

# Maggie

## Episode 1

Maggie stood in front of the infinity pool with five other women, every one of them bronzed, fully made-up and clad in bikinis and stilettos. She'd already met Chloe, Layla, Tia, Sunny and Felicia at promotional events where they'd been photographed—also in bikinis, also in full glam—on a fake beach outside of Tucson, Arizona. The show itself was filmed in the Arizona desert in late spring and made to look tropical, as if they were in Hawaii. When she'd been cast, Maggie's manager had explained the reason for Arizona: it was cheap, and warm and sunny enough that the mandatory bikini rule was easier to follow. But she couldn't help feeling excited about the prospect of hanging around a mansion with an infinity pool all day with beautiful people, even if it was in Arizona.

Maggie had recently, following her manager's advice, spent hours learning how to do her own hair and makeup—something she'd never mastered as a part of her failing career as a model-slash-actress-slash-waitress. Today, however, she'd had professional glam done one last time before she entered the bungalow and was cut off from the rest of the world. Her long dark brown hair (courtesy of clip-in extensions) was slicked back into a ponytail. She had a spray tan that made her look about three to four shades darker than she actually was, and a suitcase full of fake tanner to keep it that way for the next month and a half. She had gotten her first-ever filler injections in her lips and upper cheek two weeks prior, so it would be fresh for the show.

Maggie, Chloe, Layla, Tia, Sunny and Felicia were waiting. At five foot ten, Maggie was the tallest girl and stood above the others. She wondered if it would've been better to wear lower heels so she'd stand out less. Though maybe standing out was exactly what she needed.

The cameras watched them, and Maggie found it difficult not to look straight back at the obtrusive lenses. Despite the fact that it was bright outside, the cameras were followed around by a full lighting set-up. All of this secretly thrilled her, because these cameras were here for them. For *her*.

And then it happened. From the large main door to the bungalow, the first guy appeared. The girls all gasped and clapped, and Maggie found herself joining in.

"Hi, I'm Patrick," the man said. The host of all five prior *LoveShack* seasons, Schuyler, beckoned him to join them. Even though Schuyler was a bit of a sleaze-ball, Maggie had been so starstruck when they'd first met that she'd practically blacked out. Now, he stood opposite Patrick, who grinned at them—his teeth were shockingly white. He was handsome. Maggie imagined his stats flashing up on the screen for the viewers. Something like: *Patrick O'Connell, 24, fitness model.*

"Well, hello, Patrick!" said Schuyler. "Welcome to the *LoveShack* bungalow."

"Not much of a shack, is it?" Patrick said. The girls all laughed. The bungalow was massive, with six bedrooms, a full gym, a pool, a hot tub, and three constantly staffed bars. It was the fanciest place Maggie had ever been.

"Not so bad, right?" Schuyler clapped Patrick on the back. "And now it's time for Hot or Not. You know how it works: each of you lucky guys gets to decide if you're interested in going on a future date with Maggie, Chloe, Layla, Sunny, Tia and Felicia. We don't get to hear your reasons, just give us one word: Hot, or Not."

"Got it." Patrick smirked.

"OK, let's start." Maggie's heart pounded and her body went numb. She knew she was hot! Of course she was hot! She had spent her life being told she was hot. It was literally all anyone had ever told her since she'd recruited to be a child model as an eleven-year-old at the Topeka mall. And she'd primped and primed for this moment down to the flick of an eyebrow pencil.

"Sunny?" Schuyler grinned so wide that his caked-on foundation had begun to crack around his mouth.

"Hot," Patrick pronounced. Everyone cheered.

"Tia?"

"Hot!"

"Layla?"

"Not." Maggie stole a quick glance at Layla, a gorgeous Filipina woman with the most perfect ass she had ever seen. Layla's smile remained plastered on her face.

"That's OK, you're a Not for me, too," Layla said.

"Maggie?"

"Hot!" he declared. Maggie's shoulders relaxed; her jaw unclenched. She smiled at him.

"Felicia?"

"Not."

"Chloe?"

"Sorry, also a Not for me." Patrick smirked again. Maggie knew then that she hated him. Chloe was a Black woman, the only one on the show. He thought the white women were Hot, and the women of color were Not.

"You're a tough judge!" Schuyler said. "These women, they're all gorgeous. But you can't be in a Love Pair with all of them, sadly. So, Patrick, you could be sent to Paradise Island with Sunny, Tia, or Maggie. Viewers at home, it's up to you! Who will you set up for a romantic evening together? Remember, your choices will impact who becomes Love Pairs, competing together as a couple to win the sixth season of *LoveShack*, and maybe even find true love."

More guys arrived. There was Aaron, who looked like a linebacker and thought Maggie was Hot. Next walked out twins Bryan and Luke. They both declared Maggie Hot (and poor Layla was again a Not for both).

Then there was Theo, who was handsome but in a boring way—his face was so perfectly proportioned it was as if he'd been designed in a lab. Theo was the only dissenter; he thought Maggie was a Not. She had expected getting a Not to sting, but it hadn't been so bad after all of the validation from the other men.

Maggie's feet ached from the heels, and she resisted the

urge to wipe sweat off her forehead. Mercifully, before too long, the final man walked in.

He was the definition of tall, dark, and handsome, and Maggie felt herself wanting his approval from the second she laid eyes on him.

"And now, our final guy!" Schuyler said.

"Hey, I'm Finn!"

"Welcome, Finn. It's time for Hot or Not." Schuyler flashed his toothy grin at the women. "Chloe?"

"Hot!"

"Layla?"

"Hot!" Maggie felt relieved for her.

"Maggie?"

"Hot!"

"Tia?"

"Hot!"

"Sunny?"

"Hot!"

"Felicia?"

"Hot!"

"Wow, this must be a *LoveShack* first! You think everyone is Hot. So that means you're willing to go to Paradise Island with any one of these lovely ladies?" asked Schuyler, as if Finn had misunderstood.

"Absolutely. They're all beautiful. And I think Hot or Not is offensive and shallow, honestly," Finn said.

Had she heard that right? She wondered if the producers would go back and cut it later; she wasn't sure if they ever aired critiques of their own show.

"Wow, tell us how you really feel!" Schuyler slapped Finn on the back.

"I just think it's objectifying," Finn said, and she saw Patrick roll his eyes. Maggie smiled at Finn, surprised to find herself agreeing with him. It had been objectifying, of course. Sometimes it was hard to notice these things, because she spent her whole life and career wanting people to look at her. He smiled back; his eyes were light green and his eyelashes thick and dark.

Finn held her gaze until Schuyler abruptly segued out. "Well, that's been Hot or Not. Now, viewers at home, it's your turn. Vote for which couples *you* want to see together on Paradise Island. Their fates are in your hands, so choose wisely."

The first day of shooting was supposedly the longest, besides the finale. She'd been up since four doing hair and makeup, and it was almost 1 a.m. when they finished filming the opening party. The rest of the day was, mercifully, less overwhelming than Hot or Not. She just wandered around the bungalow, drinking and making small talk with whomever she stumbled upon.

Despite her three skinny margaritas, she shivered as they stood in line, waiting for the producers to collect their mics. She'd ended up behind Bryan and in front of Finn, both of whom she had yet to speak to one-on-one. But because cameras were off, they were forbidden from having any real conversation.

Maggie was a little drunk and very exhausted. Her eyes were heavy, and she felt the slightest bit nauseous from the cheap liquor. Before she knew what was happening and could stop herself, she let out a giant, drunk burp into the mostly silent desert night. She covered her mouth with her hand, mortified, but it was too late. Burping in front of all of these men was something out of a nightmare. Why hadn't she taken a couple of Tums before dinner? She felt like crying, but took a deep breath. It wasn't that bad. It was the twenty-first century, and women were allowed to burp! Except, were they really, in front of a bunch of men whom they were supposed to be impressing?

At least the cameras hadn't been rolling.

"You good?" Finn whispered, and her face went hot with shame.

"Yup." Except she wished a hole would open up in the ground and swallow her. "Just embarrassed."

He chuckled. "Don't be. We all had a lot to drink tonight."

The line moved forward and, because she was destined to humiliate herself over and over in front of these people, one of her heels stuck in the gravel. She stumbled, just slightly, but Finn caught her by her left arm. His body was warm, and he smelled a little bit like beer, but in a way that was familiar, comfortable.

"Steady there. It's been a long day." He was still holding on to her arm and gestured to her heels. "You can take those off, you know. We're done filming."

"Not a bad idea." Her feet were aching, and she'd already fantasized about throwing her heels—four-inch stilettos from Zara—in the garbage and never wearing them again. She turned around to look at him. He was still holding on to her arm. That had to be flirting, right? Even after her drunk burp, he was flirting with her. The thought warmed her.

She bent down to undo the straps of her shoes, but Finn stopped her. "I'll do it," he said.

She opened her mouth to protest but something about the look in his eyes stopped her.

Without breaking eye contact, he let go of her arm and kneeled down. Carefully, he took her ankle in his hand. The touch—gentle, but assured—shocked her. This guy was bold, that was for sure. He undid the straps of her heels and the rough feeling of his fingertips on her made her skin prickle with goosebumps.

Despite herself, she giggled. "Do you have a foot fetish or something?" she blurted out. It broke the spell, and she immediately regretted it.

Thankfully, he smiled at her gamely. "Come on. Ew. I'm just trying to be a gentleman." He stood up and she stepped out of her heels.

But before she could respond, Priya cut in. "What's going on here? This kind of thing is not allowed when we're not rolling. You both know that, so don't pull this shit again." But then she smiled playfully. "Flirts, both of you. Save it for later."

With that, Maggie handed in her mic. The first day was over, and she had a crush.

# Amanda

Today was her sober-versary: it'd been one year and ten months. She woke up to her alarm, and felt the familiar combination of good and bad. Good in her body. Bad because she craved amphetamines and knew she had to face another day without them.

She dressed in a Rodarte floral smock that was very *Little House on the Prairie* and looked like a maternity dress but complemented her milky (and, if she was being honest, increasingly spider-veiny) skin. She wore her so-blonde-it-was-almost-silver hair in two braids. The hair color required a monthly visit from her hair stylist, who had to triple-process her roots with organic bleach—apparently bleach could be organic—and then do a conditioning treatment to counteract the damage.

She didn't drive (her license had been revoked because of her two DUIs), so she took an Uber to set, or Jill picked her up on her way to Burbank. Today it was an Uber, and it took forever with traffic. When she got to her office on the lot, Amanda found Jill typing away on the couch across from her desk. Jill had once again brought her breakfast, so she didn't need to eat craft services. She was, without question, the best assistant Amanda had ever had. She did what Amanda asked her to do with no complaint, from picking up yeast-infection medication to standing in an hours-long line for a sample sale. Having an assistant like Jill was like striking gold.

The show Amanda was working on—*The Youth*—was not hers, technically, though she was an executive producer, writer, and was slated to direct a share of the episodes. She did her best to show up on time on days she was needed. It was her first real sober project, and she wanted to prove that she had it together, and that she was still good. It was also her first project after everything had happened with Trevor.

The show was supposed to be a Gen Z answer to *Skins*; it contained a lot of drugs and sex, but also some jokes.

Amanda had also pushed for a storyline in which one of the characters developed an Adderall addiction, because she knew it would be interesting to write, and that the writers' room would defer to her. She also hoped the press would love it and would ask her about it.

"How was yesterday after I left?" Jill looked up from her laptop. "The shoot go OK?"

"It was fine." Amanda unwrapped her bagel and took a bite. It was delicious. Another wonderful thing about no longer using stimulants: food tasted good. When she'd stopped using, she'd immediately put on twenty pounds. But it was a small price to pay, because the pockmarks on her skin were gone, the color had returned to her cheeks, and her hair was no longer falling out.

"You need to be on set in thirty minutes," Jill told her.

Though Jill was a few years younger, sometimes she felt like Amanda's parent more than her assistant.

"I need to finish this bagel first. But how are you? How is Emma?" Amanda, like everyone else in the universe, had followed the stories about Maggie's murder. She was invested because of the Jill connection, sure, but also because of her own past work with *LoveShack*—work she'd kept hidden to the best of her abilities, even from Jill. She'd since pivoted to a more high-brow brand, and that was part of it. But primarily she didn't want to be associated with all the terrible things that tended to happen to *LoveShack* cast members after the show stopped filming.

There'd been ten seasons of *LoveShack* with twelve cast members each, making it a total of one hundred and twenty people who'd ever starred on the show. And of that group, there'd been four—four!—deaths, including Maggie's. The press occasionally called it "the *LoveShack* Curse."

She couldn't help but feel that none of this—even Maggie's death, somehow—would have happened without her.

She'd met Maggie only a few times before she died, at various functions they happened to both be invited to. Maggie and Theo were some of the first reality stars to hit it big on TikTok, and had converted those followers to Instagram. They'd become something of a 2020s version of Jessica Simpson and Nick Lachey from the *Newlyweds* era, combined with a bit of Chip and Joanna Gaines's domesticity and craftiness. They filmed a lot of short content that was boring and captivating at once: Theo pulling pranks on Maggie, Maggie wrapping Theo's Christmas gifts and making him salads, Maggie and Theo half-heartedly doing the latest viral dance together. It was brilliant and vacuous.

Amanda sat with Jill and finished her bagel while Jill told her the latest.

"I can't believe they're declaring it a cold case. Emma must be so frustrated and sad." Amanda wiped her hands on the brown napkin she'd folded on her lap.

"It's awful. She's not doing well. Sitting in her room all day. She looks so thin it's scary. She doesn't eat even though I try to force her," Jill said.

"What happened to those suspects? The cleaning lady or whatever?"

Jill shrugged. "No idea. The police just stopped looking into them but wouldn't tell anyone why. Emma watches a lot of TikToks from conspiracy theorists about why the cleaning lady and her husband were definitely the killers, but beyond that I don't think we know anything."

Amanda sighed. "Can I do anything to help? I hope you're getting the support you need right now. If you ever need to take a day or a week off or whatever, you can. I'm here for you." She hoped Jill wouldn't take her up on this, though. She needed her.

"Thanks, Amanda, I appreciate you," Jill said. "I just want her to get some answers. OK, you need to get to set. Go—go."

Amanda's house in Santa Monica was described to her by her realtor as a charming mid-century bungalow by the sea before she visited it for the first time. In reality, it was a stark, modern mansion that was a ten-minute walk from the beach.

But the moment she saw it, she wanted it. It reminded her of a house you'd see in a mid-2000s horror movie—all floor-to-ceiling windows, white walls, and cement. Los Angeles was too sunny for her, and this place felt severe and chilly, even a bit creepy. She loved it. (*Architectural Digest* had once filmed a YouTube tour of her house while she was very coked up. *The Cut* had called it "the most out-of-touch celebrity house tour of all time" because, in an attempt to display her domesticity, she'd tried to cut a watermelon using a butter knife. In her defense, it was a very sharp butter knife.)

When she got home after work, the place smelled like laundry detergent. She opened her fridge, and in it her housekeeper Alejandra had left a large Tupperware of quinoa-stuffed peppers. Amanda walked over to her oven—she never used it, except to reheat Alejandra's cooking—and set it to 375°F.

Amanda was one of about seven famous actresses who was not thin. But she also wasn't fat, and she liked to remind people she was the size of the average American woman. At thirty-four and 178 pounds, her brand was centered on "you *can* be this normal-looking and work in Hollywood!" When she had created *Anxiety*, her body had become an important feature of the show, even though she hadn't planned on it being that way. Even though she was at her thinnest, gobbling Adderall by the handful every hour. But if you were going to be a normal-sized person and successful in Hollywood, it had to be a central part of your identity. It was the thing people thought was "brave." The truth was, at a certain point her body began to help her career. She stood out. It added an interesting component to any role she played (and she refused to take roles where it was the defining element of her character). When Amanda starred in anything, just existing as a regular-looking person in a TV show or movie generated think-pieces. Anything she did while not thin was considered "revelatory."

She ate her stuffed peppers at her large marble island, and flipped through the Sunday edition of the *Los Angeles Times*, which contained a column about Maggie, teased on the front page. She skimmed a profile of an architect who'd redesigned a famous home, and then a review of a new restaurant she would never try, before she allowed herself to read the essay about Maggie. The image accompanying the article was a drawing of Maggie's face, refracted dozens of times in a broken mirror, eyes fearful like a Hitchcockian femme fatale.

### *The Death of an Influencer*
#### *By Farouq Hijazi*

*In the last post on Maggie Lathrop's feed, she stands in front of a mirror, posing with a gold bottle of self-tanner. The caption reads:* love my line at @lushglow. collaborating with them has been a dream come true, i am OBSESSED with & use daily. love looking like i came from the beach when i've been inside at meetings all day. link in bio 🖤 🌴. *It had 2.9 million likes at the time of the publication of this article.*

*Unless you have somehow managed to avoid consuming any form of media for the last few months, you know that thirteen hours later, she was murdered.*

*Lathrop's death is the stuff of true crime legend. HBO is already slated to make a documentary about the murder, even though we know almost nothing about its circumstances. It will continue to be fictionalized and retold in TV shows and movies. The world—including production studios everywhere—waited with bated breath as the Los Angeles Police Department investigated the murder. Then, after only three and a half months, they announced that, with no meaningful leads, it was now a cold case.*

*It's a bizarre move, to say the least, leaving fans across the country disappointed and angry in equal measure. At risk of adding to the fever pitch surrounding this case, I'm going to outline what we know, according to the LAPD:*

*On January 29 at 9:34 a.m., Maggie Jean Lathrop, 32, was found dead in a warehouse in Culver City. The warehouse, GrayLounge, was the site of a photoshoot she was set to do later that morning with a perfume company. The cause of death was multiple stab wounds.*

*Lathrop, according to her husband, Theo Cooke, left their home early that morning for the shoot, around 7:45 a.m. Cooke told investigators he assumed she had taken a rideshare to the warehouse, though no record of a ride exists. No one from the crew was known to have been on site before the 10:00 a.m. call time, besides the director of the shoot, John Lorraine, and his assistant, Sarah Martinez. Martinez and Lorraine found Lathrop's body at 9:34 a.m. and called 911. (Martinez and Lorraine declined to comment for this story, and are not considered persons of interest by the LAPD.)*

*Adding to the intrigue, according to the LAPD, the crime scene was clean; the murder was almost certainly premeditated. They found no DNA besides Lathrop's own at the scene: no fingerprints, no blood, no hair, no skin under Lathrop's fingernails. They found no footprints or other indications that anyone else had been inside the warehouse, and no security footage showed anything besides Lathrop walking in at 8:39 and Martinez and Lorraine walking in at 9:34. The LAPD suspects the murder took place sometime between 8:45 and 9:10.*

*Early in the investigation, police announced that they'd found footage of Lathrop's housekeeper's husband, Javier Cruz, driving a half-mile from the crime scene about thirty minutes after the suspected time of death (Lucía Cruz, the housekeeper, was reportedly cleaning a client's home that morning in Brentwood). Though fans have coalesced around the theory that Javier Cruz murdered Lathrop, the LAPD cleared him of any wrongdoing after finding CCTV footage to corroborate his claim that he was at a location nearby from 8:15 a.m. to 9:00 a.m.—a location they've chosen not to disclose.*

*Javier and his wife Lucía Cruz emigrated from El Salvador in 2004 and live in Crenshaw, just east of the Culver City warehouse where Lathrop's body was found.*

*A quick search on Instagram shows that there are over 200 accounts in tribute to Lathrop or in search of answers about her death, the biggest being @Justice4Maggie, with over 57,000 followers.*

*The Justice4Maggie community is focused on how little information there is about the murder. "It's hard to comprehend," said Amy Miller, who runs the account. "Her fans have a responsibility to hold the police accountable. We need answers."*

*The many unanswered—and potentially unanswerable—questions frustrate Miller and the Justice4Maggie acolytes. "Why was Maggie at the warehouse so early? Why was no DNA evidence found at the scene of the crime?" Miller wonders.*

*Per conventional true crime wisdom, the husband is always the killer. But in Theo Cooke's case, fans have stood behind him wholeheartedly, referencing his sparkling on-camera romance with Lathrop as rationale for his innocence. The LAPD also announced Cooke is not a person of interest, but declined to provide further details.*

*The obsession with Lathrop isn't surprising. She was famous, and beautiful, and lived her life in the public eye both with her high-profile reality TV appearance and her high-earning career as a social media influencer. She was beloved and reviled, like many public figures. And her murder was brutal and shocking. So why has the LAPD given up? According to an insider with the department who asked to remain anonymous, this was a PR move gone wrong . . .*

Amanda shut the newspaper without finishing the story, mindlessly using her knife to scrape a crusted piece of cheese that had melted from one of the peppers onto her plate. Something was bothering her about the article, but she couldn't put her finger on it. Maybe it was just the feeling of shame she carried with her about all things *LoveShack*.

Or perhaps it was the fact that she recognized the name Lucía Cruz. But from where? She couldn't quite place it. She told herself to forget about it; it was a common enough

Latina name. She likely just thought she recognized it because her DoorDash driver from a few nights ago had had a similar name or something. But then she chided herself, because that was probably a racist thing to think.

Curiosity—or an attempt to absolve herself of racism?—got the better of her, and she googled Lucía. The woman did look familiar, actually. She looked through her phone contacts, typing in L-u-c-i. There it was: *Lucia Cruz Cleaning Lady*. who was that? She'd had the same cleaning lady since the beginning of time. Then it hit her: Lucía was probably the one who'd cleaned her house for two months a few years ago, when Alejandra was in Guatemala visiting her family. Holy shit. Was this the same woman? She had to imagine it was. She'd gotten the name from Trevor, and it was totally possible he'd gotten it from a *LoveShack* colleague. He was in touch and on good terms with all of them still. It was likely, even, that the same *LoveShack* person had given the cleaner's name to Maggie.

She tried to remember Lucía, but couldn't think of much. She was rarely home in those days. Before she could talk herself out of it, she opened her contact and pressed the text message button. *Hi Lucía. This is Amanda Lehman. You worked in my house a couple years ago. Was wondering if you had availability to come for the next few Saturdays to do a clean? I am short-staffed right now.* Alejandra's day off was Saturday, so this was the only thing that made sense. The house would be freakishly clean, but whatever.

Was this woman dangerous? Probably not. The LAPD had cleared her husband of any wrongdoing. But she couldn't help but feel a nervous thrill in her gut as she pressed send.

Within seconds, her phone buzzed. *I can come Saturday. What time?*

Her hands shook as she clicked on Jill's name—first in her favorites—and pressed call. Jill answered right away.

"Sorry it's so late," she said, as if she didn't call Jill at this hour three times a week.

"What's up?" Jill asked.

"Look." Amanda paused. "I just figured something out. Something kinda weird."

Jill was quiet on the other end of the phone for a second. "Yes?"

"You know Lucía Cruz? The woman who used to clean Maggie's house? And was under investigation because her husband's car was spotted near the warehouse where Maggie was killed?" She paused, waiting for Jill to react.

"Of course," Jill said.

"Well, she cleans my house too. Sort of."

She could hear Jill inhale sharply. "What happened to Alejandra? Did you fire her?"

"God no!" Amanda paced around her kitchen. "I just . . . needed fuller coverage. Alejandra doesn't work Saturdays."

"Hm. OK." Jill was silent for an awkward beat.

"I thought maybe I could ask her about Maggie. Maybe she knows something. Now that the police have shut down the investigation."

"Oh, Manda. I don't know if that's a good idea. What if she was somehow involved?" Jill sounded almost annoyed, which in turn made Amanda feel annoyed.

"Even more reason to talk to her, then. It might help us— Emma—get to the truth."

"Don't say anything to her until I can ask Emma what she thinks," Jill said. "Is that OK?"

"Whatever you say, boss." Amanda faked a yawn. "Let's go to bed. I'll see you tomorrow." They hung up, but she knew she wouldn't be able to sleep. She was buzzing. The excitement of this discovery was almost as thrilling as cocaine. Almost, but not quite.

# Emma

She was back in LaClair's stuffy office, but this time with Theo, too. It was the first time she'd seen him since the funeral, and he looked terrible, just as Jill had described. She noticed he'd put his wedding ring back on, presumably for her benefit. He'd barely acknowledged her when they'd walked in together, besides giving her a brief, lukewarm hug.

Emma had woken up that morning to a text from LaClair to her and Theo. The text just said: *Our investigators are done with the house. It's all yours. Please come get keys and documents.* LaClair droned on as he handed over the keys, alongside Maggie's important documents: bank statements; property and medical records. Theo looked bored.

"We didn't find much." LaClair's voice was gravelly and tired. "Except, well, you both probably know this: she was about three hundred thousand dollars in debt until three years ago. Mostly medical expenses from when your mom was ill, but about fifty thousand was credit card debt."

"Are you kidding me?" Emma gave Theo a questioning look, but he refused to make eye contact. Emma knew there was some medical debt from when her mom died, but had had no idea it was that much. Maggie had taken it on because Emma was still in college, and had never asked her for a cent. The idea that she was shouldering that without Emma's help, for all those years, broke her heart.

"Debts can often lead us to a motive," LaClair said. "But with her increased income after *LoveShack*, she paid it off easily. So, I don't see any smoke here. Or fire."

"I didn't know how bad it was," Emma said. "I should've helped."

"Well, none of this is relevant to her death," LaClair said. "And the only thing we found in the house was this note, tucked inside one of her planners." He handed them a photocopy of a handwritten note that said, in blocky letters, *End it, or I'll tell everyone your secret.* Emma's insides felt cold. What could that possibly mean? "But we've already spoken about it." LaClair nodded at Theo.

"It was a weird inside joke we had," Theo said to Emma by way of explanation. Was it her imagination, or was there a touch of desperation behind his smile?

"I don't understand. End what? What's funny about that?" she asked.

"We would be on calls or something with reporters or brands, and they used to take forever. When someone was going on for too long, we sometimes passed these notes to each other. Just as a weird joke." Theo toyed with his wedding ring. His explanation felt off, but she'd have to ask LaClair about it later, because Theo changed the subject. "And nothing on Javier?"

LaClair cleared his throat. "No. Like I've said, we have

footage of Javier in a different location at the time of the murder."

Emma looked LaClair in the eye. "Why can't you tell me where they were? I don't understand."

"Just trust me," LaClair said. "They couldn't have been at the warehouse."

"But you said a few weeks ago that we didn't have firm timing on when the murder took place? Maybe they—"

LaClair cut her off. "Please, Emma. Enough."

There was a moment of uncomfortable silence before Theo spoke, his voice filled with false cheer. "OK. Thanks for your hard work on this, detective."

LaClair handed Theo the keys and the documents, and stood up to shake their hands. He shook Emma's first, giving her a decisive nod. His palm was clammy, but his handshake was surprisingly firm. He then reached out to shake Theo's, and the two barely made eye contact.

As they walked out, Emma wanted to ask Theo about the house, the note, and about what he thought of the LAPD closing the investigation. But he was quiet. He looked at his shoes as they made their way down the hall to the exit. "How are you holding up?" she asked instead.

"I'm OK." He was still looking down. He opened the door for her and walked to the parking lot. "You?"

"Bad," she answered honestly. "Really fucking bad. I don't feel like I'll ever be OK unless we know what happened to Maggie."

"I'm sorry," he said, and gave her a cursory pat on the shoulder. "I know what you mean."

She considered him. The last time she'd seen him before

Maggie had died was when she'd been over at their house filming a video with her sister. Maggie had wanted to recreate a photo of them from their childhood in which they were wearing backwards baseball caps and holding large popsicles because of some viral TikTok trend. It was annoying to be in Maggie's videos, partially because people always commented things like *omg how are you even related???*, but she occasionally caved and participated when her sister bribed her with dinner.

He'd been there while they recorded by the pool, giving them feedback on the takes that Maggie's assistant filmed. It was warm out that day, in the eighties, but he wore a pair of black pants and a terry-cloth polo.

He studied the footage. "You need more of the popsicle juice on your face. Funnier that way." His brows were knit together in concentration. "Emma, do you think you can look a little less pained? It doesn't match the childhood photo."

"Fine." She was always slightly taken aback by how seriously he took these things, and how sharp his criticism could be.

He gave her a look. "I'm just helping. You didn't want to schlep all the way out here for this video to flop, I assume?"

"Theo, come on. Give her a break." Maggie turned to her assistant. "Can we do another take? We'll get more popsicle juice on our faces."

"It's my brand too." Theo spoke directly to Maggie, as if that meant Emma couldn't hear him. "Don't tell me to 'give her a break.'"

"It's fine," Emma said, trying to break the tension. "I'll look less miserable, I swear."

"Thank you." Theo shot Maggie a look. "Was that so hard?"

"Should we look into Lucía and Javier on our own?" she asked Theo as they stood outside the police station. "We could go together. I know you have a relationship with them. Maybe they would talk to us?"

"And what would they say? 'Yeah, I killed your wife'?"

Her cheeks burned. "Of course not. But we could get their side of the story, see if it really holds up? If the police got the full picture?"

"I know you miss her," Theo said. "I miss her too. But we should trust the police on this."

She sighed. "That would mean giving up on finding out who killed her, because that's what they're doing."

He ignored her. "Hey, I have to get going. I have a meeting soon."

"Whatever." What the fuck was his problem? "Bye, Theo."

He gave her a half-hearted wave and got into his Alfa Romeo. She'd always hated that car.

As soon as she got home, she kicked off her shoes and dropped her bag on the floor. She plopped herself down on her bed and opened the anonymous Instagram account she had created a month prior to do internet sleuthing. She followed a few of the #JusticeForMaggie accounts, which, as far as she could tell, were run by weird fans who had no reason to be speculating about Maggie's death. But still, some of these posts got hundreds of thousands of likes.

Maybe there was a way to use these people to build momentum.

She opened the first account, called MaggieLathropUpdates. She clicked on the latest post, which had 34,352 likes. Jesus. It was a straight-to-camera video featuring the woman, Martha, who ran the account.

"We're not talking enough about the fact that the LAPD is straight up ignoring Javier Cruz as a suspect," said Martha. Her eyes were narrowed in frustration. "I need this community to be asking: Why? Why is this supposed CCTV footage enough to clear him? I'm sorry, but there is literally nothing near that warehouse. I just don't buy it. I'm sorry, but I don't."

Emma let out a breath she hadn't realized she was holding. Should she contact this woman and ask for help?

She looked down to see she was scratching the inside of her wrist so hard she'd drawn blood. "Fuck," she said out loud, to no one.

"What's going on?" Jill said, peering into her bedroom as Emma held her wrist. "Let me get you a Band-Aid for that." It was not the first time this had happened.

"Thank you," Emma said, though she wondered if there would ever come a day when she could go even five minutes without needing something from Jill.

"What's wrong?" Jill brought her a large Band-Aid and some antibiotic ointment.

"I'm just feeling so . . ." She swallowed a sob. "Hopeless. We're never going to know what happened. I don't see a way forward here. It seems like the only real suspect is Javier Cruz, and the LAPD doesn't give a shit. Except maybe I'm just falling for these stupid conspiracy theories. I don't know."

Jill sighed. "Em, I actually have something to tell you."

"You do?" Emma said.

"Yes, but it's going to sound odd. Can you hang tight while I call Amanda?"

"Your boss, Amanda?"

"Yes," Jill said, but she was already dialing.

# Amanda

Emma and Jill sat on the couch in Amanda's office, staring at the art above her desk. It was a screen print of her vagina she'd gotten done by a celebrated avant-garde artist, and always an eyecatcher.

Amanda could see Emma had a small tremor, and wore a large Band-Aid on her wrist. Had she been cutting herself? The poor thing.

"Thank you for doing this," Emma choked out. "I honestly don't know what to say."

Amanda smiled at Emma as warmly as she could. "I'm happy to help."

"I hope this isn't weird for you," Emma said.

"Of course not. Lucía won't mind." She had no idea if Lucía would mind.

"I hope this helps me get some resolution," Emma said. Amanda was pleased with herself; she was doing a favor for someone who really, really needed it.

Amanda had every privilege in the world, she knew. She often felt that, unlike others who suffered because of their circumstances, because of their lots in life, her suffering was her own fault. Beth, of course, pushed back on this line of thinking ("Addiction is a disease, not a personality flaw"). But the only way she'd been able to maintain sobriety was by taking responsibility—by acknowledging that, while it wasn't her fault, exactly, it was on her to fix. And even her experience with addiction was one of enormous privilege. Her two stints in rehab were in Malibu, in a lovely place right on the beach. Not that rehab itself was lovely—it wasn't. But it was the least bad way to do it. She went to bed every night in a king-sized bed, in her own room (which featured an expansive view of the ocean). It resembled a fancy hotel without any sharp objects or minibar. And yes, she was detoxing, so spent the majority of her first weeks lying on the expensive tile of the cool bathroom floor, sitting up only to vomit in the lovely toilet. Still. It could've been a lot worse.

She had every privilege, every support, and then some: loving parents who put up with her shit. A lot of money. A career that seemed to be limping along after some bad and very public missteps. She felt, in equal measure, guilty and relieved when she considered her life's struggles relative to Emma's. When she considered the *LoveShack* curse, and everything it'd wrought.

"I'm here for you." Amanda squeezed Emma's shoulder. "How about you come over on Saturday? We can make a day out of it. After you talk to Lucía, of course. My manicurist is coming that afternoon and I can ask if she'll do you too. You deserve some pampering."

Was that a weird offer? Jill looked a bit confused.

"Wow. That's so kind." Emma started crying again. "Sorry, I'm a mess." Amanda offered her a tissue, and she blew her nose.

"Don't apologize." Amanda stood up to give Emma a hug. "It means a lot to be able to help."

An hour after their meeting, she received a text from Emma with a simple heart emoji. She smiled to herself and sent one back.

# Jill

Tonight was the first time that Emma had agreed to go out since Maggie had died, and Jill was nervous. She figured that reconnecting with some old friends from college would be good for Emma—it would be good for them both. Since Maggie had died, Jill hadn't done much socializing either. It sometimes felt like her entire life was now just filled with Emma's and Amanda's needs.

Their friend Sammi had chosen the meeting spot: a natural wine bar in Eagle Rock near where she and their other friend Alice lived. As a waitress led Jill and Emma to a booth, Jill could tell that Emma was also nervous, even though Sammi and Alice had been their friends for ten years. When they were getting ready, Emma had tried to leave the house in leggings and a sweatshirt. Jill had kindly suggested she change into something a little nicer, and lent her a new sweater she'd just bought herself from Anthropologie. For her part, Jill was wearing red lipstick and a green dress that matched her eyes. Her hair was de-frizzed, and she felt good about herself; she didn't want to look overdressed next to Emma.

They both considered the menu while they waited for

their friends, and Jill ordered an expensive bottle of Pét-Nat to split. Jill was excited to try it, but Emma wore a look that was seemingly intended to convey that this outing was causing her physical pain.

"Cheer up, Eeyore," Jill said. It was something that she'd always called Emma when she was in one of her moods. It was meant to be playful, but Emma just stared back at her. They sat in near silence until their wine arrived.

Emma took a sip and contorted her face. "This tastes like expensive vinegar. They must make it specifically for stupid LA millennials who pretend to like bad-tasting shit because it makes them feel interesting."

"It's not *that* bad," Jill said. She wanted to have just one night when Emma wasn't engaged in an exhausting display of ironic detachment to their surroundings. "Should we get a snack, too?" But before Emma could answer, Sammi and Alice arrived. They all hugged and settled into the booth, and Emma brightened. Jill was relieved. Maybe this evening was just what Emma needed, after all.

"Emma, it's *so* good to see you," Alice said. "It's been way too long."

"Totally," Sammi agreed. "We really missed you."

Emma smiled in a sad way. "I missed you both too. It's been a tough few months. I haven't left my house much."

"I get that." Sammi squeezed Emma's hand. "And I'm so sorry we couldn't be at the funeral."

Jill's stomach lurched. Why would Sammi bring that up? She was pretty sure Emma hadn't even noticed they hadn't been there.

"We'd been planning that trip to Oaxaca forever, and it

was all nonrefundable," Alice chimed in. Emma's expression hardened.

"We would've lost, like, so much money if we'd had to cancel the Airbnb," Sammi continued.

Jill's face flushed with irritation. If she was being honest, the fact that she and Emma hadn't been invited on the trip in the first place also annoyed her. Sammi and Alice were both in long-term relationships, and they traveled together as couples. Because Emma and Jill were both single, they were never included.

"Alright." Emma's expression was blank, tired. "Can we talk about something else?"

"Oh, OK," Alice said, jarred. She shot Sammi a quick look. "Sorry, I didn't mean to upset you."

"It's fine," Emma said. "I just felt really alone at the funeral. That's all."

"I'm sorry if we contributed to that," Alice said. Emma nodded.

"Jill, how're things?" Sammi redirected. "Are you still working on that show about those high-school kids doing drugs?"

Jill felt grateful for the new topic. "Yep. *The Youth*. It's my first time on an actual set, and it's fun but stressful. All I do is work these days." *And babysit Emma*, she didn't add.

"I'll have to check it out," Sammi said. "Also, what's the deal with Amanda Lehman? How's working for her?"

Jill took a glug of her wine and considered the question, trying to ignore that Emma was scratching her wrist under the table. "It's good. She's definitely more than just a boss; she feels like a friend, too." She didn't say the rest, which was that Amanda was the neediest boss she'd ever had. And she could be strange, too. Why had Jill never realized she had Lucía cleaning her place on Saturdays? It was spotless, for one thing. She didn't need a cleaner seven days a week. And Jill coordinated with Alejandra all the time, letting her know when Amanda would be back for dinner. Hopefully this conversation with Lucía would give Emma some closure, because it pained her to have to play into one of Amanda's weird ideas.

But at least she got to be near screenwriting. At her last job, as an assistant at a talent agency, she never got to look over scripts or be in creative meetings. All she did was get coffee for her boss and respond to emails telling people that her boss was unavailable. And at least working with Amanda was interesting, more or less. Even if Jill had spent all day yesterday driving around the Valley in search of a particular brand of smoked salmon that cost $27 per pound that Amanda just "had to have." But she didn't want to talk about any of this with her friends. It felt disloyal; Amanda was nice. And she was in a vulnerable place. And she was helping Jill's grieving best friend.

"Is that weird?" Alice asked.

"What do you mean?"

"Like, it is weird that she's your friend *and* your boss?"

"Not really." But Jill wasn't sure if that was the truth.

"It's amazing that she's still getting work. Because of, like, everything that went down with that guy," Sammi said. Jill's cheeks turned red again. She hated talking about Amanda's big fuck-up.

"Yeah, she's fine. Clearly." Jill looked over at Emma for

support, but she was scrolling on her phone. She nudged her friend under the table.

"Emma, how's work for you?" Alice asked.

"I'm on leave," Emma said. "I may just fully quit."

"I thought you loved your job," Sammi said.

Emma sighed. "I loved writing. And I guess I loved *Mrs. Ladybug*, even though it was silly. But now I'm focused on finding out what happened to Maggie."

Sammi and Alice sat in uncomfortable silence.

Jill broke the tension. "*Mrs. Ladybug* will just have to rely on some other cynical thirty-something to write engaging content about sea creatures and trains and types of clouds."

Emma chuckled. "True."

Conversation for the rest of the night, mercifully, didn't focus on Maggie, but on Alice's wedding plans, and some gossip about other college friends. Emma seemed disengaged, though not unhappy. And before the night was over, Jill finally relaxed a bit. Being with friends was fun, she remembered. She couldn't help but fantasize about what it would've been like without Emma there, which made her feel guilty. It was wrong of her to want to do anything but support Emma right now, just a few months after her sister had been murdered. As penance, she put her credit card down to pay for everyone's drinks, even though she couldn't afford it. But when the check came back, she saw that Emma had quietly added her card too, so they were splitting it. Jill squeezed her hand under the table as more guilt surged through her.

## Emma

Emma's ex, Liz, was a journalist for a local paper, and had won an award two years prior for her investigative work into the environmental impacts of an oil refinery near Santa Barbara. Emma was nervous to see Lucía again—she'd only met her a couple of times at Maggie and Theo's, and they'd never spoken much. She had no idea how to frame the conversation she wanted to have with her. So she'd panic-texted Liz about the situation and asked if there was anything in particular she should ask Lucía about.

Liz's answer came in as she was pulling up:

> hiii so don't take this the wrong way but isn't it kinda strange that amanda is inviting you over to interrogate her housekeeper? i hope you're not going down a conspiracy theory rabbit hole. i guess if it were me I would just be really honest with her about what you're looking for & maybe ask her what her experience was like dealing with the police. make her feel comfortable.

Emma's hands shook slightly on the steering wheel as she considered Liz's advice. This meeting was more than kinda strange, that was for sure. And she hoped it wasn't a mistake.

Amanda's house was sparse and modern and entirely different from the chaotic aesthetic of her office. Emma buzzed the call button at the large iron gate, and heard a click as it swung open. Amanda was standing at her open door when she walked up, waving. She wore a red corset top with puffy sleeves and a pair of low-slung, baggy jeans. While Emma appreciated her commitment to her aesthetic, perhaps this look was a bit eye-catching for a serious conversation with one's housekeeper? But who was Emma to judge? She was wearing a pair of overalls and a shirt from her old gay kickball team.

"Welcome!" Amanda said, before dropping her voice to a whisper. Her smile was too big, and it was making Emma nervous. "OK, so we've got a tiny, tiny problem." Amanda's hand gripped Emma's upper arm a little too hard. She could feel the metal of her rings against her skin.

"What's going on?"

"Do you speak Spanish?" Amanda asked.

"No, not at all." Emma had taken Spanish at her high school in Kansas. The teacher was a man who went by Señor Dawkins, and barely spoke Spanish himself. She'd essentially learned the names of different foods, as well as how to say *My name is Emma, and I like strawberries*.

"I'm *so* stupid." Amanda closed her eyes. "I somehow forgot that Lucía is basically monolingual. Whenever she's here, we speak in Spanish."

Emma recalled a vague memory of Theo, who was half-Chilean, speaking to Lucía in Spanish. "Oh shit. Can you translate?"

"I'll try," Amanda said. "My Spanish isn't amazing."

So this was going to be even cringier than Emma had feared. She considered, briefly, turning around and walking away. But she couldn't. She was too curious. Plus, the house was astonishing, and she wanted to see more. The parlor, where they stood, had floor-to-ceiling windows that let in the late-morning light. It also hosted a floating staircase, a large, singular cactus plant, and a chrome and crystal chandelier that hung from the tall ceiling. The floors were the kind of light hardwood that likely got ruined by any sort of contact with shoes.

"Wow. Your place. It's incredible."

"You're too sweet." Amanda led Emma to the kitchen, which looked sterile and unused. White marble countertops lined the space, with dark wood cabinetry providing a stark contrast. There was a large island in the middle of the space, and it was empty except for a giant chrome espresso machine.

Amanda offered her a seat at her live-edge wood table, which Emma ran her hand over. "It's redwood," Amanda said by way of explanation, before calling into the other room. "Lucía? *¿Venga acá?*"

Emma's heart beat quicker due to a potent combination of social anxiety and anticipation that Lucía might actually be able to tell them something useful. She took a deep breath, trying to prepare herself.

Lucía appeared a few seconds later. Emma barely recognized her. She'd lost weight and looked older than Emma remembered. She had dark circles under her eyes and had tied her hair into a limp ponytail. She was short, perhaps four foot eleven, and wore a sweatshirt, a pair of leggings, and knock-off Converse.

Lucía eyed Emma. *"Es bueno verla."* Her voice was quiet and her face solemn. *"Siento su pérdida."*

Emma looked at Amanda, waiting for her to translate. Amanda looked back at her, smiling. "Lucía, please sit." She pointed to the empty chair. As Lucía complied, Amanda continued. "Is it OK if we ask you some questions? Nothing too invasive, but just to get a handle on things, on your timeline of events. *¿Comprendes?"* Amanda's attempt at rolling her Rs made it sound like she was saying an L instead. *Complendes.* Emma almost winced.

Lucía gave them a worried look. *"Lo siento.* My English very bad."

Amanda smiled, but Emma could see frustration in her expression. *"Es no problema. ¿Es . . . posible estamos preguntamos . . . preguntos?"*

Lucía nodded her head yes.

Suddenly, Emma felt shy. What was she going to say to this woman? This was bizarre and inappropriate, and she should've realized that before she'd agreed to it. But she was here now, and she knew it would be best to get on with it. "Sorry! *Yo no hablo español."* Why was she speaking so loud, like Lucía was a hard-of-hearing older relative? She tried to return her voice to its normal pitch. "Amanda, can you ask her what her relationship was like with Maggie?"

Amanda nodded, her face scrunched in concentration. *"¿Todo bien con Maggie? ¿Te gusta ella?"*

Lucía looked confused. "*¿Sí? Por supuesto.*"

Helpful. Great. "Can you ask if she saw anything suspicious in the months before Maggie died? Did anything at the house feel off?"

Amanda grimaced, presumably at the prospect of translating a real sentence. "*¿Todos con Maggie . . . bueno? ¿Es nada mala? ¿Y todos con la casa? ¿Es nada . . . suspiciosa?*"

OK, so Amanda really didn't speak Spanish. Why had she misrepresented this? How did she not know her own housekeeper didn't speak English?

"*No entiendo.*" Lucía spoke slowly. Her face looked pained. "*Lo siento. Quiero ayudar, pero no entiendo inglés.*"

Amanda turned to Emma. A blush was creeping from her cheeks down her neck. "I'm so sorry. I overestimated my Spanish here." She closed her eyes. "I feel so bad for making you come all this way. Maybe we can do a Google Translate conversation?"

Emma held in a sigh. This was embarrassing. She pulled out her phone and typed: *Hi Lucia, sorry I don't speak Spanish. We just wanted any information you might have about Maggie's death, and if anything weird happened before she died.* She stopped, thinking. Should she write out this next part? She decided to go for it. *I know your husband's car was seen near the warehouse and he was taken in for questioning. Can you tell us in your own words what exactly happened?* She put the message into Google Translate and handed the phone to Lucía, who read it quickly.

Lucía shook her head in what looked like disgust. "*Mi esposo no hizo nada malo. Es una buena persona; fue solo una mala coincidencia. Ya le dije a la policía. Amanda me dijo que tenía preguntas sobre la señora Maggie, no sobre Javier. Me tengo que ir.*"

Emma looked at Amanda, hoping she understood. But Amanda just shook her head. "I think something about her husband not being bad? Or maybe that her husband is bad? I don't know."

"You no understand," Lucía said.

"I'm sorry. *Lo siento.* I don't think we do," Emma said. "Can you help us understand?"

Lucía spoke slowly. *"Lo que estuvimos haciendo ese día fue privado. ¿Entiende?"*

"I think *privado* means 'private,'" Amanda whispered.

"What was *privado*? You can trust us." Emma tried to make eye contact with Lucía, but she was looking at her feet.

*"La policía ya lo sabe. Les dijimos todo."*

"She's saying she already told the police everything," Amanda said.

Emma took out her phone and typed into Google Translate: *Can you tell us why you were near the warehouse the day Maggie died? Please. I need to know what happened. We won't tell anyone.*

She handed the phone to Lucía, who sighed. She spent a few minutes typing before she handed the phone back. *Javier has problem with drugs. Drug addiction but he gets better. He was at the methadone clinic near the warehouse where Maggie died. He goes one time each week. The police said they won't call ICE or make a story. If it about drugs in the news ICE could look for us. I'm sorry for the loss of Maggie. Please leave us alone.* Then, wordlessly, Lucía pulled out her own phone and showed it to Emma. On it was a photo of a CCTV still of Javier in a nondescript room that was obviously some sort of medical clinic. It was slightly grainy, but she could see that Javier was drinking from a plastic cup filled a third of the way with clear liquid. *"Esta foto es de la policía,"* Lucía said. She pointed to the cup in the photo. *"Metadona."* Emma nodded, guessing this meant methadone. With that, Lucía took her phone back and began to gather her cleaning supplies.

Emma felt a rush of panic. "Please, you should stay. I'm sorry to hear that about Javier. I believe you." But Lucía just shook her head and walked away, cleaning-supply caddy in hand.

"Fuck," Emma said, once they heard the front door slam. She handed Amanda the phone.

Amanda read quickly, her eyes widening as she went on. "Shit. Are we assholes?"

"Well, I just forced her to tell me about her husband's drug addiction," Emma said. "So yes, I think we are." She was suddenly embarrassed. Embarrassed to have agreed to this in the first place. Embarrassed that she'd assumed the police were being careless about Lucía when really they were keeping her sensitive information private.

"I'll apologize to her," Amanda said. "I'm sorry, I just wanted to be helpful. I didn't know about the drugs. Or that they were worried about getting deported. I didn't even know she was undocumented!"

Emma looked away. She knew what this was: Amanda was just another busybody weirdo who wanted to get involved in a high-profile murder. Even if she was famous and Jill's boss, it was still weird. "I think I should go."

Amanda looked at her. "Don't, please. I shouldn't have done this: it was stupid. But I just wanted to help."

"Why? No offense, but we don't really know each other. I should've thought this through. You're Lucía's boss, and she's terrified, and she probably felt she had to say yes to talking to us."

Amanda looked as though she was about to cry. "I fucked up. And, honestly, she's not really my employee. I only told her to start coming on Saturdays so we could get her to talk."

Emma shook her head. "Seriously?"

"I know. I'm an idiot, and I'm sorry. But I need to tell you something, for the sake of 'rigorous honesty.' It's an AA thing."

Emma held in a snort. "What?"

Amanda looked down at her hands. "Don't freak out. But I kind of, like, invented *LoveShack*."

# Amanda

"Shit. My manicurist is supposed to come in a few minutes," Amanda said, looking at her watch. "Should we get our nails done, and then I can explain everything?"

"Can you just cancel?" Emma gave her an irritated look. "You can tell me about the show, but then I think I should leave."

OK, so she was, like, *mad* mad. "I'm sorry I didn't tell you until now. The whole thing is very sensitive for me."

"Jesus, Amanda. It was a stupid reality TV show. Why does it matter? Just tell me."

She was twenty-five and working as a barista. She and Trevor were just friends and creative partners at that point. They'd written the pilot script for *Anxiety* and had an agent—a friend of her dad's whose only high-profile client was Howie Mandel, but still—yet they hadn't gotten interest in their script from any TV studios or streaming networks.

Amanda was depressed, and nursing a growing stimulant addiction. One night, after she'd taken a couple of Adderalls, she sat at home and binged back-to-back episodes of *The Bachelor*. Her nighttime routine consisted of watching a massive amount of reality TV while keeping her hands busy with some sort of craft—Trevor was never there at night because he bartended. She was really into needlepoint at the time, and liked to pretend she was a heroine in a gothic novel, working on her stitching while her brain withered away to nothing.

*The Bachelor* was just so chaste! She curled up on her shabby-chic Urban Outfitters couch as that season's Bachelor (who, as always, was some white dude ex-college football player) went on a one-on-one date with some nondescript blonde alum of the University of Alabama's Delta Gamma chapter. They stared longingly into each other's eyes as they rode horses at a ranch somewhere outside of Dallas. It seemed as if they liked each other enough. Or maybe they didn't. These people lacked any sort of meaningful interiority, so it was hard to decipher.

That's when the idea hit. What if she wrote the outline for a different kind of reality TV dating show? One where everyone had a personality. Where the audience got to be involved, playing matchmaker, instead of passively watching while blandly attractive people went on monotonous dates. She took out a pen and paper and jotted down her thoughts:

- Couples paired by viewers, doesn't matter if they hate each other
- Everyone lives together
- Put them in actually funny/tense situations
- People are smarter? Have more substance?
- More sex stuff
- Most popular couple wins. Based on viewer votes

She'd talk it over with Trevor. It wasn't the think-y millennial discourse-starter that *Anxiety* was, sure. But she was an entertainer, and she liked the idea of creating something that would make people happy. That would comfort them while they sat on their couch at night, wrapped in a blanket, high on amphetamines and extremely lonely.

"So you just pitched it, and the network produced it? I'm confused. How are you not publicly associated with this?" Emma, despite herself, was obviously enthralled with the *LoveShack* origin story. She sat at Amanda's table, eating one of Alejandra's famous salted chocolate chip cookies.

"We used a pen name. Trevor and I." She didn't feel like getting into what happened after, how she'd been pushed out and Trevor had ended up pocketing the money. That was a story for another time.

"OK, so you came up with the idea for the show. Who cares?" Emma licked a stray streak of melted chocolate off her thumb. The cookie had improved her mood more than Amanda probably deserved.

"The show is fucked up. And bad for the world," Amanda said. "I didn't realize it then, but now I do. You know about the *LoveShack* curse."

"You don't really believe in that, though?" Emma said.

"I don't know." Amanda took a piece of a cookie and popped it in her mouth. "We put people in some messed-up situations."

"Like what?" Emma asked.

"You know. Like, the challenges. The intentionally bad Love Pairs."

"I actually don't really know," Emma said. "I've only watched one episode."

"How is that possible?"

"Maggie told me not to watch. She said it was cringey and embarrassing, so I only saw the first episode a couple days ago. It was kind of amazing to see Maggie again, so alive. But still. The whole thing is weird."

Amanda thought about this. What was Maggie so afraid of that she'd told Emma not to watch? "I think you should watch the rest. We can do it together, if you want. I can give you the inside story about the show."

Emma paused, considering this.

"Maybe you'll learn something about your sister," Amanda continued.

"I think I should focus my energy on actually trying to investigate her murder. Obviously, Lucía was a dead end," Emma said.

That was a jab at her, but Amanda didn't care. Despite herself, she liked this girl. She was plucky and uncowed by Amanda's fame.

"Why not both?" Amanda said. "We can start watching now. I've got a home theater."

Emma sighed. She paused, and Amanda could tell she was considering her offer. "Fine. I guess I've got nothing better to do. But we need to apologize to Lucía. And I'm taking more of these cookies." She plucked two off the plate.

And though Amanda had a no-food-on-the-fancy-couch rule, she decided to allow it.

# Maggie

## Episode 2

"Do you think they actually let the viewers choose who we go to Paradise Island with?" Layla whispered to Maggie in their shared room. They'd been filming for four days, which made about enough content for one episode. This was the only time of day they were allowed to be without mics, and they relished it. One of the producers, Priya, had warned them in a hushed voice that the rooms *did* have hidden cameras and mics (referred to by producers as "surveillance"), so if anyone tried anything they could catch it on tape. But she'd also said they didn't use any footage or audio from their rooms unless something interesting happened.

"I don't know," Maggie responded. "But in any scenario, you got lucky. Finn seems great." Layla had been paired with Finn for her Paradise Island date, and it'd gone exceedingly well. Maggie tried to sound upbeat, as if this were a positive development that she was in no way cripplingly jealous of.

"Yeah, but every other guy still thinks I'm ugly as fuck." Layla rolled onto her back and sighed. She was still hung up on Hot or Not.

"That's ridiculous." Maggie kicked her blanket off, trying to cool herself down enough to sleep. "You're an actual model. Like, you literally get paid to model." The bungalow's off-camera interior was completely different from its glamorous exterior. They slept in twin beds and the blankets were the polyester kind usually found in cheap motels. Their rooms had no A/C, just fans, and the polyester trapped sweat.

"You're just saying that because every guy thought you were Hot."

"Am not. Also, Theo didn't think I was Hot!"

"Oh, boo-hoo. He looks like the fourth Hanson brother."

"You're not wrong," Maggie said, and Layla laughed. "None of this matters, though, because you had a great date." *With the only guy I have any romantic interest in*, she didn't add. She barely even knew Finn, and they hadn't talked much since what she'd come to think of as the Shoe Incident. Plus, it wasn't as if Layla had chosen Finn.

There was a pause, just long enough for Maggie's eyes to get heavy. She yawned.

"Do you think everyone thought I was ugly because I'm brown?" Layla asked.

Maggie had, of course, noticed that the two women of color did worse in Hot or Not. But still. Was it racist? "I really hope not. You're gorgeous, and any guy should've wanted to go to Paradise Island with you. For fuck's sake. It's ridiculous. It's like Finn said, the game is shallow and stupid."

"You're sweet." Layla's bed creaked as she rolled over.

Maggie wiped a bead of sweat from her forehead. Sure,

this wasn't the glossy dream house she'd pictured. But still—the showers had hot water. That was a luxury her Brooklyn apartment didn't consistently offer.

"I think you have a little crush on Finn," Layla said, breaking their comfortable silence. She had a note of mischief in her voice. Maggie threw a pillow at her.

"Oh my God, you're relentless! Not true. He just seems the most in touch with reality," she said.

"Well, you're going to have to pry him from my cold, dead hands," Layla said. At this, they both laughed, though it wasn't clear if she was kidding.

When Maggie's manager, Anita, had told her she should start applying to be on reality dating shows, she'd balked. These shows seemed impossibly glamorous and definitely not for broke nobodies from the middle of nowhere like her.

She was an aspiring actress, and had auditioned for every commercial, play, and TV show in New York City by the time she was twenty-eight. She was a full-time waitress with a very, very part-time acting career and an anemic Instagram page without the follower count she needed to make any real money. The only Instagram brand deal she had was with a natural deodorant company, whose product made her armpits itch and who only paid her on commission. She was in massive debt that she'd never be able to pay off with waitressing money and natural deodorant samples.

Her biggest career success was a Dr. Scholl's commercial in 2013, which played during all the daytime talk shows for years. As a result, women in their sixties and seventies occasionally looked at her with faint recognition when she passed them on the street.

"Maggie, you're twenty-eight, and you're gorgeous, but it won't last forever. And you don't have the money to get the work done you're gonna need to stay relevant in your thirties. Botox is expensive," Anita had told her one day, about six months before she was cast on *LoveShack*.

"I already got Botox," Maggie reminded her.

"Well, you're going to need more," Anita said. "You have to get out there *now*, and I think we can be honest that acting isn't working out. So it's either reality TV, or selling feet pics online."

So she auditioned for *The Bachelor* (rejected after a final interview with the producers when she refused to agree to let them list "orphan" as her job title on the chyron), *Big Brother* (a casting agent deemed her "too normal"), *Love Island* (she was too old and didn't even get an interview. Anita chided her for not knowing to list her age as twenty-three), and even *Selling Sunset* (she didn't have a real estate license). *LoveShack* was her Hail Mary. It also had a bigger viewership than any of the other shows, and its stars had gone on to have successful Instagram influencing careers.

The idea of taking a break from her stressful life and playing dress-up for a month in a fancy mansion felt exciting. Plus, it'd give her the chance to make some real money.

Every night that week there was a Paradise Island matching ceremony, where Schuyler announced which two people viewers had paired for a romantic getaway. So far, Maggie hadn't been paired, and there were only two girls left.

Viewers could match her with any of the guys who'd declared her Hot, even if they'd been on another Paradise Island date.

The two remaining girls—she and Chloe—stood side by side in front of the fire pit in full glam. She knew it was unlikely she'd be paired with Finn, and tried to tamp down any errant hope she felt.

"Tonight," Schuyler said, "we're announcing a very special Paradise Island date." He looked directly at Maggie, and she knew it was her turn. She took a deep breath, and tried to calm herself. It would be OK. Whoever it was, she would make it work.

"Maggie, the viewers have paired you with . . . Patrick!"

Except him. Fuck. The most annoying guy there. She quickly plastered a smile on her face as Patrick came barreling over to her, and gave her a kiss on the cheek. His breath was stale and sour.

Schuyler beamed. "Viewers, stay tuned. Will Maggie and Patrick become a true Love Pair? We'll find out!"

Later that night, Maggie was sitting on a couch in the bungalow with Layla. It was hard to pass the time when you were on camera. You didn't want to gossip unless you wanted the gossip shown to millions of people, and, for the same reason, you didn't want to talk about your real feelings. They mostly talked about random, non-show-related stuff: their families, their old jobs, how they felt about various prestige television shows. Stuff they knew would be too boring to make it on to the show. Finn approached them, and sat down next to Layla. She moved toward him, and Maggie tried not to wince.

"Actually, Maggie, I wanted to see if I could pull you for a sec," he said.

Maggie looked at Layla, who just nodded at her. "Sure," Maggie said. Her heart rate increased.

They made their way to the other side of the bungalow's living room, near the photos of their faces. As soon as people were voted out, their portraits were removed. But for now, everyone was still there. The cameras had followed Finn and zoomed in on them. She leaned against the wall, and he stood next to her. Their arms grazed lightly, and it sent a pleasant chill down her spine. "I just wanted to check in and make sure you were good." His voice was quiet. God, he was handsome. It was almost painful to make eye contact.

"What do you mean?"

"With, you know, your Paradise Island situation? Like, being paired with Patrick."

"I'm feeling fine about it," she said. She didn't want to badmouth the guy on camera when he hadn't done anything wrong. "I'm going to give him a chance."

"Well, be careful. The guy has bad vibes," he said. "Really bad."

"What do you mean?" she asked.

"I haven't talked about it much since I got here, but I served in the military as a field medic. I saw lots of different guys over the years, from all types of units," he said. Of course Finn was a field medic. The thought of him bandaging wounded soldiers made her heart melt, just a bit. "Most of the guys I met were solid, but sometimes, well. I don't know how to say this." He paused, running his fingers over his five o'clock shadow. He leaned over, whispering into her ear. "Sometimes you can tell when something's not right with someone. They're different behind closed doors when it's just other men around."

Maggie nodded, but her mind was racing. Was it possible that Finn was jealous of Patrick? More likely he was just looking after her, like a big brother. She needed to not have a crush on this man. "Thanks for letting me know."

"Just be careful."

"Of course." She tried to sound cheery as he turned to leave. "I will."

# Jill

Emma sat on the floor of her bedroom with a wild look in her eyes, and a freshly scratched wrist. "It's somewhere in here." She was rifling through the bottom drawer of her dresser, throwing her clothes all over the floor.

Jill sat next to Emma on the floor. "We'll find it." She began refolding the clothes while Emma threw more out of the drawer. "How much is in this emergency fund, exactly?"

"Thirty thousand dollars."

Jill nearly choked on her own spit.

"Since our mom died," Emma continued, "Maggie was always paranoid about money shit. She had this notion she was in charge if something bad ever happened again. So, like, six months ago she just gave me thirty thousand in cash. Just in case."

"That was in here the whole time?" Jill was stunned. That was a little more than half of her salary. "Sometimes I leave the apartment unlocked!"

"Ah! Here it is." Emma pulled a manila envelope out from underneath a pair of jeans.

"What are you planning on doing with this?" Jill asked.

"I'm officially quitting my job." Emma pulled a wad of

cash out of the envelope. "I'm going to make investigating Maggie's death my full-time gig, at least until the money runs out."

"Wow." This was so deeply a bad idea that Jill was rendered temporarily speechless.

"Amanda is going to help, which could be good. She has all this guilt and weird AA rigorous honesty shit because she created *LoveShack*."

"What are you talking about?"

"You should ask her," Emma said. "But I guess she sold the idea for the show with Trevor. Anyway, she can connect us to people, maybe. Or help with resources. And Liz is going to help too."

Before Jill had a chance to process this, she felt a prickle of embarrassing jealousy at the idea that her boss and Emma's ex were going to help, but she'd never been asked. "I'll help," she said.

"Great." But Emma was barely paying attention to Jill as she began counting the money. The hundred-dollar bills were crisp and clean, and Jill felt the need to avert her eyes.

"How was everything with Lucía?" she asked.

"Not good. Amanda didn't really know her at all. She spoke almost no English and was just terrified of getting deported. It was icky."

Jill's cheeks turned red. Amanda could be so embarrassing. "Damn. I should've known. But do you think she or Javier had anything to do with Maggie's murder?"

Emma shook her head. "She told me Javier was at a methadone clinic; I guess he's struggled with drug addiction.

That's why the police kept his exact location quiet. I feel like an asshole."

"You're not an asshole, but yikes," Jill said.

Emma nodded. "They're undocumented, and I bet they never even drive over the speed limit. And you wanna know something gross? I watched a YouTuber talk about how Javier has, like, a third cousin in San Salvador who's in jail for drug trafficking. And he accused Javier and Lucía of being drug mules who killed Maggie after she refused to help them bring drugs to LA or something. The whole thing is racist and absurd and I shouldn't have let myself take the bait, even from Amanda."

"Damn. I'm sorry I even suggested talking to Amanda."

"Oh, it's fine. It was actually good to talk to her about *LoveShack*. I'm just done fucking around." Emma stacked the last of the bills in a pile. "Now that we've got the keys back to Maggie and Theo's house, I should do my own search."

"I'll come with you," Jill said.

Emma looked up at her. "Sounds like a plan."

So that's how they ended up, two days later, wandering around the Calabasas house with Theo, who'd—to Emma's dismay—insisted on joining them.

Emma wanted to start looking in Maggie's giant walk-in closet, which wasn't cleaned out yet. Theo led them to it, and Emma quickly disappeared into its bowels.

"Do you need help?" Theo asked.

"No," Emma called from the closet. "I'm good."

Jill hovered with Theo around the bedroom for a couple minutes until he leaned over and whispered to her: "Should we leave her to it and go downstairs? Have a glass of wine or something?"

"Sure." Jill was relieved he didn't want to keep tabs on the search. And if she was being honest, him wanting to hang out with her was flattering. *Snap out of it*, she told herself. Theo yelled to Emma that they were heading downstairs, and she stuck her head out of the closet and gave a thumbs-up.

They made their way down the spiral staircase, Jill following Theo. His hair was longer than she'd ever seen it, and a bit greasy. He wore it under a Dodgers cap. His white T-shirt was yellowing at the collar and at the armpits. But even in the heights of whatever despair he was in, he was still the most handsome man she'd ever known. He was far more handsome than the actors on Amanda's show (who, to be fair, were either in their late teens or were late-forties former child stars who'd been enlisted to play parents and teachers).

Theo led her down to the kitchen, which had a refrigerated walk-in wine cellar attached to it. He opened the door to the cellar and invited her in; it was still full. "Maggie was really the wine person," he explained. "I'm still living in the rental, so I haven't touched any of it since she died. But we should drink something."

"Sure," she managed to say, feeling the weight of being in his company in the home he used to share with his now-dead wife, while her best friend searched her closet. Was it weird to drink with him? She figured Emma would want her to do whatever it took to keep him occupied and out of her hair.

He browsed the collection. "I honestly don't really know anything about all of this, so I'm just going to pull something with a cool label. Pinot Noir sound OK?" She said that it did, and they made their way back to the kitchen, where he poured them each a generous glass.

"So, Jill, tell me about you." Theo sprawled out his long limbs, placing his arm on the backside of the couch and feet up on the chaise.

"I'm not very interesting. What do you want to know?" She smiled, hoping to come off as self-deprecating rather than insecure. She tied her hair up into a bun at the top of her head to keep herself from playing with it and ruining her curls.

"Well, you're not from LA, right?"

"Correct. I grew up in New Jersey." She took another sip of wine.

"Really? Not the Midwest?" Theo asked. She shook her head no. People always thought she was from the Midwest, because she came off as passive and nice. It was irritating, and she felt the sudden desire to be direct with him, to prove him wrong.

"Why weren't you wearing your wedding ring when I saw you that night? At Taco?" The question was on her mind as he was wearing it now.

Theo let out a surprised bark of a laugh. "Wow. Um. I hadn't even realized I wasn't wearing it. Sometimes I just take it off when I shower or something, and forget to put it back on."

She could tell it was a lie, but he looked her directly in the eyes and she softened.

"It's hard," he continued. "I don't want to be known as this tragic character, you know? And forgetting to wear a wedding ring . . . It can look like a statement when it's not."

"I get that," Jill said.

"Anyway. Don't think I didn't notice that you changed the subject." He moved slightly closer to her. Against her will, she buzzed at the proximity. "I still want to know more about you."

"I told you, I'm boring." She moved back, putting more space between them. "Truly. I'm thirty years old, work for Amanda Lehman, and still live with my best friend from college in a shitty apartment in Mid City."

"I don't buy this whole 'I'm boring' thing," he said. "I can't quite figure you out, though. Is it because Emma takes up a lot of space? And it feels easier to stay in the background?"

Jill felt a protective twinge for Emma. "I wouldn't say she takes up a lot of space."

"No need to pretend in front of me. I was married to a Lathrop sister. I get it. Just don't get lost in her, you know?"

She gulped. As if on cue, Emma descended the stairs.

"I think I'm done for the day," she told Theo and Jill. "Let's find another time for me to do the rest of the house." They murmured their agreement.

"Find anything useful?" Jill asked in a tone she worried was too upbeat. But Emma only responded with a tight-lipped smile.

# Maggie

## Episode 3

Maggie and Patrick's Paradise Island date was that evening. They were driven separately in black SUVs to Paradise Island, and when they arrived, they were sent to separate production trailers to be made up and styled. Usually, *LoveShack* contestants saw to this themselves, but for Paradise Island nights the pros were brought in. She'd been filming for a week and a half, and the break from having to do her own glam was a relief.

Maggie emerged from her trailer and was stunned to see the "island" was just a bunch of imported white sand and a couple of fake palm trees on the banks of a man-made brown lake somewhere in the desert. A camera crew was following her to get her reaction to the glamorous private island, so she did her best to look impressed. Of course, she'd watched every prior season of *LoveShack*, so she was familiar with the edited-for-TV version of the unlovely beach she was encountering. She wandered around cupping her mouth in fake surprise while she looked at tiki torches and hammocks. Cameras followed her, capturing her every move. How could anyone expect to have a romantic date here?

The first part of their night was to be spent in the hot tub, where they'd be served champagne and chocolate-covered strawberries. She was going to need alcohol to get through this night. As for the chocolate-covered strawberries, she supposed this would be dinner. She hadn't eaten since their catered lunch, and often the producers forgot to feed them. Maggie didn't realize, when she'd agreed to be on the show, that she would be starving all the time, relying on whatever morsels were thrown her way during a challenge or in a makeup trailer. It was never clear if they were forgetting to feed them or withholding food on purpose so they would get drunker. One desperate evening, Maggie begged one of the producers, Priya, for something to eat, but Priya told her she didn't have any food. Two grueling hours later, after Maggie worried she was going to collapse in her stilettos and gown as she was filmed having one-on-ones with some of the men, she found a Luna bar of unknown origin on her bed with a handwritten note: *Don't tell.*

Maggie was dressed in a gold lamé bikini under a black silk robe. When she approached the hot tub, Patrick was already in it, sipping on his champagne and popping strawberries into his mouth. She felt her stomach grumble, and willed him to stop eating them and leave her some. As she'd been instructed earlier by a producer, she shimmied off her black robe as sexily as she could while Patrick ogled her (also per some producer's instructions, she was sure).

"Wow, you look amazing." His eyes moved all the way over her body.

"Thank you," she said, trying to sound cheery. Why was it that when men like Finn looked at her it made her feel sexy, but with Patrick, she felt gross?

"Can I pour you some champagne?"

She agreed as she got into the lukewarm tub. He handed her a glass as she sat down next to him. "Actually, can you hand me the strawberries?" she asked. "I'm starving."

"Can do. I love a lady with an appetite. You'd fit right in with my family. My mom makes the best food for game days; we're all pretty big eaters back home."

Maggie wasn't sure how to react to this, so she just said: "Cool!"

He droned on about his family's love of the Green Bay Packers as she tried to eat as many strawberries as she could.

"You're really going at those." He paused to take one of his own.

"Yep, I'm a chocolate lover," she lied. She didn't have a sweet tooth, but food was food. She wondered if the men were as starved as the women. Before she could follow up, she heard a producer yell cut.

"Guys, enough of the football talk," said Larry, a producer. "I'm bored to tears here. Can we get something more interesting? Patrick, ask Maggie about her sex life, what she likes in bed."

Patrick grinned and Maggie stared down at her hands, which were pruning in the water.

"Maggie, you're super attractive: I bet you get a ton of guys back home." Patrick took a gulp of his champagne.

"Ha, I'm not sure about that," she demurred.

He moved toward her. "Don't be modest. Seriously, what kind of guys do you usually go for?"

"Nice ones," she said. *Finn.*

Patrick burst out laughing as if it were a joke. "I mean looks-wise."

"Ha, um, I don't really have a type." She was panicking. What was the right answer? Larry, standing next to the cameramen, stared at her and gestured with both hands as if to say, *Give me more.* "I just—I usually go for athletes?"

"Athletes." Patrick nodded. "Good news for me, then. Did you know I went to college for football?"

"I had no idea." She forced herself to smile. "That's . . . um. That's hot!" Maggie wanted to die. Who was she, Paris fucking Hilton? This was a disaster. She had no idea what to talk about with him, and she probably looked like a prude. She drank down the rest of her champagne in the silence that followed.

"Can I have another one?" Maggie asked, and Patrick refilled her glass.

"I feel like we're vibing," he said as she downed half of her second glass. "Do you feel that too?"

"Oh, yeah. For sure." She nodded as enthusiastically as she could.

"Well, in that case, I'm gonna kiss you right now." He leaned toward her and she froze. When his lips met hers, she tried to activate hers in response, but felt stuck. He pulled back and looked at her, and a swell of relief filled her. But before she could even luxuriate in the kiss being over, he leaned in again, almost lunging at her. This time, he stuck his tongue into her mouth, and she wanted to gag. She could feel her chest tighten with anxiety as he pulled her onto his lap, but she followed his lead anyway, her body now somehow limp and pliant. She straddled him as he covered her neck with big, sloppy kisses, pushing her hips down onto his erection.

As he made his way back up her neck, he whispered in her ear, "You're making me so hard." She worried she might throw up. He pulled her hand down to his swimming trunks, as if to prove it to her. She untangled her hand from his grip, pulling away and putting her hand in his chest in a way she hoped seemed sexy. In response, his hands gripped her thighs, and the panic continued to rise in her chest.

"Hey, this is fun but maybe let's save it for later," she whispered into his ear as quietly as she could. He raised his eyebrows at this, but let her off his lap. She sat back down, took two deep breaths, and tried to block out anxious thoughts about how much of this interaction the mics had picked up, how much they'd show on TV.

Out of the corner of her eye, she saw a figure approaching from the shadows, backlit by tiki torches. She craned her neck to see who it was. Schuyler. Thank God. She had never been happier to see another human in her life.

"Well, hello, lovebirds." Schuyler smiled at them. His hair was slicked back and he wore a Hawaiian shirt. She felt a wave of nausea rise in her again, but this time, she was worried it was related to the champagne and hot tub and empty stomach.

"Hey, man." Patrick put his arm around Maggie and pulled her into his torso.

"While it's great to see you two getting along so

well"—Schuyler turned to face the camera and winked—"I'm here with a Choice Point."

Patrick groaned, but Maggie's heart rate quickened with excitement. Anything to get her some space from Patrick.

"Maggie and Patrick, each of you will have a very important choice to make." With this, Schuyler paused for dramatic effect. "There are two *LoveShack*ers waiting just a few hundred feet away. You choose: stay on Paradise Island with each other for the night, or switch for a mystery *Shack*er."

Before Maggie could think it through, Schuyler demanded an answer. "Patrick?"

"I'll be sticking with this beautiful lady right here." He pulled her closer. *Fuck, fuck, fuck.* It would now be much harder to do what she was going to do next.

"A man who knows what he wants, I like it. Maggie, it's up to you. Stay with Patrick or shack up with someone new?"

She paused, feeling lightheaded. "Can I have someone new?"

Patrick recoiled from her. "Are you fucking kidding me?"

"I'm sorry," she said. "I'm actually not into this." Relief rushed through her chest, her stomach, her hands.

"Wow." Patrick stood. "I'm getting the fuck out of here. Thanks for leading me on." Maggie flinched, but didn't respond. He stormed away in his bathing suit, and in the distance she saw a producer give him a towel and escort him away. She hadn't led him on; that she knew. Hopefully the audience would see that too. Hopefully she wouldn't look like a bitch to millions of viewers.

Schuyler rubbed his hands together. "I just love a good

Choice Point. Maggie, wanna see who you'll be shacking up with tonight on Paradise Island?"

She nodded. "I do." But in truth, she just wanted to go home. She was tipsy and nauseous. She didn't want to share a bed with some man she barely knew. She hoped it would be Finn, even though she knew it was unlikely.

"Here he is!" Schuyler pointed to another shadowy figure walking toward them. After a few seconds, she could see that it was Theo. Fuck. They really didn't want to make this easy for her, she thought. The one guy who had "Not"-ed her. Was this even allowed?

He gave her a big smile. It was a self-assured smile, but it also felt practiced. Nonetheless, she returned it as she got out of the hot tub and wrapped herself in a fluffy robe a producer had left out for her.

She hugged him. "Sorry I'm all wet."

"It's all good." He hugged her back, and she noticed he smelled good.

"I'll leave you two to your romantic evening in the luxury yurt," Schuyler said, and disappeared behind the cameras. A luxury yurt sounded nice right about then. After their greeting, someone yelled cut and they were brought to their glamping set-up: a white, circular canvas tent on a wooden platform. The outside was surrounded by string lights and soft uplighting, and there was a small fire pit and two Adirondack chairs. it was the nicest part of the "island" she'd seen so far. But when they were shown inside, her stomach dropped. It was just an air mattress, two pillows and a blanket.

Larry the producer let them know that at night, the camera crew wouldn't be there—the tent was filled with hidden night-vision cameras and mics so they could be "alone." There were adjacent bathroom trailers, and he told them that of course there were no cameras there, for privacy. Maggie almost laughed at this.

"You can change in the bathroom. They've left some pajamas in there for you," Larry told them, taking their mics. They both went to their adjoining bathroom trailers to get ready for bed, and as soon as Maggie walked in, she saw the producers had left her just a black lace negligee to wear to bed. She held it up, realized it was see-through, and burst into tears. God, it felt good to cry. It felt good to be alone. She was sick of feeling like a puppet, sick of being poked and prodded and told where to go and expected to comply. She cried harder and looked at herself in the mirror. Her mascara was running and her eyes were red and puffy. Before she could further examine or fix her make-up, she heard a knock on the door.

"Yes?" she said in her best non-crying voice.

"Hey, it's Theo. Are you OK? I can hear you crying from my bathroom."

"I'm . . ." she started, but couldn't hold back the tears. "I'm sorry. I'm just overwhelmed."

"Let me in?" he asked, and she complied. As soon as he saw her, he grimaced. "Oh God, are you that unhappy with this situation? I swear it wasn't my choice. But wait, actually, why did you say yes to switching if you were going to be so upset?"

She took a deep breath and wiped her tears with the palm of her hand. "No, it's not you. I just had . . ." She felt the tears coming again. "I just had a tough date with Patrick. He kind of took control in a way I didn't like." Why was she telling him this? "And then I walked in here and found that this"—she held up the negligee—"was all I was given to wear tonight. And I don't even know you, and we have to share a bed. No offense."

"None taken."

"Truly, I'm not upset with you," she said. "You're probably more upset that you have to spend a night with me."

"Why would that be the case?" Theo looked confused.

"Because you didn't think I was 'Hot.'" She blushed.

"Oh, Maggie, come on. That is a dumb thing that they made us do. I didn't mean it. I just had to choose someone. You are gorgeous, of course," he said, and she blushed more, down through her collarbone.

"You don't have to say that."

"It's true. I didn't even know I could 'Hot' everyone, like Finn did. Wish I'd done that," he said. She wasn't sure she believed him, but it did make her feel less awful.

"It's stupid," she said. "This is just a lot."

"Look, I'm sorry to hear about what happened with Patrick," he said. "That guy sucks. All the other guys hate him, too."

"Finn mentioned something about him having bad vibes."

"Oh yeah, for sure. He's an asshole."

"Well, I agree," she said. "But I'm going to look like the asshole now, for ditching him for you."

"Nah," he said. "I doubt it. But look, I don't want to make you more uncomfortable than you already are. I'll blow out all the candles in the tent before you get in, and I won't see anything. And I promise to stay on my side of the bed." Again, relief coursed through her.

"This will be the most boring Paradise Island date in *LoveShack* history." She smiled at him.

"I don't care." He was probably relieved to have the out, she realized. And as if reading her mind, he continued. "I'm honestly not that interested in anyone here—no offense. It's not you. I just want to get through this experience in one piece. I feel like a zoo animal being forced to mate in captivity."

"Totally." Maggie laughed.

There was a long pause before Theo spoke again. "This is all so different than I thought it would be."

"I know what you mean." The glamor of the whole thing was wearing off quickly. She knew, of course, that reality TV was highly staged. But she was surprised by just how much production could fake.

"Why'd you sign up to do this in the first place?" she asked him.

"Honestly?"

"Honestly."

He let out a sigh. "I was lonely and depressed. I haven't been in a serious relationship in my entire life. I thought maybe I could meet someone here."

She let that information sit. "That's surprising." Did anyone come on the show to actually meet someone? It felt like a potential positive outcome, rather than the goal. At least for her.

He just shrugged. "Oh, it's OK. Unfortunately I don't think anyone here is right for me."

She nodded. "Well, let's be friends. We can be here for each other."

"I like the sound of that," he said.

# Amanda

The thing about public apologies, Amanda now knew, was that there was no way to do them and make people believe you meant it.

You could tell people the truth, your version of the story, and everyone would think you were being defensive and underplaying your role (Trevor-related apology attempt number one). You could completely own up to everything, make yourself sound like the worst version of you, and people would think you were being performative and find a way to hate you even more because you weren't "doing the work" (Trevor-related apology attempt number two). Or you could stay silent and let your publicist make a non-statement for you, i.e. "Amanda Lehman will not be commenting on the additional accusations made against Trevor Koch at this time." (Trevor-related apology attempt number three.)

It'd been a full two years since everything had happened with Trevor, her former writing partner and former best friend. It was the anniversary of the Article, and she was lying in bed, feeling bad for herself. She forced herself to get up for the noon Narcotics Anonymous meeting, during which she'd inevitably recount the whole sorry tale once again. Jill was picking her up in twenty minutes to take her.

She and Trevor wrote the pilot of *Anxiety* together when they were college seniors, and developed the entire show as post-grads living in cockroach-filled houses in Los Feliz and Silver Lake. And, of course, in a moment of desperation before *Anxiety* had generated interest, they'd sold the *LoveShack* pitch together.

If only she'd confronted him about his first betrayal—everything that happened with *LoveShack*. Maybe he wouldn't have fucked up so badly the second time.

She got up and made her way to her closet, where she pulled out a denim Alexander McQueen dress that Trevor loved. Wearing it was like pressing on a bruise.

A thing worth noting about her and Trevor: they'd had sex twice. The first time was their sophomore year of college, when Trevor had shown up at the campus coffee shop where she worked, blubbery and sad and needy after having just broken up with some short-lived girlfriend. Later that night, he and Amanda found their way to a bar near campus—one that accepted fake IDs—and got plastered. They were both lonely, and it just happened. But sleeping together then had been a mistake. They realized this almost immediately, as Trevor lay in Amanda's single bed, their limbs still entangled.

The next time they slept together was two years and three days ago. Exactly three days before Trevor was accused of sexual assault by four women in the *Los Angeles Times*.

By the time these accusations were made, Trevor had risen to fame that was, given his behind-the-scenes role on

*Anxiety*, surprising. The women, in an exclusive given to the *Times*, laid out four similar, bizarre stories. Trevor met each woman on a dating app for celebrities. After their respective first dates, he invited each of them back to his home. This was where the stories started to diverge from one another, but the central, strange accusation remained the same: Trevor had forcibly penetrated each woman with a rose quartz dildo.

The story was odd in every way. Why the fuck did Trevor have a rose quartz dildo? Why did rose quartz dildos exist, and what kind of wellness bullshit was that? And of course, the most pressing question of all, why would he coerce these women—but not Amanda—into such a bizarre sexual act?

One of the accusers, a C-list actress, gave the most detailed description of the assault. She claimed that she and Trevor agreed to have sex, and after putting on a condom, he told her to close her eyes. Rather than a penis, she felt something cold and solid, like a stone, enter her. She screamed in surprise and opened her eyes to find it was some sort of dildo, and asked him to remove it. After twenty or thirty seconds of telling him to stop, he finally did.

Amanda first read this story while nursing a brutal hangover on that fateful morning two years ago. She had woken up at five for an early shoot, rolled over in her bed to turn off her phone alarm, and saw she had a barrage of texts from the night before with the link to the story about Trevor. Her first thought was that somehow the press had found out that they were behind the most cursed reality show in history. Or worse, that he'd completely fucked her over afterwards, and she'd done nothing about it.

But it was more awful than that by a long shot. She'd quickly popped a couple of Adderall, turned on the light by her bedside table, and read the story on her phone. And then read it again. And again. She found that she couldn't absorb the information, and her head was pounding. She took two more Adderall and four ibuprofen, and read the article again. She called Trevor, who was supposed to be at the early-morning shoot too. No answer. She texted him, and waited. She texted him again. She chugged a leftover Gatorade Zero that she found underneath her bed. She texted him again.

Yes, she should've checked in with her publicist before responding to a text from a nice *New York Times* reporter who had profiled her a year prior. But being open and accessible was her brand. Plus, she was on drugs! So many drugs! It was hard to know what to do when you were on drugs.

By the time she got to work that morning, it was clear that Trevor would not be responding to her calls (seven) or her texts (thirteen). No one on set had seen him.

Yes, in retrospect, she shouldn't have told the reporter that she knew from firsthand experience that Trevor wasn't into that kind of stuff. And almost definitely she should not have said that while she was a feminist (a strong feminist!), she was concerned that people sometimes made up stories like this to get their names in the paper. In her defense, she assumed it'd been off the record. And she was on drugs!

On that horrible day two years ago, at 11:00 a.m., the *New York Times* piece came out with her ill-advised quotes. She couldn't know then that it would cleave her life into two halves: Before and After.

She buttoned the denim dress slowly, looking at herself in the mirror. The dress barely fit anymore, and the buttons gaped around her stomach. She ran her fingers through her unwashed hair, trying to make it presentable. Her phone buzzed to let her know someone was at the door—probably Jill coming to get her. She sighed and threw on a sweater. This was her life in the After.

# Jill

Jill and Emma met in their freshman year at Kenyon in Ohio. They both auditioned for the campus improv group that was 80 percent men and 20 percent "chill" women. The improv troupe was, for some reason, named "Need Money 4 Beer." The origin of this name, to Jill's surprise, was never explained at auditions.

Emma and Jill found out they were rejected at the same time, both arriving at the campus coffee house to check the list of who was accepted. An email had told them it would be posted at 3:00 p.m., but it was 2:57 and the list was up. They recognized each other from auditions, nodded at each other in solidarity, and scanned for their names. Of course, neither of them had made it. Jill flushed with embarrassment. She looked up at Emma, who was looking back at her with a smile.

"Hey, I'm Jill," she said. "I didn't make it either." Jill's hair that day was pulled into a ponytail with her curly bangs straightened and lying flat against her forehead. Her eyes were rimmed with black eyeliner, and she wore a red fake leather jacket and bootcut jeans, overflowing from the chestnut brown Uggs she'd tucked them in to. She smelled like

Princess by Vera Wang, which she was cultivating as her "signature scent." Emma, on the other hand, wore a gray hoodie and ripped jeans; her hair—long, then—in two messy braids. She smelled like men's deodorant.

Emma smiled. "Fuck 'em. I'm Emma." She reached out to shake Jill's hand as if they were in a business meeting. Jill laughed at this but returned the handshake. "Want a coffee? I have, like, a million meal points left. And we can nurse our bruised egos."

Emma bought them both soy lattes and they made their way to the stained couches, talking shit about the improv troupe's captains, two senior boys named Dan and Chad. Dan and Chad were not funny, but did have a sarcastic meanness to them that passed as humor. They had been terrifying at the auditions: sitting expressionless, observing as everyone worked through improv scenarios together. Jill knew they'd fit right in in a sexist writers' room on a late-night show someday.

Emma laughed at all the right moments in their conversation, and as Jill took another sip of her latte, she found she didn't care at all about the improv troupe. Her earlier embarrassment had faded. "I literally wore my dad's flannel shirt that I had to beg him to send me. I also borrowed my roommate's Timberlands, which were, like, three sizes too small. And all that for them to reject me! I know I'm funny enough," Jill said, shaking her head. "I guess I'm just not cool enough."

"You seem fucking hilarious," Emma said. "You were great in the audition. But if it's any comfort, I'm gay, and even *I* wasn't considered 'chill' enough to take one of the four spots they reserve for women each year." At this, Jill chuckled.

"It's 2010! You can't just have four women in your improv troupe of twenty!" Jill said.

"Yes! And you need to have at least one lesbian!" Emma pointed her finger in the air in mock outrage. "We need to start a social movement. This is the biggest issue of our times: let Emma and Jill into your improv troupe even though we're not cool enough."

"I'm so there. I'll be leading protests around campus." Jill downed the rest of her latte. She felt the rush of the caffeine hit her system, and she knew she should get to work on an essay due the next day.

"Jill, this is lame to say, but let's be friends?"

Jill looked back at Emma. "I thought you'd never ask."

There was a knock on Jill's door. She'd just gotten back from dropping Amanda off at a Narcotics Anonymous meeting, even though it was a Saturday.

She kept trying to find time to talk to Amanda about a promotion. About a job where she didn't have to do menial stuff, but could be in the writers' room. It was something Amanda had initially promised when she'd taken the job, but whenever Jill brought it up, she got weird and evasive.

Another knock. "Come in," Jill said.

Emma poked her head in. "I think I should get back on the dating apps," she announced.

Jill couldn't help but smile. "Oh my God, yes. I love this idea."

"Slow down there," Emma said, but she was smiling.

"What brought this on?" Jill asked. Sure, it wasn't as if Emma asked her a lot of questions or was involved in the day-to-day of Jill's life like she used to be. But she was going through hell. Didn't that give her a right to make things about herself, at least for a while?

"Nothing," Emma said. "Well, not nothing. Liz started posting photos with a new girlfriend. But I swear it's not just about that."

"Let me see." In the photo, Liz, whom Jill found rigid and un-fun, looked adoringly at her new girlfriend. They were posing together in front of a cabin in Big Bear, wearing matching beanies. "You can do better than this," Jill said.

"Can you help me choose photos?" Emma scrolled through her camera roll, looking for potential options. She showed Jill one that Jill had taken of Emma during a weekend trip to Santa Barbara a year ago. Emma's face looked fuller, healthier. She wore gray overalls and Birkenstocks, and looked happy.

"I love this one." Jill took the phone and started scrolling. There was a great one of Emma at her thirtieth birthday party, which Jill had thrown for her at their apartment. It was seventies themed, and Emma had her hair blown out and looked like Farrah Fawcett. She wore a purple flare-legged jumpsuit and white go-go boots. It almost took Jill's breath away, seeing her friend like this. Seeing her happy. She showed it to Emma, who smiled. The next few photos were from Christmas that year, a month before Maggie had died. Maggie, Theo and Emma always got together with Theo's parents at the Calabasas mansion, and from what Emma described, it was always perfectly nice. That year, Emma had gotten Maggie and Theo Bobbleheads of themselves.

"Oh my God," Jill said.

"Some weird fan was selling them on Etsy. I had to buy them. Maggie laughed so hard, but Theo was annoyed."

"Annoyed? What do you mean?" Jill continued scrolling through Emma's photos. There was one of the three of them—Maggie, Theo and Emma—in matching Christmas sweaters. That would've been Maggie's doing; it was probably for some video content.

"He kinda bugged out," Emma said. "Made some sarcastic comment, I don't remember exactly what, that made it seem like he thought the joke was mean."

Jill wondered if this was another symptom of Theo's resentment of their dynamic, but said nothing. "How'd it go at the house the other day? Find anything useful?" she asked instead, hoping to sound casual. They hadn't debriefed the house search yet, partly because Jill hadn't pushed. She was still thinking about her conversation with Theo. Emma was her best friend, and yet Theo's words had rankled her. *Just don't get lost in her.*

"How much do you know about adoption?" Emma got up from the bed and began pacing around the room.

"Very little."

"I found a bunch of adoption information pamphlets. Well, specifically information about adoption and fostering," Emma said. She went to her room and came back, scattering some pamphlets on Jill's bed.

"That would've been wonderful." Jill examined the brochures. The first one was titled "Adopting in California." But she immediately sensed it was the wrong thing to say as Emma's eyebrows knit together.

"Well, Maggie always talked about wanting to have kids,

but I'd never heard her mention anything about adopting or fostering."

Jill noticed Emma was scratching her wrist again, and she gently put her hand on Emma's arm to stop her. Emma responded with an irritated look. "Is it possible she just never told you about this? Or that they were in the early stages?" Jill asked.

Emma tapped her fingers against her thigh. "I doubt it. I really think she would've told me if she was considering it. It's such a big decision, and we used to talk about this kind of stuff. We talked about everything."

"I'm sorry, Em."

Emma looked distraught. "Don't judge me for even thinking about this, OK?" She turned to face Jill.

"I would never," she said.

"What if . . . what if Theo did something to her? Because he didn't want to have a family?"

Jill squeezed her eyes shut. "Don't take this the wrong way," she began. "But you may be misinterpreting his behavior as nefarious when really he's just grieving. Would a guy who had something to hide let you look through his house and all his belongings?"

"He insisted on being there!" Emma said. "And who knows, maybe he cleaned it out beforehand."

"I seriously doubt that," Jill said.

"Something's wrong with him and this situation. I just know it."

"I don't disagree," she said. "I think he's lying about something. But I don't think Theo is your guy. I feel it in my gut." Emma nodded, but Jill could tell she didn't believe her.

# Emma

Jill took a large sip of her iced coffee and opened her notebook.

She was at a café on Melrose with Emma and Amanda for their first official "brainstorming session." This had been Jill's idea. Emma could sense her friend's discomfort about the fact that she was officially quitting her job to focus on this, but Jill was not one to be left out. Plus, she was the most organized person Emma knew.

"Let's officially cross Lucía and Javier off the list of suspects," Emma said. It'd been a week and a half since they'd met with Lucía, and her guilt about the whole thing had mostly subsided. At least she'd gotten an answer about *something* related to the case, and that was a relief.

Jill nodded. "I took the liberty of compiling a list of all of the evidence we know about so far. Anything that feels unusual, or has been noted by the police or the true crime weirdos." She pulled a couple of printouts from a folder, and handed them to Emma and Amanda.

God bless Jill.

The document said:

**Evidence**

- "End it" note from Theo to Maggie—was that really an inside joke?
- Adoption pamphlets
- Javier's car spotted near warehouse
- Emergency money given to Emma

Emma was surprised to see the last item on the list. "How is the emergency fund 'evidence'?"

Jill looked up. "Oh. I don't know. Isn't it weird that she gave you all that money only six months ago? What if she knew she was in danger?"

Emma hadn't really considered that before, because at the time, it'd felt par for the course. Maggie liked to take care of her. To mother her.

The day Maggie gave her the money, she'd just shown up at her house on a Tuesday—a rarity. Emma could count on one hand the times that Maggie had made it all the way to Mid City on a weekday.

She wore a full leather outfit and red stilettos for some sort of photoshoot. They barely looked like sisters anymore, with Maggie's surgically altered face and aggressive tan.

But Emma had long gotten used to Maggie's new appearance. She was still the same Maggie underneath it all, at least for the most part. She examined her sister as she stood in her doorway. "You look like Catwoman."

Maggie rolled her eyes as they hugged. She made her way to Emma's kitchen, helping herself to a glass of water.

"OK, don't be weird about this." Maggie opened her Prada tote and pulled out a manila envelope.

"What's this?" Emma took the envelope.

"Just open it."

Emma did as she was instructed. She gasped at the sight of all the bills. "Maggie, what the fuck?"

"I told you not to be weird!" her sister said. "It's for emergencies. You know how when we were cleaning out Mom's house, we found all that cash?"

"Of course I remember," Emma said. Their mom had stuffed hundred-dollar bills in multiple old paperbacks that lived underneath her bed. All in all, they'd found about $2,000, which was an absurd amount, given that she'd died with $1,300 in her bank account. "That was silly and so is this. How much is even in here?"

"Thirty thousand dollars," Maggie whispered, even though they were alone. "So hide it somewhere good."

"I can't take this." Emma handed the envelope back. "First of all, I'm in good shape. I have a great job. And if I needed anything, I promise I'd let you know."

"I may not always be here." Maggie handed the envelope back. Her nails were red and long and oval-shaped. "What if something happens to me, like it did to Mom?"

"It won't," Emma said. "I couldn't survive that and I don't even want to imagine it."

"Still. What if it did? Or what if the big earthquake comes and you have to evacuate? Or aliens invade the Earth and you need to bribe them with cash?"

Emma snorted. "I'll charm the aliens with my winning personality."

"Just humor me," Maggie said. "You're the most important person in the world to me. Don't tell Theo I said that, of course. But I'll sleep better if I know you have the money."

"I just figured she was being overprotective," Emma said to Jill.

"God, that's fascinating. What if she *knew* something bad was going to happen to her?" Amanda chimed in.

Emma shook her head. "Nah. She was like this. A little overbearing and anxious, but loving. At least to me. And I'm grateful for the money, honestly, because it's allowing me to focus on this instead of writing jokes for a children's show."

Jill nodded. "You did love that job, though."

"Yeah. I guess so. But who knows if I'll ever be able to get another writing job again, now that Maggie won't be able to introduce me to anyone."

"Don't worry about that," Amanda said. "When it comes time and you want to go back to work, just call me and I'll get you a job on *The Youth*."

Jill abruptly changed the subject, pointing to her printout. "How about the threatening note? Do you have any theories about that?"

"Theo said it was some sort of joke they had. But I don't know what to believe," Emma said.

"Can we look at it?" Amanda said.

"I think the police still have it."

Jill nodded. "How about finding time with Theo to go back and search the house one more time? You could ask him about the adoption—"

Emma interrupted. "I don't want us to be alone with Theo again. It just doesn't feel safe. He's hiding something."

Jill didn't return her gaze. She'd pulled a strand of her curly hair out of its clip and was twirling it around her finger anxiously. "Whatever you think is best."

Emma and Jill had originally planned to go see a movie after their session, but Emma was too wired from the caffeine and the conversation. Instead, she went home and googled the shit out of the *LoveShack* curse. The first article she came across was from a month ago, published in *Variety*.

### *The Truth Behind the "LoveShack Curse"*
### *by Elif Demir*

*Just six months after season two of* LoveShack *wrapped, cast member and runner-up Adrianne Wilbur was found dead in her Downtown Los Angeles condo. Wilbur, a recovering alcoholic, was sober for three years until she set foot on the* LoveShack *set.*

*"We all knew it was a bad idea for her to go on the show," Wilbur's mother, Leanne, said. "She started drinking the second she got to set. I don't know what happened. She was so strong."*

*According to Leanne Wilbur, as soon as her daughter left the show, she fell into a deep depression. "She was doing social media and stuff like that, but not making as much money as she thought she would. She had to go back to her nursing job. Except people harassed her on the street, taking sneaky photos of her. Sometimes patients gave her a hard time. It was very difficult."* Wilbur soon started using OxyContin—a widely prescribed opiate—that she'd begun stealing from work. It wasn't long before her employer found out and fired her. And just two months later, her brother broke her door down and discovered her dead from a heroin overdose. She was 26 years old.

On the face of it, Wilbur's death has little in common with Lawrence Pollack's. Pollack was eliminated in episode five of LoveShack's fourth season, but became a well-known alumnus of the show after he went on a tirade calling a fellow cast member a "homo" and a "f*ggot." He died just two weeks following the season finale's air date after jumping off a 60-foot rock into a river at Heaven's Falls, Nevada. *"It was a stupid dare,"* his friend Will Jackson said. *"We were drinking and being idiots."* Pollack underestimated the water's depth and hit his head on an underwater rock. He drowned before his friends could reach him.

Two deaths? A tragedy. Three? A weird coincidence. But four starts to feel like a conspiracy.

The two most famous LoveShack deaths—JoAnne Ryder and Maggie Lathrop—happened six years apart. Ryder won the first season of LoveShack and married her Love Pair, Mario Ricci. Two years later, Ryder was found dead in her car from a self-inflicted gunshot wound. Ricci described her as a *"loving, committed wife,"* but said she struggled with depression and anxiety.

Lathrop, of course, was murdered just four months ago. The case remains unsolved.

"It's a sort of chicken or the egg situation," said TV and popular-culture analyst Dolly Gallagher. "Are these cast members already unstable, which is why they get cast on the show? Or do they become unstable after their time on the show? It's no secret that casting directors for reality shows look for big personalities. Are they actually looking for people with something darker to them?"

Emma clicked out of the article before she could finish reading it. Maggie wasn't *unstable*. This was victim-blaming crap. She pulled out her phone and texted the article to Amanda. *No one has anything intelligent to say about this supposed LoveShack curse.* Amanda responded right away: *idk . . . i sort of agree with that pop-culture analyst, honestly. people who came on the show often had something to hide. it's just the nature of who's attracted to this artificial world. they got to play dress up and be caricatures of themselves.*

Emma didn't respond. She'd been so sure that Maggie didn't have anything to hide. But her confidence was slipping away little by little each day.

# Maggie

### Episode 4

"Tonight on *LoveShack*, we're about to begin our first Love Pair ceremony of the season." Schuyler grinned at the contestants as they stood in two lines in front of him on the bungalow's balcony. His hair was slicked back and he wore a Hawaiian shirt, which was his classic uniform. Despite his over-the-top look and presentation style—or maybe because of it?—fans loved him. But what the people watching at home couldn't see was the dead look in his eyes as he panned to the cameras. "Tonight's Love Pair ceremony will be a new start for many of our *Shack*ers. They'll be paired up as couples by you, our viewers. But sadly, one man and one woman will be sent home as their *LoveShack* journey comes to an end. Who will it be? Stay tuned to find out. We'll be right back on tonight's episode of *LoveShack*."

"Cut!" Priya yelled. "Ladies, you look freezing. I'm sorry, I know it's chilly. But you need to act a bit warmer so it doesn't look like we're torturing you."

"This isn't torture?" Layla stage-whispered to Maggie. Priya gave them a look.

"You get five minutes inside to warm up. And then we'll be back out here to film the rest of this. You're welcome to drink some alcohol if that will help." Priya motioned to the bar inside the bungalow. They all wandered inside and Layla walked over to the bar.

"Alright. Who's doing a shot of this crap with me?" Layla asked, pulling out the cheap cinnamon-flavored whiskey the producers kept stocked at all times.

Maggie raised her hand. "I guess I am." Theo, Luke and Finn also joined as she poured out generous shots in plastic cups behind the bar. She forced herself to look away as Layla grabbed Finn's hand. They'd been hanging out around the bungalow almost every day, holding hands and kissing and looking generally happy. It was hard to tell if Finn was as into it as Layla, but she secretly hoped the answer was no. She tried not to think about the fact that they were almost certainly going to get Love Paired for real tonight. The first Love Pair ceremony was a milestone that took place about a third of the way through the season when the cast had had some time to get to know each other. It was sometimes possible to "switch" Love Pairs, but after the first one, they were largely used as an opportunity to eliminate couples rather than reconfigure existing pairs.

Luke held up his cup. "This is at least three shots."

"Well, drink up. It's gonna be a long night." Layla held up her cup, looked around to see if anyone was listening, and whispered, "Cheers. To Patrick hopefully getting eliminated." Maggie gasped at Layla's boldness, and the boys laughed. Since their failed Paradise Island date, Maggie had heard of at least two more instances of Patrick being inappropriate with women on the show. In the hot tub two nights before, he'd somehow untied Sunny's bikini top without her noticing, and when she got up to leave, she'd accidentally exposed herself to the tub full of other *Shack*ers. Poor Sunny had cried and cried, and had refused to film for the rest of the day. And then, just yesterday morning, Patrick had told Chloe that she should consider a Brazilian butt lift if she really wanted her modeling career to take off. Chloe had yelled at him in front of the whole cast, and everyone had sided with her. Patrick sucked and they all knew it.

They clinked their plastic cups. "Cheers," they said in unison. The whiskey burned on its way down.

As the group made their way back outside, Finn was walking slowly, waiting for her. She smiled at the sight of him.

"Was everything OK with Patrick?" he asked. "I know you switched to Theo mid-date." The terrible date with Patrick was already a few days ago, but Finn hadn't approached her one-on-one since.

"Not really," she admitted.

He nodded. "I'm sorry to hear that. Do you want to talk about it?"

"Also not really," she said, eyeing the cameraman who was following them. "But I appreciate it." Before she could stop herself, she looked at him. Like, really looked—something she hadn't let herself do in a while. He wore a navy cable-knit sweater, dark jeans, and Chelsea boots, which was decidedly un-*LoveShack*, but charming and appropriate for the chilly night.

"And did it go OK with Theo?"

"Oh, you know. It was good." She kept her tone light, noncommittal. The left corner of his mouth turned up in an almost undetectable smile. Was he pleased that she hadn't full-throatedly proclaimed her love for him? "How about you and Layla? How are things?"

"They're good." He also didn't sound convinced. The cameraman, bored with their nothing of a conversation, got back in formation with the rest of the camera techs waiting to film the Love Pair ceremony.

She nodded. "Layla's the best."

"She really is."

She rubbed her hands together, trying to warm them. "Well, um. Good luck tonight."

They stood there for a quiet moment, looking at each other. Her heart raced at the eye contact, which was almost embarrassing.

And then, wordlessly, he took her hands in his, shaping them into a cup. Her heart pounded harder as he held them a few inches from his face. What was he doing? He leaned over, just slightly, and, looking up at her through his thick eyelashes, he blew on her hands. His breath was hot, and it made her weak in the knees.

"There," he said. "Stay warm."

"You, the viewers, have been voting for who you think should be Love Paired," Schuyler said to the camera. "Tonight, we'll find out: who do you think makes a cute couple? And who should be sent packing?" Maggie shivered. Layla grabbed her hand and squeezed it.

Schuyler read off the first couple to be chosen by the

viewers as a Love Pair. Sunny and Luke. Everyone clapped. And then the next sets of couples: Aaron and Felicia, Bryan and Tia. Maggie's feet ached, and she was so cold in her black satin gown that she couldn't feel her fingers. She willed this to go faster.

"Maggie, you are in a Love Pair with . . ." Schuyler paused for dramatic effect. "Theo." Maggie felt a warm rush of relief flood her veins. She wouldn't be going home. But then, half a second later, a sick feeling hit her like a slap. She was paired with Theo, not Finn. This wasn't a surprise, but something about the viewers choosing them for each other made it feel more real.

Theo came over to Maggie and kissed her cheek. His lips were cold. Theo and Maggie went to stand together on the other side of the balcony. Maggie considered her new Love Pair, and what it meant to be with someone who wasn't into her. It at least meant she could avoid creeps like Patrick. Viewers sometimes even appreciated couples who were best friends, even if they weren't involved romantically. These so-called "Platonic Pairs" could even get all the way to the end—it had happened on a season two or three years back. But it was rare.

As she stood beside Theo, she began shivering again. He did nothing to warm her.

The only contestants left unpaired were Chloe and Layla, and Patrick and Finn. She wanted Layla and Finn to stay, but she felt a pang at the thought of them becoming officially Love Paired. But it would be worth it, she figured, if she got to keep both of them. And say goodbye to Patrick.

"Revealing our last Love Pair is bittersweet for me, y'all,"

Schuyler said, speaking with a Southern drawl that Maggie had never heard him use before that sentence. "We're already like a family." Maggie almost snorted. "Our final Love Pair will be Layla and Finn. Chloe and Patrick, I'm sorry to say, it's time to pack your bags."

With this Chloe burst into tears, and all the women ran over to hug her and comfort her. Patrick stormed away, accompanied by a flurry of cameras and producers angling to capture whatever nonsense he was about to say.

"Bye, bitch!" Layla yelled in his direction, and everyone laughed. With most of the cameras diverted to the Patrick spectacle, and poor Chloe sent away to pack, Priya beckoned the rest of the cast to come inside. They all sat on the leather couches as a bottle of champagne was opened and glasses passed around.

"It's time to debrief the Love Pair ceremony. I'm going to ask you questions, but I, of course, won't be on camera, nor will viewers hear my questions. So please answer them as if they're complete thoughts and not just answers you're giving," Priya said. Everyone nodded and sipped on the cheap champagne. Maggie grimaced at her first sip. It was a step above Franzia, but not a big one.

"First, Theo. How are you feeling about being in a Love Pair with Maggie?" She looked straight at Maggie as she said it. *Thanks for that, Priya*, she thought.

"When I found out I was paired with Maggie, I was pretty happy. She's attractive," Theo said, and Maggie couldn't help but blush. "But yeah, I'm also keeping my options open, you know? It's a bit early to say what I'm looking for." Maggie's blush grew deeper, but now with shame.

Priya nodded, and then directed her questions to some other contestants, how they felt in their Love Pairs. Finally, she asked the group. "How are you feeling about Patrick leaving? I know there were some mixed feelings about him."

Layla looked around before speaking. "I'm thrilled Patrick is leaving. That guy is a creep." There were murmurs of agreement. Maggie looked at Theo, who was picking at his nails. She couldn't decide if she wanted him to say something, or stay silent. She, of course, didn't want him to tell everyone about her experience with Patrick. But it would feel good to hear him comment about how terrible he was. There was a long pause until someone chimed in.

"When it comes to Patrick, I'll just say this." Finn's voice was calm. "I know it seems like a stupid prank, but what happened with Sunny"—he motioned to her—"was not OK. I don't use this word lightly, but it was abusive. Doing something so private to her without her consent, even if it was just untying her swimsuit, is sexual harassment at a minimum, but honestly, it could be considered sexual assault. And obviously what he said to Chloe was awful. The guy was a scumbag. I'm glad he's gone."

The remaining men looked around at each other, uncomfortable. Theo raised an eyebrow slightly, but Maggie ignored him. She could feel herself beaming, and tried to tamp it down. Layla grabbed Finn and kissed him on the cheek.

Maggie wanted to cry. There was only one decent guy on this show, and her best friend was paired up with him.

# Emma

She wasn't sleeping. Now that she'd officially resigned from *Mrs. Ladybug*, her days had started once again to form a shapeless clump, made up of internet wormholes, *LoveShack* episodes, and long, fitful naps punctuated by nightmares about her sister.

She'd started a *LoveShack* group chat with Amanda, Liz and Jill, who were watching episodes alongside her. She opened the thread again, rereading the messages.

> Emma: Glad Patrick was eliminated. He was gross. I could tell Maggie hated him.
>
> Amanda: ugh. ya. i remember the producers specifically looking to cast guys like that. obvious misogynists and creeps. if they were handsome, of course.
>
> Jill: Yikes
>
> Liz: Really? Holy shit
>
> Amanda: off the record, of course
>
> Liz: 😇
>
> Emma: I know they look for extreme personalities, but seriously?

> Amanda: ya. part of the reason i don't want to be publicly associated with the show ... my original idea for LoveShack was that we'd cast people who didn't fit the mold (i.e. not just jesus-loving, normatively attractive white people). but they took it too far

She put down her phone as Jill knocked at the door. "You ready?"

Jill had started to make her go on evening walks around the neighborhood, to get her out of the house. It was rush hour, or what counted as rush hour in LA, which was basically 5:00 a.m. to 8:30 p.m. during the week. Their Mid City apartment was on a busy street, and their walk was punctuated by the sounds of hundreds of cars driving by and honking at each other.

As they left the apartment, Jill asked how her day had been.

"Oh, you know, just a blast," Emma said. "I spent the day googling adoption rules in California."

"Have you asked Theo about it?"

"Of course not." But what she hadn't told Jill or Amanda at their brainstorming session was about something that'd happened seven or eight months before Maggie had died. Emma had gone over to the Calabasas house. Maggie had a scalp masseuse coming in to "stimulate her hair follicles," and wanted Emma to try it too. It felt like a regular head massage, but Emma was grateful for some free pampering.

After the scalp thing, the sisters sat together in her living room. It was the late afternoon, and all the staff had left for the day. Theo was filming TikToks in their room upstairs. "There's something I wanted to tell you," Maggie said to her. She was eating low-calorie popcorn that Emma found flavorless.

"Yes?" Emma took a handful anyway.

"Don't freak out, but I got an abortion two days ago," she said.

Emma examined her sister's face, which was surprisingly neutral. She tried to keep her face expressionless too. "How are you doing?"

"I'm fine. It was the right thing. I'm not ready to have kids yet," Maggie said. Emma had had a few friends get abortions over the years, and they'd all had different experiences and reactions. Maggie seemed muted, but OK.

"Makes sense," Emma said. "You still want kids eventually, right?"

"Maybe," she said. "Not for a couple years, at least. I need to use my hot years wisely." This was something she talked about all the time: her looks were what made her money, and she wouldn't have them forever. Even with all the filler in the world.

"Glad you're doing OK, Mags." Emma squeezed her sister's hand. "You know, I would've come with you. If you'd asked."

"Of course," Maggie said. "But it was something I needed to do on my own. I took a couple of pills at home." She took another handful of popcorn. "OK, can we watch some shitty TV now?"

And that was it. The first and last time they'd talked about the abortion. Why would she say she wasn't ready for kids while simultaneously looking to foster or adopt? It made no sense.

"I don't think it's that weird that they were casually thinking about adoption," Jill told her.

"I disagree," Emma said. "I'm sorry, but, like, we told each other everything. We talked about this stuff all the time. She never mentioned anything like this. She said she wasn't ready for kids."

"People adopt for lots of reasons, though," Jill said. "Maybe they were just starting to think about—"

Emma cut her off. "I just can't understand why she wouldn't tell me."

"Is there a chance she just wanted to wait until she and Theo made a decision?" Jill asked. "Adoption takes a while to finalize. Maybe they wanted to start the process now so they'd be ready in a couple years."

"I guess." Emma sighed. What Jill was saying was rational, but she couldn't wrap her mind around it. "We just talked about this stuff. Really. We talked about all of it."

"People can be very private about kid stuff," Jill said.

"She was my sister. We cleaned our mother's bedpan together every day for two months. We were past privacy."

"I'm not questioning that," Jill replied. "But I think there may have been things she didn't tell you. Not secrets! Just things she wasn't . . . ready to discuss."

"It's all so weird," Emma said. "And I don't want to talk to Theo about it, of course. I don't trust him. He won't even let me go to the house alone."

"He already let you search it." Jill sounded frustrated

with her, which had been happening more often lately. Emma wasn't totally sure why: was it her focus on Maggie? Her suspicion around Theo?

"But just that once," Emma said. "And he didn't want me to search it alone."

"Would you want someone poking through our house without us being there?" Jill asked.

"Honestly, I wouldn't care. I really wouldn't."

"That's admirable," Jill said. "But not everyone feels that way. Especially a celebrity."

Was Jill giving Theo the benefit of the doubt just because he was famous? "Let's talk about something else," Emma said. "We just have to agree to disagree."

They were a few blocks from home, but instead of finding a new topic, they walked in silence.

# Amanda

The best time in her life had been, without question, the period right after college. She and Trevor were living together in a tiny apartment in Los Feliz, for which her parents footed the bill for two years out of college. It was when she and Trevor wrote the bulk of *Anxiety*. They had nothing to focus on besides writing, occasionally showing up to their respective low-wage jobs, and developing unhealthy relationships with various substances on their constant nights out.

The years that followed in their mid-twenties were harder. They were broke, and her parents had stopped paying her rent. *Anxiety* wasn't selling, and she'd come up with the idea for *LoveShack*. Their agent was excited about it, even if it was an unusual proposal from two more serious writers. Still, she sent it around, and there was real interest from a major network.

She and Trevor met the network's development team in a conference room in Century City. The space was far less glamorous than she'd expected. There was no city view, no dark mahogany conference table, no smartly dressed assistant wandering around offering coffee and Perrier. There was fluorescent lighting, a dead plant, and a Formica table. That was about it.

The network representatives sat across from Trevor and Amanda. Their agent sat at the head of the table.

"We're interested in making an offer," one of the reps told them. "We love the concept. It's simple. Won't be too expensive to film."

Amanda beamed. How was this real? Someone wanted to *pay her* for an idea she had?

"Normally we'd just buy the rights and send you on your way. But we're intrigued by you two, as a writing pair," another rep said.

One of them, a wiry middle-aged woman with jet-black hair pulled into a crisp bun, passed a piece of paper to their agent. "We need writers to craft the host script, the overall narrative. Work with production on voice-over scripts."

"Of course," Amanda said. "We're interested."

"Under a pen name," Trevor said.

"Whatever you want," a rep said.

They got low-balled in the end, of course—they were paid far lower than industry average for the rights. But getting a salary as a full-time writer with her best friend, even if it was for an embarrassing reality TV show, was exhilarating.

However, their first day on set with production was nothing short of a nightmare. They met in the same dingy conference room, but this time with the group of producers the network had assembled.

"We have our cast!" Priya, a producer who looked criminally young, told them excitedly. "Shall we review?"

"Please," Trevor said.

"Perfect. First, we've got the guys." Priya motioned toward the PowerPoint, which was projected on a screen across from the table. "This is Mack Figaroa. You may recognize him, because he's a professional MMA fighter. A big get for us." On the screen was a stocky, muscular guy who looked slightly terrifying. Amanda discreetly pulled out her phone and googled him under the table. The first thing that popped up was a news article from two years prior, titled *Mack Figaroa Charged with Aggravated Assault Outside Nightclub*. The blood drained from her face.

She raised her hand.

"Yes?" Priya said.

"Did you see this? The aggravated assault thing?" She turned her phone around and displayed the headline. Trevor kicked her under the table and gave her a questioning look.

Priya's face fell just slightly. "Do you mean to suggest I haven't thoroughly researched each cast member?"

"No! That's not what I meant," Amanda said. "I'm just a little concerned that he could be, you know, an unsavory character to have on the show."

Priya raised her eyebrows. "The good news is that's not your concern. All you two need to do is write some stupid copy about how he's going to be a 'knock-out in the bedroom,' collect your paycheck, and go home."

Amanda gave Trevor a look, which he ignored. "Understood," he said. "Not a problem."

"Excellent," Priya said. "I thought so."

# Maggie

### Episode 6

Maggie had now been on two dates with Theo, if you didn't include her Paradise Island sleepover. Two full dates, and they had yet to kiss; that was *LoveShack* malpractice and the fastest way to get sent home. There was nothing there between them, and she wasn't sure how much longer the viewers would keep her around if she and Theo continued to display whatever the opposite of chemistry was.

She imagined Emma watching her two dates and it made her want to die. Theo was exactly the kind of guy Emma would tell her to swipe left on—boring, personality-less. The kind of guy who would put in his dating profile that he was just "looking for good vibes" or that his dog was his best friend or something. She could almost picture Emma sitting next to her on the couch, lording over her matches. "No. Not this guy. I can tell he's dull," she'd say, before ruthlessly unmatching.

Finn, on the other hand—Emma would probably like Finn. She was picky about straight men, but Finn was charming, and confident, and he stood up for women.

\*

To succeed on *LoveShack*—to leave with brand deals and Instagram followers—there were two options (Anita, her manager, had explained this when she was cast). She could fall in love, or become a villain. People wanted a love story, or they wanted drama. The key was to get screen time, at any cost.

"Let's be honest, I don't think you can pull off villain," Anita told her. "Though obviously that's the easier route." Last season on *LoveShack*, a woman named Ula had managed to break up three happy couples by shamelessly pursuing the men in each couple. Her villain arc had ended with a spectacularly dramatic showdown between Ula and one of the wronged women, wherein Ula had thrown a vodka tonic in the poor woman's face. It had gone viral, and had got Ula millions of Instagram followers, a podcast called *Bitch, Please!*, and her own hard seltzer brand.

Because Maggie was more girl next door than drama-starting firebrand, her only real option was to give finding love a go.

Layla had been so encouraging, picking out her outfits, telling her it wasn't her fault that chemistry with Theo wasn't there. But still, she couldn't help feeling rejected by this man—a man to whom she wasn't even particularly attracted. Meanwhile, Layla and Finn's connection seemed to deepen every day. They'd made out a few times, and, according to Layla, were having amazing dates where they had meaningful conversations about their lives and the things they wanted from a relationship.

Maggie had taken to sitting by the propane fire pit on the balcony at night by herself, while all the other couples got drunk and flirted or fought. She was aware that this meant she was getting less camera time, and therefore the likelihood that she'd be sent home soon was increasing. As Anita said: *If you want to stay on the show, keep yourself in front of the cameras. Keep the drama flowing.* She was doing the opposite. Not only was she not producing drama, but she was avoiding it. While this was a healthy outlook to have on life, it wasn't the best when you were trying to win a reality TV show.

"Mind if I join you?"

She turned her head to see Theo, followed by two cameras, walking through the glass doors and out onto the balcony. She didn't feel like talking to him, but she had no choice.

"Sure. I'll scoot over." Maggie looked up at him as he came toward her. She could not deny that, yes, he was handsome. Even if it was in a 2000s boy band kind of way.

"I just wanted to talk to you, because . . ." He seemed nervous. Where was this going? "Because I think we've gotten off on the wrong foot."

Maggie felt herself burn with irritation, thinking of their past dates and her desperate, unreciprocated attempts at conversation. "Yeah, you could say that."

"No, I just mean . . ." He stopped for a millisecond. "I mean that I want us to start over. I feel like I've given you the wrong impression. I'm actually really into you. You're gorgeous, and funny, and smart, and I want us to make this work."

Huh.

"Wow," she managed. "That's . . . not what I thought you were going to say."

"Well, it's how I feel."

"OK." Maggie finally relaxed a bit. So he *did* like her. She felt buoyed by this.

"How do you feel about me?" he asked, not skipping a beat. For the first time, it occurred to her: had some producer put him up to this? Maybe for the drama of it? Was she supposed to confess her love for him or something, just for him to reject her?

"I honestly didn't think you liked me," she said.

Theo looked confused. "What? No! I'm so into you." How strange. He was so into her? Was he just painfully shy? It'd been difficult to talk to him up until that point. But maybe the viewers *had* paired them up intentionally. Maybe he was going to confessionals and talking about his feelings for her. Maybe he'd told the other guys when she wasn't around. It was weird that it hadn't gotten back to her, but she was happy to be hearing it now.

"I'm surprised to hear that, but I'm glad," she said, even though she wasn't sure how she felt about him. It was still nice to know that at least one man on this show was interested in her. He stood up and grabbed her hand so she'd stand up with him.

"I really want this to be a fresh start for us," he said.

"Me too," she responded, and meant it. He looked her right in the eyes, and leaned in to kiss her. It was awkward and stilted, but it was nice enough. He pulled away and smiled at her, grabbing her hand again. As he moved his hand away, he closed it on top of hers, and she felt that he'd placed something in it. She began to open her mouth to ask what it was, but something in his look quieted her.

The object was small. She guessed it was paper, folded up. Instinct told her not to unfurl her hand until she was alone. She realized, as he walked away with the cameras trailing, what he'd done. He'd left her a note.

# Amanda

Amanda was alone in her office after Jill had left for the day, ostensibly to do a rewrite of a script but really to kill time before therapy. The document was open on her computer, but she was having a hard time focusing. She kept opening new tabs on Matches and Moda Operandi to browse for things she didn't need. Then, whenever she got close to buying a Prada bag or a Zimmermann dress, she'd force herself to close the websites and look at the script again. She read and reread a too-long scene about a character on *The Youth* experimenting with bulimia, but nothing was coming to her. In the olden days, she would've opened her desk drawer, popped an Adderall or three, and gotten this done in an hour. But these were not the olden days.

Instead, she walked over to her mini-fridge, where Jill kept a supply of Diet Coke and kombucha stocked at all times. She grabbed a Diet Coke and walked back to her desk. She stared at the script again and took a large sip of her soda. She tried to pretend there was some vodka in there, or something that could help her get through a rewrite. But it didn't work.

Suddenly, as often happened in the dark moments of the

night or during a particularly bad spell of writer's block, she felt a powerful urge to open the Bad Document. The Bad Document was almost as menacing as the binder of unflattering press clips that she stored under her bed. She kept it on her drive under the name "July Receipts." She took a deep breath and decided to give in. At least it wasn't drugs. It was just Google Docs.

The Bad Document was actually a collection of all of the information she'd been able to find about Trevor since his disappearance. Some of it she'd got from a private detective she'd hired online, who'd done some research for her. Some of it she'd got from scouring Reddit and Twitter for mentions of his name. Mostly her information was from blind items she'd seen on gossip accounts.

Supposedly, he'd been spotted in Greece a few months after he'd disappeared. A few people had posted more recently that they'd seen him in New Mexico, but she doubted the veracity of that claim. Something in her gut told her he'd left the country for good. The private investigator had confirmed that he'd purchased a flight from Los Angeles to Bucharest the evening the initial sexual assault allegations had become public. From Bucharest on, no one had been able to track him.

She typed "Trevor Koch" into Twitter's search bar to see if there was anything new. Nothing came up; as always, it was mostly people posting #MeToo tweets about how they hated him. Then she went onto Reddit.

This was a familiar routine, because the truth was, she was only able to feel even a little bit OK about all that had happened with Trevor when she was actively looking for him.

When Beth, months earlier, asked her why she was searching for him, she couldn't answer honestly. That would mean telling her therapist the truth of what had happened between them, what she gave up for him. Instead, she told herself and Beth that she just wanted to take him to task for everything he did. But the thing was: she missed him. This was the sorry state of her life. She missed what they had together, and mourned what they would've had if he'd stuck around. Beth had diagnosed the root of Amanda's propensity toward interpersonal obsession as a volatile mix of an "addictive personality," borderline personality disorder, and complex post-traumatic stress disorder. But Amanda knew it was simpler than that: she was just lonely.

Until she'd hired Jill a year ago, she'd had no real friends in her life anymore. That was humiliating, so she tried not to think about it very often. It's why she could never promote Jill beyond assistant, could never get her a writing gig on *The Youth*. Because it'd mean she'd lose her closest person. Again.

But that was her reality: Trevor was gone, and, for obvious reasons, her drug friends were gone too. Before Trevor was accused, she'd had some people, mostly industry contacts turned friends, with whom she'd grab drinks or coffee. But all of them—every last one—had faded away.

Trevor took over her life, ruined everything, and then left her to pick up the pieces. But worst of all, he left her alone.

This was the thing: she'd actually propositioned Trevor that second time.

*Anxiety* had just been renewed for a fourth season, and

Amanda had been the subject of a major and very flattering profile in the *New Yorker*. They were long past the *LoveShack* writing disaster and all that'd ensued. Everything was coming up roses.

She invited Trevor over the night of the *New Yorker*'s publication to celebrate and start writing new episodes. For the occasion, Amanda had acquired, thanks to her old PA Melanie, large whiteboards and old magazines so they could collage and make a "vision board." She wanted to do this both ironically and unironically. Amanda had also procured for them an earth-shattering amount of the finest cocaine that money could buy.

He arrived at her place wearing a vintage corduroy jacket she loved, and her heart swelled just seeing him in her doorway. He was her best friend, her creative partner. He was her life.

He came in and kissed her on the cheek. "Congrats on the profile, you fucking superstar."

She laughed. "Oh, come on." She eyed the bottle of champagne he had brought with him.

"I mean it." He looked at her with a seriousness that surprised her. "It's incredible." She blushed.

Trevor plopped down on her couch, a green velvet Chesterfield she had found in an upscale antique store in Echo Park. "You know what, Amanda? I really miss being your roommate," he said. "Even though that place was too small for two adults to live in, let alone two adults who were not sleeping together." She was surprised to feel a pang at this.

"Aw, you sap." She hit him on the chest. "I miss living with you too. Though I don't miss your disinterest in doing dishes." Or when she'd gotten pushed out of the *LoveShack* writers' room and he'd taken her money. But they never talked about that, and she wasn't going to start now.

"Oh, come on. You loved it." He untwisted the metal wiring holding down the cork on the champagne. "Let's drink this, yeah? From the bottle? Like old times?"

"Yes! And I have some additional supplies." She disappeared into her room, reappearing carrying an ornate handheld mirror she had been gifted by her late grandmother. On it were four lines of cocaine.

"This is why I love you." He stood to uncork the bottle. "To you."

"To us," she corrected.

"Fine, but who's the sap now?" He popped the bottle, and they each took two giant swigs and then did their two lines of cocaine.

"There's more where that came from." Amanda wandered off to get the baggie. "For when we're deep in brainstorming mode."

They spent the next two hours in a coked-up frenzy (with a healthy dose of Adderall, for her), sitting on her antique Persian rug and cutting out things from the magazines and writing story arcs on the whiteboards.

Trevor looked up at her, nose still sprinkled with powder. "Tonight is one of those nights where I feel like we have the same soul," he said. "I know how dumb that sounds."

"I completely agree." Her heart raced, likely from all the stimulants, but also with something new—something big. Something that was just occurring to her. It was so brilliant!

Why hadn't she thought of it before? She felt the words come out of her mouth before she had made a conscious decision to say them. "Why did we, like, never . . ." She paused. He was looking at her, eyes bloodshot and a dusting of cocaine still lining his left nostril. "Why did we never try to do this thing we have as an actual, you know, relationship?"

Trevor put down his scissors. Her heart sped up even more.

"You mean, like, why aren't we fucking?" He looked at her sincerely. It was not quite what she meant, but she went with it.

"Yeah, I guess." She began pacing back and forth in front of the whiteboard, trying to calm her nervous system. "You know, we're both never in relationships. We're both straight, at least mostly. We've slept together before and it was pretty fun." The truth was, he was sometimes in relationships, but always with Romanian models he found at the Chateau Marmont or somewhere. She was always single. She sometimes hooked up with guys, usually C-list actors she suspected were using her for her fame, or drummers or bassists in third-rate rock bands who fucked all types of people but weren't as hot as the lead singers. She wasn't Hollywood pretty. She'd accepted that. But why should that stop her from being with Trevor, who was as normal-looking as she was?

"All true." He nodded his head up and down and up and down. "All true."

"And I know I'm not, like, the typical model-slash-actress that you usually hook up with, but we have good—"

"Oh, Amanda. You're hot. You know I've always thought that. It doesn't matter that you're not thin." She blushed at this, even though it was not exactly the compliment she craved.

"I was actually thinking that we are more compatible than just, you know, for sex. We could have something. We have so much fun together, just being creative and brainstorming. And think how well we work together—that we created this amazing thing with our stupid script from when we were twenty-two. We created a hit reality show. We're best friends already. We're attracted to each other. Should we just do this?"

He nodded again, this time looking at her thoughtfully—or as thoughtfully as he could muster after consuming an absurd amount of cocaine. He stood up, put his arms around her, and kissed her.

They dropped to the couch and he pulled her on top of him, and she tried to quiet her mind. Her thoughts circled back and forth. What was this? Was this just sex? Was it something more? *Just be in the moment, Amanda,* she commanded herself as he pulled down the straps of her tank top and circled her nipples with his fingers. With this, her brain was silent for just a moment; it felt so good to be with him, for him to touch her.

She pulled back and looked at him as he did this, before he moved down and put her left nipple in his mouth, never breaking eye contact. He groaned, pulling back and whispering in her ear. "I think about doing that all the time."

She felt dizzy with joy. "Let's have sex," she said, trying to sound enticing. "I mean, if you want to." She was both enjoying this and wanting it to be over, so she could think about it, play it back in her mind.

"Of course I want to." He smiled. "Let me get a condom."

"That's OK," she said, quickly. "No need." She would not be the kind of girl who demanded he wear a condom even though she was on the pill.

"If you're sure," he said, and she nodded. She trusted him. He laid her down on the couch, kneeling next to it. His face was serious and focused as he took off her shirt, then her pants. He touched her over her underwear, and she closed her eyes.

He entered her with his fingers and she inhaled sharply.

"I'm ready," she said, her voice not quite her own.

"I can feel that." He removed his own boxers and she took him in her hands.

He moaned as she guided him on top of her, and then inside of her.

It went quicker than she had expected—did coke counteract alcohol in that department?—and he finished on her stomach. He lay on top of her, catching his breath, and she moved her nails across his back.

"Did you come?" he asked her.

"Definitely," she lied.

"I'll clean that up," he told her, and went to the bathroom to grab tissues. She lay still, trying not to get cum on her couch, feeling ecstatic. It'd happened: she and Trevor were taking their relationship to the next level. It was like a dream. She smiled to herself.

He wandered out of the bathroom and threw a wad of tissues at her, grabbing his discarded boxers. "Hey, I need to get going. I have an early morning."

"Oh." She tried to hide her surprise. "So soon?"

"Yeah, sorry about that." He walked over to kiss her on the cheek.

*Be chill, Amanda.* "No worries. I'm getting tired too," she said, even though she would not sleep for about three days given the amount of stimulants in her bloodstream.

"I'll text you later." He pulled his jeans back on.

"Sounds good." She pretended to yawn as he let himself out.

And that was it. That was the last time she saw him.

(Oh, and he'd given her chlamydia, too.)

In an attempt to escape the Bad Document, she got to therapy early. But she had to wait on one of the uncomfortable chairs, and was still consumed with thoughts of Trevor. So she closed her eyes and leaned against the stiff upper back of the chair, trying to meditate. She needed to clear her head. She breathed in for four counts, held it for four counts, breathed out for four counts, and held that for four counts. She'd learned that one at rehab.

But as soon as she had settled into a meditative rhythm, she found herself disrupted by someone leaving one of the other therapy offices in the suite upstairs. Irritated, she opened her eyes as she was forced to listen to someone clomp down the stairs in what sounded like chunky platform heels. She looked down at her phone to check the time; she still had ten minutes until her appointment began. As the person emerged, she tried to look away, to give them the customary privacy that everyone at this office afforded one another. But something about this person, who was now clomping toward the front door of the office, caused her to turn her head in a way that was completely unsubtle. She recognized this woman, she realized as she watched her walk away. But from where? She couldn't place her. But it felt important. The woman was short, with long dark hair styled into glossy waves. She was indeed wearing heels—black suede with a tan platform heel—and walking to the door. Something in Amanda told her to get up and go after her.

She followed the woman out of the front door, where the valet was handing her the key to her car. And that's when Amanda realized who it was. It was Layla. Maggie's Layla. *LoveShack* Layla.

Before she could stop herself, she cried out to her, "Layla! Hi!"

Layla turned around, and Amanda could see that her eyes were puffy and red. "Do we know each other?"

"I'm so sorry to bug you. I'm Amanda Lehman." She extended her hand. Layla awkwardly returned her handshake but continued to stare at her. "I wrote and starred on *Anxiety*?"

"Oh, yeah, I've heard of it. Thanks for saying hi. Good to meet you," Layla said tersely, walking over to the driver's side of her car and opening it.

"Wait, sorry, I just . . ." She just what? Wanted to talk to her because she had seen her on a reality TV show Amanda had secretly come up with the idea for? "I was friends with Maggie Lathrop," she lied.

Layla, who had been halfway inside her car, got up and looked at Amanda. Anger brimmed behind her puffy eyes. "I'm not interested in talking about Maggie." She shut the door and turned her key in the ignition. Amanda ran over to the driver's side.

"I'm sorry, I'm confused," she said loudly, so it would break through the window. "I'm just saying hi because we had a mutual friend. I didn't mean to offend you."

Layla—the nerve—rolled her eyes at this, but let out a breath and turned off the car. She rolled down her window. "Maggie and I were not friends. I don't know what she told you, but I want to be clear about that. Sorry, I don't like speaking ill of the dead."

Amanda was stunned. She had just watched an episode of *LoveShack* where they were inseparable. Obviously, a lot happened in the editing room, but a friendship like that was hard to produce. "I'm sorry to have bothered you. You just looked like you were friends on the show."

"Look, the valet will get pissed if I just sit here. I have to go." Layla turned her key again.

"I just want to know what happened to Maggie. We're gathering information. The police called off the investigation—"

"I don't know anything about her murder." Layla's eyes filled with what looked like pity. Or maybe irritation? "The only thing I do know is that Maggie and Theo were not what they seemed. That's all I can really say."

"Wait, what does that mean?" Amanda asked.

"I have to go," Layla said. "I'm late for something." She put her car in drive, looked stonily ahead, and drove away.

# Maggie

## Episode 8

Maggie held the note in her hands, pacing back and forth in the en suite bathroom.

"You OK in there?" Layla called to her.

"Just a sec," she said, trying to steady her voice.

"I want to tell you about my date tonight," Layla said through the door. "It was so romantic that it's literally gonna make you vom."

But Maggie wasn't listening. Instead, she reread the note, flushing the toilet so Layla wouldn't suspect anything.

*Maggie,*

*I'm sorry we can't talk about this out loud, but you'll see why in just a moment. I want to propose something to you, and I hope you won't be offended.*

*Unfortunately, I don't have a romantic connection with anyone here. It seems like you might be in the same boat? Since we're paired, I hope we can come to an arrangement. Because the show's winning couple gets all the magazine covers, brand deals, and spin-offs, etc., I assume we both want to win. I believe we can make this work for both of us. I know this sounds manipulative, but we could pretend we're really falling in love. Then a few months after the show is over, we'll go our separate ways and tell everyone we had a mutual breakup.*

*It's a win-win. If you are interested in pursuing this, please say "I really like you" on our next date. Then I'll know.*

*Obviously, I'm trusting you not to tell anyone about this. Please consider this offer. I think it's a good one.*

*Theo*


Maggie ran the note under warm water in the sink, watching the ink of the letters bleed together. Her heart pounded. She ripped up the note and threw it in their small bathroom trash can, covering it with a wad of toilet paper.

She re-entered the room, where Layla was sitting on her bed picking at her split ends.

"You OK?" she asked.

"Oh, yeah," Maggie said. "Just . . . you know. Stomach issues."

"Damn," Layla said. "Do you think it was those chicken tenders from earlier? Those were gross."

"Possibly." She plopped onto her bed, thoughts racing. "Sorry, Layla, I think I need to go to bed. Not feeling great."

Layla turned off the light, and Maggie lay on her back, eyes wide open. She could not believe the gall of it—the nerve Theo had to even offer this deal to her. Why couldn't he just have done what everyone else did, and fake it a little with her for the duration of the show? He was such a pretentious prick. But at the same time, she appreciated his candor. And he was right that the winners did much better, career-wise. They earned millions of Instagram followers, as opposed to the hundreds of thousands the other contestants got. But hundreds of thousands still wasn't terrible—she could live comfortably on second-tier brand deals for at least a few years. But then what would she do with her life? She had no college education, no career prospects, no family money to lean on. She had nothing. The thought of going home to deal with her mounting debt made her queasy.

And he was right: she wasn't going to find love. Despite Finn being a bit of a flirt, he and Layla were clearly happy together. And if he actually liked her, he'd have made his move by now, surely.

But could she convincingly fake it with Theo? And what if someone—or the world—found out? She would look terrible. She would become the villain. Her manager might be pleased, but it wasn't what she wanted for herself. The central pillar holding up the *LoveShack* empire was the idea that true love was real, and it could be found if you lived among sexy singles in a mansion for long enough. If anyone discovered that she and Theo were fully faking it, it would cost her.

As Layla's light breathing turned into gentle snores, Maggie turned onto her side and tucked her pillow under her head to encourage sleep to come. She resolved to do what she needed to do.

Her date with Theo was supposed to be a sunset hike and picnic, and the producers had picked out a "safari chic" outfit for her to wear. Hopefully they wouldn't be doing serious hiking, as she was wearing wedge-heel sneakers, silky green cargo pants, and a white mesh bustier. Not exactly the best hiking gear.

As soon as she got to the mountain they'd be hiking up and received her instructions from Priya, she knew she was in trouble. The beginning of the trail was rocky and unpaved, and there was a steep incline on a bare mountain with no tree cover. Why did it always feel like the producers were fucking with her? In her outfit, it would be nearly impossible to climb to the top unscathed. She shuddered thinking of the blisters she was about to develop.

"You'll be fine," Priya told her. "The hike is like thirty minutes, max. It's supposed to be a bonding experience."

"It feels like hazing," Maggie said. "Can I at least change my shoes?"

"We don't have any replacement shoes here. Just be grateful you aren't in stilettos."

Maggie knew it was a losing battle. And as Theo's car pulled up, her heart beat faster with anticipation. About the hike or about the conversation that was to come, she wasn't sure.

As Theo got out of the car, the cameras began rolling. He greeted her warmly, kissing her on the cheek.

"Are you excited for our adventure?" he asked her.

"Yes." Maggie was surprised to find herself a little nervous. She reminded herself this wasn't a big deal: everyone faked it on these shows. "But you may have to help me, because I am wearing the worst possible hiking outfit." She glared at Priya, who was standing behind one of the cameras. Priya rolled her eyes, and pointed her finger, directing Maggie to stop looking at the camera.

The hike was both better and worse than she'd expected. Part of the trail was paved with stones, and they went slowly so she wouldn't trip on anything. It was hot, but as the sun began to set, it wasn't uncomfortably so. And conversation was more natural than it had been a few days prior.

When they got to the top of the mountain, there was an anemic picnic set up for them: two bottles of wine, two tuna sandwiches (why?), and a snack-size bag of potato chips to split. Once again, she wondered if they were being starved.

As they sat down on the plaid blanket, Theo put his arm around her.

"Want some?" He pointed to the wine. She nodded, and he poured her a generous glass. He looked at her for a long moment. "Cheers," he said.

"Cheers." She clinked his glass. He took a large sip and then looked directly at her again.

"I really want to kiss you right now." His voice was low, hoarse. Something inside her stirred, even though she knew it was just part of the act. She leaned in. This kiss was deeper and more interesting than their last, and she wondered what he was trying to communicate to her. If only they could have a few moments without cameras, just to hash things out. He pulled away, looking at her, and she almost wondered if he was blushing.

Before she could lose her nerve, she leaned in and whispered to him, "Theo, I really like you." If he wanted to do this fake relationship thing, why the hell not?

He looked back at her, eyes wide, and she tried to read him. Hopefully he was relieved. He smiled back at her, and grabbed her hand. "I really like you, too."

She woke up the next morning feeling hungover, but she wasn't sure if it was from the three glasses of wine or the intense date the night before. When she had returned to her room after the hike and picnic, Layla had grilled her. Maggie pretended that she was on cloud nine, retelling the events of the night as they appeared to the outside world, without any additional information about what was going on under the surface. What were all those years of expensive acting classes for, if not this? Layla seemed convinced, because mid-conversation, she was clearly beginning to drift off to sleep. It was not exactly the behavior of a suspicious friend on high alert.

It was a competition day, which meant that the producers would force them into some uncomfortable, gross, or degrading game that took four or five hours to film in the hot desert sun. A few days ago they'd filmed a game where each contestant had to perform oral sex on bananas (the women) and papayas (the men) and got scored on their "technique."

Usually, at this point in the season, the competitions were aimed at breaking up settled couples. It was boring when there were too many happy people; the audience wanted drama. Maggie knew she should've been nervous for what was going to be a humiliating game that she was contractually obligated to participate in on national television, but since she had made the arrangement with Theo, something in her had relaxed. The emotional stakes of their coupledom were as low as they could be.

"We're here right now to put your Love Pairs to the test," Schuyler said as they lined up on a patch of fake grass outside of the bungalow. They stood as instructed, men in a line behind the women. "Today's competition is called Smooch or Dare." There were audible groans from multiple contestants.

"Cut!" Larry yelled. "For fuck's sake. We're going to have to reshoot that. You can't groan when we announce the games. Let's take it from the top."

"We're here right now to put your Love Pairs to the test," Schuyler said again, in the exact same cadence. "Today's competition is called Smooch or Dare. You're probably wondering what that means." There was a dramatic pause. "Ladies, today you're in the driver's seat. You will get to decide if you want to smooch—for at least five seconds—a randomly selected male *Shack*er. If you say no, you will have to undertake a dare that the rejected *Shack*er chooses for you. But be careful, the dares will get spicy!"

*Yawn.* The dares would be something stupid, like jump in the pool naked, or lick whipped cream out of someone's belly button. It would be nothing worse than she'd already done on the show, she figured. Last week she'd been forced to massage Luke's feet for twenty seconds in a similar game.

"First up, we have Tia. Are you ready for Smooch or Dare?"

"I guess so." She stepped forward, wearing a white one-piece bathing suit with huge cutouts displaying her perfectly toned stomach. While they were obligated to wear bikinis every day, exceptions were made for revealing one-pieces.

Schuyler handed a large hollowed-out disco ball to Tia. "In here, you have the names of all five remaining *LoveShack* men. Pick one, and then you'll be asked: Smooch or Dare." Tia reached into the disco ball and pulled out a name, reading it aloud.

"Theo," she said, looking bored.

"OK, Theo, you're the lucky man. Now, Tia, the choice is yours: Smooch or Dare. Kiss Theo for at least five seconds, or go for a Dare." Maggie wondered, with passive curiosity, what she would choose. She marveled at the fact that she felt no possessiveness over Theo.

"Smooch?" Tia said, as if it were a question.

"Well then!" Schuyler practically squealed with delight. "Shots fired. Maggie, how are you feeling?"

What was the right response here? "I'm secure in my Love Pair." She hoped it sounded like something someone in a real Love Pair would say. "Yeah, I'm not too worried. But enjoy!" She winked at Theo and Tia, hoping this appeared sufficiently bitchy.

"Meeee-OW!" Schuyler said. With that, Theo and Tia kissed for the required five seconds. It looked chaste, which Maggie supposed was a good thing for keeping up appearances.

"Tia, how was that for you?" Schuyler asked as soon as they pulled away from each other.

"Um, it was fine. I prefer kissing Bryan," she said, though Bryan was shaking his head with irritation that she'd chosen Smooch.

"OK, Maggie, you're up next. Pick a name out of the disco ball." Schuyler handed it to her. She rummaged around and chose a small piece of paper. *Finn*, it said. She read the name out loud. Of course it was Finn. In another life where she wasn't in a fake relationship with Theo, and where Layla wasn't in a real one with Finn, she would've jumped at the chance to kiss him, to see if there was chemistry.

"Are you excited, Finn?" Schuyler asked. Finn looked startled, almost. Schuyler continued. "OK then, Maggie: Smooch or Dare?"

"Dare." She'd known from the second the game was announced that she'd choose Dare. But she especially knew she'd choose that option now, given that she couldn't kiss her best friend's Love Pair.

"Risky move!" Schuyler said. "You sure?"

"Yes."

"OK, Finn, come on up here." Schuyler handed him a second hollowed-out disco ball. "Please choose a dare." Finn walked up and dug his hand around the disco ball, drawing a piece of paper. Even though there was nothing to be nervous about, Maggie's chest tightened.

Finn looked at the piece of paper and ruffled his short brown hair, showing off his muscular arms. She was trying to read his face, but he wasn't giving anything away. "Uh, wow. It says: 'Make out with the person you selected for fifteen seconds, and use tongue.'"

"Wait, so even though I chose *not* to kiss Finn, I now have to kiss him for longer? With tongue?" she asked, trying to sustain outrage, though part of her was excited.

"That's right!" Schuyler chuckled. "See, I told you you

were taking a risk. Layla, how are you feeling? I know you and Maggie are close."

Layla looked as though she was about to cry. "It's fine." Her voice wavered. "I know it's not a choice either of them would have made on their own."

Guilt spiked in Maggie's stomach. She couldn't bring herself to look back at Layla as Finn stepped toward her. "Is this OK?" he asked her.

What was she supposed to say? She had no choice, so she nodded.

He leaned in, put his hands behind her head, and pulled her into him. To her shock, he kissed her deeply, with control. Desire swelled inside of her. Without thinking about it, she put her arms around his neck and kissed him back, now with reciprocal intensity. This went on until he moved away just slightly. She looked up at him, his eyes boring straight into her. She worried the kiss was over, but he pulled her body close to his, and returned his lips to hers.

Finally, when one of the other cast members coughed, she came back to herself. She pulled away to see the rest of the cast and the producers staring at them, stupefied. Layla was shaking her head, her arms crossed and eyes narrowed.

"Wowza!" Schuyler said, and Maggie felt hot with panic. Had she really just done that in front of all these people? On national TV? Yes, she had. She, with obvious pleasure, had kissed the guy with whom her best friend was paired. Schuyler continued, "You guys were going at it for at least a minute. I think a kiss that long in a competition may be a *LoveShack* first! Theo, how was watching that for you?"

Theo shot Maggie a confused look. Though not yet well versed in the subtext of his expressions, she understood it meant: *What the actual fuck is wrong with you?*

"As I've said," Theo began, his face blank, "I have serious feelings for Maggie. So it doesn't feel good."

"I'm sure." Schuyler clapped him on the back. "Layla, how about you?"

"I'm just confused." But she sounded more angry than confused.

Finn cut in, and looked at Layla. His face crumpled. "I'm so sorry. I lost track of time. You know how these things are. No one told us when the fifteen seconds was up. You mean a lot to me, Layla. I would never intentionally hurt you."

Layla rolled her eyes at this, pushing back tears. "That sounds like bullshit." A loaded silence followed.

Maggie turned to Layla. "I'm so sor—"

"Not now. Please," Layla said. "I had no idea you were that kind of person."

"I'm not! Or, I don't know what kind of person you mean, exactly, but I'm not a bad person. It was an accident." Maggie was rambling.

Tia jumped in. "How the hell was it an accident?"

"It just was." Maggie was holding back tears. "I'm sorry. I never wanted to hurt you, Layla. I promise."

Layla turned away, shaking her head. Tia hugged her. Everyone stood silently, waiting for someone else to speak. She could see Larry's face: he was annoyed that no one was storming off or willing to go low. But it was too awkward for Theo to say more, and Finn wasn't exactly able to comfort Layla.

"OK, fine, cut," Larry yelled. "Everyone take five." A producer grabbed Layla for a pull-aside, and they walked away.

Maggie tried to find Theo, but he was already making his way back to the bungalow. She sat down on the grass to give her feet a break. Without realizing it, she angrily dug her nails into her left thigh until they left welts.

It was going to be a long rest of the season.

# Emma

She, Jill and Amanda sat on the plush couches in the theater room at Amanda's house as she scratched the inside of her wrist. They'd just watched an episode of *LoveShack* together, and besides the fact that it was gross to watch her sister make out with random men on television, the latest episodes of *LoveShack* had unsettled something in her. Maggie committing herself to Theo, her future husband, just before making out with Finn—her best friend's Love Pair—was wrong.

Amanda grabbed a handful of popcorn and offered Emma the bowl. "Hear me out," she said, her mouth full. "What if someone from her cast had something to do with her murder? You should reach out to them. Interview them or something."

"Maybe," Emma said. Jill put her arm on Emma's to stop her from scratching. Emma nudged Jill in an attempt to get her to leave her alone. "Do you really think that's possible?"

"I don't know." Amanda crunched on a popcorn kernel. "Something has to be deeply wrong with you to go on that show in the first place. Maybe they were mad that she won."

Emma decided not to point out that her beloved sister was one of those people Amanda thought had something "deeply wrong" with them. "If anyone from the show killed her, it had to be Theo. There's something not right about him. You can even see it on the show," she said.

"I know what you mean," Amanda said. "Honestly, there's something weird about his on-camera relationship with your sister."

Jill looked annoyed. "I don't think he killed her. But I agree that something is off. More with Maggie, though, honestly."

The truth was, the person on the screen barely resembled the sister Emma knew. Maybe that was why Maggie had told her not to watch in the first place. Maggie's sunset date with Theo had been odd; it was like watching two animals engage in a strange mating ritual she couldn't quite comprehend. The version of them she saw on the screen bore no resemblance to the actual couple she knew in real life. In real life, it was almost as if they operated as business partners and friends rather than lovers. But on the show, it was full-on lovey-dovey. Plus, there'd been a full 180 from the previous episodes in which they seemed to almost dislike each other. Now, they looked madly in love.

That is, until Maggie and Finn had kissed.

On the drive home from Amanda's, Emma stared straight ahead, her left eye twitching with exhaustion. Jill was sitting shotgun, and had been oddly silent since they'd left Amanda's.

Emma gently pressed the brakes, cruising to a stop at an

oncoming red light on Crenshaw. The other bizarre thing about that night had, of course, been Amanda's retelling of her encounter with Layla. Emma knew it was stupid, but it was almost too much to bear that Layla—someone Maggie had known well, but whom Emma had never met or even known about before watching the show—had been right here in Los Angeles, all this time. Even though it seemed that Layla now hated Maggie, she'd known her. Maybe Amanda was right, and she should try to talk to Layla and the others. If nothing else, they could fill in the blanks.

As she watched the light turn green, she accelerated until she approached a backlog of cars waiting at the next light. Jill moved the dial on the stereo to the local public radio station and they listened in silence to a story about lemurs going extinct in Madagascar. There was traffic, though it was well past rush hour. She hated driving in LA, and couldn't get used to it no matter how many years she'd lived here. The traffic at all hours, the strip malls, the highways to more highways in the middle of a city. It was a far cry from the roads she'd driven on as a teenager in rural Kansas.

Emma's first car was a '94 Corolla, which she inherited from Maggie after her sister moved to New York. It was her favorite of all the cars she'd ever owned; though it had no heater or air conditioning, she and Maggie had jerry-rigged it with a cassette-to-iPod system.

Maggie got her license at sixteen, and the night she passed her driver's test, she picked Emma up from her after-school studio art class (Emma was terrible at art, but as a young, closeted kid in Kansas, it was about the only game in town when it came to meeting other people who were even remotely like you). Emma shrieked when she saw Maggie pull into the parking lot of the strip mall where she took the class, and everyone in the quiet studio had startled. But she didn't care. Having a sister with a license was going to be life-changing. Finally, she'd have someone to drive her to concerts in Topeka, a place she only went a few times a year, but which regularly hosted indie bands she liked.

Emma put away her canvas and paint set and ran outside to meet her sister. Maggie was in the driver's seat and her boyfriend at the time, Kevin, sat in the passenger's seat, even though it was his car. The Corolla wouldn't come into Maggie's possession for another few months.

"Oh my God. Let me see it!" Emma said, and Maggie, on command, produced her license. "Of course you look amazing in your license photo. How is that even possible?"

"She looks so good there, right?" Kevin agreed.

"Who cares." Maggie smiled. "I just can't believe I finally have a license."

"Now you'll just have to convince Mom to extend our curfew," Emma said.

"Yeah, right. Plus, where would we even go after ten p.m.? It's not like anyone invites us to anything," Maggie said, and Kevin laughed. Emma had to agree with this logic, but it was still exciting.

"True. But Tegan and Sara are playing at the Jayhawk in April and I really want to go."

Maggie looked in the rearview mirror at Emma. "Mom will let us. We never do anything social." Even though Maggie was a literal model, her only real friends in school were Emma and Kevin. Maggie had met him in third-period history class their freshman year, and he'd asked her out. He was a band geek, but also happened to be handsome. Emma had always liked him. Emma had a few more friends than Maggie, but they were mostly the theater and art kids, and they were not throwing ragers.

Emma never understood why Maggie had no friends in school, given that she was prettier than all the other girls and looked straight out of *Sweet Valley High*. When Maggie tried out for the cheerleading squad, and then the dance team, and then mock trial (a lesser but still popular kid-adjacent activity), she was rejected from all three. Her mom would always comfort her by saying the other kids were just jealous. And maybe they were. Maggie was stunning, and that was intimidating. Plus, the Lathrop's Salvation Army hand-me-downs didn't help, though Maggie now occasionally took them shopping with her modeling money (Maggie at Abercrombie & Fitch, Emma at Hot Topic and Delia's).

But Maggie was also a classic people pleaser, and sometimes Emma wondered if people could smell it on her. If they were repulsed by it.

As Emma parked in a spot near her apartment, she thought more about this. When she and Jill got out of her car, it finally dawned on her why the latest episode of the show and hearing about Amanda's run-in with Layla had felt so strange. It was because she'd never known Maggie to do something so unlikeable before—not even once. Maggie hated disappointing people, her friends most of all. And yet, she'd humiliated Layla by kissing Finn like that.

When they got back to the apartment, Jill went straight to

sleep. Emma collapsed onto their living-room couch, an Ikea sectional they needed to replace. She opened her phone and pulled up Layla's ShackWiki bio. She scrolled through her basic stats: she was thirty, married to a man Emma had never heard of named Paul Chen, a start-up founder. They lived in Los Angeles. She was the host of a podcast called *ShackTalk*, which Emma surmised was some sort of *LoveShack* debrief show—a classic career move for the less successful *LoveShack* alumni. There'd been four seasons since Maggie and Layla's, and she'd hosted a podcast for each of them. She scrolled down, but there was nothing useful, just a blurb about Layla's role as a brand ambassador for a keto cereal company.

With this, she shut her browser, and opened a text to Liz. *I want to find this woman Layla Reyes. She was on LoveShack with Maggie. Can you help me track down a number or an email or something?* As she pressed send, her left eye twitched again. All of a sudden, she was bone-tired. Even though she meant to get up and brush her teeth and make it to her own bed, she curled up against the couch cushion and fell asleep.

When Emma woke up the next morning, it was somehow 11:00 a.m. She saw that Jill had placed a blanket over her. She turned over to the coffee table where Jill had left a note saying she was off to set and that there were waffles in the freezer if she wanted them. She grabbed her phone, which she of course had forgotten to charge. It was at 9 percent. She had two missed calls from Liz.

Immediately she sprang into action, running to her room to plug her phone in and call her back.

Liz answered right away. "I got a hold of Layla."

"That was fast." Emma sat against her bed and smiled.

"I literally emailed 'hello@laylareyes.com,'" she said. "And said I was a reporter, and that I'm working with you, and we were trying to reach her."

Emma laughed. "Well, thanks for doing that for me."

"She is willing to talk. But she is insisting that she talks only with you, and only off-the-record, which I assume is fine—"

"I'll talk to her," Emma said.

"Well, it's not that simple. She just flew to London. She's filming some sort of celebrity international house-hunting show for a few months and wants to talk in person. She gave me her assistant's number for you to schedule with."

"Does that mean she wants me to come to London?" Emma asked. It was a strange request, but it seemed like their only option. "It's fine, right?"

"It's a long way to go for a conversation."

"True. But my gut says she knows something," Emma said. "And she's willing to talk."

"Oh, another thing," Liz began. "I'm not a detective, but given that she and your sister had a falling out, I'd consider that a possible motive. So maybe meet her somewhere public."

"I doubt that this five-foot-two woman killed Maggie," she said. Maggie had a good six inches and thirty pounds on Layla.

"I'm just saying."

"Fine. I'll meet her somewhere public."

After she hung up with Liz, she called Layla's assistant.

"She wants you to come this Sunday, when she has a break from filming," the assistant said.

"Like, as in this coming Sunday?"

"Yes."

"And why does it have to be in person?" Emma tucked her phone in between her shoulder and her ear and started googling flights on her computer.

"I don't know. She's paranoid about stuff like this."

Emma wondered what that meant. "I'll be there." With that, they said their goodbyes. She started a to-do list on her phone's notes app:

1) *Buy flight to London*
2) *London Airbnb/hotel?*
3) *Tell Jill and Amanda*

She got up, feeling jittery. Finally, finally, after months of stagnation, they were getting somewhere.

# Jill

It was the final day of filming on *The Youth*, and the main character was overdosing on fentanyl. Sonya, the teen actress who was playing her, had a faceful of ghostly white makeup, meant to make her look nearly dead.

"This is like a goddamn afterschool special," Amanda hissed. Jill nodded, not wanting to talk over the sounds of the actress's screams as another character "revived" her using Narcan.

"I just want to be dead! Let me die!" the actress wailed. The scene really *was* overwrought, though Jill wished Amanda would just leave it be.

Jill decided it was time to get lunch, mostly because she didn't want to hear Amanda's commentary. Amanda's bad mood had put her in one, and the back of the set, where they'd been sitting for hours on two folding chairs, was dark and dingy. She whispered to Amanda that she was going to go to Sal's to get them chicken Caesar wraps (they ate them every day), and Amanda handed over her black Amex (as she did every day). Jill made her way off the set, and when she got to the parking lot, she relaxed. Her daily lunch run was the one time of day that was hers to spend alone.

*The Youth* filmed in Burbank, on a soundstage that was made to look like an average American high school. She usually drove twenty minutes (forty minutes with traffic) from the set to Sal's, which was in Studio City. Her cherry-red Prius from 2004 got good gas mileage, but her commute to and from Burbank and her lunch trip cost her about a quarter of her salary each month.

When she pulled into the parking lot of the strip mall where Sal's was located, she rolled her windows up and turned off her car. Sal's had a line snaking out the door, which wasn't unusual. As she waited for their sandwiches and sipped her smoothie (she never got a smoothie on her own dime), she opened Twitter. She followed reporters, critics, celebrity gossip accounts and TV writers—anyone who might have something to say about Amanda. Today, the Twitter universe seemed mostly focused on a bad tweet from some *Washington Post* reporter calling Cher overrated. She swiped up to close the app before something caught her eye: *@insiderealitytv247: Theo Cooke spotted getting cozy with mystery man.*

A man? Who was this person? She double-tapped on the photo to open it and zoom in. It was Theo holding hands with a guy and kissing him on the cheek as they walked down the street. The man was short compared to Theo, and looked quite a bit older than him—perhaps in his fifties. He had a bear vibe, maybe—a certain rugged masculinity that was popular in the gay community. She had no idea Theo was queer; she'd never heard him talk publicly or privately about his sexuality. The mystery man wore large sunglasses and a baseball cap, so it was difficult to see what he actually looked like. But he wasn't the kind of person, woman or man, that she'd expected Theo to end up with. She was almost impressed that he'd found a regular-looking person to date. She copied the link to the tweet and opened her texts with Emma. Would Emma want to see this? Yes, she definitely would. Emma had just deleted Twitter in an effort to spend less time going down internet rabbit holes, so she might not come across it unless Jill sent it to her. But it was also possible that this photo would send Emma spiraling, and that it would only make her hate Theo more. Jill hesitated for a moment before deleting the draft text as the cashier called out her order number. She'd figure it out later, after work.

Emma wasn't there when Jill got home around six. This was unusual—Emma, even months after Maggie's death, rarely left the house on her own. She'd left Jill a note saying she had to run an errand at the bank. While Jill waited, she poured herself a glass of wine, sat on the couch, and deliberated about whether or not to tell Emma about the tweet. Even after downing half a glass of cabernet, she still had no idea what to do.

As Emma put her key into their front door, Jill seized up with dread. She had to make a decision.

"How was your day?" Jill asked as Emma walked in.

Emma sat down on the couch. "Weird, honestly. But not bad weird. I wanted to talk to you about something if you had a moment."

"Of course."

Emma looked hesitant. "Wait, why don't you tell me

about your day first? Sorry, I should've asked before I jumped in," she said. But Jill could tell from her face that this was a diversion tactic.

"Out with it," Jill said.

"OK, fine. I'm going to London."

"London! That's great, Em."

Emma looked down at her feet. "Like, tomorrow."

"That's soon." Jill heard a note of skepticism in her voice. "You're going to use the emergency money?"

Emma nodded. "There's more than enough left, and I have to do this. You remember Layla? Maggie's ex-friend from *LoveShack* who was weird to Amanda?"

"Yes." Jill sipped her wine. God, this was classic Emma. Or classic Emma in the last few months—impulsive, self-centered, obsessive, and sure that everyone around her was as engaged in the minute details of Maggie's case as she was. When was the last time she'd even asked Jill about her day, not in a perfunctory way, but a genuine one?

Not to mention that Amanda had offered Emma a writing job which happened to be Jill's dream job and Emma had never even acknowledged it. She probably hadn't even registered it, or how it would feel for Jill. But Jill chided herself. That'd been a week ago already, and she needed to get over it.

Jill felt a pang of guilt at her unkind thoughts. *Of course* Emma was going to be self-centered after going through a major trauma. Jill needed to be supportive, unconditionally. Or, if she was going to have conditions, they needed to be about Emma's safety and well-being.

"Liz reached out to her. She wants to talk to me, in person. She's filming some show right now in London." Emma's voice was measured, which Jill knew was intended to make everything sound casual.

Jill took in the news. "Wow. That's a big deal. You'd be going alone?"

"Yes. Unless you wanted to come," Emma said.

Jill held in a snort. "Well, I have to work. I can't just go to London on a day's notice." It came out a little sharper than she'd intended.

"I know you do. That's why I didn't invite you in the first place." Emma sounded defensive.

"Sorry. I shouldn't have said it like that." Jill let out a breath.

"What's your deal, though?" Emma said. "You've been aloof this whole week. What's going on?"

"I guess I'm a little annoyed. About the Amanda thing." The words came out of Jill's mouth before she could reconsider. She was supposed to be being unconditionally supportive, and instead she'd admitted she was irritated with Emma.

"What Amanda thing?"

Jill looked down at her hands. This was so embarrassing. "It's stupid."

"Just tell me."

Her face felt hot. "It's just that Amanda offered you that job in the writers' room, if you ever want one. On *The Youth*."

Emma blinked. "I honestly don't even remember that."

"Of course you don't!" Jill felt a flash of real hurt. She

needed to tell Emma the truth or she would maybe explode. Unconditional support would have to wait. "You don't pay attention to anything that isn't Maggie-related. Of course you didn't notice that she just went and offered you my dream job, even though I work so hard for her, doing every little inane thing she asks—"

Emma cut her off. "Whoa. Where is this coming from? I didn't ask her to say that. And I didn't say I'd do it!"

"It's just so classic," Jill said. "It's like I fade into the background when you're around. And mostly I'm OK with that, but sometimes it really hurts."

Emma shook her head. "That's not true. I'm your weird butch friend and you're the normie one. You're the one who people actually understand."

Oh, Emma. How wrong she was. Before she knew what was happening, Jill felt hot tears run down her cheeks.

"Why are *you* crying? You just yelled at me!" Emma said.

"I don't know." Jill wiped her tears. "I'm sorry. I don't mean to yell. I just want things with us to be . . . I don't know. Easier. Like how they were. I hate fighting with you." Emma was silent, so she continued. "It's just that if you paid attention, you'd know that I would kill for an actual TV writing job. And you had one! And just threw it all away." She'd rarely spoken this honestly to Emma before. Or to anyone, really.

Emma turned away, shaking her head. "I didn't know you felt that way. You know, Maggie could've helped you, too. She could've connected you to a writing job."

Jill let out a sigh. "That's not what I wanted. I just mean

that you had a good life. I just want things to go back to how they were between us. Before all of this."

"Things will never be how they were." Emma's voice was cold, distant. "My sister was murdered and I'm a different person now. It's up to you whether or not you can handle it."

# Emma

By the time Emma got to her Airbnb in London, it had been two days since her fight with Jill. They rarely argued, and when they did, the iciness never usually lasted this long. She was almost impressed that Jill had it in her to keep it up. But now, with the distance of an ocean between them, Emma wasn't sure how to break the tension. After she unpacked her stuff—hastily chosen sweaters and scarves and jeans for the cold and rainy early London summer—she opened WhatsApp to message Jill. *I hate it when we fight. I'm sorry I haven't been paying enough attention to our friendship. I also want things to be normal with us, and I want to get back to my life. I just need a little time. I hope you can understand that.* She pressed send, and collapsed backwards onto the bed, kicking her shoes off.

When her eyelids got heavy, she jolted upright. She needed to stay up to beat the jet lag that was threatening to consume her. It was 3:00 a.m. in California and 11:00 a.m. in London. She hadn't left the country since a trip to Costa Rica with Jill a few years ago, and she resolved that in the days before she was supposed to meet up with Layla, she'd explore. She'd chosen an Airbnb in Shoreditch upon Amanda's recommendation. It was a lovely studio, with a propane fireplace, giant windows, and a comfortable bed with a luscious white duvet. It was the only time she'd ever traveled by herself.

The first order of business was getting caffeine in her system, so she googled nearby cafés. She found one that was a couple of minutes away, and put on boots, burnt-orange wide-leg pants, a black turtleneck, and an oversized wool blazer. She actually felt cute for the first time in recent memory. Even her paleness looked less worrisome now that she was in the UK—she felt more like a heroine from a gothic novel rather than a depressed thirty-something. Maybe living in LA around a bunch of perennially tan fitness freaks was not good for her self-esteem.

Once she arrived at the café, she ordered a scone and a large black tea with milk (cow's milk! Did that exist in LA anymore?) and chose a seat by the window. Perhaps it was the exhaustion from a twelve-hour international flight, but she felt light and buzzy, stupidly happy to be somewhere that was not California. Why hadn't she thought to take a trip sooner?

She opened her notes app so she could plot out what she wanted to say to Layla. As the caffeine hit her system, she typed a few questions. The first and most obvious was, of course: *What did you mean when you told Amanda that Theo and Maggie weren't who they said they were?* She jotted down a couple more: *Did Maggie say anything concerning/worrying about Theo? Was Maggie happy when she and Theo began dating? Is there anyone who had it in for Maggie?* She continued to think about her meeting with Layla as she finished her tea and scone. It was dry and tasteless, but she kept hearing Jill's voice in her head, telling her she needed to eat.

Afterwards, she wandered around the neighborhood for another hour, stopping in vintage stores and bookshops and feeling a sense of happiness that was so alien to her now. She bought herself two books and a few grocery items—some apples, a block of cheddar cheese, and a packet of oatcakes. Real food. Jill would be proud.

After a late dinner, she decided to pay a visit to a famous lesbian bar in Soho that she'd seen featured in some gay travel TikTok months ago. It had been a while since she'd been to a bar, let alone a gay bar. Jill was always offering to go out with Emma so she could meet women, but the idea of dragging her oppressively straight friend to gay bars felt unfun. She had a few queer friends she'd made in LA right out of college in a gay kickball league, but they'd lost touch as the years went on. It was always easier to hang out with Jill or Maggie rather than make an effort to socialize with people she didn't know as well. She'd always coasted along having a few close friends rather than a big group.

The lesbian bar was on the top floor of a three-story building in the middle of Soho. It was sweaty and dark and loud. She took a seat at the bar on a red pleather stool and ordered a drink. Emma had never gone out to a bar by herself before, and was surprised at just how comfortable it felt. She didn't even feel the urge to play on her phone. It was fun to watch people: the couples making out on the dance floor; the early-twenties crowd dipping their toes into the world of lesbian nightlife; the older regulars sitting and laughing together. The bartender brought her a pint of beer, and she sipped it as she continued to people-watch.

"You're not from around here, are you?" a voice behind her said.

Emma swiveled around on her barstool to find an attractive woman leaning over the bar, martini in hand. "How could you tell?"

"Just something about you," the woman said. She had long blonde hair streaked with a bit of gray, and wore a black silk tank top. She looked to be somewhere in her early forties. She was taller than Emma, which was rare, though she had curves and Emma was an ironing board. Was she being hit on? It'd been embarrassingly long since she'd experienced this. Emma hadn't considered herself a human for the last few months, and it was grounding to be reminded of her own desirability. Of the material fact of her body.

"I'm American. But I'm humiliated that it was so obvious." Emma took a sip of her beer.

"Why? Americans are hot." The woman tossed back the rest of her martini. "I'm Ollie."

"I'm Emma. Can I get you another?" She was really doing this. Ollie agreed, and Emma flagged down the bartender. They talked for a half-hour or so, giving each other the information people at loud bars usually exchanged: hometowns (Ollie was from Leeds but lived in London); jobs (Emma said she was a writer, which wasn't technically true anymore, but Ollie didn't probe. Ollie, for her part, was a social worker); what Emma was doing in London (work trip, she lied); kids (Ollie had one who lived with her ex half the time). It wasn't the most scintillating conversation she'd ever had, but it was nice. It felt good to play the character of a normal person.

After Ollie had finished her martini and she a second beer, Emma got up. "I think we should dance," she said, and Ollie agreed. They made their way to the dance floor, the pleasantness of the evening and the two beers giving her a buzz. They danced for a few minutes before Ollie leaned over and kissed Emma. She tasted like lipstick, and olives.

Emma wasn't exactly surprised by her own boldness—she used to do this all the time: pick up women in various social settings. But she was proud of herself, nonetheless, for asking Ollie to come home with her. As they exited the taxi together, Emma took Ollie's hand and led her up the stairs to her Airbnb. Emma fumbled with the code to the door as Ollie stood behind her, running her hands up and down Emma's hips. But as she went to open the door, she realized that it was slightly ajar. Had she left it that way in her jet-lagged daze? Her laptop and passport were in there, she realized, panicking and pushing the door open wider.

"Shit," she said. "I left it open."

Ollie grabbed her hand. "It's fine." She kissed Emma's neck. "Sometimes the locks on these Airbnbs are weird."

Emma walked in, trying to focus on Ollie. But the place felt disturbed in some way, as if someone had come through and tried not to move anything.

It was when Emma sat down on the edge of her bed that she smelled the faintest trace of a familiar perfume in the air. She kissed the base of Ollie's jaw, trying to detect if it was her perfume. But she wasn't wearing any scent, or at least none that Emma could smell. She heard a noise—a quick, quiet set of footsteps—that sounded as if it could be coming from the bathroom or even the closet. They pulled apart from each other as adrenaline rushed through her. "I think someone broke in," she whispered in Ollie's ear. Ollie nodded in agreement, her eyes wide with fear.

Emma left Ollie on the bed as she quietly got up and turned on the light. She grabbed an umbrella, holding it behind her as a bludgeon while she tiptoed to the closet. She flung the door open, but no one was there. Just toilet paper and an ironing board. Her heart pounded as she walked toward the bathroom. As she got closer, she could feel that someone was in there. She closed her eyes, steeling herself, and approached the door. But before she could open it, the door swung open. Emma shrieked. Ollie shrieked.

"Surprise!"

It was Amanda.

Thank God. But, also, what the fuck? Emma dropped the umbrella, and it made a loud noise as it landed on the floor.

"Oh my God, you look like you saw a ghost. I'm sorry, this was supposed to be fun. I didn't mean to be in here when you came in, I just really had to pee. And then I thought it'd be funny to pop out from your bathroom." Amanda laughed and hugged Emma, who stood motionless.

"But how . . ." Emma was almost unable to speak. "How did you get in?" Her heart rate was slowing, but her hands still shook.

"Remember? You forwarded me the details to your Airbnb so I could tell you about all my favorite spots."

"Are you just here to, like, hang out?" Emma's voice sounded calm, but she was angry. The adrenaline was starting to fade, and she felt faint.

"Ha, I wish," Amanda said. "I have a few meetings set up here about a potential BBC adaptation of *The Youth*. Which is super exciting, since we're always stealing shows from them and not the other way around. But I decided to come early to surprise you!"

"I see," Emma said. OK, so Amanda hadn't followed her across the globe just to hang out; that was somewhat reassuring. Maybe this was just a weird surprise gone wrong on an otherwise normal work trip. Or maybe it was the most obnoxious thing that had ever happened to her. It was hard to say. "Sorry for freaking out. I'm just a little on edge right now."

"Emma, do *not* worry about it. I'm excited to spend some time with you over here. When you're not dealing with Layla, of course," Amanda said, leaving the bathroom. Then Emma remembered she'd brought a woman home with her. Fuck.

"This is awkward, but, um, this is Ollie," Emma said. Amanda raised her eyebrows in a knowing and irksome way at the woman still sitting on her bed.

"I'd better be going." Ollie got up to leave. Emma could tell she recognized Amanda from the look on her face.

"Oh my God, don't go on my account!" Amanda said. "Please. I didn't mean to interrupt."

"No, it's OK. I'll give you some time to catch up," Ollie said, slipping out. She didn't ask for Emma's number.

"I'm sorry about that," Amanda said. "She was hot."

"Yeah, she was." Emma didn't even try to hide her irritation. But Amanda wasn't registering it.

"I'm so wiped from my trip. I know this is super

obnoxious to say, but flying first class isn't what it used to be. Now it's like flying coach was in 1998. Just terrible. The food was basically trying to copy Balthazar's menu, but in, like, a sad way. The first course was this inedible salmon—"

Emma cut her off. "So are you staying with me?" She said a silent prayer that the answer would be no.

"Of course not. In this tiny place? I've got a room at the Hoxton. It's only a few blocks from here."

"Gotcha." She wondered what Amanda had told Jill about her surprise trip to London.

"What do you want to do tomorrow morning?" Amanda asked. "I can get us a rezzy somewhere for brunch?"

"Honestly, I was going to go to the Tate Modern. Which I know you've done a million times." Emma figured if she could get rid of Amanda for the day, maybe she could cool off and forgive her for scaring the shit out of her and interrupting the only hookup she'd had in the past many months.

Amanda paused, pursed her lips and wrinkled her brow, as if deep in thought. "I know what we should do." She smiled conspiratorially. "You go to the Tate in the morning, and then in the afternoon, come hang out in my hotel room. I'll get us a million things from room service—their restaurant is amazing. My treat. We can watch the rest of *LoveShack*, if you want."

While it wasn't originally what Emma had planned, exhaustion was creeping in as the terror from chasing this would-be intruder faded, and the plan didn't sound so bad. Plus, she needed to watch the rest of the show before she met up with Layla.

"OK," Emma conceded. "I'll be there."

# Maggie

## Episode 9

It was late, and Maggie was alone in her room, taking off her make-up and thinking about her day. As she removed one set of fake eyelashes, she found herself missing Layla. It was strange being alone at the end of the night, with no one to process or to joke around with about all the stupid shit that happened. But after Maggie's kiss with Finn, Layla had requested a room switch and the producers had granted it. Her new roommate for a time had been Tia, who was nice enough, but had been eliminated two days ago. So now Maggie was on her own. It'd been almost a month of filming, and she was lonely.

The producers had arranged a one-on-one chat for her and Finn earlier that day, to discuss the kiss. They sat together by the pool, their feet over the edge, while cameras lingered on their faces, bodies. Maggie had worn her best bikini: a light blue Melissa Obadash with gold buckles; she'd found it on Poshmark at 75 percent off. It was still the most expensive thing she owned. She'd curled her hair and applied a hefty dose of self-tanner the night before so her tan would be fresh and even.

Finn, for his part, was wearing a retro-looking bathing suit that hit mid-thigh—the kind she loved. His dark hair was combed back and he was perfectly tanned from the weeks they'd spent in the sun.

"I take full responsibility for the kiss," he told her as he splashed water on his muscular arms to cool himself down. Her eyes landed on the smattering of dark hair on his chest that she found unbearably sexy. She looked away quickly, hoping she wasn't blushing. "Obviously you're a beautiful woman, but I'm paired with Layla. We shouldn't have done that. It was a mistake."

"Totally," she said. "One hundred percent." But the words felt hollow even to her own ears.

"And I apologized to Layla," he continued.

She nodded. "I said sorry to Theo. And I've tried to apologize to Layla, but I think she hates me now."

"I wish this had never come between you two. I wish it hadn't happened at all." He sounded so sincerely regretful that her throat tightened with anguish. Clearly, no part of him wanted to be with her. She didn't want to cry, so she said nothing, instead kicking her foot absentmindedly in the water like a five-year-old.

"I think we should just restart, you and me," Finn said. "Pretend this never happened. We can be friends."

"Sure." She willed this conversation to be over. It was humiliating.

He stood up and she followed his lead. They paused there, and she could tell that Finn was thinking about saying something else. But he must've thought better of it, because he stayed silent as his gaze lingered over her body. She tried to read his expression, but he went to hug her. She relaxed into him, trying not to enjoy the feel of his bare torso against her. As he pulled away, his left hand grazed the tie of her bathing suit bottom so quickly that she wondered if she'd imagined it.

She was removing her second set of eyelashes when she heard a faint knock at the door.

It was probably Priya, doing a round with the next day's schedule. She walked over to the door, and opened it. To her surprise, it wasn't Priya. It wasn't any of the producers.

It was Finn.

She took a sharp breath in. They were only allowed in each other's rooms in the presence of cameras, and he wasn't accompanied by one. He wore gray sweatpants and a plain white T-shirt, which was the most casual she'd ever seen him. She looked down at herself self-consciously, realizing she was wearing an old college sweatshirt of Emma's and plaid pajama pants. She was about to speak and ask him what he was doing standing outside of her room when he put his index finger over her lips to shush her.

"Don't say anything," he whispered, his breath hot on her ear. "Can I come in?" She opened her door wider, checking that no one was lingering in the hallway to catch him walking into her room. If they were found out, they'd be sent home. Maggie ushered him in before remembering that the room was bugged with cameras and mics.

But clearly he'd anticipated this, as he pressed himself flat against the wall near the door as she shut it.

"Turn off the circuit breaker for your room, in your closet," he whispered. "All of the cameras and mics will stop working. Since it's late, we probably have about thirty minutes until they notice."

Doing what she was told, she went to her closet and switched off the power. Everything went black all of a sudden, and before her eyes could adjust, she felt panicked. "Finn, what are you doing here?" Maggie tried to keep her voice down as she left her closet. "And how did you know how to turn off the power?"

"I'm here to see you." He found his way toward her in the dark. "And I've been exploring some of the guys' rooms – we all have these power switches. I tested it out the other night in mine. It took a camera tech forty-five minutes to show up to fix it. The guy told me the cameras and mics don't work at all if the power's off."

"Wow." Maggie was stunned by the extent of Finn's research. "So, what do you want?" Against her will, she felt herself almost pulled toward him, his warm body strange but welcome in her room.

"I wanted to talk."

"About?" She moved closer so they could speak more quietly. Her eyes were adjusting, and she could make out the faint outline of him a few feet away from her. It dawned on her that they were alone. Truly alone. No prying eyes of their fellow contestants, no cameras. The absence of onlookers was a fact erotically charged in and of itself.

"Us. I wanted to talk about what's going on between us."

"You just told me earlier today that the kiss was a mistake," she said.

"I said that because I've been trying to make it work with Layla. I thought that'd be the right thing to do. And I think Layla is amazing. But it made me sick to say those things, because they weren't true. And I couldn't live with myself if I never told you how I actually feel. Which is that I like you, Maggie. I really, really like you."

Her heart sped up. She felt dizzy. She hadn't realized, until he'd said it, just how much she'd wanted to hear those words come out of his mouth. "Do you mean it?" An image flashed into her mind of their conversation earlier that day. She'd been so humiliated.

"Of course." He moved toward her.

"But what about Layla? What about Theo? I can't just abandon him."

"Whatever you have with Theo, I respect that. But I think what we have is bigger than this stupid show. I know you feel it too. There's something here."

"I wish you could've just told me how you felt earlier in the season, before everything with Layla got serious. Because everyone will say I stole you from her, that I'm a cheating bitch who broke Theo's heart. People will despise me. I can't live with that. And no one will come after you because you're a guy."

"I understand. You're right. I should've been braver. But you know how hard it is once you get Love Paired. You have all this momentum; the viewers are rooting for you . . ." He trailed off. "That's why we're not going to do anything in front of the cameras. What if we just continue in our Love Pairs as they are, and act disinterested in each other, and after this is over, we wait a little and then get together? We're both based in LA, we can try to actually date without cameras or stupid games or Paradise Island. Just the two of us."

Maggie considered this. It wasn't the worst idea. That way, she wouldn't have to violate her agreement with Theo or become a villain. But still. "I can't do that to Layla," she said. "Even though she hates me. I'm not that kind of person."

"I know you're not," Finn said. "That's why I like you so much; you're kind. But I promise, the second we get off this show, I was going to break up with her anyway. Even if I hadn't met you."

Then they were both quiet for a moment, and she felt her resolve melt. What she knew was that she wanted him. And he was right there. She wanted it to be OK to want him.

With this, he walked closer to her, so their bodies were almost touching. Anticipation grew inside of her. He was right. There *was* something between them. Something she'd sensed the very first time they'd met, when he'd subverted the stupid Hot or Not game. It was not only that he was attractive; there was something about him that felt comfortable, and normal. She felt around him the way she'd always wanted to feel: both respected and desired at the same time.

She leaned in closer to him, and his lips grazed her forehead.

"Wait," he said, and she looked up at him. "Before we do this, I want to know that this is real. That it's as real for you as it is for me."

"Yes, it's real. I swear," she said. She was just going off a feeling, an attraction, but she hoped it was real. She wanted it to be real.

He grabbed her waist and pulled her into him. They kissed, delicately at first, and then with more intensity as she put her arms around his neck. He backed up onto her bed, and she followed him, straddling him and taking his shirt off. He took the bottom of her sweatshirt in his hands, lifting it over her head and throwing it on the floor. He kissed the inside of her neck, and made his way up to her left ear, sucking on her earlobe until she surprised herself by letting out a moan.

"You liked that." He said it not as a question, but as a statement. He lay down on his side and she followed him.

"I did." Her voice was breathy and uneven as Finn moved his hands to her waist, untying the drawstring of her pants. She felt an almost literal hunger for him as he pulled her cotton underwear to the side and moved his fingers against her. The tension in her body grew and grew and she almost couldn't bear it any longer, letting out a sharp breath as he moved on top of her.

"I just want you to feel good." His voice was hoarse as he removed her pants and underwear.

She sat and looked up at him as she pulled his sweatpants down and his boxers with them. "Do you have a condom?"

"Yes." He got up to fish it out of the pocket of his discarded sweatpants. He was so beautiful it almost hurt to look at him like that, naked in silhouette in the dark. He laid her back down on the bed.

Every part of her body responded to him as they moved slowly together, and then more quickly.

When they were finished, he lay on top of her for a moment,

and she felt the strangest thing—the prick of tears forming in her eyes.

"What's wrong?" Finn asked. "Did I do something?"

She shook her head no. "Not at all. It's just . . . this is a lot to process. Sorry, I have no idea why I'm crying. I'm not really upset, I promise." The feeling of genuine intimacy—rather than the pretend intimacy she'd been performing with Theo—was overwhelming. It was bizarre to switch between the two.

"I understand." He tucked a piece of her hair behind her ear. "Is it OK if I get up? I have to get back to my room before the camera tech shows."

"Of course," she said.

He put his clothes back on and kissed her on the cheek. "I meant everything I said. I want us to do this for real when we leave the bungalow."

"I want that too," she said.

"Goodnight." He opened her door and slipped away. As he shut the door, she lay flat and still on her bed. It was dark, and once again she was alone.

# Amanda

Tears streamed down Amanda's face as she turned off the TV. She looked over at Emma, who was fast asleep next to her in her king-sized bed at the Hoxton. After watching another two episodes of *LoveShack*, Emma had had enough. Amanda had convinced her that they should watch *When Harry Met Sally . . .*, which, unbelievably, Emma had never seen.

Amanda was obsessed with *When Harry Met Sally . . .* She had seen it at least twenty-five times after watching it for the first time on TV when she was in middle school. She begged her parents to buy it for her on VCR, and then on DVD when that became a thing. She liked to rewatch it every year on or around New Year's Eve, or whenever she was in a moment of need, or whenever she was with someone—in this case, Emma—who hadn't seen it before. Every single time, she cried like a baby watching the final scene, when Harry made his speech to Sally about all the very specific ways he loved her, and they kissed as "Auld Lang Syne" played in the background.

Rewatching *When Harry Met Sally . . .* had—thankfully— all but cured her of the anxiety she'd felt about Emma's less-than-thrilled reaction to her surprise trip to London. Amanda knew that she was lonely and bored, and that it was clouding her judgment. She was relieved that Emma had warmed up to her presence, though. Their afternoon and evening together in the hotel, watching TV and eating room service, had been cozy and relaxed. And Meg Ryan walking through Central Park with Billy Crystal always did the trick.

Amanda pulled the covers aside and tiptoed out of bed, careful not to disturb Emma, and stepped around the discarded trays of cold room-service food—french fries, spag bol, steamed broccoli.

She wasn't tired. Maybe her two-hour nap during the middle of the day hadn't been the best idea. She decided to go for a walk in the neighborhood to clear her head and tire herself out. She threw on a large olive-green Rejina Pyo trenchcoat over the black nightgown she wore, and donned an old pair of rubber Chelsea boots from Rag & Bone.

It was drizzling when she stepped outside, and the rain in the cool night air felt good on her face. She loved London, she really did. It was 8:30 p.m., and the streets were filled with people coming and going: young professionals getting off a long day of work; couples heading to dinner; students meeting up with friends.

As if on autopilot, she ended up at one of her favorite spots from when she'd lived in London for the half-season they filmed of *Anxiety* there—a place they'd been dozens of times. It was their post-set hangout, and they'd gotten to know the bartenders, especially the ones who'd make their drinks extra-strong. It was called the Bixby and the interior was wall-to-wall exposed old red bricks. She hadn't been inside a bar since she'd gotten sober, but she couldn't help herself. It was an old haunt, one she missed. Plus, a not-insignificant part of her hoped that the cute bartender still worked there—the one she'd slept with a few times when she was a regular. She wasn't trying to reignite that particular old flame, but a little validation could go a long way at a time like this.

She pushed the door open, and the warm air enveloped her. She looked around and realized George, the bartender, a tall bald guy with sleeve tattoos and thick black-framed glasses, was indeed working. Excellent.

"Holy shit. If it isn't Amanda Lehman in the flesh!" he said. "So good to see you! Let me make you a drink." He came around the bar and gave her a bear hug. Sweat pooled on her forehead as she took in the smell of gin and stale beer. What the fuck was she doing here, at a bar? She so badly wanted a vodka soda. She wanted to get obliterated, to black out, to turn her stupid brain off for just a few hours. She wondered if that desire would ever go away. The older alcoholics and addicts said it never fully did, although the feeling dulled. But she wasn't there yet.

"It's so good to see you, too! No thanks on the drink." Her hands were as clammy as they'd be if she was about to go cliff diving. She hadn't expected it to be this intense to be in a bar. She'd been to a few parties at fancy restaurants—premiere after-parties, mostly, and a holiday party—where alcohol was served. She always forced Jill to come along, though, as a sort of accountability mechanism. But she hadn't yet stepped into a full-fledged pub, let alone one where no one was watching her to make sure she didn't do anything stupid. She wiped her sweaty hands on her jacket. They were shaking a little, so she stuck them in her pockets. "Could I just get a sparkling water?" God, it felt so lame to be sober. Flirting sober was going to be especially humiliating.

"Coming right up," he said, and she tried not to look too closely at his very capable hands as he opened a can of seltzer and poured it into a glass with a flourish. They made a few minutes of small talk—he asked her what brought her back to London; she asked him how his niece was doing.

At some point, she stopped sweating. "I got sober, you know. Hence the sparkling water."

"Good for you," he said. "That's wonderful."

"Yeah, you probably remember that I wasn't exactly measured in my substance use when I was living here," she said. He laughed gamely, without agreeing or disagreeing.

"You know, I just saw your bloke a few days ago. Can't remember the guy's name. He came in here—same nostalgia bug as you, I guess. We talked for a few minutes, had a nice chat," George said as he replenished her sparkling water, adding a little splash of lime syrup.

"My bloke?" She laughed. "You're mistaken. I don't have—I've never had—a bloke."

"No, I mean your best friend, the guy you used to work with back on the show. What was it called? *Depression*?"

"*Anxiety*. And I assume you mean Trevor? That's not possible. He's been . . ." She racked her brain for a euphemism for *hiding due to being canceled and possibly in trouble with the law.* "... out of commission. He doesn't come out in public anymore."

"No, it was definitely him," George said. "He looked different, but it was him. I remember, because I was jealous of him when you two used to come in together all the time. Thought you were dating." He smiled at her.

"I'm flattered," she said. Perhaps this was just a way for him to check that she didn't have a boyfriend?

"Sounds like you're not in touch?" he continued as a customer ordered a pint of Tennent's. Amanda felt another strong pang of desire for a drink. She grabbed her seltzer and lime and took a large sip. She would call her sponsor in a moment. Or maybe Jill. She silently cursed herself for not paying for her assistant to come along on the trip. She needed to get out of there; it was too much. And she didn't want to explain everything about her situation with Trevor.

"I should get going," she said. "Probably not the best thing for me to sit in a bar as my desperation to have a drink escalates."

"Right, fair enough." He smiled at her. "It was good to see you."

"You too." She gathered her purse and coat and stood up.

He gave her a funny look. "I promise it was him. He has a shaved head now, and a mustache and the like, but he was pretty much the same. He had on that ratty denim jacket with Prince's face on the back." George poured a swig of gin into a glass for an impatient-looking older guy. Amanda's heart sped up; the Prince jacket was classic Trevor. He was almost never without it.

She was having a hard time comprehending this. "Are you sure?"

"Absolutely. One hundred percent." He scribbled something on a napkin.

Amanda's mind raced. "Did he say anything about what he was doing? Or where he was staying?"

George shook his head. "Don't think so."

She had to get out there. She had to look for him. But even if Trevor *had* come into the pub a few days ago, he could be halfway to Antarctica by now. "Thanks," she said. "I should get going."

"No problem." He wiped his brow with the back of his hand. "Take this." He handed her a cocktail napkin with a number on it—his, she assumed. "If you want some company while you're here."

"I'll keep it in mind." She folded up the napkin and put it in her pocket. At that moment, Brad Pitt could've handed her his number and she wouldn't have cared. The only thing on her mind was Trevor. If he really was in London, she needed to find him.

# Emma

When Emma woke up, it was 4:14 a.m., and she had no idea where she was. She looked around, rubbing her eyes. She felt someone next to her, and turned around. It was Amanda, fast asleep. Then it all came back to her: she'd fallen asleep in Amanda's hotel bed last night while they watched *When Harry Met Sally* . . .

She extended her arm onto the bedside table and felt around for her phone. She had 25 percent battery and a text from Jill. *I'm sorry, Em. I should never have brought up the job thing. I love you and will always support you no matter what, and I know you care about me, too.* Emma sighed. There was a follow-up text: *And please be safe in London! I know you need to do this, but take care of yourself.* The thing with Jill was it was impossible to stay mad at her. Emma opened her phone to check that she was still sharing her location with Jill. She drafted a response and sent it. *It's OK. I'm sorry for being defensive. Promise I'm being safe. My location's still shared with you so you can see where I'm going with Layla. I'll be fine. xoxo.*

As she clicked send, her phone began buzzing with a call from Liz. She got out of bed, remembering only after that Amanda was sleeping and she should probably be quiet.

Amanda stirred, but thankfully didn't wake. Emma threw on last night's clothes and ran into the hallway, calling the elevator and taking it down eleven stories to the lobby. She texted: *One sec*.

Liz answered on the third ring. "Hey, Em," Liz said. Emma heard someone in the background, presumably Liz's new girlfriend. Liz whispered to the person: "Baby, just on the phone with Emma about the photo. Give me two minutes."

"What's up? It's the middle of the night here. Is everything OK?" Emma's voice was still sleepy.

"Oh shit. Sorry, I totally forgot you were in London. I just called to gossip. Let's talk later."

Emma sighed. "No, it's fine. I was up anyway."

"Well, I'm sure you saw the photos of Theo and the mystery guy—"

"Excuse me?" Emma said. What was Liz talking about?

"The mystery man that Theo was photographed with? Holding hands?" Liz continued, speaking fast. When Emma didn't respond, she kept going. "The internet was going crazy. I know I'm terminally online but it was hard to miss."

"I deleted my Twitter last week," Emma said by way of explanation. "And I've been slacking off on scouring the internet because I've been dealing with this London trip." She asked Liz to pause so she could pull up the photo in question on her phone. It was as if all the air had left the room. She recognized the mystery man. "What the hell is this?"

"Did you know he was queer? Part of me is, like, I guess this is good. You never see reality TV stars being open about this. But on the other hand, he's moved on extremely quickly. How are you feeling?"

"One sec." Emma pulled the phone away from her ear and looked at the photo again, using her thumb and pointer finger to zoom in. "Detective LaClair," Emma said out loud, to no one. Her stomach dropped. She dug her nails into the inside of her wrist and scratched. She felt dizzy, as though she was going to faint. How was this possible? It wasn't possible. She was confused. Yes, that was it—she must've been mistaken. It was the jet lag. She forced herself to look at the photo one more time. It was definitely LaClair: he had the same wiry goatee Emma remembered. She held in a scream, trying to breathe.

"Huh? Who's that?" Liz asked.

"It's the fucking detective. Who worked on Maggie's case."

"Are you sure?" Liz asked.

"Yes, I'm sure!" Emma paced around, her wrist stinging from where she'd attacked the raw skin.

"That is bizarre and inappropriate," Liz said. "Plus, this guy is very much a regular-looking person. And Theo is . . . well. Theo's gorgeous."

"I don't understand what I'm even looking at." Emma examined the photo again. Theo and Detective LaClair, side by side, holding hands. Theo kissing him on the cheek. On the streets of LA. Her hands shook violently.

"It's probably a conflict of interest for me to write a story, but can I tip off a colleague about this? For obvious reasons, a detective having a relationship with a victim's family member is serious malpractice."

"That's a good idea," Emma said. They could learn more while she kept her hands clean.

"I'm on it," Liz said. "Are you OK, though?"

"I don't know," Emma said. "It's really fucked up. It's horrible to think that they were maybe flirting, or even sleeping together, while he was being questioned about his wife's . . ." The word "murder" got caught in her throat.

"It's odd that he hasn't been fired," Liz said. "Given how high-profile the case is, you'd think this would be a serious HR issue for the LAPD."

"True. And if they're hooking up or whatever, why didn't Theo do anything to stop him from declaring it a cold case so early?" Emma pinched the bridge of her nose to stifle the headache that was growing between her eyebrows.

"Or maybe he closed the case early because they started seeing each other," Liz said.

Emma's stomach lurched. Why hadn't she thought of that? "Do you think it's possible? Like maybe this was some sort of set-up? Theo killed Maggie and wanted to cover it up, so he started dating LaClair so he'd stop looking into it?" Last night's room-service feast was threatening to come back up.

"That's one possibility," said Liz. "But maybe they met and fell for each other and he closed the case early so they could date without all that muddy conflict-of-interest business."

Was this actually happening? She took a deep breath. "This is so gross," Emma finally said. She couldn't think of anything smart to contribute to this conversation.

"We're going to figure this out," Liz said. And for a second, Emma loved her again. Competent, smart, no-nonsense Liz.

"I feel useless. What can I do?"

"Just hang in there until we get this out to the public. I'll call my colleague now."

"OK." Emma sniveled, and they hung up. She would go and wake Amanda up to tell her, even though it was the middle of the night. And then she would call Jill.

*Theo.* She couldn't believe it. Or maybe she could believe it, because she'd always had a bad feeling about him. He was a fucking monster. A sociopath. Her rage was blinding, and singular. Whatever Theo had done wrong, she would find out. And she would make him pay.

"Are you OK?" the receptionist asked.

"Not really." She scratched her wrist and it stung.

"Would you like one?" He slid over a pack of cigarettes. She looked at them. She'd smoked maybe two cigarettes in her life, both times when she was drunk in college.

"Sure," she said, for some reason. She needed something to do with her hands. With a nod, he handed her one, and a lighter. She walked outside the sliding doors into the cold, rainy London night. She wasn't wearing a coat, or even a sweatshirt, but the shock of cold on her bare arms felt good.

It took her a few tries to light the cigarette, because it was windy and her hands were trembling. Once she finally got it lit, she took a deep drag. The smoke hit the back of her throat and then her lungs, and she coughed hysterically. It was disgusting.

She threw the cigarette on the ground, stepped on it, and walked back inside.

# Maggie

## Finale

The lights in the stuffy confessional room were so bright that Maggie worried they'd induce a migraine. This would be a disaster just one day before the finale, so she closed her eyes and massaged her temples as she waited on the red velvet love seat for Priya to make her way to the small studio. Beads of sweat pooled on her lower back, staining the pink satin dress she was wearing.

Usually, Maggie or other cast members were sent to the confessional room following an elimination, or in advance of a major event. And of course, if there was any drama unfolding that involved them, they were made to spend a lot of time there. Since Maggie had apologized to Theo after her too-long kiss with Finn, they'd been relatively drama-free. As such, Maggie hadn't done as many confessionals as the other cast members recently. She averaged two or three a week instead of once or twice a day. This wasn't something she minded, of course, though she wondered if her over-the-top shows of affection for Theo were boring viewers. Perhaps in the confessional room, under one-on-one scrutiny, it would be obvious that her relationship with Theo was bullshit. She also hadn't done a confessional since she and Finn had had sex. What if the producers knew, and were waiting to blindside her until they got her alone? Her ticket to winning was ensuring no cracks slipped into their façade.

"Sorry I'm late!" Priya swung open the door, and a cameraman followed.

"Can I get some water?" Maggie said.

Priya called it into her walkie talkie. "Water to confessional room number three." They made small talk until a bottle was delivered. Maggie took three giant gulps.

"Ready?"

"Yep." Maggie unstuck her dress from the small of her back.

"So how do you feel going into the final with Layla and Finn?" Priya asked.

"It feels amazing to be in the final. I'm so happy with Theo, he's wonderful, and to get to be in this together right until the end is a blessing." She smiled as widely as she could. It was almost strange how easy this lie was for her to inhabit.

"That's sweet." Priya looked bored. "How about things with Layla? Is it weird to be here with her given that you're not friends anymore?"

"I have a lot of respect for Layla." Maggie chose her words carefully. "There aren't any hard feelings about us not being super close anymore. That's just life. I'm focused on deepening my connection with Theo right now."

"Maggie, this is super boring. Can you give me

something?" Priya asked. "I like you. I want you to get camera time. That's how you'll win this thing. But I need more."

"Oh, um. I'm sorry." Her cheeks turned red.

"How about this: I know you have chemistry with Finn. It's really fucking obvious. Is there something there?"

"No!" Maggie practically yelled. She needed to tamp it down. "We already covered this. No. Absolutely not. That kiss just happened because we lost track of time. I know Finn feels the same way." Her cheeks were now burning. It felt as though Priya was staring at her. Was she staring?

"Alright then." Priya was still bored, but Maggie breathed a sigh of relief. "Fair enough. So my last question: Why should you and Theo win this over Layla and Finn?"

"Theo and I should win this because . . ." Shit. What was she going to say? Priya stared at her. "Because I'm falling for him." The lie escaped her mouth before she had a chance to think it through. On reality TV dating shows, for whatever reason, there were entirely different milestones for couples than in the real world. Her manager had explained the unwritten rules for her before she'd left for filming. First, you expressed to each other that you felt a "connection." After that, you had your first kiss. Then, you dated for a bit. And then—this was the big thing—you said you were "falling" for someone. This was the precursor to saying, "I love you," which was a milestone only the most advanced couples ever reached. In reality TV parlance, falling for someone was a big deal.

"Well, that's something!" Priya beamed at her, having secured the confession she wanted. Maggie smiled back.

"That's so sweet. Do you think you're going to say the L word soon?"

"Yes. If it feels right, I might tell Theo I love him."

To Maggie's surprise, the last week of the show went off without a hitch. She and Theo continued with their comfortable on-camera rhythm: they spent most of their dates talking about how much they liked each other, and how strong their connection was. They didn't talk about much else, and Maggie worried that viewers would notice. But continuing to reaffirm their feelings for one another without actually discussing anything of substance before making out for three minutes (no tongue) seemed to work just fine.

She had almost begun to think of the night she'd spent with Finn in her room as a weird, hot dream. Whenever they saw each other, he barely looked at her, he was so absorbed with Layla. This made Maggie nervous, though she tried to ignore it.

Now, here they were, at the finale. This came after days of prep and rehearsals with the producers. Unlike during the rest of the show, they were meticulously blocked—shown exactly where to stand at every given moment. The finale was the show's cash cow. It brought in more viewers than the Oscars, and therefore earned the network more advertising dollars than any other episode. They were also primped and had full glam done by a team, which was both a relief and incredibly awkward. It was a relief because she was sick of doing a full face of makeup and styling her own hair every single day and night, with no breaks. She had multiple burns on her hands from playing fast and loose with her curling iron, and her skin was rebelling against a constant regime of self-tanner, primer, foundation, concealer, contour, blush, and setting mist—and her rosacea had come back, which meant she needed more of those things. It was a vicious cycle.

But it was awkward because it meant that she had to spend the entire day with Layla, mostly in silence. She wanted so badly to think of something to say to her, but she couldn't think of anything. *Sorry for kissing your Love Pair for too long* felt stupid and was a lie, especially since she'd then gone and had sex with Finn. So she said nothing. Layla, for her part, made no effort to initiate conversation.

After they had been waxed, tanned, manicured, made up, and styled, they stood clumped together on the balcony of the bungalow. Maggie wore a long yellow ball gown embroidered with tiny crystals and her hair (well, some of it was her hair, most of it was extensions) was styled into old Hollywood waves. "We're going for America's sweetheart here," the stylist had told her. The dress wasn't her style and didn't fit quite right. There was no use arguing, though—it was on loan from a famous designer who'd paid to have it worn on the show. So the stylist had artfully pinned it and she hoped no one would be able to tell. Theo was wearing a classic tuxedo and his long hair was down, parted in the middle and slicked back.

For Layla, the stylist had gone for a sexier look instead. She was wearing a metallic silver dress with a deep V-neck that clung to her curves. Finn wore a deep maroon tuxedo jacket with a silver pocket square to match her. They waited for a lighting adjustment so Schuyler could read the viewers' vote totals and crown the winning couple. It was freezing, and they looked ridiculous standing there in their formal attire, as if they were the finalists for prom king and queen. Which, if she thought about it, wasn't far off.

Maggie couldn't help but look over at Layla and Finn. They were huddled together to stay warm. Finn stood behind Layla, rubbing her arms with his hands. She tried not to stare as she burned with jealousy.

For their part, she and Theo were holding hands weakly, both of their palms clammy. Maggie's teeth chattered.

"Layla and Finn," Schuyler began, "you're a gorgeous couple. Tell us a bit about your journey here. What was your favorite moment?"

"My final date with Finn was amazing," Layla said. "I'm a huge animal lover, and getting to visit a dog shelter and play with the puppies together was incredible. We want to adopt a dog as soon as we're back home." She pulled Finn into her and kissed his cheek. Maggie wanted to crawl into a hole.

"You're moving in together?" Schuyler asked.

"We're talking about it," Finn cut in, smiling at Layla. Maggie tried not to grimace. They were talking about moving in together? Theirs would be a tougher breakup than she'd imagined, if it happened at all.

Then Schuyler nodded to Finn. "How about you, Finn? What was the highlight of your time here?"

"My favorite moment," Finn began, "was getting to spend some special alone time with the person I care about most." Maggie could've sworn he looked right at her when he said that. It sent a chill down her spine. Layla hadn't seemed to notice.

"Care to be more specific?" Schuyler asked.

"I think I'll keep the specifics between us. I'm not going to reveal anything for Brownie points. Things that are private between two people should stay private," Finn said. This made Maggie blush.

"Well, OK, then!" Schuyler clapped his hands together. "Whatever that means. So, Maggie and Theo, how about you both? Best memory here? I know you two just said 'I love you' for the first time a few days ago."

Theo beamed at Maggie. "We did," he said. "It was an incredible moment. One I'll always treasure."

"Oh, absolutely." She smiled wider. Her face was numb. "I agree."

After a few more minutes of inane back and forth about their highs and lows, Larry, from behind the cameras, signaled to Schuyler, whirling his index finger around in a circle to say *Wrap it up*. "Well, I won't delay any longer," Schuyler said, and butterflies grew in Maggie's stomach. This was almost it. It was so close to being over. Win or lose, she was excited to be done pretending. It was exhausting. And she was excited to give things a shot with Finn, without the prying eyes of cameras—if he still wanted her.

She visualized Schuyler saying their names, and how good it would feel. She could finally pay off her debt. She'd make a real career as an influencer. She could help Emma out—be her safety net. And if she lost . . . well, then all of this would have been for nothing.

She closed her eyes. *Please*, she prayed. She wasn't

religious; she didn't believe in God and never had. But on the off chance that a God existed, now would be the time to evoke Him (or Her). *Please let me and Theo win. I need this.*

"The winner of *LoveShack* season six is . . ." Schuyler pulled a notecard from a pocket inside his jacket. He paused, clearing his throat. She tried to discreetly wipe her sweaty left hand on her dress. The pause was getting longer. Was he trying to torture them? He winked—just slightly—at them, and that's when she knew.

"Theo and Maggie!" he bellowed.

Maggie's heart pounded in her ears, and for a moment, she was a marionette. It was as if something or someone had taken over the movement of her body. It wasn't unpleasant; she felt her jaw drop, she felt herself jump into Theo's arms. She felt him kiss her squarely on the mouth, and she felt herself kiss him back. Confetti fired from cannons Maggie hadn't even known were there. "Viewers fell in love with your love story," Schuyler said, delivering his pre-written lines. "The purity of your connection. Your journey had its ups and downs, but you never wavered from one another. You inspired America!"

"We fucking did it," Theo whispered in her ear. She looked back at him, her gaze steady. Yes, yes they had.

She couldn't have known, of course, just how much winning would change everything about her life. If she had, maybe she would've taken a second to let the final moments sink in before it all happened.

# Jill

Amanda was half an hour late to their coffee with one of *The Youth's* producers. Jill had been forced to entertain this man for the past half-hour, but small talk was wearing thin and he was clearly irritated.

Amanda hadn't responded to Jill's texts or emails all day yesterday, besides a *no can u handle?* when Jill had asked if she was going to send back post-production notes on the first episode of the season. Jill's mind raced. What if Amanda was mad at her? Or worse, what if something bad was happening? Perhaps she'd relapsed.

She finally called Amanda, who picked up right away. "I'm in London!" Amanda sounded cheery, as if this was a normal and exciting update. "Sorry, I would've liked to give you some notice, but didn't want to risk ruining the surprise. For Emma, I mean."

"What are you talking about?" She tried to keep the anger out of her voice.

"I surprised Emma! She was sort of weird about the whole thing, but we're hanging out now."

"What do you mean you surprised her? I don't understand."

But Amanda ignored her. "I shouldn't have done it that way, probably. I realize that now. But it was meant to be fun."

"Jesus Christ," Jill said under her breath.

"What was that? My connection's bad."

"I think I'm losing you." Jill hung up. She was furious, and nothing productive was going to come from staying on the phone.

Giving Jill no notice so she could surprise Emma in London? It was batshit. And now Jill would have to do damage control on her behalf with this producer. After the disastrous coffee, she spent the rest of the morning stewing in Amanda's office and eating her boss's fancy Erewhon granola out of spite.

She went home early. If Amanda was going to randomly go to London, she was going to leave at six thirty and not feel bad about missing a night shoot. So she sat on her couch, waiting for dinner to cook on the stove, feeling irritated. Emma called her—almost definitely to talk about Amanda's "surprise." She clicked ignore, feeling guilty. But the last thing she wanted to do was debrief Amanda's antics with Emma right now. Or worse, hear about their amazing dinner at Dishoom or an afternoon wandering around Selfridges.

*Can you pick up? I need to talk to you about something.*

Jill stared at the text message from Emma for a few seconds before she put her phone down. She took a deep breath, and opened her phone to draft a text. *Just sitting down for dinner. Can I call you in a few?*

She sat at her table and put her phone on Do Not Disturb

to stop the incessant buzzing. She'd call Emma back after she ate something. She sat down at the kitchen table with a bowl of chili she'd just made, and scooped sour cream on top of it. But before she could dig in, the doorbell rang.

Leaving her chili untouched, she opened the door and made her way downstairs.

"Who is it?" It was dark, and she could barely see anything. The light in their hallway was out, and their landlord had neglected to replace it. "Hello?" Her voice echoed, but there was no response. Her heart started beating a little faster. Call it post-Maggie paranoia, but she hated being alone in the dark.

"Hello?" she said again. Silence. The hair on her arms stood up. She was just about to turn around, run back to her apartment and lock the door when she heard a voice.

"Emma?" the voice said. It was familiar, but she couldn't quite place it.

"It's Jill," she responded. When the metal grates of the front door came into her line of vision, she realized who it was: Theo. She unclenched her fists and her heart rate slowed. But why was he at their apartment? On a random Friday?

"Sorry to just show up like this." He sounded jittery. "Is Emma home? There's something I wanted to talk to her about."

"No, she's not here. Sorry," Jill said. "Did you try to call her? Text her?"

"It's something I didn't want to discuss on the phone," he said. How odd. "It's not that urgent." She doubted this, given that whatever it was had prompted him to show up at their place for the first time in history. As Theo stood behind the closed door, she could see through the grating that he was wearing a pair of black jeans, white shoes, and a crisp white T-shirt. He looked really fucking good, as per usual. She looked down self-consciously at her own Target tank top and decade-old leggings.

The awkward silence continued until she broke it. "Do you want to come in for dinner? Emma won't be back tonight, but I just made chili, and I have enough for two. Nothing fancy, obviously."

He stood silently behind the door for a moment, and her heart dropped with preemptive embarrassment. She had just invited a celebrity/influencer/male model into her home for vegetarian chili, and he, of course, now needed to find a polite way out of it.

"I'd love that," he said. "Thank you."

Even though Theo was shoveling bites of chili into his mouth, Jill stared down at her own bowl. She willed herself to eat this meal she had been so hungry for just moments ago, but Theo's presence in her apartment had, for some reason, diminished her appetite.

"This is delicious," he said, mouth full. She forced herself to eat a bite. "And your apartment," Theo continued, swallowing. "It's great to finally see it. It's really sweet. Reminds me of the place I lived in right after college." Jill felt a prick of irritation at this. Jill and Emma were in their thirties, and this was the most adult and expensive place they'd ever lived. But to Theo, it was a generic shitty apartment that reminded him of his pre-fame days. Nonetheless, she managed a smile.

"We like it." She took another bite, looking sheepishly at their mismatched bowls and spoons, which they'd purchased from Goodwill a few years back.

"Shit," Theo said, and she looked up to see that he'd spilled a large brown spot of chili on his probably quite expensive white T-shirt. Jill sprang into action, running to get a stain remover stick she kept in her purse.

"Good thinking," he said as she handed it to him. To her surprise, he pulled his shirt over his head, placed it on his lap, and began to attack the stain with it. Jill stood behind him, shell-shocked, even though she had seen him without a shirt hundreds of times: on *LoveShack*, on the cover of magazines, in his modeling campaigns for various men's underwear brands. He had the body of a Greek god, that she knew. But seeing him without a shirt in the flesh—the profoundly sculpted muscles of his shoulders and back, the ripple of his abs as he turned around to ask her if she had a washcloth and soap—was a near-spiritual experience.

"Yes." Jill tried to quiet the stirring inside her. She grabbed a washcloth and ran it under hot water in the kitchen sink. Before she could turn around to give it to him, he rose from his chair and came up behind her—close enough that she could feel heat from his body.

As he took the washcloth, his fingers grazed hers. After scrubbing his shirt, he sat down at the table and continued eating the chili with gusto. His shirt was now discarded over the back of another chair, and she tried not to look at him.

"Do you want another shirt?"

He looked at her, his face a mixture of confusion and amusement. "No," he said. "I'm good. Just letting it dry."

They continued eating their meal in relative silence, as she struggled to think of things to talk about with him. He seemed content with the silence as he took hearty bites of the chili, and she did her best to finish her bowl as well.

"Let me get that." She grabbed his empty bowl alongside hers, and brought them to the sink.

"Don't do those now," he said. "Do you have a beer or something? I really need a drink."

"Sure, yeah. I have a couple in the fridge." She wandered over to grab two of Emma's IPAs that must've been in there for three years and were probably flat. He must have been really lonely to want her company this badly. She handed him a beer anyway.

He was still shirtless as they moved to the living room. He patted the seat next to him on their stupid Ikea couch, beckoning her to sit there. "I feel like I'm making you nervous," he said as she sat down, careful to leave a good amount of room between them. "Did I do something wrong?"

"Not at all." But her cheeks turned bright red, and she instinctively pulled her hand up to face. He pretended not to notice and took a swig of his beer. "Is everything OK?"

"Not really. But let's not talk about that right now. Can we talk about you? I need a distraction."

"Sure." Except what was there to talk about? "Though there's not much going on here at the moment because Emma and Amanda are in London. Work's been quiet."

He raised an eyebrow. "What're they doing in London?"

"Actually, Emma is meeting up with—" For some reason, she stopped herself. "Emma and Amanda both have work meetings."

He nodded. "I thought Emma was taking time off?"

Shit. She was a terrible liar. "Well, yeah. She's figuring out her next steps. So I'm just here alone while she's gallivanting in the UK."

"Alone? You don't have a boyfriend or something?"

She shook her head no. If she didn't know any better, she'd think he was hitting on her. Could it possibly be that Theo, husband-of-the-dead-sister-of-her-best-friend, was into her? What about the guy he was just photographed with? She tried to push the thought out of her mind. It would be rude to ask about a tabloid photo. "No. I've been single for a while," she said.

"I'm surprised to hear that. I'd think guys would be knocking down your door," Theo said, just as she was taking another sip of her beer. She almost snorted it back up.

"Not exactly." She chose not to elaborate. It was a strange thing for one of *People*'s Sexiest Men Alive three years running to say to someone who was, all things considered, a normal-looking woman. Instead of pointing that out, Jill said nothing. So they sat there together, silence hanging between them.

"Can I say something?" he asked. "I don't want to make you uncomfortable or anything, but I've always really liked spending time with you." He moved toward her, his right tricep making light contact with her left one. They were now sitting so close together on this big couch—so close that goosebumps appeared on her arms and legs.

She looked away, trying to think of how to respond. "I like spending time with you, too," she settled on. Except they hadn't ever spent much time together. But it felt like the right thing to say, given the circumstances. She turned back toward him, and his eyes locked with hers. *Do not fuck your best friend's murdered sister's widowed husband, Jill. Do not do it. Do not do not do not.* As he leaned in and kissed her, the image of Theo and the mystery man flashed into her mind. And yet, she did nothing to stop him.

Theo and Maggie's wedding had been a garish and uncomfortable affair. It took place exactly three months after Maggie and Theo won *LoveShack*, and was filmed at a mid-tier resort in Rancho Mirage. Emma was, of course, beside herself that they were getting married so quickly. She asked Jill to be her plus one, and on the drive from LA to the desert complained the entire time—about Maggie and Theo barely knowing each other, about the rashness of the decision.

Jill was also recruited to be a sort of bridesmaid stand-in. Maggie only asked Emma and a few friends to be bridesmaids, but the producers wanted footage of Maggie getting ready with a large group. So Maggie, Emma, Jill and some of Maggie's friends spent the day in a hotel room as two hair and makeup artists tended to them.

"Em, I can't convince you to get your hair and makeup done, too?" Maggie asked, her lips puffier than they'd been just a few weeks prior. Though it'd only been three months since the show, her appearance had changed dramatically. With the money she'd made from winning and from the incoming brand deals, she'd had her lips done, semi-permanent hair extensions put in, had started working out with a personal trainer, and exclusively wore gifted designer clothes.

"Absolutely not," Emma said. "I'll look ridiculous. I'm already wearing this ugly dress." She pointed down at her blue chiffon gown.

Maggie looked hurt at the jab, even though she of course hadn't picked out the bridesmaid dresses. She hadn't even picked out her own dress, a princessy Carolina Herrera gown with a strapless silk bodice and a puffy tulle skirt that trailed for almost five feet behind her. ("It's just like Maggie to not push back when the network picks out a heinous dress," Emma had said earlier that day.) "Suit yourself." Maggie fluffed her skirt and looked away. "Just reminding you that you'll be on national TV in front of millions."

"They'll all be looking at you, not me," Emma said. "No one cares about the bride's soft-butch sister."

"Hey, that's not necessarily true," Jill chimed in. "What if the future Mrs. Lathrop is out there, looking for her knight in shining armor? And you—an absolute vision in pale blue chiffon—are just what she's been waiting for?"

Maggie and Emma both laughed at this, and the tension between them temporarily lifted. But when the cameras came in, Emma stiffened. She looked as if she was being held hostage when a producer asked her to button up the back of Maggie's dress as they filmed them. Emma almost broke out in a laugh as Maggie was instructed to put on her tiara, but Jill shot her a look.

After they had finished getting ready and Jill was released from her fake bridesmaid duties, she took a seat in the second row. There were only about forty people in attendance, and most appeared to be Theo's family and some of Maggie's and Theo's friends. None of Maggie's extended family—cousins or a great-aunt they had in Kansas—showed.

As Theo walked down the aisle, flanked by both of his parents and followed by three cameras and a drone, Jill marveled at the fact that the camera crew and production team outnumbered the wedding guests by about two to one. Emma had told her earlier that they were sending in extras to be in the background of the reception later that night. Forty people an epic party did not make.

Theo wore a tuxedo and had his long hair trimmed to fall just below his chin. He looked as if he was auditioning to be the next James Bond. No wonder Maggie was marrying him after knowing him for only a few months. He smiled placidly at his bride as she walked toward him. He looked happy. Or happy enough.

As the violins played and Maggie made her way down the aisle, Jill felt her heart swell at the sight. Maggie's smile was so big. And so white. How were her teeth so white? There was probably some special dentist that LA's nouveau riche went to to bleach their teeth while getting a lymphatic drainage massage. As Maggie continued her march down the aisle, Jill caught a closer look. She was surprised to see tears streaming down Maggie's face, creating almost imperceptible streaks in her foundation. Something about this sat uncomfortably with Jill, even though she knew they were happy tears. But after watching Maggie and Theo exchange personalized but somehow still banal vows (Theo to Maggie: "I vow to always bring you your morning coffee in bed before asking you for anything;" Maggie to Theo: "I vow to not judge you for spending more time than me on your hair every day"), Jill had promptly forgotten about it.

Jill hadn't spent much time in the years that followed thinking about Maggie and Theo's wedding. That was, until she and Theo lay in her bed after having just peeled their naked bodies away from one another. It was then that she couldn't stop replaying the wedding in her mind: Maggie's tears as she walked down the aisle; Theo's serene-bordering-on-ambivalent look as he gazed back at her. Their tepid kiss after saying "I do." Tepid was also the best way to describe the sex Jill and Theo had just had. Jill didn't want to admit to herself that she had pictured sex with Theo differently (or even that she'd pictured it at all. Had she had a crush on him all this time? Sure seemed like it). She tried not to feel offended that he hadn't even been able to finish. Or, honestly, that he'd barely been able to get or maintain an erection at all. Was she that repulsive? And if so, why have sex with her in the first place?

"I'm sorry about that," he said. She turned to look at him, and was surprised to find his face contorted as if he was about to cry.

"Don't apologize. It's not a big deal." She could barely focus on whatever was going on with him, because she was paralyzed with extreme, sickening guilt. Emma would never forgive her for this. And she deserved that.

She wanted to scream at the Jill of fifteen minutes ago. She couldn't lie there any longer, and gave in to the urge to spring out of bed and put her clothes back on.

As she dressed, she saw that for his part, Theo's eyes were glassy as he stared at the wall.

"I'm feeling super tired." Jill needed him out of here.

Theo took a deep breath and nodded. "I'm heading out. Don't worry." He slipped out of her bed, and dug around for his clothes. Jill grabbed her phone to have something to look at that wasn't Theo's naked body. She turned it off Do Not Disturb and saw she had another three missed calls from Emma. Shit. She had completely forgotten to call her back. She texted Emma, trying to block out from her mind that Emma's brother-in-law was getting dressed in her room.

The phone rang again, which startled both Theo and Jill. It was Emma FaceTiming her.

"Stay there," she instructed Theo. "I need to talk to Emma." She threw on a sweatshirt and slippers and made her way to the living room and answered the phone. "Emma, what the hell. Are you OK?"

"Not really." Emma's voice sounded choked. She looked exhausted. "Why did you take so long to pick up?"

"I was busy, I'm so sorry."

"I have something important to tell you," Emma said.

Jill thought of Theo in her bedroom. "Can I call you back in, like, ten minutes? I have someone over and I'm being rude. Amanda told me about the stupid surprise."

"It's about Theo," Emma said.

"Theo?" Jill's heart pounded. Did Emma somehow know about her and Theo? It had *just* happened. That was impossible.

"Yes. Check your messages. He was photographed

holding hands and kissing the cheek of the detective responsible for investigating Maggie's murder." She sounded angry. Jill's phone dinged with the photo, which of course she'd already seen. "That's Detective Daniel LaClair."

*So she doesn't know about us,* Jill thought. Relief flooded her body. But as she processed what she'd said about Theo and Detective LaClair, her hands began to shake. How could that be true? Maybe she'd died, and this was hell. That seemed as plausible as anything at this point. "What . . . what does that mean?" she asked.

"Well, I'm not totally sure. But in any scenario it's not a good look for either of them. The relationship is completely inappropriate. Liz's colleague is writing a story about it. This needs to become public." Emma was speaking quickly, manically. "We need to stop him. He's somehow responsible for all this, I just know it."

Jill propped up her phone against a large pot on their kitchen counter. "No." She shook her head. "There has to be an explanation."

She was interrupted as the door to her bedroom swung open and out barged Theo, wearing his chili-stained T-shirt, boxers, and, for some reason, nothing else.

"I promise you there's an explanation," Theo cried, breathless. "There's an explanation for everything."

Jill felt a powerful urge to slap him across the face.

"Who's that?" Emma asked. "Wait. Is that Theo? Jill, what's going on?"

Before she could answer, Theo interjected. He ran over to the phone and yelled into it: "Emma, please, give me a chance to clear things up about Daniel. About everything. I can explain." He sounded like he was about to cry.

Emma was silent for a long moment. On video, her face looked ashen. "Theo, what are you doing at our house? In your boxers?"

"Emma, we'll talk about it later. And Theo, put some fucking clothes on," Jill said, trying to ward off the humiliation and panic that were settling inside of her. She had never done anything so terrible in her entire life, and now Emma knew that the guy who was maybe sleeping with the detective who'd failed to solve Maggie's murder was hanging out in his underwear in her house. She thought she might be sick. "Theo, you have exactly three minutes to explain yourself. And after that, you need to leave," Jill said. Theo looked at her, surprised at the anger in her voice, his eyes pleading. She ignored him as a headache pounded behind her left eye.

"Are you dating Detective LaClair?" Emma asked him.

All the color had drained from Theo's face. "It's what I came here to talk about. I just got a call from a reporter. But I feel like you're not going to believe me."

"Just fucking tell us," Jill said.

"It doesn't make me look good. But I'm not a bad person."

"You've got two minutes and thirty seconds to tell us what's going on." Jill was surprised at the strength in her voice. "Don't think I'm not counting."

"I've been dating Daniel. I'm—I'm gay," Theo blurted out.

"You're gay? As in, like, bi?" Jill said.

"No, I don't think so. I'm just gay." He started to cry in earnest now.

"But you . . . you were married to my sister," Emma said.

*But we just had sex*, Jill thought. *Well, sort of.* Why would he come over to her house to seduce her, and then come out ten minutes later?

"Our marriage was complicated," Theo said through tears. "There was a lot about us you didn't know."

"Such as?"

"It's difficult to explain," Theo said. "I wanted to be straight. I wanted everyone to think I was straight, at least. I was in denial for a long time. And by the time I started to figure it out, I'd already established this super-hetero brand."

Emma was crying now too. "Did Maggie know you were gay?"

"Eventually." Theo sniffled. "Not right away. We had an arrangement. A business arrangement. We were partners. Dear friends and partners, and that was enough for us. I really did love her, even though it was mostly platonic by the end."

"Holy shit," Jill said.

Emma was momentarily silent before she spoke. "I don't even know how to begin to process that. An arrangement? Your marriage was fake?"

"Yes." Theo's voice was quiet.

Jill could hear through the phone that Emma was scratching her wrist. "So Maggie lied to me. To everyone. This whole time," Emma said.

Theo hung his head. "I'm so sorry. I didn't want you to find out this way."

"Also, why are you standing there in your underwear?" Emma asked. "I assumed it was because you and Jill had just hooked up, but now I'm confused."

"We did have sex. Or, I don't know, we tried," Theo said. Shame coursed through her. "I'm sorry, Jill. I came here to tell Emma about Daniel, and ... I don't know. With that photo circulating, I was outed before I was ready. I guess I just wanted to try the straight thing one more time, just to be super sure. And Jill, you've always made me feel safe."

Great. The only hot guys that wanted to sleep with her were gay men who wanted to make sure they were fully gay.

"Don't make this about Jill, or about getting outed." Emma's voice was suddenly furious. "Why were you sleeping with the detective? Was it because you were afraid he was going to find something out you'd rather he didn't? Was it because you wanted him to think you were innocent when really you aren't?"

"No! It's true, I didn't want him to keep investigating me. But I didn't kill Maggie, I swear." His voice cracked. "I didn't expect it to go this far. And now he's going to get in trouble and I don't know how to end it."

"Your relationship woes are not our problem," she said. "Why would you want him to stop investigating you if you didn't kill Maggie? That makes no sense."

"It's just that the police were obsessed with me at first. They were interrogating me every day. I was scared. They always think it's the husband. And our marriage was fake! What if they found that out? That's not a good look for me. But it wasn't me. I promise."

"I feel thoroughly unconvinced," Jill said, and Emma nodded in agreement. But that was a bit of a bluff. The bumbling guy in front of her didn't seem like a murderer.

Theo looked at his feet. "You have no idea how awful it felt. The police were constantly calling, searching the house. I had no privacy. It was terrible."

"So how did this thing between you and Detective LaClair start?" Emma asked.

"Well, we were spending a lot of time together, obviously," Theo said. "With him interviewing me and stuff. I don't know why, but I could just tell he had a thing for me. And eventually he told me he was gay, but that he wasn't out at work. I don't think he'd ever gotten that kind of attention from someone like me. Sorry if that's obnoxious to say."

"It is," Jill said.

Theo ignored this. "And I just started flirting with him in the hopes he'd back off. And he really . . . responded to it?"

Jill again felt the urge to slap him. "Continue," she said instead.

"It started just as, like, flirty jokes and stuff, but then it escalated. He told me he was developing feelings for me, but that it would've been a conflict of interest to pursue anything. I should've put it to rest then, but I didn't."

"And this entire time, you didn't want the police's help to find out who killed Maggie?" Jill asked.

"Well, of course I wanted that. But Daniel was telling me that they had no leads, that the case was a lost cause, that he just wanted it to be over so we could be together."

"That is so vile," Jill said.

"I'm not proud of it. But I wasn't thinking clearly; I was scared. I didn't want to go to jail."

Jill knew that Emma was going to burst. "So you seduced this closeted guy because you knew it would give you power over him? To get him to stop investigating your fake wife's murder? That might be the most fucked-up thing I've ever heard," Emma said.

"I actually like him," Theo said pathetically. "He's only the third man I've ever slept with."

"I don't care," Emma said. Even through FaceTime, Jill could tell she was furious. "You should've known better. You never should've done this."

"I still don't understand why you wouldn't just cooperate with the investigation. Especially if you're as innocent as you claim," Jill added.

Without warning, Theo burst into tears again. "I *am* innocent!" he cried. "I don't know how to make you believe me."

"You have to see that your story makes no sense," Jill said.

Theo's dramatic sobs sucked the air out of the room.

"Save it for the trial," Emma said.

"For the trial?" Theo sounded alarmed. "What do you mean?"

"Well, for one, you directly interfered with an investigation," Jill said. "I think that's considered an obstruction of justice. Not to mention that what you've just told us will absolutely make you the primary murder suspect." She had no idea what she was talking about, but it felt good to say it.

"I'm going to tell the reporter everything," Emma said.

"Fuck." At this, Theo began to cry harder. "Please don't, Emma. If you have any love or respect for me at all, please don't talk to the reporter."

Jill stared at Theo, feeling queasy. How had she been so attracted to him just thirty minutes ago that she was willing to betray her best friend? How had his naked body been on top of hers, and his tongue on her—no. She couldn't think about that. He'd used her, just as he'd used LaClair. She felt both disgusted and disgusting, and looked away.

After a few moments, Emma spoke, relieving the tension. "Theo, you need to go to the police. You'll tell them everything you told us. They can decide what to do with you and what to believe."

"What's going to happen to me?" Theo asked, through sobs.

"Who knows," Jill said. "Get a good lawyer."

Theo sniveled, wiping away his tears with the palms of his hands. "I'm innocent." They both ignored him, and he gathered his stuff to leave. He was still crying as he walked out the door. They sat in a moment of loaded silence on FaceTime.

"Jill, I need to process this," Emma said, her voice tinny on Jill's phone speaker. "I think I'm in shock. We can talk later about why you thought it was a good idea to sleep with my brother-in-law." She didn't even sound that angry, just defeated. And tired.

As they hung up, Jill realized she was crying too.

# Amanda

It was a stroke of brilliance, really, that had led her to the doorstep of her old dealer, Charlie. She realized she still had his number from the olden days, when she was in London filming *Anxiety* and discovered that it was harder to acquire Adderall from actual doctors than it was in America.

Charlie lived in a Brixton third-floor walk-up, and he sold every stimulant under the sun to an upscale clientele. When she lived in London for those months, she'd become friends with him—they would get fucked up on speed and go watch his friends DJ at underground EDM clubs. One time, he had even somehow acquired Quaaludes for them (vintage!), and they'd spent all night snorting Adderall to bring them up, then Quaaludes to bring them down, then some coke to level them out, and then some more Quaaludes just for fun. It was one of the top five most fun nights of her life.

She had texted Charlie last night, planning to meet up at his place like old times. Obviously, she hadn't led with the fact that she was now sober. But if Trevor was in London, there was one certainty: he'd hit up Charlie for coke. Charlie had the best cocaine in the UK, and Trevor—if nothing else—liked good cocaine. And if he was willing to do something like walk into an old bar where he could be recognized, maybe he'd be comfortable hitting up an old dealer.

"Amanda, love." Charlie swung open his door. "You never write, you never call. I was beginning to worry I'd never see you again." He beckoned her in, kissing her cheek.

"I literally just got to London." She once again left out that she was no longer doing drugs and was planning to flush the ones he gave her straight down the toilet. It was possible he'd have seen something on the news about her getting sober, but dealers never asked too many questions about stuff like that. If you were buying, they were selling. He also didn't seem like the type to read the tabloids.

"Alright, fair enough," he said, and they climbed the rickety stairs to his unit. She was about to buy drugs for the first time in almost two years.

The worst events of Amanda's life occurred in the two-month period starting when she found out about Trevor, to when she went to rehab for the first time, to her eventual relapse. That morning, before she made her way to Charlie's, she forced herself to reread the Worst Thing Anyone Had Ever Written About Her, a profile in *Vulture* that recapped every unforgivable thing she'd ever done (besides her *LoveShack* involvement, which they'd blessedly not been able to dig up) and made her unhirable for a while. She reread it from time to time, whenever she felt as if she was in danger of using drugs again. Given that she was going to her dealer's house, she figured preemptively revisiting the article was a good idea.

## *The Rise and Fall of Amanda Lehman*
### *by Natalie DeLong*

*Amanda Lehman's mugshot isn't her best photo. But it's not her worst, either. That honor belongs to a photo snapped by paparazzi as she steps out of a West Hollywood bar. In it, her eyes are bloodshot, her hair limp. She wears a leopard-print bodysuit that doesn't do much for her doughy figure. What makes it memorable, though, is that she's throwing up. She's puking on the street. So when Lehman's mugshot arrived a few months later, it looked downright flattering.*

*The photo is almost as infamous as Britney Spears's 2007 shaved-head-umbrella-attack meltdown, and her mugshot almost as notorious as Lindsay Lohan's 2007 one.*

*But an aughts anorexia-chic starlet Lehman is not. Her brand reflects the early-to-mid 2010s, when hipster millennial college grads in therapy ruled the world.* Anxiety *was exactly the type of upper-middle-class white feminist comedy that dominated the culture of the era. And Lehman was its poster child.*

*So when she began spiraling—in a fantastically public way—it came as a shock for many. Lehman isn't a* Mickey Mouse Club *alum who is hounded by the paps. She is someone the* New Yorker *once heralded as "the millennial spokesperson." She went to Brown University. She isn't thin or classically beautiful.*

*So how did the rising star's career implode so spectacularly? Well, for one, drugs. Suffering from a very public drug addiction at the height of one's fame can be a quick career ruiner. But people forgive drug addictions all the time. What they don't forgive as quickly, especially for self-proclaimed feminists, is defending serial rapists.*

*After the* Los Angeles Times *published an investigation detailing how her best friend and Anxiety co-creator Trevor Koch sexually assaulted multiple women, Lehman was quick to come to his aid. "Trevor couldn't have done this," she said to the* New York Times. *"He's my best friend. I know him better than I know myself. I'm sorry, but it's just not possible. I don't know who these women are, or why they're doing this, but it's sad. It's disappointing."*

*What ensued was mass outrage online directed at Lehman that almost overshadowed the outrage at Koch. #FuckAmandaLehman trended for weeks. But instead of backing down, Lehman doubled down. She told the* Hollywood Reporter *that she didn't care if she "never worked in this town again. When your best friend is accused of these terrible things and you know he didn't do them, you have the obligation to stand up for him." For his part, Koch disappeared after the investigation became public. He issued no response to the accusations and never showed up to the Anxiety set again. As many have since pointed out, nothing looks guiltier than fleeing your life and job.*

*Lehman always had a reputation for being kooky, but after Koch got #MeToo'd, her behavior escalated. Stories ran about Lehman showing up to film Anxiety "rambling and incoherent." She became a meme after flubbing her lines while presenting an award, eyes glassy. After it leaked to the press that she attended a meeting with network executives while "very obviously high," she fired her agent, publicist, and manager.*

*Days after, she overdosed on a combination of meth and heroin. When she left the hospital, she was bombarded by press and paparazzi, sans publicist. Reportedly, she told the group: "I didn't want to die. I just wanted to feel nothing." She was then arrested just a week after her overdose for drunk and disorderly conduct, and spent a night in county jail. She received a court order to go to rehab for 30 days, which she spent at a facility in Malibu.*

*When she left rehab and hired a new publicist, she apologized for her defense of Koch. "I am truly sorry for any hurt I caused. As an addict, I'm doing my best to take responsibility for my actions. I was using drugs heavily when I made the decision to support Koch. I regret my choice to do so. I condemn sexual assault in any form. #BelieveWomen." But the public was not having it.*

*Social media activist Serena Campbell went viral in a video eviscerating Lehman. At the time of publication, it has over 4 million likes. "Amanda Lehman was always the epitome of white capitalist 'feminism.' I'm sorry, but we're not buying your apology. It's going to take more than you going to rehab for billionaires for us to care about you again."*

*Then Lehman and her team went silent. Sources close to Lehman confirmed she was spending time in her palatial Los Angeles home, writing the new season of* Anxiety *alone. That was, until two weeks ago, when the network canceled* Anxiety, *after previously having renewed the show for another season. Lehman was spotted just hours after the announcement partying in West Hollywood, high and drunk. Her team released a statement admitting that Lehman had relapsed and was going back to rehab.*

*It's hard to know where rock bottom will be for Lehman. Perhaps she's already there. With no hit TV show, no creative partner, and a very serious addiction to overcome, one thing is certain: a tough road lies ahead.*

The events of her relapse haunted her most of all—before she fell asleep, the second she woke up, and in any of her time alone, really. Images from her subconscious forced their way out as if they were blinking lights inside a dark dive bar.

As she walked up the stairs to Charlie's place, it happened: her palms became clammy, her vision blurred. *Not now. Please, not now,* she pleaded with herself as Charlie opened his door and they walked to the same couch she used to sit on in a past life, when he would count out pills for her and she would pay him in cash.

It was then that the images started playing on a loop in her mind: the phone call from the EP, saying they'd had enough and were canceling the show. Begging, pleading with him, asking for one more chance—she was sober! Didn't that count for anything? Calling Trevor again and again, sobbing. Straight to voicemail, as per usual. Calling Samson. Dinner with Samson. A first martini. A second, a third. The heady feeling of relief and invincibility and shame that accompanied finally using again. Dancing at the Eagle, coke in the bathroom with Samson. More cocaine. Then more. Then back to Samson's house.

Charlie's voice drew her out of herself. "Want something to drink?"

"Oh, no, I'm good," she said as he led her to the couch. She sat down and wiped her palms on her Stella McCartney joggers. "I can't stay for long." A voice inside of her told her, very clearly: *Get out of here.* Before she could move, more images came back: her final three lines of coke. Her left arm going numb. Pressure on her chest. Samson insisting she was fine. Calling 911 on herself. The ambulance. The aspirin the medics had her take. A heart attack. Realizing it was a fucking heart attack.

"You OK?" Charlie asked her.

"Actually, sorry, I'm not feeling so well. I should get going."

"But you just got here," he said.

She stood up, but felt dizzy. She sat back down. "Yeah, I just . . ."

"What is it? Just tell me."

She paused, considering her options. Fuck it. "This is fully insane, I'm aware, but I came here to pretend to buy drugs from you so I could try to extract information about Trevor. Because I heard he's in London, and want to know if that's true. And I figured you would know." Her old dealer stared at her, but she continued. "I'm sober, and have been for a while. And it's overwhelming to be back here, at your place. Not that I care what you do with your time or to make money. To be clear."

He looked surprised. "Wow."

"Yeah," she said.

"Well, it would be a pretty big breach of my clients' confidentiality if I gave you any information about anyone. Privacy is everything for me."

"I assumed as much. I just had to try." What a humiliating endeavor this was.

"Let me finish," he said. "I saw what happened. I know what Trevor did to those women."

"Yep." She looked down, not wanting to make eye contact. He probably also knew she had defended him.

"And I know that your show was canceled. And that you got sober. A couple of times, right?" Charlie said.

"Yes, though I like to think that this time it's sticking," she said.

Charlie sighed. "Amanda, I've never known what to do with you."

She smiled, even though she knew it wasn't a compliment. "Same, honestly."

"You didn't hear it from me, but he's not going by Trevor at this point," Charlie said. "He's going by Tom." He took out his phone. "And he looks different. I'm texting you his number. But again, you didn't get it from me. If he finds out, you're fucked. I'll make sure of it." Ah, there was the Charlie she knew.

Her hands trembled as she opened her phone to a text from Charlie. "I can't thank you enough. Really."

"Don't mention it. Just . . . do whatever you need to do."

She couldn't believe it. She got up again, this time steadier on her feet. He walked her out.

"I'm proud of you." He hugged her goodbye. "For getting sober, I mean."

"Thank you." She felt tears well up in her eyes. Her *ex-dealer* was proud of her and she was crying? For fuck's sake. "It means a lot."

"Be careful," he said as he walked her out. "He's not a very happy person right now."

Before she could ask him for more details, he shut the door.

# Maggie

## Post-Finale

The weeks following the show's finale had been the strangest and busiest of her life. The second that filming was over and they were handed their phones back, she turned hers on to see she had gained hundreds of thousands of Instagram followers. Thousands of comments populated her profile with adoring words for her and Theo. It was invigorating; she couldn't stop refreshing her page to watch her follower count go up.

*We love u and Theo omgggg.*

*u guys are so cute I just want to see u get married!!!!! and have babies obvs.*

*BEST Love Pair EVER.*

She spoke to her agent and manager the second she could, and Theo spoke to his—though they agreed not to share the truth about their relationship with them. Theo and Maggie set up shop at her apartment on La Brea for the time being. The first order of business would be figuring out how to maximize publicity in the moments following their big win. They needed to be in the same place all the time so if paparazzi followed them, they'd see that they were spending time together. They needed to look cozy, and intimate, as if they were honeymooning. What followed was a whirlwind: magazine covers, talk show invitations, photoshoots.

Still, she saw Finn as much as she could. After filming, she was worried he would choose to stay with Layla and forget about their plan. But the second production wrapped, he'd texted her: *I'm in this, Maggie. I want to see you.*

Before he went on *LoveShack*, he'd worked as a fundraiser for a veterans' health nonprofit. One of his former donors had asked him to dogsit for their goldendoodle in their mansion in Sherman Oaks for a month, so Finn and Maggie met there and played house every night.

It was a Tuesday, and Finn was cooking spaghetti and meatballs while she sat at the kitchen island.

"I'm making you spaghetti squash," he said. Maggie was trying to lose three pounds before her appearance with Theo on *The View* in two weeks. "With turkey meatballs." He looked cute in a blue gingham apron, his hair messy and glasses on.

"Sounds perfect." She looked in her calorie-counting app to see how many points this would cost her.

"You're obsessed with that app." He motioned to her phone. "Truly, you don't need to lose any weight."

She rolled her eyes. "Easy for you to say. You're a dude. You can lose ten pounds by imagining doing a push-up."

"Not true," he said. "But still. I know you're under a lot of pressure, but I wish you knew how perfect you are."

"Ugh, stop. You flatter me." She got up to kiss him on the cheek.

"I feel like I've known you for my whole life," he whispered.

"I know what you mean," she whispered back.

"It's wild that it's so easy between us and we've only known each other for a few months. Is it insane that I feel sure about you?"

Maggie looked at him, at the food, at the house. At the goldendoodle, Marci, who was eating crumbs off the ground near their feet. If she squinted, she could almost pretend this was her real life. She'd only been seeing Finn in earnest for a few weeks and while it'd been a good few weeks, was she sure about him? Every part of them was physically compatible. The sex was the best she'd ever had. And he was doting and attentive and lovely. But was she *sure*? It was a little early for that. Was this his way of asking her to "dump" Theo?

He was looking at her expectantly, so she smiled and took his hand. "We're getting there," she said.

His expression faltered. "What does that mean?"

"I really like you, but it's a bit early." And she wasn't ready to end the arrangement with Theo just yet.

He let go of her hand. "You know I got asked to do an entertainment tour with other reality stars for active service members stationed in Germany and Kuwait? I said no. Because I didn't want to leave for a month while we were just getting started."

He looked so hurt that she couldn't possibly point out that she'd never asked him to do that. Instead, she took his hand back in hers. "Finn, believe me. You're the best thing that's happened to me in a long time." Then, before either of them could say anything else, she kissed him on the mouth. To her relief, he relaxed into it, kissing her back.

It was the next day that debt collectors started ramping up their calls. She owed money on two credit cards in addition to the mind-numbing amount from when her mom was dying. She thought it'd be easier to pay things off quickly once she got back from the show, but the $30,000 prize hadn't gone far, and while brand deals were coming in, it took a while to actually get paid. She'd gotten two calls just that morning from collection agencies, because she hadn't been able to make her minimum payments in the last few months before she'd been on the show. The collection agencies had somehow found her new address already, and she was getting three or four letters a day, stamped with big red phrases like "URGENT" and "ACTION REQUIRED."

She opened a text message to Emma, one she'd started and stopped drafting a million times: *Em, I'm in trouble. I have a lot of debt from Mom's medical bills. I'm sorry I never told you. I know you don't have a lot of money, but I need help making a monthly payment until I get paid from these brand deals.* But, as always, she deleted it before she could hit send. She couldn't burden her sister with this—especially as she was barely scraping by too. Maggie was the older sister. She should be able to take care of things.

"You look stressed." Theo eyed the collection letters that lay across her counter. They were meeting to review a few of the brand offers that had come in over the past couple weeks. The first was from a sunscreen company that didn't want to pay them, but wanted them to join an all-expenses paid influencer trip to Belize. That sounded nice, but it wasn't what she needed, which was actual money.

"I just don't see how we're going to make anything off of this," she said.

"Yeah," he agreed. "I was hoping we'd be able to do this fake dating thing for a few months and cash out. But it's harder than I thought." They'd gotten a few additional offers from small-time brands, but the totals would basically cover her rent and nothing else.

"Maybe we should just take the deal with the online gambling people," she said. A website called Place Your Bets was offering them a small amount of money to star in digital ads. They'd be filmed wearing bathing suits, sitting by a pool and playing on their phones. It would be easy money, but felt gross. Plus, it wouldn't be a good look for the brand they were hoping to establish.

"I guess," Theo said.

As if on cue, Maggie's manager Anita called. Maggie answered and put her on speaker. "Here with Theo," she said. "We were actually just talking about how we're not liking the offers coming in."

"We need to make more money," Theo said. "What you've sent us so far isn't enough."

"Well, you're going to fucking love this," Anita said.

# Emma

"Please yell at me," Jill said. "I deserve it." Jill was clearly crying, and Emma was exhausted.

"I can't," Emma said. This was the first time they'd spoken on the phone since she'd FaceTimed Jill to find Theo half-naked at their apartment yesterday. Jill had been calling incessantly even though it was the middle of the night for her. With nothing better to do before her meeting with Layla in an hour, Emma finally answered. She wanted to get worked up about Jill sleeping with Theo, but she was just so drained. Drained from Theo's confession about his arrangement with Maggie, about his relationship with LaClair, about his sexuality. Drained because her best friend had slept with her brother-in-law even though he'd gone to their house to come out, ostensibly. It would've been funny if it wasn't so awful.

Emma lay in bed, phone on speaker, and scratched her wrist. "I don't think there's anything you can say to make this better."

"You're doing that thing; you're shutting down instead of telling me how you feel," Jill said.

"God, Jill. Enough."

"I can literally hear you scratching your wrist. You shouldn't be alone right now." Jill was still crying.

Emma stopped scratching and stood up to look for a Band-Aid. "I don't know what you want from me. I wish you hadn't slept with Theo. I wish I was more surprised. But I have to go. You should go to bed, it's late."

"Please, don't go." Jill was crying harder.

"I'm hanging up," Emma said. Even though it was ten in the morning, it was dark in the apartment; she hadn't turned on any of the lights. She made her way to the bathroom and found a large Band-Aid in the bathroom's first-aid kit, and put it on her wrist. She looked at herself in the mirror, and found she looked almost as bad as she had in the weeks after Maggie had died. She splashed water on her face and applied a coat of mascara. This would have to do, because she was going to meet Layla in a half-hour.

Emma sat on a bench in Regent's Park as Layla approached, wearing a white fur jacket, a gray turtleneck, high-waisted flare jeans, and heeled white patent-leather boots.

Emma stood up to greet her. Were they supposed to hug? Probably not. She extended her hand instead, before realizing it was trembling. But Layla took it, and didn't seem to notice; her handshake was firm.

Layla gave her a once-over. "Sorry I'm late. God, you look nothing like your sister." Emma looked down at herself: the corduroy jacket and cargo pants, the Converse High Tops. It was the opposite of how Maggie would've shown up anywhere. "I don't mean that as an insult," Layla continued. "She was gorgeous, but you've got your own thing going on."

Emma chuckled as they sat down on the bench. "Thanks, I guess." Her heart pounded with nerves as she turned to face Layla.

"So, how can I help you?" Layla said. "I assume you want to know all of Maggie's dirty laundry?"

*Not really*, she wanted to say. But instead, she went with, "I guess that's why I'm here."

"I don't know how any of this will help you, but I know things about Maggie she'd probably rather I kept quiet. That's why I wanted to talk to you in person, instead of with that reporter or whoever that woman was. I know it's sensitive."

"I get that," Emma said. "I appreciate that you were willing to talk at all. I'm just trying to learn everything I can. I'm hopeful that you can help me get to the bottom of this."

"Well, first, I assume you know that Maggie and Theo's relationship was, um, how do I say this politely . . ." Layla paused. "It was a sham. It was fake?"

Emma sighed. "I just found out, but honestly I haven't processed it yet. It's absurd. Like, Theo was my brother-in-law. I did Christmas and Easter with him for three years. I know his parents. I was at their fucking wedding. They own a house together."

"I'm so sorry," Layla said. "I can't even imagine what this is like for you."

"The one thing I'm stuck on, that maybe you can help me understand, is what was in it for Maggie? Theo, I get. He was closeted and scared. But a fake relationship? I have no idea why Maggie would do something like that."

Layla looked at her empathetically. "I don't know for sure. But did she ever talk to you about her medical debt?"

"No," Emma said. "But I found out about it from the LAPD."

"We were roommates, you know. For most of filming. And she used to talk about things with your mom. About the financial burden she'd taken on. My guess is that she was desperate."

Emma sighed. She felt like crying, but was so exhausted that her tear ducts seemed unable to produce anything. "But why not just do a fake boyfriend-girlfriend relationship? Why get married?"

"Well, remember: they made a lot of money from the network for that, I'm sure," Layla said. "But I don't know. Maybe it felt safe to her, to be in that fake relationship with Theo. Low-stakes, I guess. I'm sorry. I'm sure it's awful to learn about all of this when she's not here to explain everything herself. She used to tell me how close you guys were."

"I wonder whose idea it was," Emma said.

Layla sighed. "At first, I'm sure it was just a ploy to win the show. Which I don't fault her for, honestly. As you clearly know, there have been, like, two successful couples to come from the ten seasons of the show. So it's not as if everyone else isn't also, shall we say, *overselling* their connections in order to win votes. And the winners of the show do so much better than the rest of us, career-wise. Maggie never needed to move to a foreign country to film a house-hunting show for cable."

"True," Emma conceded.

"Honestly, they made great content together. She was on magazine covers all the time. She had lucrative brand partnerships and ad campaigns. She had her own fucking toothpaste brand. She and Theo were operating at a different level than me or any of the other cast from our season. Maybe she was just afraid of losing it all. I know I would be."

"Was she going to be with him for the rest of her life just to move her career forward? For fuck's sake." Emma blew her nose into a tissue Layla had offered her. "She was ambitious, but not *that* ambitious. Or that's what I thought."

"I don't understand it, honestly," Layla said. "You knew her better than I did."

Emma sighed. "Yeah. Though I wish you'd told the police. This does feel relevant given . . ." She couldn't bring herself to say *given that Maggie was murdered in cold blood*.

"Do you think Theo could have done it?" Layla asked, as if reading Emma's mind.

"I don't know." And she didn't. Was he really depraved or smart enough to pull off killing Maggie and leaving no trace of evidence?

"For what it's worth, I really can't see him doing something like that," Layla said. "I think, if nothing else, she was his cover story. And his cash cow. Sorry if that sounds crude."

"No, I know what you mean." And though the characterization disturbed her, part of her felt sorry for Theo. Sorry that he was so uncomfortable in his own skin that he needed to fake something like this for so long. "Is there anything else you think I should know about Maggie? Stuff that happened while you were filming the show, or whatever?"

"Have you ever met Finn? From our season?" Layla asked.

"Briefly, at the funeral," Emma said. "But I've seen the show, I know he was your Love Pair."

"That he was," Layla said, an edge of bitterness in her voice.

"I'm sorry about that kiss thing," Emma said. "I know it's weird to apologize on behalf of my sister. But it made me feel icky. And now it makes sense why that looked way more passionate than any of her makeouts with Theo."

Layla snorted. "I guess you really have no idea." She shook her head.

"No idea about what?" Emma asked.

"They were fucking. Finn and Maggie. During and after the show. He's who told me about Maggie and Theo's arrangement." Layla stared at her fingernails, as if this didn't matter to her at all. Emma tried to act calm, even though she wanted to scream. Did she actually know anything about her sister? Who was she really, with a made-for-TV relationship and a secret lover?

"I'm so sorry. That must have been awful for you," Emma said.

"It was," Layla said. "I know it's dumb, but I really did like Finn. And for what it's worth, I don't have a lot of anger toward him anymore. He wasn't a bad guy. He just loved Maggie, and not me."

Emma nodded her understanding. What a week this had been. She wanted to get back to America, back to her bed, close the blinds and sleep for three days straight.

"This sounds petty, but it was like Maggie just had to have everything. She needed to win *and* get the best guy on the show," Layla said.

"I understand," Emma said, though she didn't, not really. "Is it worth reaching out to Finn? Would he know any other bombshell secrets about my sister?"

"I'm not sure," Layla said. "I haven't spoken to him in years. I have no idea if he and Maggie were still in touch even. But it's probably worth trying." She took out her phone. "Sending you his number, if you want to reach out."

Emma saved the number.

"Sorry I couldn't be of more help," Layla said. "I actually should get going. But Emma, thanks for reaching out. And coming all the way here. I know I wasn't the nicest to your friend."

Emma had almost forgotten about Amanda and Layla's tense interaction. "Don't worry about it," she said.

Layla stood up to leave, and they hugged goodbye.

"You seem like a more genuine version of your sister," Layla said.

Emma wanted to cry again. She understood that Layla was angry with Maggie, but it hurt.

"I don't know about that," she demurred.

"Well, I do. And I just . . . I hope you can move on from this. You deserve to have your own life." Layla started to walk away.

"Thanks," Emma said. But Layla was already out of earshot.

# Maggie

### Reunion Episode

The network was offering them $1.5 million each if they got married on live television within three months: $1.5 million. Each! It was baffling.

Apparently, the show's ratings had been stellar; she and Theo were fan favorites.

At first, Maggie laughed at the prospect of getting fake married. Carrying on a fake relationship was uncomfortable enough; getting married would be far more bizarre. But $1.5 million would change her life. She could pay off her debt, and she would have a good amount of cushion to start her influencing career in earnest. She wouldn't have to involve Emma in her money woes. Plus, if fake dating was something that she and Theo were good at, maybe they'd excel at being fake married, too.

He'd finally told her a few nights ago what she'd long suspected: he was queer. She wasn't sure if that meant bi, or gay, but she was pretty sure he wasn't interested in having a real relationship with a woman.

"I know that we live in the twenty-first century, but is it

so bad that I want to keep my sexual orientation private? I'd like to make this influencing thing work. It's all I've ever been good at. And I don't want to be an *LGBTQ influencer*," he said with thinly veiled disgust.

"Why not? What's wrong with that?" Except, did she really want to talk him out of this? Wasn't she more valuable as a part of a couple?

"It's just such a narrow market. Plus, think about all the death threats and crazy people. We can appeal to middle America as a couple in a way I never could alone."

"Don't you want to be with someone you're actually attracted to? Someone you have a connection with?" she asked.

"I'm still figuring out what that looks like for me," he said. "Plus, can't we do both? Sleep with whoever we want to, see whoever we want to? We'd just keep it low-key and quiet."

But she wasn't sure how she could do that to Finn. It would break his heart.

Two nights before the show's reunion was set to film, she decided it was time to tell Finn. It was the third night in a row he'd been staying at her place in the last week, and they were sitting together on her futon in their pajamas. Her feet were propped up on his lap and he was three-quarters of the way through his second beer. It was the best time she could think of to broach this.

"There's something I wanted to talk to you about." She steeled herself. He looked at her excitedly, which made her heart sink. "I want to keep up this thing with Theo for a little bit longer."

Finn's face fell. "What does that mean?"

"It's gotten sort of complicated with money stuff."

He looked at her, brows knit. "I'm just surprised. I assumed you were ready to move on and stop pretending."

"I am, Finn." She moved toward him on the futon, taking his hand. "I want to see where this thing between us goes."

"Me too." But his expression didn't match the sentiment. "But it'll be impossible if you're publicly with someone else."

"I promise we'll figure it out. I just need more time," she said. He seemed mollified, so she continued. "Have you heard from Layla?" He'd broken up with her right after the show ended, but they were all about to reunite tomorrow for the first time.

"Oh, she'll be fine," Finn said. "I'm talking to her tomorrow before the reunion. Just to explain my feelings more, and confirm we're not going to hash this out in front of the cameras."

"OK," Maggie said, though this news made her nervous.

"It'll be fine," he said. "I just want you to get moving on this Theo breakup. I want us to get started on our real lives together."

"I want that too, I really do." Her heart pounded, because she knew it was time to go in for the kill. "But the network is offering us one and a half million to get married on TV."

He let out a sharp breath. "Are you fucking kidding me?"

"It wouldn't be real, of course," Maggie said. "We've talked it over, and we're on the same page. We'll get the marriage annulled in a few months."

"That would be a terrible mistake." Finn pulled away from her. "You're living a lie. It's only going to get worse."

"Finn, I need the money," she said. "I need it really badly."

"I could help you out a bit," he said. "You could live with me until you get on your feet financially. I'm probably going to start taking on some hours again at the veterans' nonprofit if influencing doesn't take off for me. You don't have to do this."

"I do, though," she said, her voice quiet. She couldn't take his money, his charity.

His expression hardened. "I can't believe you're doing this to me."

"Finn, we just started seeing each other." She knew she sounded desperate, pathetic. "I really like you, but I can't throw this kind of money away. I promise it's temporary."

"You can't keep saying that!" he yelled. This was the most angry she'd ever seen him, and he almost looked like a different person. His neck had gone red and splotchy and his eyes were bloodshot. "We've been together a month and a half now, and this was not the deal. You're being manipulative and cruel. You're using me."

Tears welled in her eyes. "I'm sorry you feel that way."

"*'I'm sorry you feel that way,'*" he repeated back to her in a mocking voice. She turned away as if he'd smacked her. After a few seconds, he stood up and began gathering his stuff. "I can't do this anymore."

"Please," she said. "Don't leave."

"You're breaking my heart."

"Finn, come on," she pleaded. "I can't just throw away one point five million dollars."

He ignored her, slamming the door on his way out.

*

The next night, she told Emma about the wedding.

"Jesus, Mags. I haven't even met Theo yet." Emma was cooking eggs, and dropped the spatula she was holding. She turned to look at Maggie, who was sitting at the kitchen table in Emma and Jill's apartment. "Isn't this all a bit fast?"

"Yes, it is." Maggie had anticipated this reaction. "But the network is paying us so much. And I could really use the money right now, honestly. We'll just get divorced if it doesn't work out. It'll be like a regular breakup but with paperwork."

Her sister looked slightly disgusted. "Is that really a good mindset, though? For a marriage? I don't want you to get hurt."

"Don't worry," Maggie said. "Truly. I know what I'm doing here. I promise."

Emma had invited her over for dinner, but Maggie was on an eggs-only diet Theo had read about somewhere. She needed to lose seven pounds before the wedding. Emma scrambled the eggs with some cheese, looking unconvinced but slightly placated. "Marriage is a big deal. Do you think you're ready?"

"Yes." Maggie tried to sound emphatic. "I really love him. I've never felt love like this before." The lie slipped right out of her mouth. It really did get easier with time. She hated being dishonest with Emma, but in some ways it was easier than telling the truth: she was in massive financial trouble, her acting career was dead, and this influencer stuff was harder than she'd thought it'd be. This was her only option, but Emma would never accept that. Emma would try to convince her there was another way.

Emma finished scrambling and grabbed a plate. She looked at Maggie, sizing her up. "Are you sure?"

*I have all this debt. All this responsibility,* she wanted to say. *I'm protecting you.* But Emma would insist on helping pay it off. She'd forget about screenwriting and get trapped, just like Maggie. She couldn't do that to her sister, so she plastered a smile on her face. "I'm sure. When you know, you know."

The reunion show was the crown jewel of every reality TV empire. That, at least, was what Priya said. The viewership was often five or six times that of an average episode—the finale notwithstanding. Priya jabbered about all of this at Maggie, while she sat getting her makeup done before the reunion show (she and Theo were the only cast members who got their own trailers). She asked Maggie if she'd been in contact with any of her castmates after the show, wondering how things were with Theo. Anything to feed Schuyler so he could ask the most obnoxious questions possible.

After the makeup artist set Maggie's makeup, she and Priya made their way out. Priya needed to bother other cast members for their leftover resentments and updates.

"Someone's here to see you!" Priya held the door open for the mystery guest before she left. Maggie hoped it was Finn, because they hadn't resolved anything from their fight about her and Theo's wedding.

To Maggie's surprise, there was Layla, looking incredible in five-inch heels and a red leather skater dress. Maggie got up out of her chair to give her a hug.

"Save it." Layla shook her head.

Maggie froze. "Is something wrong?"

Layla rolled her eyes. "Yes, something is obviously very fucking wrong, Maggie. Finn just told me. He told me everything."

"Told you what?" Maggie tried to remain calm.

"Oh, don't play dumb. Please. Show me at least that much respect."

"Layla, I'm so sorry. I really—"

Layla put her hand up. "I mean it. Stop. Don't apologize like you care about me. I just want to understand."

"Understand?"

"Why Finn? You could've had any guy on that show, and you chose Finn. Was it because he liked me? You didn't want me to have any semblance of happiness or success?"

Maggie was silent, trying to strategize. Part of her was relieved; at least Finn had seen enough of a future with her that he'd felt he needed to tell Layla about them.

"Are you just going to stand there silently?" Layla asked.

"I'm so sorry. Just please don't bring this up on camera tonight. I promise we'll talk about it. I'll tell you everything. I just can't do it tonight." Maggie's chest was tight with panic.

Layla shook her head. "I owe you literally nothing, Maggie. Seriously. Why would I protect you? It's an insulting suggestion, honestly."

*Think, Maggie. Fucking think.* "You're going to look like the villain," Maggie said, her voice as calm as she could make it. "I hate to say it, but it's true."

Layla scoffed at this. "What does that mean? Why would *I* look like the villain?"

"First of all, you're going to break Theo's heart. He'll be devastated." Maggie said a silent prayer that Finn hadn't told Layla about her arrangement with Theo.

"I know you don't have a real relationship with Theo," Layla said. "But nice try." Jesus. Finn really had laid it all out there. Had he done that because it'd be a clean way to expose her?

"Theo's a nice person. He doesn't deserve to be exposed on TV," Maggie said. Layla again rolled her eyes. "But seriously, Layla. You're going to look bad."

"I don't think so," Layla said.

Maggie knew then that there was no other way out of this situation. She had to go low. "You know Theo is queer. That's why we're doing this. If you tell everyone the truth, I'll accuse you of being homophobic. Of outing him before he was ready." She felt nauseous with shame.

Layla was silent, and she and Maggie stood there for a painful beat before she spoke. "You disgust me, Maggie. You're the only one outing Theo tonight. I can't believe you'd pretend this was about protecting him when it's about protecting your money."

Maggie took a deep breath, trying to hold in her tears. "Please, I'm begging you. Let's not do this tonight in front of everyone. After this, we'll get a drink. I'll explain everything. I promise."

But Layla was already walking out the door.

# Jill

Emma opened the door to their apartment, her duffel bag thrown over her shoulder. The dark circles under her eyes looked worse than they had after Maggie had died.

"How was your flight home?" Jill stood up to hug her.

Emma dropped her bag. "I can't do this pretend-to-be-normal thing with you."

Jill's heart sank. She'd held on to some hope that Emma would come home and they'd hash things out.

"We don't have to. It's OK if you want to scream at me," Jill tried. "I can take it."

"I don't have the energy for that right now, either," Emma said. "Though you deserve it."

"Is there anything I'm allowed to talk about?" Jill knew she'd fucked up, but she was still irritated with Emma's disinterest in discussing the state of their friendship.

"I need some space," Emma said. "I'll sleep here tonight, but I'm going to live in the Calabasas house for a while. Maggie's estate lawyer OK'ed it with Theo. It's the least he can fucking do." The mention of him sent an unhappy shiver down Jill's spine.

Emma hated that house. She must've been desperate to

get away from Jill. She tried to change the subject. "How'd it go in London?" Her voice was artificially bright; she was close to tears.

"God, Jill, just stop," Emma said. "I don't want to talk about any of this with you."

"I know you're mad, but I want to talk to you. It doesn't have to be now. But I'm in this with you," Jill said. "Even if you hate me right now."

Emma looked back at her, her face blank. "Whatever. I'm jet-lagged, I need to sleep."

"I'll let you sleep, but one thing I did want to ask—did Amanda say why she was staying in London? Now that you're gone, and all."

"How would I know?" Emma began walking to her room, but Jill followed. "She had some meetings or something."

"Huh. Her calendar is totally clear. She called me yesterday to tell me she'd be extending her trip, but didn't say why. It's becoming an issue at work: people are getting annoyed."

"Well, maybe just ask her," Emma said. "I'm sure it's fine. She probably just wants a vacation."

"I guess," Jill said. "So you're not going to tell me how it went with Layla? I really want to know, Emma. I care about this."

Emma walked into her room and threw her bag on her bed. She opened it and began to haphazardly throw her clothes into her hamper or back in her closet. Jill grabbed one of Emma's shirts and began to fold it, but Emma shooed her away and she retreated to the doorway.

"You can talk to me," Jill said. "You can't just hold it all in."

"Why would I talk to you, of all people? The amount of lying Maggie did was so fucked. Theo being closeted and sleeping with LaClair is beyond fucked. But you're a liar too. You went behind my back and had sex with him! I can't deal with more lies right now."

Jill blushed. "We didn't really, um, have sex. He couldn't . . . you know."

Emma cut her off. "Ew. I don't want to hear about this. Honestly, Jill, I hope you got whatever fucked-up validation you were looking for from him."

"Validation?" Jill was suddenly angry. "He's literally not interested in women. I'm sorry I fucked up. But don't act like I have some weird obsession with Theo."

"Jill, come on. All you care about is people liking you. It's just sad," Emma said.

Tears welled up behind Jill's eyes, but she didn't know how to respond. She wanted this horrible conversation to be over. She wanted to cry alone in her room. She wanted to stew in self-hatred and then have a large glass of wine and go to sleep. "I hate this. I don't care about Theo, I really don't. I love you, and I don't want to fight," she told Emma as she turned to leave the room.

Emma didn't respond; she just shook her head and shut the door.

# Amanda

The three dots appearing and disappearing: it was what she saw when she closed her eyes before she fell asleep, and it was the first thing she thought about when she woke up in the morning.

The dots had only been there for a few seconds after she'd texted Trevor's new number the first time, but it was enough to keep her going. When she'd started trying to find Trevor, she'd never imagined that he'd feel so far away from her that the three dots on her phone indicating there was someone on the other end, typing back, would feel like the most intimate thing in the world.

As soon as Charlie had given her his number, she'd texted him: *It's Amanda. I'm in London and I want to see you. Please answer me.*

Those three dots had been enough to keep her in London. They were so close; she could feel it. So she'd now been at the Hoxton for a week since Emma had left, and it'd been days since she'd had any work meetings on the books. Her time was filled with trips to all of her and Trevor's old haunts in London—their favorite café, the little bookstore, the Indian restaurant—but he was never there, and no one else had seen him. After a week of nothing, she caved and booked a flight home.

It was her last night, and even though she knew it was useless, she decided to contact him one last time. *The Bixby tonight at 7. Meet me there? Leaving London tmrw.* He never responded.

At 7:06 p.m., she pulled open the door to the pub. In her Chloé houndstooth pantsuit, she made her way through the crowd, scanning for Trevor. She tried not to be disappointed that he wasn't there.

She was happy to find George behind the bar again. She waved at him and he smiled at her as he finished with another customer.

He brought her soda water and lime, and they spent the next twenty minutes or so chatting. Eventually, she picked up some fish and chips from the shop down the block and brought it back to eat at the bar. It was surprisingly pleasant. George took a few of her chips and told her about his niece, who was finishing preschool, and his punk band called Orion's Belt, which had a small following in the area. She found that she wasn't yearning for a drink.

"I want to believe you walked back into the bar to see me," he said. "But I have to ask: Why are you here?"

"Oh." She laughed. "I was hoping to see someone, but I don't think he's coming." It felt both good and bad to say it out loud. Once again, Trevor had left her hanging out to dry. It was predictable, and she was getting bored of it.

"He's an idiot, then."

"It's not like I got stood up," Amanda said. "To be clear."

"Of course. That would be a ridiculous thing to do to someone like you."

"True," she said, and he laughed.

They made more conversation as she unselfconsciously dug into her fish and chips. She found she wasn't even sad that Trevor wasn't there, wasn't sad to be sober. She was growing warm in the cheeks, animated by good conversation and greasy food. She even felt a little excited when George handed her another soda and lime and their fingers grazed.

"What time do you get off work tonight?" she asked him.

"Eleven," he said. "I would ask if you fancied a pint, but I suspect that's not an appropriate thing to suggest to someone who doesn't drink."

"Correct," she said. "Though I wouldn't mind hanging out and not drinking." It was her last night, and she was feeling bold.

"That sounds fun." He smiled. "What would we do?"

"Oh, this and that. I make a mean Shirley Temple."

"Well, in that case . . ." he said, and they laughed.

She dipped her final chip into ketchup and licked her fingers, tasting the remnants of salt and oil. She imagined Trevor walking in and seeing her, confidently hitting on a cute bartender. Would he be jealous? She pushed the thought out of her mind. This wasn't about him. Fuck him.

"I'm going to go back to my hotel room now," she said. "And then, around eleven thirty, you're going to come over."

He smiled. "I like the sound of that."

She slipped him her extra hotel key and stood up. And before she lost her nerve, she pulled him in close, kissing him on the mouth. His stubble felt nice against her face and he had this good, clean smell that some part of her animal brain had continued to associate with him even though they hadn't seen each other in years. Kissing him felt more comfortable than it should have. Better than it'd ever felt with Trevor. "More later," she whispered as they pulled away from each other.

"More later," he agreed.

She smiled as she gathered her purse and her coat from the back of the chair, her face pleasantly warm and lips a little swollen from the kiss. What an unexpected and welcome turn of events this was.

As she put her coat on, she felt a tap on her shoulder. George's eyes widened. It was then, as she saw his expression, that she knew what was happening.

Her heart pounded and she turned around.

It was Trevor.

# Emma

Emma sat on her dead sister's couch, rereading the short article that Liz's coworker had written about Theo and LaClair. Emma had spoken anonymously to the reporter for the story, and Theo was pissed.

## *Reality Star Theo Cooke Admits to Relationship with LAPD Detective*

*Cooke described himself as a "gay man . . . trying to figure things out"*
*By Sasha Montague*

*Theo Cooke, influencer and winner of season six of the reality dating show* LoveShack, *has admitted to carrying on a sexual relationship with Los Angeles Police Department detective Daniel LaClair after the two were photographed together in Los Angeles.*

*LaClair, 56, was investigating Maggie Lathrop's death on behalf of the LAPD. The detective declared it a cold case after only four months. Lathrop and Cooke met as contestants on* LoveShack, *and were married for three years before she died from fatal stab wounds in January of this year. Sources, who requested anonymity for fear of retribution, say Cooke, 34, initiated the relationship with LaClair as an attempt to end the investigation into his wife's murder. Cooke insists he began the relationship to explore his sexuality.*

*"[Cooke] didn't want the police to look into him too closely," said one source knowledgeable about the situation. Cooke admitted he started the relationship so the detective would cut the investigation short, according to the source. According to the LAPD, Cooke is now under investigation for obstruction of justice.*

*University of Southern California Law Professor Timothy Belden said that, if found guilty, Cooke could be convicted of tampering with an investigation, a crime which could result in up to 10 years of prison time. LaClair has been placed on administrative leave while the department investigates potential wrongdoing. The LAPD did not respond to multiple requests for comment.*

*"Pursuing a relationship with Daniel LaClair was a grave mistake, and I sincerely regret this lapse in judgment. It was never my intention to impede the investigation into my late wife's death. This was a misguided attempt at exploring my sexual identity, and for that I apologize. My actions were never malicious. I was and am a gay man who's trying to figure things out. I hope the LAPD will choose to reopen the case so her assailant can be brought to justice," Cooke said in a written statement.*

*This is a developing story and will be updated as the situation evolves.*

This was, predictably, blowing up. She'd seen hundreds of tweets about it, and it'd made national TV news. Suspicion about Theo's role in Maggie's death was mounting, which was oddly satisfying. Finally, people were paying attention to him. Even some of his fans had turned on him online, commenting things like *Fuck you creep* and *You don't represent the gay community* and *Don't use queerness as a shield* under his recent posts. A reality TV gossip account had posted a paparazzi photo of a stricken-looking Theo taking out the trash in sweatpants and three-day old stubble with the caption *Reality bites*.

Her "brother-in-law" was a liar, and the public was catching on. Since their FaceTime confrontation after he'd slept with Jill, Emma had started to understand that Theo probably hadn't killed Maggie. He was too vapid to do something so evil.

Of course, after the story ran, Theo had sent an angry text. *Emma, what the fuck? Why would you talk to the reporter about this? I asked you not to. Going to the press never helps anything. This is sensitive for me, which you of all people should understand. I wasn't ready for my identity to be debated on national TV.* She questioned whether or not to respond. Yes, she'd gone on the record, but it'd been anonymously. And she hadn't told the press about his sham marriage to her sister, which she considered generous. Plus, he had no way to verify it was her.

She took a deep breath and drafted a text to Theo. *I don't owe you anything*, she wrote. *You're a liar and I hope you're held accountable for this. Don't feed me some sob story about coming out when we both know what really happened.* She pressed send before she could talk herself out of it. Jill called her, as if intuiting that she was spiraling. Jill had called six times over the last few days, and texted dozens more. She ignored the call, and then opened Jill's contact and pressed mute. It was a petty thing to do, but she needed space.

Then she sent another text. *Hi Finn, it's Emma Lathrop. Can we find a time to meet? I have some questions about my sister's life, and I was hoping you could help.*

He didn't respond right away, which gave her another hour to stew in her fury at Theo and Jill. But then her phone pinged with a text. *Sure, Emma. Good to hear from you. I'm happy to chat. On the phone or in person?*

*Let's meet in person,* she replied. *Coffee? Dinner?*

He responded a few minutes later. *Want to come for dinner next week? I've got a new pizza oven I'm testing out.* She paused to think about it. Was it weird that he wanted her to come over when they'd only met at the funeral? But then he texted again: *Is that over the top? Lol. I just feel like I know you from all the things Maggie's said over the years.*

That piqued her interest. So he'd stayed in touch with Maggie. Had they, perhaps, continued sleeping together? She'd have to find a tactful way to ask.

Emma, in her new, empty life at the Calabasas house, was making a habit of exploring the place, and sorting through her sister's stuff. Maggie's clothes were all still there, plus her wine collection, a small office and a glam room that also remained untouched. She started by cleaning out Maggie's massive closet, dividing things into piles: donate, keep, sell.

Emma wasn't a clothes or makeup person, but she wanted a few things with sentimental value. And she figured she could sell some of Maggie's fancier stuff and donate the proceeds. Today, Emma would explore Maggie's glam room, where she got her hair and makeup done and kept hundreds of products. She walked down the hall on the plush white carpeting and opened the door.

The room smelled of Maggie, specifically of the Le Labo perfume she'd wore every day after she'd made her *Love-Shack* money. Emma walked over to the vanity and found the perfume, spraying a small spritz into the air. Emma and Maggie had used to joke that Maggie had got rich just so she could afford her perfume habit.

Emma had learned of Maggie's perfume obsession on a belated birthday trip to New York for the first time thirteen years ago, when, for Emma's seventeenth birthday, Maggie bought her a plane ticket to come visit. Most of the money Maggie made then went toward her rent, which by New York standards was cheap, but by Kansas standards was exorbitant. Thus, it took her a little over a year to save the $250 for the plane fare. Emma was so excited for the trip that she'd created a countdown calendar for it, hanging it above her desk in the room she used to share with Maggie.

Emma flew out on Friday after school at the start of spring break. It was her first time on a plane, and she had a blast. The little TVs, the free soda—thrilling.

Maggie met her at JFK, where they took the AirTrain to the subway to the bus. It was also her first time on public transportation, unless you counted the school bus. Maggie seemed like an old pro, even though she'd only lived there a year. Emma watched in amazement as the subway lurched and Maggie stayed put, even though she wasn't holding on to anything.

The only real ideas Emma had about New York City had come from *Friends* and *Seinfeld*. So when she got to Maggie's railroad apartment in Bushwick, she was shocked. It wasn't shabby chic, like Rachel and Monica's place in *Friends*; it was just shabby. Maggie lived with eight roommates, and they didn't have a living room or working heat. There was just one bathroom, and even when the shower was turned all the way up, it let out an anemic trickle. When Maggie led Emma into her tiny room, Emma marveled that it was the size of a large closet.

"Less work for this piece of shit to do." Maggie kicked the space heater which lived on the floor next to her bed. "But yeah, I wasn't exaggerating."

"And you pay six hundred and fifty a month to live here? I don't get it."

"Well, it's near the subway. And Bushwick is cool." Maggie flopped on her bed and kicked off her shoes. They sat side by side on Maggie's bed for hours, catching up on their lives: Emma had a crush on someone in her math class; Maggie had a callback for an Office Depot commercial, and her least favorite roommate had moved out after getting a role in the chorus of a Broadway show.

"There's this lesbian bar I heard about in Gowanus," Maggie told her as she painted Emma's nails a royal blue. "If you want to go?"

Emma had come out to Maggie on the phone a few

months prior ("You've always been so authentically yourself," Maggie had said. "I'm proud of you." It was exactly what she'd needed to hear), and now Maggie was trying to plan a full evening of gay nightlife for her.

"I'm not twenty-one. Neither are you," Emma said, though excitement prickled through her at the suggestion.

"That's fine. We can borrow IDs from a couple of the girls here. I do it all the time."

"You do?" It was strange to think about Maggie's life here—drinking at bars, going to auditions, riding the subway.

"Yeah. Let's go. I think it'll be fun. Plus, you can show off your new manicure." Maggie giggled at the shade of the garish blue she'd painted Emma's nails.

Maggie kept her clothes in trash bags underneath her bed, and, after dumping all of her earthly possessions out onto her comforter, picked out an outfit for Emma: fishnets, a frayed black denim miniskirt, and a red tube top. Emma had to admit, it was perfect. She even had knock-off Doc Martens to wear with it.

That's when Maggie showed her the perfume collection she'd amassed. It was mostly made up of drugstore knock-offs of designer perfumes, but she had one prized possession: Juicy Couture's Viva La Juicy. Maggie let Emma spray a bit on her wrist to smell it. It was sweet, floral, and not at all subtle.

"Isn't it incredible?" Maggie asked.

"Definitely," she lied. The bottle was rectangular with a fake crystal stopper, topped with a pink bow. Attached to the bow were two charms: a "J" for Juicy, and a little terrier dog. Emma held the little terrier in her fingers.

"Take it." Maggie removed the charm.

"Really?" Emma asked, and Maggie nodded.

She stuck the charm on her keychain where it lived until she was in her senior year of college, when she transferred it to a necklace.

Many years later, for Maggie's thirtieth birthday, Emma bought her sister a bracelet and attached a matching terrier charm on it, which she'd hunted down on eBay for an exorbitant amount of money. Since Maggie had died, Emma hadn't removed her necklace once. When she found herself playing with it, she tried to remember the trip: that first time on the subway, the smell of roasted peanuts, the taste of her first good bagel. It helped a little. Not a lot, but a little.

Her phone dinged, and the sound brought her back to the present. Theo had responded. *Em, it was complicated with your sister, like I said.* God, it was irritating that he thought he could call her "Em." *I don't know what to tell you. Maggie and I made a business decision, and we knew it would work only if we didn't tell anyone. Not even our management knew. Still shitty of you to go to the press . . .* She put her phone down. She couldn't read any more.

# Amanda

Trevor was there with her, in the flesh, in their old favorite pub. It didn't feel real. He looked emaciated. He had a shaved head, a mustache. He wore his usual denim jacket with Prince on the back and a sweatshirt underneath, and black Doc Martens. He looked as if he hadn't seen the sun in years.

"I'll leave you to it," George said.

"I'm so sorry," she told him, remembering their plan for later. "Let's reschedule."

Had Trevor seen them kiss? She put the thought out of her mind as she pulled him into a tight hug. "Is it really you?" She could feel his ribcage through his sweatshirt.

"Can you make less of a scene?" Trevor whispered, escaping the hug.

"I'm not making a scene," she said, wounded.

They left the pub together, entering the cool London night. Trevor walked at a clip, staring straight ahead. He pulled the hood over his head. "Sorry I interrupted your date."

So he *had* seen them kiss. Her cheeks burned. Why was she so embarrassed? "It wasn't a date."

"Sure," he said, picking up the pace.

"Where are we going?" she asked.

"Piccadilly. Where I'm staying. Somewhere private."

"Trev, I can't believe it's really you."

He ignored her. "Why are you in London?"

"I had some work meetings." She was slightly out of breath from how fast they were walking. "I promise I wasn't stalking you. But I really wanted to find you."

"Oh, I'm aware."

She felt a burst of shame. "I missed you."

"I missed you, too," he said, and it made her heart speed up. That was something, at least. She considered, not for the first time, whether she was in love with him. The strong rush of emotion at hearing even the smallest validation from him made it seem as if the answer was yes. But it was also possible she was so fucked up that even a tiny bit of male attention was enough to make her feel something. That's what her therapist would say.

They walked in an awkward silence for the next minute before Amanda couldn't take it anymore. "I have to admit, I'm a bit confused. I thought you'd be happier to see me. Given that you've been living like a bandit."

Trevor's hands were balled into fists, and he was cracking his knuckles one by one. "Happy to see you? Sure. But I didn't disappear with the intention of being found, so you have to see why I'm a little disturbed. Do you want to explain why you've been chasing after me since I left?"

"I've been trying to find you. That's not 'chasing.'" Her heart clenched with the sting of this.

"Oh, come on. I know you hired a private detective."

"I . . ." She wanted to explain, but found herself without words. It felt like a punch in the gut. "That was months ago. I really just wanted to find you. I was worried." Tears formed in her eyes.

"Please stop crying," he said. "I wish you hadn't come to London to look for me."

"I didn't!" she said. "I'm actually working on this new TV show and had some meetings out here. Plus, my friend Emma was here to look in to her sister Maggie Lathrop's death, and I wanted to support her, because Maggie was on *LoveShack* a few seasons ago."

"Oh, I know all about Maggie Lathrop." He chuckled. "Your guilt about *LoveShack* has always been so over the top."

She ignored him. "Why are you laughing? Someone died. For the fourth time. Someone from our stupid show."

"You always take so much responsibility. Has it ever occurred to you that maybe the world doesn't revolve around you? That maybe Maggie's death has nothing to do with you at all?"

"I'm not saying it does. But also, what do you know about Maggie Lathrop?"

"More than you'd think," he said. "Let's get to my place and I'll tell you."

They walked in silence for another three blocks, until he led her through an alley to the back of what she recognized to be the Ritz-Carlton. She was stunned—it probably cost £2,000 a night. Even she wouldn't spend that kind of money on accommodation. Two security guards opened the door for him, and he led Amanda to a service elevator. The elevator let them out on the fifth floor, and they walked quickly until he got to his suite. She was surprised to see it had its own sitting room, with tufted baby blue couches and gold wallpaper. It wasn't her taste, and wasn't Trevor's, either.

"How can you afford this?" He ignored her, so she continued. "Look, I can tell you're really pissed at me, but can I just say I'm glad to see you? Even if it took me tracking you down for years. I'm just glad you're alive."

He sat down on the couch, and she sat across from him. "This is so like you. You never know when to just stop. Going to Charlie to get my number? That's insane." Her expression probably betrayed her surprise, because he kept going. "You know, that was just a guess. But from the look on your face, I can see I'm right."

"Don't be mad at Charlie," she said. "I made him tell me."

"There are so many worse things to be mad at you about, Amanda. Like that private detective you hired contacting me nonstop for fucking months. I had to delete all my email addresses and change my number. He tried to pay off my mom so she'd tell him where I was. Why would you send someone like that after me?"

"I was just trying to find you. You're making it sound like I was doing something bad," she said. "I'm the one who should be mad at you. You basically ruined my career."

"I never told you to defend me in the press. I would never have asked that of you."

Now she rolled her eyes. "Come on. Of course I was going to do that. You're my best friend and I was in a vulnerable place. We'd just had sex. I thought I knew you better than those women." This was humiliating. "Plus, I was using. I wasn't thinking straight. What did you think was going to happen?"

"Please don't play the victim here," Trevor said. "I left my life, my home, my job, my friends, everything. I didn't ask you to defend me. I wouldn't have asked you that. It was never about you. You always make everything about you."

Cowed, she stared at her shoes. "OK."

Trevor continued, his anger building. "Don't 'OK' me, Amanda. Why are you really here? Do you want to make me feel guilty for leaving? Or maybe you want to find out if I actually did all the things I was accused of?"

"Come on, let's not do this. It's me you're talking to, not the *Times*. I'm sure you did what the women said. Why would you run away for so long if you hadn't?"

He snorted. "Wow. So if I did those things, why are you even here?"

This made her pause. Why *was* she there? What did she want from him? Suddenly, those questions felt of actual, immediate importance. "I'm not a hundred percent sure," she admitted. "I guess I thought I could convince you to come back. Like, even if you did assault those women, I don't understand why you ran away. It's not like getting canceled is even that big a deal anymore. Everyone gets canceled. I got canceled for defending you! And I'm working again. You just need to apologize and say you're going to get help and then quietly reemerge after six months. It's not that hard."

He laughed bitterly. "I'm not coming back. I don't want to be burned at the stake. I'm not interested in that. And I'm not going to apologize. I'm not a rapist or an abuser. That's all bullshit."

"So you're disputing everything the women said?"

"I'm disputing the idea that it was nonconsensual."

"So you consensually penetrated each of them with a rose quartz dildo?"

"Yes." He sighed as if she was some sort of idiot.

"Why would they all have come forward, then? Why would they have lied about it?"

"I don't know. Attention? Pursuit of cultural capital?" Trevor said.

She grimaced. It was as if someone had kidnapped the real Trevor and replaced him with some incel loser.

There was a long silence as she figured out what to say. "Can we talk about something else? Like what you think you know about Maggie? Or maybe you can tell me why you're living in the Ritz?" It was bonkers that she hadn't been able to find him until now. He'd been right there, in Piccadilly, all this time. She'd imagined him in some former Soviet bloc country, living in a hovel.

"Why not live here? I make enough money, and people here are discreet. It's the kind of place where oil barons live with their mistresses. Stuff like that. Good security—I can go in through the back entrance. I don't leave much."

She cackled. "God, you think you're so important, that people would be harassing you on the street if you walked around without your hood up or came in through the front door. It's embarrassing."

He rolled his eyes at this. "Again, you literally sent a private investigator after me. I wanted privacy."

"I paid some random guy I found online a thousand bucks to look for you. Don't flatter yourself."

"Still."

"How can you afford to live here?" she asked.

He sat silently for a moment. "I'd rather not get into it."

Was he dealing drugs or something? Trafficking women? "Are you kidding? Can you just tell me how you get to live like a king while existing without any footprint—"

"Ethereum," he said. "Selling Ethereum."

Was that some sort of new drug? She was trying to remember if she'd heard anything about it in rehab. "I'm not following."

"Cryptocurrency. Like Bitcoin." He rolled his eyes. "I was holed up after everything happened, and I started spending time on Reddit. I learned all about crypto. It's actually amazing. It's the future of all commerce. It's untraceable and there's so much opportunity there. It's going to change the world. It's already changing the world."

She stifled a laugh. "Seriously? You're a crypto bro now? You've always been money-obsessed, so I'm not surprised."

"What's that supposed to mean?"

"Come on. Don't play dumb. You know what happened with *LoveShack*."

He gave her a look. "Don't be a conspiracy theorist."

"Oh, please. You got me kicked out of that writers' room, admit it. You were all-too-willing to be whatever they needed, to turn a blind eye to all the fucked-up stuff. And now look at what's happened. Four fucking people are dead! And you know what I think? I think the

*LoveShack* curse is bullshit. It's not a curse if it's the very logical result of the show's actions."

He snorted. "You got kicked out of the writers' room for being a pain in the ass."

Maybe there was some truth in that. She remembered sitting next to Priya during a writing session on *LoveShack*, watching back footage from the fourth episode. One of the contestants, the MMA fighter Mack with an aggravated assault charge, was predictably volatile.

"We've paired him with Shelby for Paradise Island," Priya began, "because she's a virgin. 'Saving herself for marriage' situation. Which we're going to reveal later in this episode." It turned out the viewer votes didn't matter. The producers paired whoever they thought would cause the most chaos.

The date was worse than Amanda had predicted it'd be. After an awkward Paradise Island date, like all couples, they were forced to spend the night together in the fancy tent with only one bed. He surprised Shelby by getting into bed naked, and when he moved toward her, she screamed, clutching the cross that hung around her neck. The producers and Trevor laughed.

"I feel bad for her," Amanda said, before she could stop herself.

Priya looked at her. "You do? Because she's in bed with a very attractive naked man?"

"Because she's clearly being violated," Amanda said. Trevor kicked her under the table.

Priya rolled her eyes, and the footage kept rolling. Matt

leaned over to kiss Shelby, but she backed away. "Hey, what the fuck?" he said.

"I don't want this," Shelby said. "Can you give me some space? Put on some boxers?"

"Stuck-up bitch," he muttered.

Shelby cried and cried, and the camera lingered on her face.

Priya pressed pause. "Any snarky voice-over ideas here?"

"How am I supposed to write something funny about this?" Amanda said.

Priya pursed her lips. "If this is so hard for you, I think you should leave."

"Seriously?" Amanda looked at Trevor for reinforcement, but he was staring at the table.

"Yes. All you do is come in here and complain. For a comedic writer, you've got no sense of humor about any of this. I think Trevor can handle it on his own."

"Come on. Don't do this," Amanda said. Their contracts stipulated that they'd be paid 25 percent up front for the rights and for their initial writing work, but would get the rest of the money after completing the voice-over script for all twelve episodes. "Trevor, can you, like, vouch for me?"

He just shrugged.

"I should've never accepted your apology about *LoveShack*," Amanda said. After she'd been fired, Trevor had continued. He'd been fully compensated, and because she hadn't been, he'd got a nice bonus equaling roughly the size of what would've been her remaining salary. When she'd confronted him about it, he'd apologized but had said there was nothing he could do. He'd then taken her out for a nice dinner and had bought them a lot of cocaine. Because she'd been twenty-four and stupid and probably in love with him, she'd let it drop. "And I should've blown the whistle on all the messed-up shit we did to those people, but I was scared."

"God, you really think *LoveShack* is any worse than any other reality show? Grow up." He ran a hand across his shaved head, and she could see that his nails were yellowed and bitten down to the quick. "You think those people died because of you? Because of us? You're a narcissist, Amanda."

"I'm a narcissist? Are you kidding? I'm not the one who went into hiding because I was scared of some bad press."

"I was wrongly accused," he said. "I told you that. I didn't want to stick around just to get crucified."

"I see you're not going to own up to any of this rape stuff. So I'll leave. But can I ask you something stupid?" Amanda said, before she could lose her nerve. He said nothing in response, so she kept going. She took a deep breath. "Why not me?"

"Why *not you*?" Trevor asked. "What are you talking about?"

"Why didn't you do the . . . the dildo thing to me?" Her cheeks burned.

"What do you mean?" This was the first time since they'd reunited that he seemed genuinely taken aback.

"I don't know how I can ask this more clearly. Why didn't you—consensually or nonconsensually—penetrate me with a goddamn rose quartz dildo?"

"God, Amanda, is this what it's all been about? You want

to know why I didn't fuck you with a crystal dildo?" He rubbed the knuckle of his right index finger across his brow in exasperation. "Because I can, if you want."

"Oh, shut up. I'm just trying to understand."

He considered this for a moment, and then spoke. "It just wasn't something I'd enjoy doing with you."

"And why is that?" she asked.

"Oh, come on, don't make me spell it out," he said.

"I'm genuinely at a loss here, Trevor."

"It wasn't like that with you. I only did it with women who I thought were sexually open-minded. Obviously, I was wrong, because they were actually not chill at all."

"You need help," she said.

"Maybe so. But you need to move on," Trevor said. "I really do have a lot of love for you, Manda, but this is pathetic. I'm not going back to deal with industry idiots who all think I am some sort of serial rapist. I'm not going through a Hollywood kangaroo court."

"Believe me, I'll be moving on." She said this with more conviction than she felt. "But when did you become this cartoon villain?"

He snorted. "That's rich, Amanda."

"I wanted to find you because the idea of spending the rest of my life without my best friend felt too painful." Her voice cracked. "But this has obviously been a horrible idea."

"Amanda, if I'd wanted to be found, I would've gotten in contact," he said, a bit more gently. She had no idea what to say to that, so they both sat silently for a beat. "I think it's time for this reunion to end."

"I agree," she lied, swallowing down tears. It was

masochistic, but the idea of leaving and never seeing him again made her feel slightly ill. "But first, tell me what you know about Maggie. If you actually know anything."

He sighed. "First, can you tell me why you're so invested in this?"

"Emma Lathrop is my friend. I owe it to her to use my power and positionality to help."

He laughed. "Oh, your 'power and positionality.' How brave."

"Shut up, Trevor.'" She was suddenly enraged. "I'm trying to help my friend find out why her sister was killed. That's all."

"Might be good to focus on yourself for a little while instead, eh?" He chuckled.

Had he always been this much of an asshole? She wanted to smack him. "What is wrong with you?"

He smiled, but it was a menacing, cruel smile. It made her stomach churn. "Look, I just hope inserting yourself into other people's problems continues to be meaningful for you."

"Oh, fuck off. I'm leaving. I won't stay here while you ridicule me." Her hands shook violently as she walked toward the door. "And I don't believe you know the first thing about the murder. About any of it."

"I don't?" he said.

There was a spark of malice in his expression that scared her. "Please tell me you weren't somehow involved."

"God, no. You really think I'm a monster."

"Please just tell me what you know."

Trevor smirked. "It's ridiculous, but I'm in a group chat

with this murder-y guy who definitely killed Maggie. He's obsessed with her."

She gripped the door handle. "Excuse me?"

"You heard me." He stood up and walked closer to her.

"I don't understand." She turned around to face him.

"Someone added me a while back to some 'canceled men of TV' Telegram group chat and I look at it from time to time because it's fucking hilarious. All these sad-sap morons. Lots of guys from *LoveShack*, funnily enough. It's a real who's who of the most pitiful men of Hollywood."

"Charming. But I'm sure you couldn't find anything the police didn't." She turned back around. But she still wasn't leaving. Why wasn't she leaving? Why couldn't she bring herself to actually go? She willed her legs to move.

"Well, your private detective didn't find me, and you could," he teased. He had a point. "I'm just trying to be helpful. Feed your new hobby. Look in to that guy Patrick from her season of *LoveShack*. He writes deranged shit about her in the group, like, daily. 'She was a stupid cunt, she's a fake bitch and a liar, she deserved to die.' The whole nine yards."

"That makes no sense. Why would he do that in a group chat?"

"He's a moron. That's what I was saying. It's actually funny how stupid and pathetic these guys are. They think the Telegram app is 'encrypted' and therefore nothing they say is traceable. Who knows. Anyway, as pleasant as this has been, you should probably go now."

She paused while she let this news sink in. She could have snapped back at him that he was obviously one of these pathetic guys; he was no better than they were. Or she could've asked more questions about Patrick.

There were so many more things to say, but she had to get out. So finally—finally—she turned the doorknob, and walked away.

# Maggie

### Reunion Episode

The entire *LoveShack* cast sat together on the giant beige couch at the center of a Glendale soundstage, women on one side and men on the other. Though Maggie had spent almost two months on-camera filming the show, having the mic on again under the bright lights made her claustrophobic. She felt the urge to bolt, but instead crossed her legs, as if strapping herself down on a gurney. Anything could happen, and she'd just have to sit there. Layla or Finn could confront her on camera, Patrick could throw a fit, anyone could reveal her relationship with Theo was fake—she would still be contractually obligated to sit in her seat or risk a lawsuit from the network.

Schuyler emerged, speaking to the cast. "Hey, team. I've missed you! Have you missed me?" Everyone shuffled uncomfortably. "Wow, OK. Not feeling the love tonight! That's OK."

"Can we just get started?" Finn asked. Maggie wished she'd found a moment alone with him before the show had started filming, to smooth things over. But the producers had whisked Maggie away right after Layla had left her trailer to film some B-roll, and she hadn't got the opportunity.

"Yes, let's dive in!" Schuyler said. "Actually, let's start with you, Finn, America's hottest veteran. How is life post-*Shack*? Are you and Layla still together?" Maggie clenched her jaw. Why'd he have to call on Finn first?

"We're not, no," Layla cut in.

"Oh, is that so? Do tell!" Schuyler said.

"It's not an exciting story," Finn said quickly.

"I disagree, actually," Layla said with a tight smile.

"Care to explain?" Schuyler said.

"It was me; it was my fault," Finn said. "There's someone I reconnected with out here. Someone I'm trying to get to know more. Layla is great; it had nothing to do with her."

"Interesting." Schuyler clapped his hands together. "An old flame?" Maggie's heart pounded. What was Finn going for here?

"Um, not really." Finn, usually so composed, turned red. "I don't want to say just yet. Things are super private between us. And I don't know where we stand at the moment."

"Cryptic!" Schuyler said. "Layla, how are you feeling?"

"I'm not surprised," Layla said. "Finn was very willing to throw me away for a new, shinier object."

"Women aren't objects," Finn said. "That's a hurtful way of talking about this situation."

"Please spare me." Layla rolled her eyes. "If you actually cared about women, you wouldn't have been such a piece of shit to me."

Although Maggie didn't enjoy watching Finn get raked over the coals on live television, it didn't seem as though

Layla was going to tell on Maggie and Theo, at least not yet. She felt some part of herself relax. She imagined she was sitting next to Finn, that she could take his hand.

"I'm sorry, Layla," Finn said, changing tactics. "I really am. I messed up. You have every right to be angry."

"Whatever," she said. "I'm done talking about this. It's stupid." Layla turned to Maggie and gave her a look that could've only been described as murderous. But Maggie understood that it meant: *You're in luck, bitch, I'm not going to come for you. Tonight.*

"Well then!" Schuyler said, changing the subject as his teleprompter scrolled on. The screens around them lit up with the *LoveShack* logo, and Maggie knew flashbacks were coming. "It was a season of highs and lows, romance and betrayal, love and lust. Let's take a look at the shocking twists and turns on this season of *LoveShack*."

A highlight reel began. The cast stared, enraptured with the footage of themselves. There was Luke, licking whipped cream out of Chloe's cleavage. There was Theo, blow-drying his hair. There was Felicia, crying after getting eliminated. There was Maggie, straddling Patrick—*shit*. She cringed at the memory. It was her, in her bikini, looking uncomfortable as Patrick gripped her thighs so tightly that she couldn't move. Then there was the Choice Point, and her choosing Theo. It was strange to see herself on the screen, so vulnerable and scared. She looked over at Patrick, and could see his fists were balled. More clips played: the cast members at an elimination ceremony; Layla and Finn on a date at the animal shelter; Bryan jumping into the pool naked.

"What a season!" Schuyler said as the video wrapped.

He began questioning Luke and Chloe about the whipped-cream incident, and Maggie tried to breathe. She hoped to get out of this reunion unscathed, with just a softball Q & A session with Theo at the end. But just as the tension in her shoulders released, Schuyler switched gears.

"So tell me, Patrick. Looking back, does it still hurt that you got ditched by Maggie during your Paradise Island date?" he said. Maggie's cheeks reddened. She pictured herself getting up and walking off the stage, never to engage with this stupid franchise again. It would feel so good.

"Definitely not," Patrick said. "Let's just say that maybe Maggie had her fun that night. She wanted a ride on all the bicycles, if you know what I mean."

Before she could stop herself, she cut in. "I'm sorry, what does that even mean? Are you guys supposed to be the bicycles?"

"I mean, you saw the clip."

"To be crystal clear, I chose Theo because I was not, and will never be, interested in you. You're a loser. I only kissed you back out of pity. That's all it was." God, it felt good to just say it.

"For all the viewers at home," Tia chimed in, "I just wanted to say, Patrick really is the worst. I'm team Maggie all the way here." There were murmurs of agreement and snaps from the rest of the women, including, surprisingly, Layla. Maggie couldn't help but smile.

"Fuck you all," Patrick said. "I'm not going to sit here and be insulted by a bunch of ugly whores."

Maggie was shocked to see Patrick actually walk off the stage; he must not be worried about a lawsuit from the network. "That's the best you could do?" Layla called after him. "There are plenty of things it makes sense to call us, but ugly isn't one of them."

The rest of the reunion was a breeze, comparatively. Maggie and Theo gushed about how in love they were, doing as much PDA as they could handle. Chloe and Bryan were interviewed about a petty disagreement between them. Schuyler botched some teleprompter line-reads. And when the producers gestured to him to wrap up, Maggie breathed a sigh of relief.

After surviving the reunion, the cast was forced to attend an after-party at the restaurant owned by a TV chef who had a major cooking show on the network. Maggie was still getting used to this aspect of her new fame: now, it mattered where she went, because someone like a famous TV chef would want her to be seen at their place.

By the time the cars dropped them off at the restaurant, Maggie's feet were sore, and she was sick of wearing her dress and a full face of makeup. She wished she were home, lying on the couch with Finn. But she had to at least make an appearance at the after-party, especially if she wanted to keep the network happy. She prayed that there would be no more run-ins with Layla or Patrick. Patrick was apparently so angry about their on-stage confrontation that he'd thrown a chair at the wall in one of the dressing rooms.

The party was on the back patio of the restaurant, and it was lit up with twinkly lights and a stone fire pit. Waiters came through with hors d'oeuvres, and she grabbed the first thing that came her way—little black balls on a couple of potato chips. It was delicious: salty and briny. And it was the first non-egg meal she'd had in days.

"Enjoying that?" Priya asked. Maggie had been so engrossed with the food that she hadn't noticed her old producer come up behind her.

"Yes, it's amazing." Maggie licked her fingers. "I've never had that before. Do you know what it is?"

Priya broke into a laugh. "You're so cute. It's caviar on a potato chip."

Maggie wanted to die. "Oh," she said. "Yes, obviously. Sorry, I've never had caviar before."

"You're about to enter a whole new universe." Priya handed her a glass of champagne from a waiter's tray. "Cheers to your new life."

As they clinked their glasses together and sipped their champagne, Maggie tried not to say anything else humiliating. Finn approached her, and her heart sped up. She hadn't talked to him since the botched conversation about her intention to marry Theo.

"Can I grab you, Maggie?" he asked. Priya eyed them suspiciously, but Maggie ignored her.

"Sure," Maggie said. It was doubly annoying that he was mad at her, because if he wasn't, she'd grill him about why he'd told Layla everything about them, and about her fake relationship with Theo. But she didn't have the upper hand right now.

She followed his lead through the restaurant and out the front. "Where are we going?" she asked.

"I want to talk somewhere where people won't see us," he said as they walked down Santa Monica Boulevard.

Maggie checked behind her shoulder, relieved that no one had followed them.

The night was cool, and it felt good to be walking, even though her feet hurt. "Finn, I'm really sorry. I know that marrying Theo will hurt you."

He sighed. "I want to forgive you, I really do. I know the deal with you and Theo. I know you need the money. But you have to admit you're gaslighting me."

"I'm gaslighting you?" Her heart pounded.

"You tell me you're into me but then your actions say otherwise. It's fucked up."

She sat with this for a second. "I think gaslighting is a strong word. But I'm sorry you feel that way." Was it gaslighting to question whether or not she'd really gaslit him? She wasn't sure.

"See, you can't even say you're sorry. You're just 'sorry I feel that way.' Do you see why that's fucked up?"

"I am genuinely sorry," she said. "I know this sucks for you. But it's one and a half million, and it's not real, I—"

He cut her off. "You know what? I don't want to hear it. I'm leaving. I'm done." Before she could process what he'd said, he started walking back to the restaurant.

Her heart pounded. No no no no. This was all wrong.

"I love you," she yelled, shocking herself. It'd just slipped out. She couldn't—she wouldn't—lose him. She needed to make him understand how much she cared, even if it was a little premature to be declaring her love.

He stopped where he was. She could see his shoulders visibly untense. When he turned around, there were tears in his eyes. His voice was quiet, almost a whisper. "Maggie, I love you too. I've loved you since the first day I saw you at that stupid Hot or Not game with your kind smile and your gorgeous eyes."

"Wow, Finn." She was filled with relief, even though his description of her felt a little . . . generic? As if he was reading from a script. Had he really fallen in love at first sight?

"That's all I wanted to hear from you, honestly," he continued. "I just needed to know that you loved me. That one day it will be us walking down the aisle. That we will start a big, loud family together. We'll make up for everything you never had growing up. We'll watch Royals games and do backyard barbecues and play board games and put the sprinklers on for the kids to run through . . ." He trailed off. Did he mean all of that literally? It sounded nice, but she wasn't sure she even wanted kids. Now was not the time to debate this, she figured. He ran over, pulling her into a hug. She couldn't help looking around to check that no one saw them.

"We can make this work," she said. "I know we can. I just need some time."

"You promise you'll annul the marriage, like you said?" He grabbed her hand. She relaxed into him, and he put his arm around her.

"I promise."

He nodded, but his eyebrows were furrowed. "And the only time you'll kiss Theo or do anything sexual with him will be at the altar? Nothing else?"

"Of course." It was a slightly annoying question, given that she'd already told Finn that Theo was gay.

At that, he kissed her square on the mouth. She melted a little bit. It was going to be OK.

# Emma

She sat at Maggie's desk and examined it, running her fingers across the grain. It was L-shaped, and the wood was bleached oak. She opened the drawer where Maggie stored her important documents, like tax stuff, but also her letters and cards and planners. She'd already looked through the drawer every morning that week—it'd become a ritual. It made her feel closer to her sister, though it also reminded her of being seven years old when she'd leaf through Maggie's diary when she wasn't home.

There were birthday cards from Theo's parents and a few of her friends. It was sweet that she'd kept those, but they didn't contain anything useful. She opened Maggie's planner from the prior year, which she'd only used a few times. She willed something useful to materialize, even though she'd already read through it many times.

In December, Maggie had written out her weekly appointments: *9am cookware photoshoot – 393 Dawson Ave*. Maggie and Theo's short-lived cookware line had been discontinued when their spatulas had been recalled for containing lead. That day, she'd also written *2pm Dr S consult*. Dr. Schwartz was Maggie's trusted plastic surgeon who did all of her injectables. It was all so normal, so unhelpful. She closed the planner and pulled out Maggie's holiday cards that she'd received just six months ago. The first one was from Theo's *LoveShack* friend Bryan, who now had a wife and cute kid. The family posed together in front of some apple trees, wearing fall clothes and looking happy. A pang of sadness hit her in the gut—for Maggie, and the life she'd never get to live. She turned the card over and looked at the next one, which was from Maggie's agent. And then there was one from a famous chef, and one from another LA influencer couple they were friends with. She returned them to the drawer, and picked up the planner to put it back too. But as she held it, she realized the back cover was much thicker than the front.

She'd already examined the inner pockets on both covers a million times, and they were empty. But this time, she lifted the back flap and felt around the corners, just to be sure something small wasn't in there. It was then that she felt something—some thick paper—stuck to the cover. Her heart beat quickly as she ripped the flap off and began peeling the paper off. It took her a second to realize what it was: an envelope. The envelope glue had melted and stuck to the inside of the planner. Emma opened it and pulled it out. The police must've missed this when they'd gone through Maggie's stuff.

It was addressed to just Theo, which was weird. She examined the return address to see if it provided a clue as to who it was from or why Maggie had kept it. The address in the top left corner read *23 Louder Ln, Unit B, Tempe, AZ, 85202*, but there was no name. Emma felt the blood drain from her face as it dawned on her: she knew the blocky handwriting. She opened her phone to check the photo of the threatening note Maggie had received. *End it, or I'll tell everyone your secret.* It was the same fucking handwriting.

If this was really Theo's handwriting and the note was an inside joke between him and Maggie, why would he have written a letter to himself from Arizona? And why would Maggie have kept the envelope? This had to be related to her murder. And if it was the envelope the note was sent in, who would've been stupid enough to include a return address on it? Maybe it was fake. But there was no way in hell Theo had written the note. Had the police even done a handwriting check? Probably not, she realized. Theo had gotten to LaClair so early on in the investigation.

She sent Theo a text with a photo of the envelope with: *Why would you lie about this???* She stared at it, turning it over in her hands, willing it to give her more information. And then it dawned on her.

The note was clearly from someone, to Theo, threatening him to end "it"—what was "it"?—or they'd tell everyone his secret. Which was, she now understood, that he was queer. Of course.

She googled the return address. 23 Louder Lane was a small apartment complex five minutes away from the Arizona State campus, and the White Pages indicated a 31-year-old man named D. TRUMAN lived in Unit B. She texted Liz: *Just found this in Maggie's stuff.* She attached a photo of the note, plus the screenshots of her Google searches. *No clue who D. Truman is.*

Liz responded right away: *I'm on it.*

Theo's text also came in. *I couldn't tell them it was addressed to me or they'd know I had a secret. I guess it doesn't matter now, but I'm sorry for lying. I have no idea who sent it or why, but I think they wanted me to "end it" with Maggie.* And then: *My lawyer says I can't talk to you anymore, so don't contact me.*

Emma ignored Theo and texted Liz back. *Should I turn this in to the police?*

*Yes*, Liz wrote. *ASAP.* Emma's heart pounded.

# Amanda

Emma answered on the second ring. "Manda? Everything OK?"

Amanda looked at her watch and realized it was 11:12 p.m. She was out of sorts from jet lag, and everything that had happened in London with Trevor. "I didn't realize how late it was. I can call you tomorrow."

"It's OK. What's up?"

Amanda had scheduled an emergency appointment with Beth for the next day, and had gone to two Narcotics Anonymous meetings since she'd been back. She hadn't even told Jill she was home, even though she'd been calling incessantly. Amanda felt that urge to crawl out of her own skin—a feeling she used to fight off with amphetamines. She wanted to claw at herself, to take a scalding hot shower until her skin was red and raw. She needed to do something, anything, to make the feeling go away. "I think Patrick from your sister's *LoveShack* season may have had something to do with her death," she said. Best to rip the Band-Aid off.

"Yeah?"

"I found Trevor in London. Trevor Koch. And he told me about this situation with Patrick—some sort of 'canceled men' group chat they're both in. Apparently Patrick is a real creep and is saying violent, horrible things about Maggie."

"Holy shit. Do you have screenshots?" Emma asked.

Amanda sighed. "He wasn't particularly cooperative. I don't have any more information, sadly. But we can do some research into Patrick."

"I'll talk to Liz," Emma said. "So what happened with Trevor? I didn't even know you were looking for him."

"I couldn't help trying to find him." Amanda was surprised to hear the truth come out of her mouth. "It was stupid, though."

Emma was silent for a moment. "Are you OK?"

"Just tired," Amanda said. "I feel a little bit like a dog who caught its tail. I'm not sure what I was hoping for." She sounded dejected, she knew. "You should just be prepared that all of this won't necessarily make you feel better. Finding out who killed Maggie isn't going to bring her back."

"Of course, Amanda. I know. But what happened over there? You don't sound like yourself."

"Really. I'm fine." She wasn't.

"I'm here if you need anything," Emma said. "Call me any time."

When they hung up, Amanda sat on her bed. Before she knew it, tears clouded her eyes.

## Emma

"Did you sleep?" Liz asked over the phone.

"Not a wink." The adrenaline from Amanda's call the night before had kept her awake. She'd immediately texted Liz the information about Patrick, and then spent the rest of the night staring at the ceiling.

"Same," Liz said. "I think I figured out who D. Truman is."

"That was fast." Sweat broke out along her hairline.

"Go to Patrick O'Connell's Instagram. His handle is DJPatDaddy," Liz said.

Emma opened the app, and found him. It seemed like a run-of-the-mill DJ Instagram—he had 149,000 followers, and the requisite shirtless pictures in Miami and Ibiza playing for crowds. "What am I looking at?"

"Go to tagged photos. It's the second-to-last post."

Emma's palms went clammy as she scrolled. The post in question was a photo of Patrick, standing next to moving boxes. Someone named Dante Truman had tagged him, and the location Tempe, Arizona. *New crib with the roomie LFG*, read the caption. Emma's chest constricted. So Patrick had lived on Louder Lane with D. Truman. "Oh my God, you're a genius. What do we do?" She'd already notified the police about the envelope. They'd sent an officer to the house to collect it, but she still hadn't heard anything about them reopening the investigation.

"I'll do some light research on him. And we'll go from there," Liz said.

Emma agreed, and they hung up.

She then spent a dazed hour on the phone with the LAPD, getting shuffled from office to office before finally getting connected to the interim detective replacing LaClair and explaining Patrick's connection to Louder Lane. She still had no idea why Patrick might want Theo to end things with Maggie, or how he knew Theo's secret.

As she got off the call, a text from Finn came in. He offered to pick her up later that afternoon. She'd forgotten she'd made plans with him, and she didn't feel like spending time with someone new today. She wanted to brainstorm how to find out more about Patrick; Liz was going to come over after work tomorrow to discuss it. But maybe Finn would have some context on his castmate.

When he got to the Calabasas house around six, she buzzed him through the gate into the massive driveway. He drove a red Tesla, and as he got closer, she saw he was dressed casually in a gray hoodie.

"It's good to see you again. Under slightly better circumstances?" He smiled warmly as she got in the car, and she remembered how she'd liked him at the funeral. He drove out of the neighborhood in the relaxed but aggressive manner she associated with straight men who believed unwaveringly in their own competence.

They made polite small talk for a few minutes, and Finn

talked about a project he was working on—some sort of Instagram thing where people could donate to create care packages for kids with enlisted parents. They got to his place quickly; it was only ten minutes away. In Los Angeles, that was like being roommates.

"Wow. You live so close," she said, and he nodded.

"Yep. It's true. I once saw some stupid tabloid article calling this slice of Calabasas 'reality star row.'"

"That's nauseating." She was pleased when he laughed at this. "When was the last time you were there? At Maggie and Theo's?"

"Oh. I actually haven't been there since right after they bought it, I think," he said.

"You've got a good memory, then," she said.

"What do you mean?" he asked.

"Well, you remembered where they lived. You didn't ask me for the address."

"I'm good with stuff like that." He turned red. Maybe she'd embarrassed him.

They got out of the car and she followed him inside. His place, compared to Maggie and Theo's, was modest. It was a chalet, built into the side of a hill. He led her to the backyard, where there were chairs and a table set up by the pool.

"This is a great place." She liked it way more than her sister's. It felt like somewhere an actual person lived.

"Thanks," Finn said. "I like it."

"My sister always had so many staff around. It felt totally different than this." She took a seat.

"I'm not really like that," he said. "I appreciate having the place to myself. Having all those staff is kind of exhausting." He offered her a beer, which she accepted, and began heating up the pizza oven.

"This is great," she said. "Thank you for having me."

"My pleasure," he said. "I really miss your sister. It's nice to hang out with you." This made her want to cry, but she took a sip of her beer instead. Was this the moment to mention that she knew he and Maggie had slept together? She couldn't decide, so she said nothing. Maybe after she drained her beer it would feel easier.

"It's nice to hang out with you, too," she said.

He smiled. "Let's grab the dough from the fridge. I bought it from this great bakery nearby. We can add toppings in the kitchen."

She followed him back into the house, and they decorated their pizzas with various ingredients. Emma chose mushrooms and red onions, and he put pepperoni and burrata on his. She was impressed that he, a random straight man who lived alone, had purchased burrata for them.

As they made their way back out to the pizza oven, she saw him eyeing her wrist. She'd forgotten to put a Band-Aid on before she left.

"That looks painful," Finn said.

"Oh, it's nothing," she said, embarrassed. "A bad habit. I scratch it unconsciously. After Maggie died it got a lot worse. It's gross, I'm sorry."

"Not at all," he said. "We all have our things. I'm a big nail-biter." She looked over at his hands and could see that his nails were, indeed, quite short.

"That's way more normal," Emma said. She could see that her wrist was bleeding again.

"Let me get you something for that. Stay there." He came back a minute later with some gauze, Neosporin, and a wrap-around bandage.

"Oh my God, this is so unnecessary."

"Please, let me bandage it for you. I was a military field medic," he said, and she relented. He carefully applied Neosporin, the gauze, and then the bandage, wrapping it around her wrist. It was such a tender moment; she wondered if this was what it would've been like growing up with an older brother. Or what it might've been like if Theo had been Maggie's real husband, not just a reality TV show husband.

"Is it OK if I ask you a few questions about my sister?" Emma said as he secured the end of the bandage. "Layla Reyes told me some things and I wanted to check with you about them."

"For sure," he said. "Hopefully she didn't assassinate my character too much."

"Nah, don't worry. But she told me that you and Maggie were . . . Sorry, I don't know how to say this. You were hooking up?"

"Oh," Finn said. "What exactly did Layla say?"

"That you were sleeping together. For a while during and after the show."

"Wow." Finn scratched his head. "If you count hooking up for a few months after the show wrapped as 'a while' then sure." So it was true; they'd hooked up. "It all stopped after they got married."

Emma nodded. It was bizarre to think that after her sister had gotten back from filming, she'd been plotting an elaborate ruse with Theo all while sleeping with Finn.

"Layla had this over-the-top jealousy thing with Maggie," Finn continued. He got up to check on the pizzas, and she took a sip of a new beer that Finn had given her to replace her empty.

"Did you ever see Maggie, even after you were hooking up? Were you friends?" she asked.

"They need, like, two more minutes." He turned the pizzas around in the oven. "But to answer your question: very rarely. She and Theo were pretty busy doing couple stuff. They didn't have a huge circle of friends. I know some of the others from the show were sort of, like, 'Wow, they think they're better than us.'" Why wasn't he mentioning that Theo and Maggie had a fake relationship? Maybe he thought she didn't know and was trying to protect her. But didn't Layla say Finn was the one who told her?

"It's OK, Finn," she told him as he sat back down. "I know about Theo and Maggie. That they were in a fake relationship. You don't have to pretend."

He tipped his chair back and sighed. "Yes, I was wondering if you'd bring that up. Not Maggie's most ethical move, that's for sure. But I couldn't keep seeing her after they got married, even though it wasn't real. It just felt wrong."

"Did you have feelings for her?" she asked.

"I did, honestly. I was pretty heartbroken that she kept pursuing the thing with Theo." He paused, and took a swig of his beer. "It must be painful to think about your sister lying for so long."

"It is. But I want all the information; I want to know everything," she said. "That's the only way I'll ever get answers about what happened to her."

He nodded solemnly. They sat in silence for a moment, but it wasn't an awkward silence.

"Sorry to keep badgering you, but what do you know about Patrick from your season of *LoveShack*?" she asked. "I've found some concerning stuff about him, and I think he had something to do with her death."

Finn considered her question. "Well, I hate to say this, but it's definitely possible. He was pissed off at her for choosing Theo over him. He's the worst. We've all cut him out. He's toxic."

"I completely agree. Did you know he's now a DJ in Tempe, Arizona?"

Finn cackled. "That's amazing. Can't say I'm surprised."

"Anyway, we're looking into it."

Finn finished the last dregs of his beer. "Let me know if you find anything."

After this line of invasive questioning about Maggie, which he'd taken like a champ, she felt eager to switch gears. "Are you feeling good about the Dodgers?" she asked. This was her go-to conversation-starter with straight dudes in LA.

"I'm actually a Royals fan," he said, getting up to retrieve the pizza. It smelled so good, and she was surprised how hungry she felt.

"No fucking way. You know me and Maggie are from Kansas, right? The Royals are my team too."

"Ah, that's right! So you understand my pain." He placed her pizza in front of her. It was beautiful: the crust was perfectly cooked, and the cheese was bubbly.

"Why are you a Royals fan?" she asked.

"I was born in Kansas City. We moved around a

lot—military family—but it stuck with me." He handed her another beer. This would be her third, which was the most she'd drunk since Maggie had died. It felt good to be tipsy. She couldn't remember why she didn't do this more often.

"It's a pleasure to meet a Royals fan in any form in Los Angeles. Sometimes Maggie used to get a suite when they played the Dodgers. It's a shame you never joined."

He smiled as he rolled a pizza slicer across her pizza for her. "That would've been a lot of fun. But you and I could go the next time they're here."

"I'd love that." She grabbed her first slice, and took a big bite. It was hot, and lightly burned the roof of her mouth, but she didn't mind. "This is so fucking good."

"Thank you." Finn took a bite. "I'm excited to use this thing more often."

"It's too bad you and Maggie didn't stay in touch," she said. "She loved pizza. Especially a homemade fancy pizza like this. It was her favorite thing. She never let herself eat carbs, except sometimes she'd allow herself some pizza."

He nodded. "That's awesome. Well, not the no-carbs part, but the pizza part."

They sat for another beat in silence, before he jumped in with another joke about the Royals. They talked the team's prospects for a while, and she looked down at her phone to see she had three more missed calls from Jill that'd gone straight to voicemail as she hadn't turned off "mute notifications" for her contact yet. She opened her phone and sent Jill a text: *Please, enough. Can you just leave me alone?*

They ate the rest of their pizzas and chatted about Finn's care packages project. Her mind was elsewhere, on Patrick, but he'd been so kind to host her and feed her that the least she could do was act curious. Finn asked her what she was doing work-wise, and she avoided the question as best she could. Besides the work talk, the conversation flowed, and being around him made her feel closer to Maggie in a weird way. She found herself wondering if this was the beginning of an actual friendship.

She hoped it was, at least.

# Jill

It was a warm night, and she was on a run. Jill had been captain of the varsity cross-country team in high school, but she hadn't done much running as an adult until recently. Since Emma had left and was ignoring all her texts and calls, she'd taken it up again, going for long runs around her neighborhood after work. It was the only thing that tamped down the feeling of self-hatred that had settled inside of her. She was four miles into her run, and finally the noise in her brain had quieted. She passed the Los Angeles County Museum of Art and the *Urban Light* sculpture that lived outside. It was swarming with tourists on this warm night, but was beautiful at dusk. She decided to stop and walk through the lampposts, lined up in narrow rows.

The last time she'd been to the museum was with Emma, a few years ago. They weren't really museum people, but they lived close by and felt guilty for never going. It had been a rare rainy day in LA, and there was nothing else to do. They wandered around a Robert Mapplethorpe retrospective, whispering among the black-and-white photographs.

"I'd fuck him," Jill said as they passed a self-portrait of Mapplethorpe.

"I'd fuck her." Emma pointed at a photo of Patti Smith from 1975.

"Then, or also now?" Jill asked.

Emma considered this. "Both, I guess. Why not? Patti's a legend. I couldn't say no." They wandered around a bit more, before Emma continued. "Who's the oldest person you'd have sex with?"

Jill chuckled. "Great question. Glad we're having this very serious conversation about art." She thought about it for a second, and then it came to her. "Harrison Ford."

"Perfect answer," Emma said. "Timeless pick." They both laughed, and a woman nearby shushed them, which only made them laugh harder.

She missed her friend. The very friend who'd just told her to leave her alone.

She sat down on the steps outside of *Urban Light*, her sweaty running shirt sticking to her body. She took her phone from the armband where it lived during runs. She opened her messages, and clicked on Emma's name. Finally, after drafting and deleting a text multiple times, she hit send. *No, I'm sorry. I can't leave you alone. I can't take this anymore. We need to talk tonight.*

# Maggie

*LoveShack: Where Are They Now?*

"Sadly, for many of our Love Pairs, a happy ending on the show doesn't always mean a happily ever after," Schuyler said, his voice booming as if he was speaking to a crowd, even though they were just filming in Maggie's living room. "That's not the case for Maggie Lathrop and Theo Cooke, who are America's favorite couple and remain madly in love. But has anything changed since the cameras stopped rolling more than three years ago? Tonight, you'll find out as we get up close and personal with Theo and Maggie for a very special episode of *LoveShack: Where Are They Now?*"

Maggie sat in her glam room as her stylist put the finishing touches on her look for the day. Her extensions looked ratty unless styled by a professional. Gone were the days of Maggie doing her own hair with a thirty-dollar curling iron in her bathroom. She now spent thousands a week on her hair, but according to her Instagram, she achieved her look using only overpriced "miracle" hair products that her followers could purchase at a 20 percent discount with the code MAGGIE20.

Her phone pinged as she sat trying not to move so her hair stylist wouldn't burn her ear with a curling iron (it'd happened three times in the last two months. She was fidgety). She looked down and saw a text from Finn, and opened it.

The plan for that day was for the network to film her and Theo making dinner together, and then Schuyler would sit down with them in their living room, and they'd do an "intimate" interview. Never mind that she and Theo hadn't cooked a meal, let alone eaten together, in the course of their entire "marriage." They were going to make a lasagna, which they would then promptly feed to staff or throw out because it had too many carbs. But making a green smoothie or riced cauliflower tabbouleh didn't have the same homey feel, the producers insisted.

She'd had to cancel on Finn, because the shoot wouldn't be over until nine or ten, and she had work to do after—two sponsored content posts to queue up for her grid for that week. She'd procrastinated telling him, and now he'd texted her back: *Fine.*

"Sorry, can you look up?" her hair stylist asked.

"Sure," Maggie said as she put her phone away.

Things had been tense with Finn since he'd bought a house not far from hers in Calabasas.

She'd gone to see it a few days before, and Finn had ordered sushi to celebrate.

"This is so good," Maggie said, mouth full, sitting at a

makeshift table made of cardboard boxes. She knew she was overcompensating because he'd been in a mood all night, but she couldn't help herself.

"I just wish that one time we could go out to dinner together," he said. "Be seen together in public. This isn't normal, what we're doing. What you're doing."

She chewed and swallowed. "I know. It's not fair to you. But it's only a couple more months. Just until this new athleisure thing has settled down."

He shook his head. "Come on. Don't bullshit me. You're always saying, 'Just after this, we're right around the corner and then I'm ending it.' And it's never fucking true. I can't do it anymore."

They had this fight like clockwork every few months. But Finn was never going to leave her, and some part of her understood this. It was always an empty threat. He'd moved so close to her house, for God's sake. Close enough that she felt a tiny bit suffocated. "Don't be like this." She set her chopsticks down and moved toward him, putting her arms around him.

He shrugged her off. "I don't get it. Why won't you just leave him? Move in here."

"I will leave him," Maggie insisted. "It's just complicated with our business. Which impacts you, too."

His expression darkened, and she knew she'd gone too far. A couple years ago, when he was struggling careerwise, she'd begun quietly introducing him to a few brands that she and Theo had decided for one reason or another not to work with. And now, with her help, Finn had built a respectable influencing career. He could afford a

$2-million-dollar house in Calabasas. "I never asked you to do any of that," he said.

"Of course not. But I'm just saying. It's complicated."

He looked her in the eyes. "I'm sick of it, Maggie. I mean it this time."

"I know, Finn." She took his hand, and he let her. "I promise, it's almost over."

As the lasagna cooked in their oven, Maggie and Theo sat next to each other on their couch, which had been moved by the production team to get better lighting. Schuyler sat across from them.

"So, Maggie and Theo, you're three years into your marriage. How is married life?"

"It's amazing." Theo grabbed Maggie's hand. "I'm the luckiest man alive."

Maggie squeezed his hand back and looked at him with her best adoring gaze. She could basically do this on autopilot, even though she was stressed about Finn and how she was hurting him. She wondered how much longer her "marriage" with Theo could go on. She thought about the threatening note Theo had gotten, telling him to "end it" or he'd be outed. Was it possible Finn was behind that in some way? She chided herself for even thinking it. This was Finn: of course he hadn't and wouldn't do something like that. He was a good guy. A really good guy.

But still, it was truly unhinged behavior, and she knew it had something to do with her. She knew it was a paranoid move, but made a mental note to give Emma the emergency money she'd withdrawn for her, just in case something ever happened. She never wanted Emma to get stuck like she'd been after their mom had died.

Schuyler asked them a few more questions about how in love they were before segueing into the brand-heavy portion of the evening, and she refocused on the interview. "So, lovebirds, tell us about your new partnership with SWEATT."

They'd only agreed to do this godforsaken special for a lot of money and prominent product placement of their new athleisure line. "We absolutely *love* working out together," Theo said. "And we wanted to create amazing clothes—for men and women and nonbinary people—so couples could have fun moving together, and look good doing it." She held in a laugh at his use of the word "nonbinary," as if he was some sort of LGBTQ rights champion. What he actually was was a deeply repressed man who'd been fed the line by the SWEATT PR person.

Maggie recited her own lines from the PR person. "We really wanted to show that you don't have to sacrifice comfort for fashion when it comes to working out. And we wanted to make these clothes size-inclusive, too." Never mind that the sizing only went up to fourteen.

After the required product placement, Schuyler asked a few more questions about their life together, ending with the one that every interviewer asked them. "So, is there any talk of . . ." Schuyler mimed cradling a baby. "I know fans are desperate for you to have a little one. That kid sure would be cute!"

Maggie looked thoughtfully at Theo, as if this was the first time they'd ever been asked this. Now that she'd officially decided—at least to herself—against adopting or fostering, she tried to shut down the idea of a baby any time it was raised.

But Theo wanted a kid, albeit for all the wrong reasons. He was worried their influence and followers from *Love-Shack* would wane, and a child opened up a whole new world of opportunity. The parent-influencing market was the biggest area for growth on social media. He'd even gone so far as to get fostering and adoption information for Maggie to review—he wanted them to take in a child from a "disadvantaged" community in LA. He thought it'd make them look like engaged citizens who cared about helping underprivileged children. He'd even suggested that they could hire around-the-clock nannies so they didn't have to really invest in raising a child together. It was disgusting on every level, and she'd rejected the idea. And it'd reaffirmed that it was time to be done with Theo.

And yet, she hadn't ended it.

"We're not ready yet," Maggie said. "Though maybe at some point."

"Tick-tock! I think that's your biological clock I just heard." Schuyler laughed at his own joke. "Just kidding!" he said, though he wasn't. It was true. She was thirty-two, and Finn was determined to have at least three children with her, so she had to get moving. She'd gotten pregnant accidentally—it was Finn's, of course—about six months ago, and had decided to get an abortion. It wasn't the right time to have kids with someone who wasn't her fake husband. She was OK with her decision, but Finn was so set on starting a family ASAP that she hadn't told him. Some part of her—deep down—was still a little unsure about the kids thing, even though she'd agreed to it.

But Finn was perfect, she reminded herself. He was hot, he was smart, he was thoughtful. He loved her. They had great sex. So why hadn't she broken off her fake relationship with Theo yet? She tried not to think about it too hard. She told herself it was just a matter of ensuring that they were set up professionally before she did that, because the brand deals and career opportunities they got together, like the one with SWEATT, would dry up. And, of course, Theo would have to agree to an "amicable" divorce, though she assumed he would. Yes, theirs was a beneficial business relationship, but the plan was always to get divorced. They were established enough now. So why wasn't she just going for it?

Theo grabbed her hand, and smiled at her. "All in good time," he said.

# Emma

By the time she and Finn had finished their pizzas and beers, the sky was darkening.

"I should probably be going," she said.

"Sure," Finn said. "I'll give you a ride."

"Mind if I use your bathroom before we leave?"

"Not at all." He recited directions to the guest bathroom.

Tipsy, she made her way down his hallway, and turned the doorknob at the far end of the hallway on the right as he'd instructed. But it wasn't a bathroom—it looked like the master bedroom. He'd probably meant another door. But she really had to pee, and she was curious about Finn's rich-person bedroom.

But the master bedroom and bathroom were both average—no jacuzzi tub, no sauna. As she sat on the toilet, she saw Jill had texted her an hour ago to say she wouldn't leave Emma alone, that they needed to talk tonight. What was she going to do, show up at the Calabasas house? Emma could respond and say she wasn't home, but she was pissed. Jill was not respecting her boundaries, and it would serve her right to show up when Emma was out.

She put her phone down on the bathroom shelf above

her head as she stood up to flush. After she washed her hands, she dried them on the hand towel and went to grab her phone, knocking something down as she retrieved it. The object was shiny, and gleamed in the light. She bent down to pick it up. She felt it in her palm before she saw it, and even then, she knew immediately what it was. A terrier. It was a tiny silver terrier charm.

She tensed. Maybe he had a girlfriend who had Viva La Juicy? Who had left the terrier charm here? Yes, that must've been it. But then she remembered just how hard she'd had to work to track down the stupid terrier charm she had given Maggie for her thirtieth. Juicy didn't make the charms for the bottles anymore.

Or maybe the charm was Maggie's, and Finn had seen her more recently than he remembered. That was possible. There was definitely some logical explanation. She relaxed her jaw, realizing she'd been clenching it. She clutched the charm. If it was Maggie's, she wanted to have it. She searched in her mind for the last time she'd seen Maggie wear it, and a memory emerged of her sitting with Maggie as she took off the bracelet while getting ready for an awards show. That was—what—two, three weeks before she was killed? Maybe Finn had just forgotten that Maggie had been over at his place right before she died. She wished she hadn't had those drinks. They were making her feel fuzzy.

She would figure it out later. In the meantime, she was happy just to have the charm back. It was a relic of a happier time in her life—a time when she still had her sister. When she could focus on tracking down stupid, sentimental gifts on eBay rather than investigating a murder.

For now, it was best to just go home and get some sleep. She opened the bathroom door, realizing it'd gotten completely dark since she'd gone to pee. Shit, how long had she been in there? She walked toward the light streaming under the door from the hall. Had she closed the door to the bedroom?

"What are you doing?" Finn asked from somewhere in the dark. She jumped back, startled. Fuck. He'd found her lurking around his room. This was embarrassing.

"Hi, sorry." Her palms were clammy from the surprise. "I was confused. I thought the bathroom was on the right all the way back. I just used this one. Didn't mean to pry or anything."

"It's the other door," he said.

"Shall we go?" she asked, her voice artificially cheery.

He stood still. "Emma, why are you really here?"

"You invited me for pizza." Her stomach dropped. Something in his voice worried her. "I'm sorry. I really didn't mean to intrude." He walked over to turn on the light, though didn't open the door. He didn't say anything, but looked upset. "Hey, I really apologize for invading your space. That was weird of me. I'm really tired now—can we head home?"

He let out a sigh. "Sure. Let's go."

She relaxed, following him as he opened the door. "I can also take an Uber, if it's too much trouble."

He turned around. "I don't mind." She realized he was staring directly at her right hand, which was closed around the charm. "What's that?"

"Nothing," she said too quickly. "A tampon." A tampon? Jesus.

"A tampon?" He walked toward her, grabbing her wrist—the wrist he'd bandaged just an hour ago—and unfurled her palm. "Didn't think so." She let out a stunned cry at his forcefulness. He took the charm from her hand. "God, you played me." He shook his head. "I almost fell for it."

"I didn't play you," she said, her voice shaky. "I don't understand."

He looked as though he was about to cry. "Why'd you have to go poking around? I liked you, Emma. I really did."

"I need to go. I've had a nice time though—thank you." She walked toward the door, and he didn't make any move to follow her. But as she turned the knob, he lunged for her, gripping his hand over hers. "Please don't touch me." She started to cry and her body shook. "Just let me go home. I only wanted the charm. It means nothing. It's nothing. You can have it back."

He looked at her sorrowfully, but still gripped her hand. "We both know you're going to walk right out of here and tell the police."

She tried to make her voice sound calm, assured. "It's not worth anything. It was maybe thirty bucks on eBay. Just an inside joke with me and Maggie. I won't go to the police."

He just stared at her. "I don't give a shit about the charm. Obviously."

She tried half-heartedly to wrench her wrist away from him, but he held on. Her heart sped up. Something very, very bad was going on here. "Then what's the problem? Why are you still holding on to me?"

He said nothing but narrowed his eyes at her.

She slowly moved her free hand to her back pocket, where her phone was. "I'm just gonna take out my phone and call an Uber."

But he grabbed her other wrist and twisted it until she shrieked. "You're not going anywhere. You need to tell me what you actually know."

She cried harder. "Know about what? About Maggie? You and Maggie? I truly know nothing, I swear."

He shook his head and gripped her wrists even tighter. "You're just as manipulative as she was."

"You're hurting me," she said through tears. "Stop it."

He laughed. It wasn't a full-throated laugh, but a small one. A mean one.

It was then that some animal instinct in her took over, and, with all of her strength, she wrenched herself away from his grip. She moved to open the door, but he blocked her, putting his body against the door.

"No," he said. "You're not leaving." They stood there for a dreadful moment as he apparently considered what to do with her. Gone was the Finn she'd shared beers with, who'd cooked her an individual pizza, who'd talked about his love of the Royals. His eyes were bloodshot, and filled with a fearful rage she would've never guessed he possessed just twenty minutes ago.

Before she realized what was happening, he threw her whole body against the floor. She screamed as her head made contact with the side of the bed frame. Her vision blurred and a searing pain followed. She wailed.

"Please be quiet." His voice was steady, as if he was trying to focus. "I'd rather not gag you."

Her head hurt terribly. It was the worst pain she'd ever felt—worse than when her appendix had almost burst in the third grade. She pulled her hand up to the place where her head had hit the bed frame. It was wet with blood, and she cried out.

Finn walked over to a drawer and grabbed a pair of socks to use as a gag. "I didn't have to gag Maggie. She cooperated. This doesn't need to be difficult if you cooperate, too."

Even through the haze of the head injury and the three beers, Emma knew she was fucked. She tried to comb through her tangled thoughts, to make a plan. "So you killed her," she said, tears running down her cheeks. "Why would you do that? What could she have possibly done to deserve it?"

His breathing was ragged as he walked over to her. "Your sister ruined my fucking life."

"And how did she do that?" When he didn't answer, she continued. "You know, I had no idea. Even after finding the charm. There was no reason to do this. I was convinced it was Patrick."

Finn moved his weight onto her, holding her down. "I didn't want to do it. I really didn't." Her head throbbed, but she told herself to focus. "It was the worst day of my life. I loved your sister. But what she was doing to me was wrong. I couldn't live with it."

"With what?" She made a half-hearted attempt to stand up, but he just pinned her down, his knee on her stomach. She wasn't going to be able to match his physical strength, that much she knew. Best to save her energy. But for what, she wasn't sure. He leaned over her, untied his shoes, and pulled his shoelaces out through the eyelets of his fancy sneakers. He tied a shoelace around her wrists, and she forced herself not to cry out. Finn had abandoned the gag and she didn't want to remind him that she could scream. Then he took his other shoelace and bound her ankles. Tightly.

"I miss her," he said. "I really do. Losing her was the worst thing I've ever been through."

"Losing her? You killed her," she said, before she could stop herself.

He gave her a pained look. "She left me no choice."

"So you were together? For how long?"

"More than three years. Since we finished filming *Love-Shack*. And you know what? We were perfect for each other. We had everything. But she couldn't give up her bullshit thing with Theo, and she strung me along for years. Do you understand the pain of that? The gaslighting? The emotional abuse I endured?"

"Abuse?"

He leaned on her harder. "She would tell me: 'This thing with Theo makes sense financially—you don't understand. I love you, but I can't end it just yet. I will soon, I promise.' It was psychological torture. It was abuse."

"You're cutting off my circulation." Emma's voice sounded choked and desperate. She started crying again. Finn was about to kill her unless she figured something out. "Can we make a deal or something? I promise not to say anything. I will do anything you want. Please, just let me go."

"Absolutely not," he said.

"Please," she said. "Please." But he ignored her, and stood up. To her surprise, he left the room. She breathed more easily without his knee on her stomach, but her head pounded. She was probably concussed.

She heard Finn rummaging around outside the room, and realized, with a jolt of adrenaline, that her phone was still in her back pocket. She contorted her body, trying to reach it with her bound hands. She couldn't stretch much farther than her left hip, and her back twinged in pain. Finally, she gave up. At her failure, she cried even harder.

When he came back into the room, he carried with him a large blue tarp which she recognized as the one that'd been covering his stack of pizza oven firewood outside. He unrolled it on the floor of the room, and pushed her onto it. It was covered in little wood chips that dug into her back.

Nothing good would come from this, she knew. *Stop crying,* she told herself. *Think.*

"This doesn't need to be difficult for you," he said. "I don't want you to suffer."

"You don't want me to suffer? As you, what? Kill me?" Her words somehow came out clear.

He ignored this as he arranged the edges of the tarp so it was maximally spread out.

"Here's what I'm confused by. Why didn't you just break up with her? If you loved her, why would you kill her?" Emma asked.

He sat down on the floor next to her, and looked her in the eye. "I knew if she was alive I wouldn't be able to live without her. I could never truly move on."

"That's sick," she said. She knew it wasn't smart to poke the bear, but it'd just slipped out.

"Maybe. But you know she got pregnant about a year ago?"

Emma nodded.

"She got an abortion and hid it from me." His voice cracked with emotion. "I wanted that baby with her. I wanted a family. She knew it would ruin me, and she did it anyway."

Emma swallowed. She had to try to keep him calm, keep him talking. "I'm so sorry. That was wrong of her."

"It was," he said. "She took everything away from me."

Emma didn't know what to say to that, so she said nothing.

Finn stood back up, leaving the room again. As soon as he was out the door, she rolled over onto her side, squirming desperately to try again to get her phone out. After about thirty seconds of this, she realized she was never going to succeed. She was furious at herself for failing to do this one thing to save herself.

But before she could figure out what to do, Finn came back, and he was holding a large kitchen knife. She shrieked. So he was really doing this.

"Jesus Christ, you're hurting my ears," he said. "Can you just be quiet?"

"Help!" she screamed. "Someone please help me."

"No one can hear you out there," Finn said. "Try to relax. It's almost over."

She squirmed harder, and screamed again. She screamed so loudly that her throat became raw. She screamed until she ran out of breath. She could've sworn the house shook with the sound. Finn just sat there, staring at her. "She never loved you." Emma's throat hurt. "If she loved you, she would've left Theo. She would've started a family with you." She was grasping, she knew.

Finn looked as if he was going to spit on her. "You have no idea what you're talking about. She never told you about any of it."

"I knew her better than anyone," Emma said, breathless. She worried she might throw up from the physical exertion and the concussion. "And you were never it for her. Because if you had been, it would've been an easy choice to leave Theo."

Without warning, he slapped her across the face. Her vision blurred from the impact and the right side of her face was on fire with pain.

"She loved me until the end," he said. "How do you think I got her to come early to the warehouse that morning?"

She needed to keep him talking until she figured something out. "You tricked her?"

"You can't imagine the pain I was in," he said. "I finally realized that our life together was a lie. So I told her we needed to talk, to meet me there early, before the photoshoot. I wasn't lying: we did need to talk. It was a terrible thing, what I did. But it was the only real choice I had."

"No," she said. "It wasn't. You don't have to do this to me, either."

"I'm afraid I do," he said. "Try to breathe. If your muscles tense while the knife is in, it's even more painful. We want this to go quickly. I don't want you to suffer. Two or three stab wounds at most. You'll start to feel numb after you lose enough blood. Maggie wasn't in pain at the end, and you don't need to be either."

"People . . . people know I'm here," she lied, her breathing labored as she struggled against the shoelace binding her wrists. "Lots of people. They're going to know you were the last person I saw."

"I'll take my chances," Finn said. "The way I see it, if you get out of here alive, I'm going to jail. If you never get out of here, I have the chance to make up something believable."

She closed her eyes, catching her breath. He began setting up a workstation as he held her down with one knee. She squirmed against him with all her might, but it was no use. He put on a pair of winter glove liners he pulled from a box under his bed marked "SKI"—she supposed in order to obfuscate any fingerprints. Then he ran to the bathroom and came back brandishing a women's shower cap. He gathered her hair into it in order to prevent stray hairs from getting everywhere, she assumed. The cap could've easily belonged to Maggie, and her stomach turned at the thought.

Finn was slow, methodical. Resourceful. Ex-field medic through and through. But it was taking way longer than she expected. She had no idea how much time had passed, maybe five or ten minutes. If she could just reach her phone, it'd all be OK. But she couldn't. She kept squirming, but he stopped her with one final movement, digging his knee hard into her stomach. It knocked the wind out of her and she retched.

As he readied the knife, she knew there was nothing she

could do. Her body relaxed. She thought about Maggie, how scared she probably was right before the end. How alone. Tears streamed down her face, but she was silent.

"Good girl," Finn said. "Just relax." He kneeled over her and lifted the knife. Without thinking, she bucked her knees against him, and he stumbled. Some survival instinct was kicking in. She wanted to die peacefully—she really did—but it was impossible; her body wanted to fight. "Emma, enough." His voice was calm but firm. He got back on top of her, but this time his knees held her down. He reached up another time, and before she could comprehend what was happening, the knife was inside her. It was red hot, as if someone had just stuck her with a fire poker. She heard a scream, loud and piercing. It was a few seconds before she realized it was her own.

"No," she cried. "Please no." He lifted the knife again, and moved toward her. She closed her eyes, waiting for it to pierce the muscle of her abdomen. She was no longer afraid of the pain, because this was it. It was going to be over soon. She was losing massive amounts of blood. She started to count backwards from ten, hoping to lose consciousness sooner rather than later. She began: *Ten, nine, eight—*

All of a sudden, she heard a clunk, and opened her eyes. Her vision was fuzzy and the room was a mass of shapes and colors. Before she could understand what was going on, Finn's body collapsed on top of hers, his knife clattering to the side. The weight of him was heavy, almost suffocating. She wanted him off her.

As she struggled beneath him, she saw a figure moving behind his head. A woman? Or was that in her imagination?

She blinked, willing her vision to clear. And then, after a few seconds, everything came into focus.

It was Jill, in her running clothes.

She was staring, wild-eyed, as she held an iron in one hand. Why was she holding an iron? Was this a dream?

"Emma!" Jill screamed, picking up the discarded knife. "Oh my God, Emma. No. No!" But Emma was drifting. Was this a hallucination? Jill wailed, and Emma heard her on the phone. "Yes, it's an emergency. Someone has been stabbed. Please come quick. Yes, the assailant is still here. Out cold. Three-twenty-two, Canyon Park. Come soon. Please come."

Jill moved toward Emma and threw Finn's knife somewhere. She placed her hands on her stomach. "Ow," Emma said as Jill applied pressure.

"Please stay awake," Jill said. "Help is almost here. I know it hurts, but I have to do this. That's what they told me."

"Who?" Emma's eyes began to close.

"The police. They're coming," Jill said. "You're going to be OK. Just stay awake."

Emma smiled at her. "I'm awake," she said. "I'm happy to see you."

Through tears, Jill laughed. "I'm happy to see you too," she said.

"What the fuck?" Finn said from a few feet away, holding his head. "Who are you?" he asked Jill.

"That's Jill," Emma said, her voice weak.

Finn stood up, wobbly on his feet. "I really wish you hadn't hit me in the head."

"Don't hurt her," Emma cried. "Don't touch her."

But Finn lumbered toward Jill, trying to get ahold of her. The head injury had unsteadied him, but he was so much larger than her. He lunged at her, but she dodged him. Emma tried to scream, but no sound came out of her mouth.

"I called the police," Jill protested as Finn continued to try to grab her. "They're on their way." He circled around her, getting a little steadier on his feet.

He held his head, wincing, in the spot where, presumably, Jill had hit him with the iron. "I'll say there was an intruder, and that he ran away when he heard the sirens, before he could kill me. We were all having a lovely dinner and then he broke in. Helps that I'll have a visible head injury." With what looked like considerable effort, he charged toward Jill. She shrieked and ran out of the room with Finn right behind. She opened the bedroom door, slamming it behind her. Finn stumbled, caught off-guard as the door shut in his face. But with an angry grunt, he opened it again and chased her out.

Emma wasn't sure how much time had passed, but Finn and Jill were gone. She knew she didn't have long left to live. She rested her head on the ground, when she saw it: the knife. It was underneath the bed.

After another few minutes, Finn came back in with Jill, dragging her by the hair. She shrieked so loudly that Emma felt it in her bones. He wasted no time, throwing Jill down on the tarp next to Emma, who cried out again in pain.

"I really wish I didn't have to do this," he said. "But I need the knife." As Finn kneeled down to look under the bed, Emma closed her eyes, surprised that she could taste the salt of her tears. She hadn't realized she was still crying.

"Found it." He lumbered over to them, knife in hand. Jill screamed a loud, shrill scream that woke Emma right out of her stupor. She kicked her legs at Finn, but it wasn't enough.

"Please, stop yelling. My head fucking hurts." He kneeled down on top of Jill, and put his hand over her mouth. Within seconds, he cried out. "Jesus. Did you just bite me?"

Jill screamed again, this time even louder. He stood over her, holding her down beside Emma. Emma closed her eyes. She couldn't watch him kill her. *I'm so sorry, Jill*, she wanted to say. But she didn't have the strength, so she tried to tell Jill telepathically. Before she could finish her thought, she heard a banging noise. Jill yelled again, and she wanted to reach out to grab her hand.

For some reason, what she thought of in that moment—the moment before she was surely about to die—was a night, years ago, after they'd first moved to LA together. Emma was working as a copywriter at an ad agency, and Jill was nannying. Sixty per cent of their income was going toward rent and, for the most part, neither of them could remember why they'd moved to LA in the first place. In that phase of their lives, Jill would make them large pots of lentils and rice on Sundays that lasted the week, and they'd supplement this with peanut butter sandwiches and grilled cheeses. But on this particular night, the night that came back to Emma, they had a feast: her company had had a board meeting earlier that day, and after the various board members went back to their homes in Beverly Hills or

Greenwich or Sun Valley, they left behind a tremendous amount of food from a fancy Mediterranean place. After her coworkers went home for the evening, Emma packed up the leftovers—the maitake kebabs, the dolmas, the beet hummus, the baklava—and took them home. It felt like winning the lottery.

There was nothing remarkable about this night, besides the food. There was no particular reason that, on the edge of death, Emma's brain should bring her there. That night, Jill and Emma sat at the same Ikea kitchen table they sat at every other night (well, really, it was a desk that they used as a table), and they had the same conversations as they did every other night (work sucked, dating apps sucked), and they drank the same wine they drank every other night (Two Buck Chuck, which was actually $2.99). Nevertheless, as Emma lay on the ground in Finn's house, bleeding out, she found herself there. She wondered if she was dead, and this was some weird version of heaven. Sitting with Jill in their apartment, just the two of them, drinking cheap wine and eating leftover dolmas—that was heaven. She realized the pain was gone; she somehow couldn't feel anything. For just a moment, she let herself believe she was simply sitting with her best friend at their kitchen table.

But the banging noise got louder, and it roused her. She remembered where she was: bleeding, on the floor. On Finn's floor. Finn, who'd murdered her sister. Jill was still crying for help. What was that noise? She wished it would stop. She wanted to rest. She wanted to tell Jill: *It will be OK. I love you. You are my family.*

Just as she was drifting off, Emma thought she heard someone yell "POLICE!" from behind the door. Now she really must have been hallucinating. Someone was trying to break down the door. She heard the sound of Finn's knife falling to the floor. She heard Jill's sobs.

"Finn Thompson, you're under arrest," a voice said as the door came down. The last thing Emma remembered was Jill squeezing her hand. Then everything went black.

# Jill

In the ambulance, Jill's hands were shaking uncontrollably, and her limbs were numb. The medics immediately hooked her up to an IV, which she was told contained a sedative.

"You're in shock," the medic told her. "It's OK. You're fine. A little bruised, but you're going to be OK."

"Will Emma be OK?" she asked, waiting for the sedative to hit. "There was so much blood."

"I don't know," the medic answered. "I won't sugarcoat it. She did lose a lot. We'll find out more when we get to the hospital. Who is a good emergency contact for her?"

"Me," Jill said.

"Well, once we get you checked out, you can ask the nurses for an update." Jill nodded at this, already drowsy. Her eyes closed, and sleep carried her away.

She slept as if she were dead, dreaming of Emma's screams, of the blood. Of the look of pity on Finn's face as he threw the iron at her—not pity for her, but for himself.

Except she wasn't dead. Her eyes fluttered open and she took in her surroundings. White light flooded her vision, and she heard a repetitive beeping sound. For just a moment, she panicked. The beeping disoriented her, made her feel like running. *You're safe now,* she told herself, blinking the sleep out of her eyes.

She looked down to see someone had changed her into a hospital gown. On her wrist was a plastic band that said her name and date of birth.

"Good morning," a voice said.

With considerable effort, Jill sat up. Her body was sore everywhere. She found a nurse standing over her, checking her vitals. "Is it actually morning?" Jill croaked. It was still dark out.

"Just about," the nurse said. "It's four thirty. I'm on morning rounds."

"Where am I?" she asked.

"You're at Cedars Sinai. Someone must really love you, because after you got here last night, we got a call asking us to upgrade you to one of our VIP suites. You were wheeled in here around one a.m."

"Whoa." She examined the room more closely. There was a mahogany entertainment console with a flat-screen TV and a gaming system, two large leather couches, and a small kitchen with stainless-steel appliances. "How is Emma? How is she doing? Is she OK?"

The nurse looked at her. "The woman you were found with? I don't know. Let me ask. I can't give out any information without her family's consent, and if she's not awake, then—"

"I'm her next of kin," Jill interrupted. "She has no family. It's just me."

"OK," the nurse said. "Why don't you go back to sleep for a couple hours, and I'll try to find out."

As soon as the nurse suggested this, Jill realized she was somehow still tired. Her sedative-laden body couldn't resist, and her eyes fluttered closed again.

When she woke up a few hours later, a doctor and a new nurse stood in the back of the room.

"I'm Dr. Bhindi. How are you feeling?"

"A little sore." Jill gestured at her left arm, which was covered in bruises. "And my ribs hurt. But I'm OK. I'm worried about Emma. Do you have an update on her? My friend Emma?"

Dr. Bhindi sighed, and the color drained from Jill's face.

"Please just tell me. I can take it."

"I'm not in charge of her care," Dr. Bhindi said. "She's in critical condition. But she's alive."

Jill burst into tears, relieved. "Thank fucking God," she said. "Sorry for cursing."

The doctor handed her a tissue. "That's OK, you can curse. You've been through a horrific trauma," Dr. Bhindi said. "I've requested that Emma's attending physician pay you a visit later today. We'd like to keep you here for one more night, for observation. Your blood pressure is still higher than we'd like it to be, and when you're up to it, we want to do a few X-rays to make sure you didn't break a rib. It says here on your chart from your initial conversation with the emergency responders last night that your assailant threw you on the floor, and hit you with an iron. Is that correct?"

"Yes." Jill swallowed, trying to block out the image of the fight with Finn. "But please just send in Emma's doctor as soon as possible."

Dr. Bhindi nodded her promise.

When the doctor left, Jill found her phone, which had been moved to the table next to her hospital bed. Someone had charged it. Over just ten or so hours, she'd accumulated about five hundred texts: from her parents, from Amanda, from random people at work, from basically everyone she'd ever known. The showdown with Finn had made the news.

First, she called her parents, who sobbed at the sound of her voice and said they were flying out to LA the next day to take care of her. Usually she'd resist, but having her parents baby her for a few days sounded nice.

Next, she called Amanda, who also cried, and then gave her a play-by-play recap of the news coverage.

"Finn's in jail, and there's some amazing footage of him doing a perp walk. The police have done, like, fifteen press conferences about it. They're clearly panicked that you both seemed to have figured out it was Finn who killed Maggie and they had never even looked in to him. Also, less important but I thought you should know, your LinkedIn picture is all over the news."

Jill chuckled at this.

"Oh, and do you like your suite? I had you upgraded."

"Yeah, it's lovely," Jill said. "I mean, all things considered."

Finally, Amanda asked about Emma. "On the news they say she's in 'critical but stable' condition. Have you been able to see her?"

"No, and no one is giving me any information. I'm

supposed to get a visit from her doctor today. But Amanda, I was there. It was horrific. She lost so much blood. I thought we were going to die. I really did."

"But you're here, Jill. You're still here. You did it. And hopefully Emma will be OK too," she said.

Jill wiped her tears. "I hope so."

"I'm so sorry this happened," Amanda said, and Jill could hear she was crying. "I'm sorry for creating this horrible TV show. I let the genie out of the bottle. The 'LoveShack curse' is real, and this proves it. Just look at me and Trevor, and everything that happened with us. Everything that I touch turns to shit."

Jill sighed. "Amanda, I love you, and I hope that's not weird to say since you're my boss. But you need to move on. Yeah, *LoveShack* is fucked up, and they cast fucked-up people. No offense to Maggie. But it's not on you, and honestly it never was. You're only responsible for yourself, and for what comes next."

Amanda was quiet for a moment. "Thank you," she said. "Thank you, Jill. You've always been too good to me."

An hour or so passed before Emma's doctor visited. He knocked, but was already walking in before she could answer.

Jill sat up in her hospital bed. "Are you Emma's doctor? Is she OK? Can I go see her?"

He nodded. "Yes, I'm Dr. Schubert. And yes, she's going to be OK. But a full recovery will take a long time." A rush of both relief and fear flooded Jill's stomach. The doctor continued, "We had to induce a coma. She received two blood transfusions last night, and then went into an emergency surgery. We conducted a laparotomy, and were able to reconstruct part of her small bowel."

"What does that mean? Is she OK now?"

"It's a serious procedure, but it went well. The plan is to move her from the ICU to a regular ward in a few days if she experiences no complications."

"When can I see her?" Jill asked.

"I expect we'll wake her up in about forty-eight hours. You can see her then," he said.

"OK," she said. "I'll be there as soon as I'm allowed."

Amanda picked her up from the hospital that night, in an Uber. "I'm so glad you're OK." Her eyes were misty. "Although I still have so many questions. Like how did you find Emma? And how is she doing?"

"Well, let me get in the car first." Jill hugged Amanda, who kissed her forehead. It was a gesture that felt almost maternal.

As they got in the car, Amanda grilled her for updates on Emma's condition. As they sat in traffic on the freeway, Jill told her everything she knew, and Amanda nodded solemnly.

"How did you know where she was? And that she needed help?" Amanda asked.

"Well, we'd been fighting since . . ." Her voice trailed off; she didn't want to admit to hooking up with Theo. "Anyway, we'd been fighting. And I was sick of it. I wanted to make up. So I went over to the Calabasas house, where she was staying. And she wasn't there."

"How'd you know where to look next?"

"She's been sharing her location with me since forever. I mostly forgot about it until the London trip, when we'd had a fight, and I was kind of panicking and checked it a lot to make sure she was OK. So when she wasn't at the house, I remembered and checked it. Not to, like, stalk her. But I was curious. Emma hasn't exactly been a social butterfly lately. I was wondering where she was at nine thirty p.m. on a Tuesday."

"And she was at Finn's?"

"Yes, though obviously I didn't know it was Finn's house at the time. But it was so close I thought I would just drive by—"

"Really?" Amanda asked. "Wow. That is creepy, even by my standards."

"Emma never sees anyone except you, me and Liz. Like, ever. I don't know, something felt off. I guess I panicked. I needed to see her, I needed to make up with her, I needed to make sure she was OK. I wasn't thinking straight. Or maybe I was, because I found her. And when I got close, I heard noise coming from the house—screaming. I decided to go inside. And he'd already stabbed her." It was weird, talking about it. It didn't feel real.

"I'm so sorry you had to see that." Amanda took her hand, and they sat in silence for a few moments. Traffic was picking up. "Do you want me to come over? Or do you want to come back to my place? So you don't have to be alone."

"I think I'm OK," Jill said. "Might be nice to have a few hours to myself before my parents show up tomorrow." Amanda nodded at this, but looked wounded. "Thank you for the offer, though. I think I just need some time to process on my own."

"I get it," she said.

They talked about other things through the rest of the drive back to Jill and Emma's place, including Amanda's encounter with Trevor. But Jill could barely focus. She looked out the window, at the city, all the people moving about as if it were a normal evening.

"I'm just so glad you're OK," Amanda said as they rolled to a stop in front of Jill's apartment building.

"Me too," Jill said.

"When do you think you'll be back to work?" Amanda asked. "No pressure, obviously. I can come check in on you until you feel better."

"I need some time," Jill said honestly. "And I don't think I can do the assistant thing anymore. It really hurt me when you offered Emma a writing job on *The Youth* when you'd never given me the same opportunity." Maybe getting assaulted by a deranged reality star acted as a truth serum.

"I'm sorry," Amanda said. She looked pained. "That was thoughtless of me."

"It's OK," Jill said. "I care about you, but I think we need to move forward in a different way."

Amanda nodded, clearly holding back tears. "Of course. And look, Jill, I only offered Emma the job because of my own stupid guilt about *LoveShack*. Not that she's not talented, I'm sure she is. But it had nothing to do with you and what you're capable of, which is beyond anything I could ever offer you. When all of this dies down, I'm going to get you a writing job on the show of your dreams. If that's what you want."

Jill smiled a little. "Thank you for saying that, Manda. I appreciate it."

"Just take care of yourself." Amanda squeezed Jill's hand, and then it was her turn to be the one holding back tears.

She said goodbye, and as she opened the car door and walked out into the early-evening air, she felt a surge of gratitude. She was OK. Emma was going to be OK. She waved goodbye, and as the Uber pulled away she looked up at her building. She would go in and lie down, but not yet. First, she wanted to go for a walk. It was glorious to be alive, and the night was young.

# Emma

Recovery was slow, and boring. Jill visited almost every day, and sometimes Amanda came too. Their college friends had shown up a couple times, as had Liz and her new girlfriend, Toni, who Emma hated to admit was cool.

Her stomach muscles were completely fucked up, and she needed to relearn how to use her entire core. So she spent an hour in physical therapy every day, which was grueling. But her PT was hot, so she made Jill give her a haircut and bring her some mascara.

Her doctors also had her doing sessions with a trauma therapist twice a week. She wasn't sure if it was helping, but she couldn't deny that it was nice talking to someone who wasn't Jill. The therapist suggested she write a letter to Maggie, to put down all the things she wanted to say to her, to ask all the questions she still had. But Emma felt embarrassed by the idea: it was just *so* sincere.

Instead, without really thinking about it, she'd started to leave voice memos for her sister. When she saw a TikTok that she would've sent to Maggie, she recorded a voice note. She did the same when a new true crime podcast came out about her murder, and got everything wrong about their childhood (she knew it was a bad idea to listen, but she was bored. And curious). And she sent one when she was thinking about how Maggie went to a friend's ice-skating party in the fifth grade, and fell and chipped her front tooth. It took her mom a couple months to save up for a new one, so Maggie walked around for a while with a jack-o'-lantern smile. The pictures from that time were hilarious.

It was a Saturday, and it was her third week in the hospital. She had another week or so before she could go home. It was quiet; she had no PT on weekends. Jill was coming in twenty minutes, even though Emma had insisted daily visits weren't necessary. It was an unremarkable day, no different than her others in the hospital, except that it would've been Maggie's thirty-third birthday. She'd asked Jill to bring a cupcake and a candle, so they could mark it.

While she waited for Jill, she opened the voice memo app on her phone, and pressed record.

"Mags," she began. "Happy thirty-third. I really miss you. And I'm still furious at you. If you were here, I would yell at you. But you're dead, so I can't. Lucky you, I guess. If you were here, you'd also have to answer all of my questions. So you can be happy you get to avoid that. Because you lied to me a stunning amount. There was so much I didn't know about you, it turns out, but maybe thirty-three would've been the year you came clean about everything. Or not, who knows. The good news is, I'm alive. That's your birthday present: me not being dead. Or maybe you'd want me to die, so we could hang out together wherever you are, which is probably nowhere. But that would be a depraved thing to want, so I hope not. Anyway, I don't have anything new to say, and Jill is about to get here. I wish an afterlife did exist so that these messages were going somewhere, rather than just taking up storage on my phone. But I never believed in any of that shit and I don't think I can start now. So happy birthday, Mags. I love you a sickening amount, and I always will."

*Two years later*

## ***The Curious Case of Finn Thompson***
### *By Farouq Hijazi*

*Obsession with celebrity murder trials is hardly a new phenomenon in Los Angeles, but not since the O. J. Simpson trial has it reached such a fever pitch. I'm referring, of course, to the trial of Finn Thompson, which begins on Monday. The trial will take place over two years after his reality TV costar Maggie Lathrop's murder, which the Los Angeles District Attorney's office claims Thompson committed. He's also on trial for allegedly stabbing her sister Emma almost seven months later.*

*The District Attorney's office has released a list of witnesses who will testify against Thompson, a former combat medicine specialist in the United States Armed Forces. Its roster includes Emma Lathrop, her roommate, Jill Friedman, Amanda Lehman, creator of the hit TV show* Anxiety *and friend of Emma Lathrop, and Patrick O'Connell, a Love-Shack cast member who claims Thompson forged threatening letters from him and impersonated him online as an attempt to frame him for Lathrop's murder.*

*It is widely expected that the defense will argue that Maggie Lathrop's widower, Theo Cooke, killed his wife because he was afraid she would out him (Cooke has said in interviews since her death that he identifies as gay). Cooke is a year into a sixteen-month sentence for his role in obstructing a murder investigation. He admitted to pursuing a relationship with former Los Angeles Police Department Detective Daniel LaClair in order to avoid becoming a subject of the department's investigation. LaClair was the chief investigator in Lathrop's murder, but declared it a cold case after just three and a half months. He is still on administrative leave and awaits a disciplinary trial.*

*Last month, Emma Lathrop and Jill Friedman sat for their first public interview on the investigative primetime TV show 20/20. Both alleged that Thompson carried on a longstanding romantic relationship with Maggie Lathrop, and that he'd admitted to Emma Lathrop that he killed her sister before he attempted to kill her, too.*

*The interview was widely seen as a move by the prosecution to drum up sympathy for their narrative about the events surrounding Maggie Lathrop's death.*

*Thompson has amassed a sizable community of supporters who question the validity of Emma Lathrop's claims, siding with Thompson in claiming that Cooke killed his wife. "He would never do this," Lorraine Johanssen said, wiping tears from her eyes during a recent interview on the local news. Johanssen runs TikTok and Instagram pages in support of Thompson under the name Finnocent. "We've followed him for such a long time, and I just know he's not that person. He cares about women. He cares about all people."*

*Emma Lathrop has called Thompson's on-camera feminism a "front." "[Thompson]'s very invested, even when he was trying to kill me, in the narrative that he is this 'wronged' guy, who was 'gaslit' so badly that he had no choice but to end my sister's life. He was so comfortable weaponizing the language that marginalized people use to describe their experiences of abuse and oppression. But he murdered Maggie in cold blood. He premeditated the whole thing and planted evidence to attempt to frame an innocent person. I urge every fan to remember that someone's public persona doesn't always align with who they are behind the scenes."*

*Finnocent's Instagram page has amassed over 400,000 followers since it was created following Thompson's arrest.*

*"If anyone doubts that Finn killed Maggie and stabbed Emma, listen to the audio of Jill's 911 call that night. Then try to say they're making this up," said Amanda Lehman. 20/20 used a snippet of the leaked 911 audio in their interview with Friedman and Emma Lathrop, and since the episode aired, the clip has trended on Twitter.*

*Lehman has been one of Emma Lathrop's and Jill Friedman's most vocal defenders in recent months. Friedman used to work as Lehman's assistant.*

*When asked if Thompson had anything in common with Trevor Koch, who co-created* Anxiety *with Lehman and was accused of sexual assault by multiple women, she was candid. "Frankly, yes. Our TV show was this feminist thing that Trevor thought he could hide behind. [Thompson] thought about himself like that too."*

*Finnocent* creator Johanssen criticized Lehman, who previously defended Koch. "She's trying to clean up her own image," Johanssen said. "Trevor Koch and Finn Thompson have nothing in common."

Lehman is now working on a memoir about her relationship with Koch, who has been missing for four years.

Emma Lathrop declined to respond to multiple requests for comment, only providing a short written statement to the Times:

"Finn Thompson killed my sister and tried to kill me and my best friend. I am confident the District Attorney's office will prove this in court."

Is her confidence well placed? The entire world is waiting to find out.

# Emma

*A year and a half later*

People were staring at her. It was in that annoying way where she could feel their eyes on her, but when she looked over they averted their gaze and pretended to be doing something else. She was used to it, though: the whispers and nervous hellos, the awkward eye contact.

Plus, she was not the most famous person there. Not by a long shot.

She gripped her flute of sparkling apple cider and scanned the room for Jill, finally locating her friend by the charcuterie table. Jill wore a red velvet dress and four-inch heels that didn't even get her close to Emma's height. Her curly hair had been blown out by one of London's top stylists, a woman Amanda had hired to prep the bridesmaids for the big day.

For her part, Emma wore a menswear-inspired pantsuit she'd splurged on after her first royalty check from *Loudmouth* had come in. The show was a semi-autobiographical dark comedy she'd co-written with Jill, and had already been renewed for two more seasons. It was easier than it should've been to sell the *Loudmouth* pilot to a major streaming network, and she had Finn's attempted stabbing to thank for that.

As she approached Jill and the charcuterie table, she heard the light clanging of a fork on a glass flute. "Hi, everyone," Amanda said, standing at the front of the room. Her wedding dress was next level bizarre: bright yellow with puff sleeves and shoulder pads, a drop waist, feathers sewn onto the hem. Some designer had had it custom-made for her, and it had never felt clearer to Emma that money couldn't buy taste. But still, she looked happy, and George looked happy, and that's what mattered.

"Thank you for being here." Amanda grabbed George's hand. "You know, I hate to talk about this, but after everything fell apart for me—when I hit rock bottom—I thought I'd never recover. I thought my career would be over. I thought everyone in the world hated me, and that I'd never find love again. So I want to raise a glass to George. Who would've thought that this cute bartender from East London would be the one to bring me back to life?" She held up her flute and the room followed. "Thanks for being my second chance."

The room cooed, and despite herself, Emma got a little teary.

"Amanda, we have the most beautiful life together and I'm grateful every day you came back for me." George gazed at her adoringly. "So, cheers to you, darling."

Emma had gotten used to fancy dinners by this point. It was wild how quickly one adjusted to things like that. With her half of the proceeds from the house, which Theo had sold right before he went to prison, plus her earnings from *Loudmouth*, she was living comfortably in a three-bedroom house in Highland Park. Jill was nearby, in Eagle Rock, living with her boyfriend of almost a year, Elijah.

Emma hadn't undergone a full transformation, Maggie-style, but she'd started getting her hair done at a very expensive queer salon on Franklin. Her clothes were mostly vintage pieces she'd had a "stylist" curate for her (Liz's wife, Toni, had a semi-popular thrifting Instagram page and was in the process of rebranding herself). She'd even bought a coveted pair of vintage Alexander McQueen combat boots.

Since Finn's trial had been wrapped up a year and a half ago, she'd started therapy for PTSD. Her therapist was an expensive psychoanalyst Amanda had recommended, but it was working. She was writing, she was dating, she was taking care of herself. She'd even done a couple of group sessions with Jill to process the impact of Maggie's murder on their friendship.

And *Loudmouth*! It was her greatest joy. Critics had called it "the American queer *Fleabag*" and "surprisingly funny." It was about a woman struggling to come to terms with her sister's mysterious murder while trying to find herself in LA. She and Jill had written it in the feverish days after she'd come back from the hospital, in the run-up to Finn's trial. At that time, they were becoming more and more famous by the day—the *60 Minutes* interview, the articles that ran 24/7 about the murder and Finn. They knew they had one big chance to sell something, and they took it—with Amanda's help, of course.

Jill and Elijah sat across from Emma at a long table near the bride and groom.

"Who would've thought?" Jill looked over at Amanda, whose head was resting on George's shoulder. The wedding theme was "sober punk rock/old-fashioned opulence," and they'd both gotten "'TIL DEATH" tattooed on their left shoulders right before dinner had begun.

Emma took a bite of lobster ravioli. The wedding reception was in an Italian restaurant in the West End and the food was delicious. The room was dark with gilded paneled walls and the waiters wore leather trench coats hand-selected by Amanda, and looked like something out of *The Matrix*.

One of the *Matrix* waiters was, at that moment, surreptitiously taking a photo of Emma and Jill as they shoveled food into their mouths.

Emma rolled her eyes but reached across the table, grabbing her friend's hand. "Who would've thought?"

# Acknowledgments

As a lover of books, getting to write my own with some of the best of the best is one of the greatest gifts of my life. Thank you, firstly, to the brilliant Emily Griffin at Century. Your diligence, creativity, and patience know no bounds. Thank you for believing in this book. To Alexandra Machinist, my wonderful agent: it is a thrill to work with you. You're a powerhouse, and your genius is only matched by your sense of humor. Sarah Harvey, I'm so grateful for all you did to get this book out in the world, and for your kind and thoughtful edits. Thank you both for making *People Pleaser* a reality. And thank you, Katherine Flitsch, for your supremely helpful feedback and for making sure I didn't include too much embarrassing millennial stuff in here.

Claire Simmonds, thank you for investing in this book and for your enthusiasm. Thank you, Jess Muscio, for your hard work and vision for *People Pleaser*. I loved having your partnership on this book. Laurie Ip Fung Chun, Alice Brett, and the rest of the team at Penguin Random House UK, I am so grateful for everything you did to whip *People Pleaser* into shape and to get it into the hands of readers. And to Richenda Todd, can you tell that math was not my best subject in school? Thank you for sorting me out.

Thank you to Lisa Krämer and the team at Goldmann Verlag for your enthusiasm about *People Pleaser*. I'm thrilled this story will get an audience in Germany.

Thank you to Eve Gleichman, without whom I simply could not have done this. Getting to reconnect and spend time with you through this process has been one of its biggest joys. You've done too many kind and generous things for me to even begin to enumerate here, but suffice it to say that I appreciate you more than I can properly communicate.

Noa Fleischacker, thank you for being my earliest reader and for taking me seriously without taking me too seriously. I think that discussing each character's enneagram was my favorite part of writing this book. Your feedback was essential to the development of these characters, and I am so grateful.

Jennifer Close, your generosity, patience and enthusiasm made me feel like I could do this. Your edits were invaluable, as well as the space you create with your workshops. Thank you for helping me take myself seriously as a writer, and for giving me a writing community.

Asha Elias, what would I do without you? Thank you for being my writing BFF: an early reader of the messy stuff, a support system, a reality check, and a friend. Thank you for being in it with me.

Kati Eisenhuth, Cliff Jacobs, Mayuri Chandra, Eileen Connors, I am so grateful for your feedback on early drafts and for all you did to shape this book.

Maya, Josh, Turbow: you were the first people I told I was going to do this, and your enthusiasm and curiosity gave me enthusiasm and curiosity of my own to see it through—thank you, I love you. Francine, Sarah, Zoe, Leah, Daniela, Adina, Ruth, Naomi, Howie, Cooper, Rachel, Jacob, Ben, Benjy, Rex, Vera, Abby, Kayla, Jacqui, the rest of the Ukiah/Guerneville gang, and anyone I missed: you enrich my life every single day, I love you, and being in community with you is the greatest thing. Thank you.

Kari, thank you for being the best damn therapist in the entire world (sorry to all the other therapists, but it's true). Thank you for not getting upset when I tweeted about you going to Burning Man. But most importantly, thank you for letting me fall apart when I need to, for meeting me where I'm at, and for believing in my ability to do this. This process sucked in so many moments, and you were there. Thank you.

Mom, your enthusiasm and love for this book is just the best. Thank you for being my momager, for taking all of my panicked phone calls (from the beginning of time, but especially now), and for giving birth to me. Thank you for reading Bachelor Nation News so I don't have to. I'm sorry Brandon and Serene didn't work out. I love you. And Lisa Orlandi, thank you for manifesting!

Dad, thank you for helping me maintain a sense of humor through all of this, for your support, and for raising a child who is apparently Scottish enough that she wrote a book for a UK audience. The pint of Tennent's is staying in, even if inaccurate. I love you.

Zainab, Russell, Vicki, and Aaron, I am the luckiest person in the world in that I have six total parents. What are the odds? Love you all, and am endlessly grateful that you exist.

Mahri and Anna, you're the world's best sisters. I'm so happy you're not reality TV stars who get murdered. Thanks for loving this book, reality TV, and Taylor Swift (the Big Three). I love you.

To my extended family—all my aunts, uncles, cousins, and especially Bareket (who, along with Anna, was born after *The Chocolate Wolf* was published and therefore didn't get her day in the sun), I love you all.

I dedicated this book to my paternal and maternal grandmothers—Mary Stewart and Barbara Cohen. Barbara was a Jewish children's book author and the person who made me want to be a writer. Mary, another woman of words, passed away as I was writing this book. I miss her every single day. This book is for them (and for Golda and Florence, too).

And finally, Gabe. You are, as they say, S-tier. Sorry about the honeymoon. You're the best thing in my life, and I love you.